A SPELL OF DEATH

BLOODBORNE PATHOGENS | BOOK THREE

C. RENÉ ASTLE

A SCARLET FEVER

Second Edition. September 1, 2020.

ISBN:

To my parents, who gave me a curiosity about the world and a love of story. To George, Mary, Amanda, Mark and Susan - the Other Writing Group - who gave me caring critiques and constant encouragement. To Amy, Alana and Jeannette, who gave me their eyes and ears.

CHAPTER ONE

Gabriel struggled against the taloned fingers clasped around her forearms, tearing into her flesh. Under the acrid scent of sulphur was the copper tang of blood. Her blood. But not just hers. She made sure of that. Her palms itched as the crimson liquid dried on them. A crooked smile twisted her lips before a magnesium-bright flash seared her eyes, temporarily burning her tormentors from her sight, though their haughty visages were imprinted on her brain. Cold and harsh, the light still burnt her skin and scorched her hair.

Blinking, she saw it was a cruel halo of magic cast by the spear of one of the archangels who yet stood on the right side of Good. The light waned slightly, and his faced loomed over her. Their kind were neither male nor female, yet both. But he had clearly picked a preference, as had she.

"You're finished." His words were crisp and sharp.

A keening howl rent her ears and pierced her heart: her beloved grey guards — her gargoyles — being corralled and subjected to petrifying magic. The aching sound suddenly stopped, leaving an icy burn in her veins. She craned her neck, trying to lay eyes on them, their leathery wings and corded muscles. But all she saw were glimpses of grey lumps. Casting her gaze around, she glared at those who held her, then returned her attention to the man who carried the three blades. He wore the Moon on his head, like an upside-down bow strung between two horns, its silver dull in the faded light. He stepped closer.

"You can't kill me." Gabriel tipped her chin up, pulling her head back as he reached a bloody hand towards her, the fingers of which were wrapped around her blade. Her soul yearned for it as her own blood dripped down its dark facets. But instead of cutting her again, his knuckles ran gently along her cheek.

"I know." His eyes were flecked with red and infused with gold like the circle of death he held in his other hand. "But we can take your power and lock you away. Keep you from spreading your disease across the world."

"You think darkness and dungeons scare me?" A sneer she didn't quite feel played across her lips. "After you kicked me out of your gilded cage, your master put me in enough prisons. Yet here I am. Do your worst." She expected some retort from him. Instead his jaw clenched, and he stepped out of her field of view. A shard of pain pierced her back and an echoing scream tore from her mouth as she collapsed, and the light dissolved. She expected darkness to flood in to fill the space. Instead there was nothing.

CHAPTER TWO

The shadow hunkered behind the dragon, her black-gloved hand resting lightly on its haunches. It seemed a grumpy sort, but it couldn't complain about her presence, given that it was made of stone. The creature capped the mausoleum rooftop she'd clambered onto to get a view of the cemetery. She slid her gaze sideways to the dragon. Cocking an eyebrow, she didn't think the person who'd topped their eternal resting place with a disgruntled dragon would mind her taking refuge there. Keeping her breath measured and her pulse even, she lay flat against the cold stone, all of her hidden except the bit from the eyes up to her hood. She imagined herself a torpid squirrel or half-asleep bird. Nothing but a shadow — nothing to draw the attention of the netherworld creatures gathered below.

A gentle breeze rustled the branches of the tree beside her. Far off, the muted sounds of a city that never slept continued to count out the witching hours, when all good folk should be snug in their beds, or grumbling about jobs that kept them away from the comforts of home and hearth.

An owl hooted and flew up from a branch behind her. Startled, she glanced over her shoulder but couldn't see what disturbed its rest. The muscles around her ear twitched as she strained to hear without moving; she picked out rustling, thumping, a whapping sound. Some vagrant perhaps, settling in for the night.

The dampened trill of blade clashing on blade reverberated through the caverns of stone in the cemetery, up to the mausoleum roof, and brought her focus forward as the battle below picked up again. These creatures of darkness and death appeared to be doing her work for her. Maybe if she watched and waited, she could keep her weapons — and her hands — clean. Her muscles, tense with anticipation and eager to enter the melee, were seizing up, and starting to ache from constraining pent up adrenalin. At least that's what she told herself. But the shadow

3

wasn't as young as when she'd joined the Hunters, finally passing her grandparents' tests. Laying on cold rock in a night that presaged rain, or worse judging from the temperature and the ring around the moon, didn't help. She glanced at said moon, while trying to roll a shoulder without actually moving it. Her grandfather had taught her to read the weather and care for her weapons. Her grandmother had taught her about good and evil, about the things that lurk in the dark. And how to kill those cursed things.

She almost gasped when the moon dimmed and the stars blinked out as if a blanket of deep indigo had descended. Only her training stopped her and kept her still. She blinked. Light returned to the night and everything was as it should be — the few stars that shone brighter than the city lights speckled the sky and the ringed moon still hung pregnant, though dim.

Imagining things. Not good. But she couldn't quite shake the gnawing fear; tendrils of wild hopelessness and heavy dread had pressed into her chest in that split second, and their echoes coursed through her veins.

She castigated herself for getting spooked by shadows, hearing her grandmother's disappointment that she let her mind wander from her purpose. She refocused as more sounds of battle rose from the scene below. One bloodsucker lay wounded, blood seeping from a gash in his shoulder. So much the better, less work for her if the thing bled out. Though that was unlikely; more like it would die a slow, painful death, since the weapons would not be off-the-shelf swords and guns. The ammo would be poisoned, the blades laced with silvery venom. Enough to fester anyway. Unbidden, a random memory came to mind of training sessions in her grandmother's garden, lifting her lips into a smile before turning them into a frown. Tears formed in her eyes. She let a tear slide down her cheek, but when another followed it, she inched a black-gloved hand up to wipe them away. They would blur her vision.

Action, not crying, her grandmother had taught her, before the slaughter that had taken both grandparents. A massacre that had left blood, pain, and a shadow.

Action, that's what I need. Enough lying on a roof in the cold and the damp. The shadow shifted, reaching a hand towards her blade, ready to join the fray.

Then the scene below changed again. The shadow pursed her lips, angry at herself for getting distracted yet again.

One creature was dead...or seemed to be. The one in the priest's body. He was a strange one, a type of creature her grandmother hadn't covered. The werewolf and mad vampire had fled, taking the wounded, undead man with them. The other vampires that had come with the priest peeled away and scurried back into the night.

Those that remained crowded around the body of the woman at the centre of the night's ritual. The shadow's eyes narrowed at some tug on a thread of memory, but she didn't have time to puzzle out its source as the vampires below shifted.

As they came into the halo of light, the shadow's breath caught in her throat. One of the vampires turned, the pale planes of her face struck by moonlight.

Mina. The shadow stared for a minute, her mind churning. Then she slipped off the mausoleum roof and into the darkness. She needed time to digest this new nugget of information. *Mina Sun's a vampire.*

CHAPTER THREE

The old clock beside Cam's bed ticked, boring like water drops into Mina's skull. Her gut twisted as another silent grimace played across her roommate's face. *Former roommate*, Mina reminded herself. A twitch of Cam's eyebrows hinted at pain though her injuries were already healed.

Mina wiped a stray strand of hair away from Cam's forehead, noting again the new tattoo on her neck — marking her indelibly as a vampire even without the song trilling in Mina's blood: cellos and windchimes. She traced the black lines with her thumb. None of the others, who stood gossiping in the living room, recognized the image, but it looked to her like an ankh with a pointed end. Except the top was too flat and filled with a blackened circle. It certainly was nothing like the only other tattoo Cam had, the one she'd asked Mina to do: a discreet, rainbow-hued dragonfly that masked a scar Cam never talked about.

A tremble passed through Cam, and Mina reached down to pick the afghan up off the floor, intent on wrapping it around Cam's sleeping form. At least, Mina hoped she was sleeping. "I'm sorry," she whispered, placing her lips on Cam's fevered forehead. Her lips pulled into a frown of worry, she clutched the afghan to her chest and turned at a sound behind her.

Brett came into the room, pausing just inside the doorway. "Sorry. I —" He glanced at the washcloth he held in his hand, then back at her. "I thought I could clean off some of the blood." He nodded towards Cam.

Her gaze flashed from him to her roommate. "Thanks." Looking back at Brett, she forced a small smile to her lips at the concern in his sad eyes and tight mouth. "You're already doing so much more than the others." She glanced down the hall at the meager gathering in their little living room, and the anger welled up again. They'd wanted to kill her friend. They probably still did though now they simply refused, oh so politely, to take Cam back to the Sanctuary and the healers there. Cam was tainted, they said. Glaring at them, her frown came back, more of a scowl this time, as Rhys walked down the hall towards her.

"How is she?" the Librarian asked, his pale blue eyes sliding to Cam, as he tucked his right hand into his left armpit.

"How should I know?" Mina savoured the tartness in her voice, hoping it would soothe the beast inside. Instead it soured in her stomach.

"No, I don't suppose you would know, having no experience with sacrifice, however unsuccessful." Rhys' sad gaze shifted from Cam to her. Even though she'd had her fill of riddles, she bit back the comment which formed in her throat and pressed her tongue to her fangs to quell the ever-simmering anger.

Rhys paused, mouth partly open. "I meant that literally," he said, as if he'd read her mind. "You have no experience with people who sacrifice others." He nodded at Cam. "Or those who've been set up as the lamb. Few do."

"Do you?" Her curiosity piqued despite her anger, Mina peered at Rhys. She saw the worry written around his eyes as well, and in the lines of his face. *Or maybe it's sadness.* She recalled with a guilty jolt that Dar's death was still fresh. She didn't know the entirety of their relationship but it was more than vampire and researcher. Tears welled up as a wave of hopelessness washed over her. "We've lost so much," she said, then startled as Rhys lay a hand on her shoulder. She flushed — she'd spoken aloud.

"And you don't want to lose her too."

Mina peered into his watery eyes. "Do you know what's wrong with her?"

Rhys tilted his head. "Not exactly. My best guess is she's caught in some kind of limbo she needs to find her way out of."

"You don't know how to get her out?"

Rhys shook his head slowly. "No. There's a lot I don't know. But sometimes, just sometimes, I know how to find out."

"Can you find a cure for her?"

"I can look." He sighed. "But I can't promise." He took his hand away and clapped it against his other one. "In the meantime, the conclave wants to...have a conclave to discuss things."

Mina waited for him to go on. "About what?" she asked when he didn't, an edge coming back into her voice as she crossed her arms over her chest.

"Your friend, and what to do about Jack, and whether to worry about Night at all, given that the sacrifice didn't come off." He nodded towards Cam again. "I think you need to be in that discussion."

A hollow pit expanded in Mina's stomach, soon filled with guilt. In the cemetery, standing in the icy rain, surrounded by death and bloody muck, she'd been forced to choose: go after Jack or get Cam to safety. It had seemed the only choice at the time, but now worry about Jack's fate gnawed at her. She swallowed the tears that caught on the lump in her throat. "They can all crowd in here then."

"Bee and Seema believe the Sanctuary is a better location for a meeting of the conclave, even if it is greatly diminished." His voice faded to a whisper. "They say they'll start in an hour, with or without you." He clasped his hands in front of him. "But as I said, you should be there."

"Why? What difference will it make?" She turned back to Cam. Hearing Rhys' heavy sigh, she looked back.

He reached out, placing his hand on her shoulder, then dropped it. "We all know you're special."

"Don't you mean strange?"

"No, I don't."

His blue eyes pierced deep as he gazed at her. She looked away, towards the living room then at Cam. "You might be the only one."

"Not the only one." Brett rose from the bed and came to stand beside her. She saw Cam's face and arms were now clean. "It's okay. I can stay, watch over her." His lips formed a sad, crooked smile, before he leaned in to lay a light kiss on her temple. "I have your number, if anything changes."

"I can't ask you to do that."

"You didn't, I offered. I have nowhere else to be." His warm hand came to rest on her lower back, nudging her towards the door.

Mina glanced at Rhys, then gave Brett a small smile. With all that was going on, she'd seriously neglected him of late. She frowned; she had no idea about his life outside of his job and being a familiar. She'd have to fix that when she had a chance. Reaching out, she ran a thumb across his forehead — it hit her that the worry lines tracing across his brow weren't about Cam at all.

"Thank you." The words were barely audible, but he smiled before turning to Cam.

Sparing a final look at her friend, Mina turned to Rhys. "Fine then. Let's go discuss shit."

"We need to find the Blade of the Sun." Rhys voice was so low even he barely heard the words over the squabbling vampires. And the eerily quiet werecat...she had clearly heard him. She shifted in her crouch, her Madeira eyes flicking to him, the flecks of gold sparking like fire. Even though she was currently human, her sharp face still appeared feline. He cleared his throat and tried again, louder this time, fighting against the pit at his solar plexus that weighed him down. "We need to find the blade. The one from the drawing of the three blades." The vampires quieted this time, and either looked at him sidelong or shuffled a bit away. The pity in their eyes turned his spine to steel. His lips pressed together. Pity was not something he was used, and he was not comfortable with it. Scorn, distaste and curiosity he'd grown accustomed to, but not pity. He snorted. Without Dar to forge a path, if pity got their attention, it would have to do.

"Night is coming, and it's the one thing that might stop her. Or so the ancient texts allude."

"I thought you said they were cryptic." Mina glanced up at him from where she sat on the floor. There was a tension in her eyes but no pity. "They spoke in riddles."

"They do, but the riddles speak of the Blade of Sun conquering Night."

"They also say the blade is broken, the pieces sent to the corners of the earth." Seema stood up from her crouch, keeping her eyes fixed on him. "Locked in a prison of puzzles. Besides, we stopped Night." She slunk towards him. Someone had found her clothes, and threads in the loose pants glinted in the low light. Her eyes narrowed as she neared him, crinkling crow's feet at the corners. "Or, should I say, *I* stopped her. Don't you remember, old man? I cut the head off her herald."

Rhys adjusted his bowtie, then met her gaze. "That means you stopped the herald. I believe...." Knowing his voice was quiet, too timid, he cleared his throat again. "Night still comes."

"You're starting to sound like Mike." Her voice was hard, but there was softness in her face as she peered at him.

He looked down between his shoes and her bare feet for a second, and debated giving up, going home to curl up with his cat, Grey, a large book in one hand and a small Scotch in the other. But the steel remained. He forced himself to meet her eyes again, and they stared at each other for long seconds, Rhys unable to decipher what was going on in the feline's head. Despite her human form, her gaze hinted that she was thinking he'd be good for dinner.

"Mike turned out to be right." Mina's voice was quiet, but Seema sent a sharp glance at her before returning her attention to Rhys.

"The Blade of the Sun is a myth," she said. "A figment of some long-lost writer's lost mind. Maybe you're losing your mind too." Her voice was quiet and even. "Grief can do that to people."

11

"That's a low blow." Mina stood up and came forward, pulling her shoulders back.

Rhys gave a brusque shake of his head then stood even straighter. It caused his back to moan but let him speak louder without clearing his throat. "You're a figment of people's imagination. Sometimes even myths forget they're based on something real. But yes, grief can drive people to do crazy things, like beheading the only creature who knows anything about Night."

"And what would you have had me do?" Sparks flared in her eyes again as they narrowed even further. Her lips pulled back into a feral snarl.

"Enough snipping." Bee stepped forward from where she'd been leaning against one of the Sanctuary's pillars. He turned his head to meet her gaze; with both Dar and Jack gone, she was the only one left with the power to corral the conclave. "What evidence do you have that Night comes?" Her words were rough and quiet, hinting at how tired she was.

Rhys shrugged. "What evidence did we have for Angelos, for the gargoyles? Rumours until the dying started."

"We no longer have the people to spare for hunting down rumours." Bee examined her hands and seemed about to say something more but didn't get the chance.

Instead Seema spoke again, shaking her head. "You're wrong, ignoring the most clear and present danger. And your blindness will get people killed."

"Well, if I'm wrong, what do you suggest we do?" He kept himself rigid as he spoke.

She took a step back, rocking on her feet, which she refused to clad in shoes despite the cold. Her knees bent slightly, as if she was preparing to kick him in the head. Instead she said something he didn't expect.

"Hunt the wolves. Kill them."

"What? There was only one with the herald, and it took off with...Lin." He fidgeted with his bowtie again. "What danger is one wolf compared to Night?"

"Not one wolf. All the wolves. Wipe their cancer from the earth."

"You don't mean that."

"They're a plague."

Mina gaped at the woman. "You can't kill an entire species. That's genocide."

Seema lifted a shoulder in a lopsided shrug. "Why not? They did it to us, and if Night is coming — IF — they're the army that will pave the way. Gargoyles make a statement but wolves are the foot soldiers."

"But...there are good wolves," Rhys said.

Seema stared at him, her expression unreadable. "The only good dog is a dead dog."

"You're both wrong." Bee stepped between him and Seema, breaking the standoff. Rhys allowed himself to slouch a bit, letting the tiredness seep into his bones again. Once more, he wished Dar was there.

Seema turned her fiery appraisal on Bee. "What do you mean?"

Bee didn't flinch or back down. "We go after Jack."

Seema snorted. "He's lost, skewered with a poisoned blade." She tempered her tone, her voice softening into its normal lilt, as Mina glared at her. "He's likely dead already. The sooner you accept the loss, the better." Rhys watched, trying to remain neutral and out of the way as he waited for the strike. Bee's nostrils flared and Mina stepped towards the Were with a clenched fist. But the blows didn't come.

Instead Bee spoke, her voice quiet but hard as steel. "You're not one of us. You don't get a vote." She turned to the conclave, and it hit Rhys again how diminished they were, how beaten up they appeared. "What say we?" She went around the assembled vampires, asking for their vote, and as she did, a spark of life came into them again.

Then the voting stopped, as Bee waited for Mina to answer. She looked from the Were to him to Bee. "You can do whatever you want, but I need to find out what's wrong with Cam, and how to fix her." The other vampires looked at her like she'd just suggested she needed to drink a cup of silver.

"Jack's one of us," Bee said. "He's family."

A tear trailed down Mina's face; she made no move to wipe it away. "I know. And we need to find him. But she's my family too." Rhys saw the tension in her eyes as she looked towards him. "Besides, she was there. She might be able to tell us about what the herald was planning, and whether Night still is a threat. Maybe where they might have taken Jack."

Looking at her, Rhys was sure she just wanted to save her friend, not support him, but he latched onto the flimsy thread anyway. "If Dar were here—"

Bee interrupted him. "But he's not here, is he?" she snapped. "He went and got himself killed."

"Bee!" Adeh said, his eyes going wide.

"I'm sorry, but it's true. He abandoned us, and for what?"

The firmness in Rhys' voice was surprising even to him when he spoke. "To stop Night. Dar knew that was the priority. He knew it was the right thing to do."

CHAPTER FOUR

Mina stepped into Jack's room, her booted foot landing softly on the polished concrete floor. She forced herself to let go of the breath she was holding as moths fluttered in her stomach. Glancing at the bed, her cheeks flushed as a memory of Jack's lips whispering across her skin surfaced. Of course, she'd been in the room before, but this time, without Jack, she was an interloper entering a forbidden inner sanctum. *What secrets could I find out about Jack, what does he keep bound tight in that sad soul of his, behind his shuttered eyes?* She inhaled sharply at the thought. *Maybe I don't want to know. I have enough angst of my own.*

She took another stuttering step forward, into the grey half-light, then stopped.

"What is it?" Rhys asked.

Looking over her shoulder, she saw he hovered in the doorway. "You could come see."

"Oh, no, I couldn't violate Jack's personal space."

But it's okay for me to do it. Mina's eyebrow lifted, then she returned to the thing that had made her pause. Bending to pick it up, she pressed it to her face as her jaw clenched. Her nose twitched.

"Have you found something?" Rhys asked.

"Hmm." Fabric muffled her voice, and she pulled it away and sniffed back the tears that were making her nose run.

"What? Is it the printout?"

Mina shook her head. "A hoodie." She pressed the garment to her face again, drinking in Jack's smell. Warm and woodsy. She could almost hear his blood song: woodwinds and brass.

"Not what I'm looking for," Rhys said. She turned and made a face, but he ignored her. "Keep searching. We need that piece of paper." With the others dismissing the need to find yet another arcane blade, Rhys had asked her to help him search for a printout Jack had mentioned, purported to show the Blade of the Sun. Perhaps because she was glad of any excuse to put off her next stop — supper with her brother, Dale, and his family — she agreed to scour Jack's room for the slip of paper. Behind her, Rhys coughed, wet and phlegmatic. "I can't find the website it came from anymore. It seems to have disappeared from my history."

Mina sighed and tossed the hoodie on Jack's bed before stepping over to his desk. Usually pristine, it was strewn with a sheaf of papers, as if abandoned in the middle of him working on something. She ran her fingers over them, fanning them out. Notes in his handwriting were interspersed with sketches.

"He's an artist," she whispered, her eyebrows twitching in surprise at the intricate ink drawings. Behind her, she sensed Rhys finally cross the threshold and a few seconds later he came to stand beside her. She didn't know if it was his curiosity or his impatience that had gotten the better of him.

He peered over her shoulder at the drawing she'd picked up. "A kusarigama. Clever boy."

"A what?"

He looked at her, eyes shining with boyish glee. "That's what he got the Smiths to make, something to take down a winged creature...the weapon he decided he needed when I told him the gargoyles would grow wings." The half smile slipped from Rhys' face and the light left his eyes. As his gaze returned to the drawing, his voice became quiet. "And it was almost enough."

Mina's index finger traced the chain that ran between a scythe-like blade and what appeared to be the business end of a mace, then she shifted the paper aside to reveal the ones underneath. Shuffling through, she saw nothing that looked like the printout Rhys was looking for.

"It's not here." Glancing around the spartan room, she didn't see any more loose scraps of paper. Even the rubbish bin was empty.

"Don't be so hasty." Rhys cast his gaze at the notebook exposed by her rifling. He lay his hand on it almost reverently, then opened it.

16

Mina's stomach fluttered again as she recognized what he had. "That's his journal."

"Don't worry. I'm not going to read it." He peered at her over his glasses. "Unless you want me too?" Mina's mouth opened and shut, but he looked away before she answered, and flipped through the pages. "And this..." He tugged at a small slip of paper Mina had missed.

"This is where he would keep something he didn't want everyone to see," she said as he unfolded the paper, revealing another detailed drawing in delicate lines of black ink. "But why wouldn't he?"

"The Blade of the Sun." Rhys adjusted his glasses, shifting them down his nose.

"I thought we were looking for a printout," Mina said, as he reached over and turned on the lamp, placing the sheet on the desk where she could get a better look at it. It was a hoop, with etchings all along the circumference.

Rhys rotated the paper on the flat surface as he squinted at the image. "It almost looks like...no, not Sanskrit." He stood up and sighed. Mina looked at the scribbles and noticed another set off to the side. Writing, even though they looked like wavy lines to her. But these were familiar wavy lines, though she couldn't place where she'd seen their kin before.

"There's a language Jack knows that you don't?"

Rhys' gaze slid sideways. "There are many things Jack knows that would surprise you." He craned his head as he rotated the page. "It's not the printout, but it is intriguing. This is much more detailed." He tilted his head the other way. "And I doubt it's drawn from imagination." He glanced at her. "So, what did he find out that he didn't share?"

"But it's just a circle. It's not a blade." She tipped her head sideways, trying to dislodge the niggling sense of familiarity looking at the drawing. "Maybe it wasn't important enough to share."

Rhys ran his pinkie finger over the lines of script Mina couldn't decipher. "See this." He pointed to a particular scribble. "I'm pretty sure it means Sun, but the rest of this is like code ciphered in a dead language written in an archaic script."

"I'm glad I'm not the only one who can't read it."

"Oh, I can probably read it given time. The shapes are familiar." Rhys folded the paper and opened the lapel of his jacket.

"That's Jack's." Mina reached out to stop him. "It might be private."

Rhys paused and looked at the paper, raising a bushy eyebrow. "I doubt it's some ode to a long-lost love." He tucked it into his pocket. "It might be the clue we need to find Jack, to find the blade. To survive the coming of Night."

Jack was drowning in sludge and deafened by a thundering howl that roared through his head like a motorcycle. He blinked, trying to clear the bleary grey from his eyes. The blurriness dissipated but the grey remained: he was surrounded by a bleak landscape painted in shades of slate, charcoal, gunmetal. He tried turning around to pinpoint where the sound was coming from, but it was like swimming through cement. Squinting, he forced his strained eyes to pick out shapes in the greyness. As he finally reached 180 degrees in his turn, something slammed into his cheekbone and he staggered back. The wail of anger that escaped him was muted, as if his ears were filled with water. He clutched at his shoulder and gasped, both at the sharp bolt of electricity that coursed from some wound he didn't remember receiving and from the figure in front of him.

Still writ in tones of grey, a creature of ethereal beauty paced the slate ground. She...he...Jack didn't know. Small breasts swelled on the torso, covered by films of black cloth fluttering in a wind he didn't feel, but an inhumanly large bulge between the legs spoke of masculinity. *They* seemed to have no problem moving in this desolate topography. Long limbs, human-like, stalked back and forth, though the legs tapered into hooves. A flash of light tore the charcoal sky, and a shriek pierced Jack's eardrums. He collapsed on his knees, hands on either side of his head, but that did little to dampen the sound. Glancing up, he saw the creature's face was elongated, the mouth open. At that moment, pearlescent wings appeared behind it, flapping in fury, causing Jack to fall back. They turned to him, obsidian eyes boring into him.

In the vacuum of sound that filled the air when their scream stopped, Jack caught a high, quiet noise: a whimper. It wasn't coming from the creature in front of him, but the only other thing in the dismal terrain was a lump of taupe. A rock. Then the rock moved, and Jack caught sight of a face he thought he should know but couldn't place. For a few long moments, pleading eyes stared at him from behind a curtain of dark curls before his attention was drawn back to the winged creature.

They opened their mouth again, and Jack braced himself for a repeat of the spear of sound. Instead, the creature strode to loom over him and spoke sibilant words, dove grey words that didn't belong in this sere environment. They tipped their head, jutted out their chin. The tone implied a question, but Jack had no answer. It was all Babel to him. A snick sounded, and a blade appeared in the creature's entirely human hand. A blade Jack recognized, its oily obsidian tugging at his soul.

So this is the end. Not in fire or in ice. Just grey. Jack peered at the last face he would see. Then the silver lightning flashed across the grey clouds again, this time accompanied by quicksilver rain. He spared a glance at the sky and thought he saw shapes moving against the charcoal. The creature also looked up and started a keening wail, before turning back to him, a cold fire burning in their eyes as they clutched the obsidian blade in their fingers.

Jack gasped again as pain seared through his shoulder. Then the world went from grey to black.

A scream echoed in her ears and lightning flashed across her eyelids. She tried to open them to find the source, but her leaden lids refused to lift, leaving her trapped in darkness. She had no qualms with the darkness; it was the nothingness she hated. And she needed the souls that thrived in sunlight to feed her power. As chaotic visions played in her mind, she struggled to remember the time before now, but it was lost in searing red pain and impenetrable gloom. She had a vague memory of a tuneless melody and a hushed conversation, followed by words whispered in a warm, rich voice to an empty room. But she hadn't been able to pick out the sense of them, and she'd soon fallen asleep, or passed out. The effect was the same: frustrating lapses of memory and annoying gaps in her knowledge of events swirling around her.

But even though she still couldn't see, she knew she was being watched. The shape of the man formed a silhouette in her mind's eye. *Is he guarding or surveilling?* she wondered as she crept her senses outward. She lay on a bed too lumpy, her head on a pillow too flat. A heavy blanket weighed down her enervated limbs. She struggled to breathe the stale air, feeling like she was drowning, though her body barely moved. What little air she drew in was laced with tantalizingly familiar odours, but only one stood out.

Blood. Her sense of death told her this was a man with blood on his hands. *I can use that,* she thought with a smile, but her frozen lips refused to move. *What did you do, Angelos?* A scream welled up in her chest, but it died into a silent snarl, and the other being — the soft and seductive consciousness that still lurked at the edges of her senses — quelled and scurried back into the abyss.

Tamping down her frustration, she refocused on her watcher. The man spoke soft words and she swore her ears tweaked in response, even though she couldn't make any part of this body move as she commanded. The rhythm and cadence of his voice, pitched slightly lower than normal, told her he was reading her a story. But the words were foreign, gibberish. Every once in a while, the beat slowed, and his head nodded, but he would jerk awake in that second before true sleep. Then he would return to watching her again, resuming the litany he'd kept up with barely a pause, despite her lack of response. He'd been there since that other woman had left. The woman who left her warm with love and hot with anger in equal measure. The vampire. Everything about the woman — the voice, the scent, the warmth of her touch — was like a memory just out of reach. In her mind, she saw flashes of colour, black hair, red lips. When she grasped at the image, she felt her finger twitch. She honed all her focus on that digit, infusing it with all her will. *Move*. Any movement was a step out of this prison of darkness.

Nothing. If she could scream, she would have. Then the man paused, and she strained her ears, trying to learn why, not wanting to go back to the cage of silence. Something clinked against something else, then the man started speaking again. The ebb and flow of his voice as he read his story was like a lullaby, threatening to drag her into sleep again. Into that impenetrable darkness. She breathed deeply, fighting the lethargy, and sighed out the sleep from behind her eyes. The eyes that refused to obey, that wouldn't open to look upon this world.

She coaxed the finger to twitch, to draw him closer, but the body still refused to comply, and he stayed where he was. Unable to move, unable to see, she reached out again with her other senses. Underneath the staleness and blood, there was a faint aroma of rosemary and lavender, with an undertone of vanilla. The latter she identified as coming from the man beside her. His breathing was deep and slow, and heat radiated from him, pulsing with his heartbeat...a beat that was slightly off. The chair he sat in creaked every now and then as he shifted. Beyond that were trills and beeps and bangs of a chaotic world outside the darkness that shrouded her.

She tried to speak, her frustration so strong her thumb almost moved as she visualized clenching her hands into fists, but

21

the sound came out as a rasping of breath. But that breath tore at her ragged throat.

The man's words slowed, stuttered and then stopped. And then silence fell. She hated the silence, but it gave her a question to hold on to: why had he gone quiet. Even out beyond the walls was quiet. Although she couldn't see, she knew the sun had set and night blanketed the city. Her night.

She was brought back by a clapping sound that almost caused her to jump...if she were able to move. *The book snapping shut*. Loose wood creaked against loose wood and she sensed a shift in the air as the man stood up.

A shuffle of fabric over carpet, then she sensed his presence, a silhouette of grey against the darkness in her mind's eye. He leaned over her. A hand, warm and dry, came to rest on her forehead. It stroked a strand of hair away.

"She walks in beauty, like the night / Of cloudless climes and starry skies; / And all that's best of dark and bright / Meet in her aspect and her eyes; / Thus mellowed to that tender light / Which heaven to gaudy day denies."

Poetry, she realized. *How quaint.*

The man paused in his recital. "I can never remember the rest." Then a thumb trailed down her cheek. "I wish you'd wake up. Mina's sick with worry." Her stomach clenched as the man took a step back, leaving a void in the warmth. The light filtering through her eyelids became painfully bright with his shadow gone. She squeezed those eyelids tight against the burning light, willing him to come back, and swore her finger twitched again.

Again, she focused her will on opening one eyelid at a time, but neither of them listened to her. Instead they were even heavier, dragging her back again into the dark abyss of unconsciousness.

No, not again. She managed to finish the thought before the darkness claimed her once more.

CHAPTER FIVE

"You've hardly touched your food." Aunt June slurped another mouthful of japchae before continuing. "Is everything alright?"

Mina froze, her left hand stopped twirling her chopsticks while her right paused under the table. The dog still found the morsel it held, licking at her fingers until she pulled them away, wiping them on her pants. She brushed aside thoughts of Cam lying catatonic and Jack in the clutches of his maker — or worse — and smiled weakly at June. "I'm fine. Tired is all. You know, work, school." Glancing from Dale to his wife Hana, her gaze passed over the kids, Maggie and Liam, before coming back to June. She was starting to understand Jack's insistence that being dead to her family would be easier. He was supposed to help her with that. *Who else can help me die if he's dead?* She swallowed against the tightness in her throat. *And what if I don't want to be dead?*

"How's your roommate?" Hana asked, taking another bite of carrot before looking at her sidelong.

"Yes, you should bring Cam by sometime." Dale smiled as he twirled noodles around his chopsticks. "It's been so long since I've seen her. Well, other than..." He stopped, stuffing the noodles in his mouth instead.

But Mina knew the last time he'd seen Cam: their mother's funeral. "I'll mention it." Her stomach churned as she stared intently at the food on her plate. "She's just been a little, um, busy lately." She swallowed and forced a smile to her lips as she turned away from her brother's questioning gaze. "How's rugby, Maggie? Your dad says you're pretty good."

"It's awesome!" Without further prompting, Maggie regaled Mina with more information about the sport than she ever needed to know, giving her a five-minute reprieve from the grilling of her aunt and sister-in-law. Unfortunately, Maggie eventually ran out of steam. "I do get a bit banged up though, which Mom doesn't like much." She slurped the last of her noodles before pointing at Mina's bruised cheek with her chopsticks. "Like you." She smiled, exposing the gap in her front teeth.

Mina's hand came out from under the table, where the dog had taken a break from eating her supper, and her fingers grazed the tender skin on her cheek.

"Maggie! It's not polite to point with your chopsticks." Hana frowned at her daughter before turning to Mina. "How *did* you get that scrape?" Her head cocked sideways, a look of concern affixed to her face. Her expression appeared as if it could slide away at any second, to be replaced by another one lying underneath. There was an unexpected coldness there. Mina sunk lower in her chair. She'd always had a warm relationship with her sister-in-law, and she knew Hana had been trying to get her to come over for supper for weeks.

"I..." She stuttered as her mind flashed to a scene of obsidian eyes and crimson blood. "I fell when I was out running. Icy patch." She dropped her hand to her throat, where she'd still had a bruise that morning, acquired when Angelos, the Herald of Night, tried to choke the life out of her. That mark had faded more than the memory, but it was still shades of green and brown. She tugged up the cowl of her turtleneck.

Beside her, Hana's heart beat a tad faster, and she tsked. "That's too bad. It looks like it's healing well, anyway. But you need to be careful out there. There are dangerous people on the streets."

"Thanks, I can take care of myself." Mina neglected to mention that she was the dangerous one now. The table went silent again, an interlude to eat. Mina played with her food, twirling and untwirling noodles, listening to the staccato of Hana's metal chopsticks clack against the plate, underpinned by a pulse that beat a touch too fast. Mina glanced at her sister-in-law. *She's definitely pissed I haven't come by sooner.* The rhythm of Hana's heartbeat sounded out her irritation. These biological tattletales were becoming familiar to Mina. She'd heard something similar in the cemetery. Cam. She put her chopsticks on the table. *I shouldn't be here, pretending to eat, with Cam lying comatose at home. And Jack god knows where.* She started to push her chair back, but Hana moved first.

"I didn't realize it was so late." She looked at the clock over Mina's head. "I have to get to work, unfortunately. The morgue never closes, and we've had a fair few strange deaths lately."

"Hana." June's voice was sharp. A small frown on her lips, she looked from Hana to Liam and Maggie. In that moment, Mina saw her mom reflected in June's face. Mina followed Hana's lead and stood up from her own chair.

"They know very well what their mom does." Dale placed his hand on his wife's arm.

"She helps catch the bad people," Liam said, before spearing the last piece of kimchi.

"You've been working too hard lately." Dale ran his hand down his wife's back. "You need to be more forceful. Say no. Tell them you need more backup."

"I know." Hana bent over and kissed him, causing the kids to make faces. "But the wicked never rest. And it looks like Mina needs to leave anyway."

Mina shifted, shrugging a shoulder and giving Hana a half smile as her sister-in-law peered at her. "No rest for the wicked, as you say."

The shadow kissed her husband goodbye. But she wasn't a shadow yet. That came later. When she left the house, she was on her way to a rewarding if grisly job as a pathologist, puzzling out how people met their unfortunate ends. It was a career for which she was imminently qualified, one that couldn't be contested as unnecessary, and the work occurred in a place where even a spouse didn't just drop in for a surprise visit.

It was only after she drove away, after she turned a few corners and donned the ink-black garments, and slipped into the night that she became a shadow. It wasn't every night. Some nights she was just a medical examiner. Some nights she was a wife and mother. She clung to that truth to bury her guilt. That, and the fact that her real nocturnal vocation kept the bogeymen in the shadows. With her.

No, some nights she didn't lie. But not tonight. Tonight, she was a hunter. She pulled onto a quiet side street at the edge of downtown, parking in the shadow of a building, before throwing her bag into the back. As she started to crawl over the centre console to join it, her phone beeped. She paused, then shimmied the rest of the way into the backseat before pulling it out. It was her weather app, letting her know it was clear skies ahead. Lies, she thought, glancing out the window as she contorted into her dark uniform.

Too bad wasn't the reply from her contact in the Brotherhood that she hoped for. She trusted those mad monks about as much as she trusted a vampire, but they had resources she didn't. Despite her grandparents being better teachers, she'd gone through one of their training programs. She'd kept in contact, and this morning had asked if they any solid information to back up — or dismiss — the rumours swirling around yet another new creature stalking the night. Or knowledge of what had happened to the beasts of grey death that infested the underground just a short while ago.

Nothing. All was quiet.

Too quiet.

But that left her free to pursue her own plans. Find Mina Sun and figure out what the hell she was doing running around with vampires, werewolves and the one remaining creature of grey flesh and corded muscle.

Nestled under an overhang, both to hide in the shadows and keep off some of the misting rain, she hitched her cowl up a little higher to cover her face below the nose. She felt naked without it on but knew pulling the mask on full would attract the attention she sought to avoid. As she leaned against the building opposite Mina's apartment, settling in to watch, her phone pinged. She cursed herself for forgetting to silence it. Glancing at the display, she saw one of the Brothers had indeed responded to her request. Her lips pressed together, but luckily it was a text, so she didn't actually have to talk to him. Flicking open the message, she scanned the details: new creature, new vampire, same evil.

She sighed then silenced her phone. The Brothers were being secretive. But then she'd been cagey herself, not wanting to reveal the nature of her hunt — to find Mina — given their suspect methods and brutal research practices. She'd have to share more details if she wanted to get anything useful out of them, a tit-for-tat she wasn't ready for yet. First, she wanted to figure out if Mina needed to die.

She glanced back at the apartment on the fourth floor. Having only been inside once, she still had an impeccable mental model of the space. The window that opened into Mina's bedroom was dark, as was the main room beside it. The blinds to the other room were shut, but she swore a faint glow escaped between the slats. Though it was hard to tell beyond the streetlights and signs. She shook her head. She'd already called the roommate and got no answer: asleep or screening.

She tapped her fingers on her thigh, considering her next move. Mina's sphere was small, being busy with school — which was closed at this hour — and work.

The boss. Sam. She'd met him a few times. He'd seemed a reasonable sort, despite the tattoos. The shadow looked up and down the street. She pulled out her phone again and entered the name of the shop. A couple of blocks away, and if the listing was correct, she had fifteen minutes. She snugged her backpack on and started off at a jog.

The shadow opened the door to the quiet shop as a woman with kohl-lined eyes and dark red lipstick was leaving. Her gaze followed the woman for a few seconds, making sure she continued on her way, then she glanced around the shop, confirming the owner was the only person left inside. She put on her innocent face as her gaze travelled over the wall, perusing the examples of work that were displayed, easily pegging Mina as the artist for some of them. She returned her attention to the man behind the counter, who had his back to her.

"Excuse me," she said from just inside the door. The man spun his head over his shoulder, betraying his surprise at not being alone, before he settled himself and turned around properly to greet her.

"How can I help you?" He placed the pen in his hand neatly next to the sketchbook on the counter. "Shop's about to close." He peered at her through frameless glasses. Neatly trimmed blond hair gave way to grey at the temples, and tattoos covered his neck before disappearing under the collar of a properly pressed dress shirt. His tie matched his vest which matched the stripe in the shirt.

She took a tentative step into the shop and assembled her face into a mask of worry.

"I hope you can help me. I'm looking for Mina Sun. I know she works here." The man's eyes narrowed, and he tilted his head, exposing a faded tattoo on his neck. *A vampire familiar.* Reflexively her eyes tensed. She forced her expression to relax as her gaze went from it to his face. It might be harder than she thought to get information out of him, but she still had to try — she'd inherited her grandfather's tenacity. She took another step forward.

"We haven't heard from her, and we're worried." She formed her lips into a frown. "I'm Hana, Dale's wife."

CHAPTER SIX

Rhys pulled his hand away from the damp wall that had stopped his fall. The pad of his thumb stung, and his joints ached, but, looking at his palm, the rough brick hadn't drawn blood. Resting his hand on the wall again, he tested his leg, gingerly placing his foot down. The ankle he'd turned on the old, uneven cobblestones of the laneway was cranky but held his weight. In a way, he was lucky the lane was narrow, barely wide enough for the hand carts whose wheels had worn grooves at the edges in centuries past. It meant he'd been able to reach out and catch himself.

But the walls were damp and slimy. Running his palm along his corduroy pants, he told himself it was rain and moss, since the passageway surely never saw the sun. He couldn't actually see what coated the wall in the weak glow cast by the neon signs scattered at irregular intervals along the alley. Continuing along the lane, he soon reached a T-junction. To his right, the passage disappeared into heavy darkness, an utter absence of light. To the left, the Chinese characters for a pharmacy flickered like an SOS. He pulled out his phone in the hopes it would serve as both flashlight and map. In his less cantankerous moments, he grudgingly admitted the phone was a truly phenomenal gadget. In his more curmudgeonly moments, he cursed the infernal thing to hell, back to the demon that spawned it.

He stared at the dot indicating his present location and the blue pin showing his destination. He sighed and turned into the narrow alley on his right that oozed darkness, being completely shrouded from the neon light. There weren't even any windows to break the monotony of gloom. The few metal doors were all closed against the night. The acrid smell of fresh urine mingled with rotten garbage. His phone cast a ghostly blue light in a small arc in front of him.

"Why do secret entrances have to be in dismal locations?" he said to the rats. Just then, a skitter passed behind him, and he froze. "It's only a rat." He refused to look, refused to think there was nowhere to run in the narrow passageway. Not that he could run anyway, his ankle reminded him with a twinge. A flicker of adrenalin coursed through his body. He cursed Dar for pushing him to the periphery of his life, away from danger. It left him with few skills to fight back, if needed. A thud echoed along the narrow passage. He cursed Dar for dying and leaving him to face the danger alone. He breathed deeply and squashed the fear, pressing it down. "I will not go gently," he whispered to the darkness, and it seemed to him the darkness whispered back. Pulling himself up straighter, he continued, approaching the dead end he sought.

A metal door appeared, dim in the darkness. It looked like the others, except for the knocker and plate. The black knocker was simple enough, shaped like a horseshoe. The plate was a similar plain black. But the mouth that held the knocker in place was that of a dragon, flames licking up the side of its head. Made of the same black-coated metal, it was barely visible in the weak light of his phone. With his free hand, Rhys lifted the heavy knocker and let it fall on the plate. The sound tumbled down the alley, causing a frantic skirmish of sounds behind him. He glanced to his right, debating turning around. He banged the knocker again, a couple of times in quick succession. The alley behind him had gone silent. Too silent. Rhys swallowed and closed his eyes. Then he slid his phone into his pocket and turned around, choosing to meet his fate head on.

He opened his eyes, just as a strong arm reached around him and dragged him into a now-open doorway.

Rhys breathed deeply, sucking as much of the astringent scent of cloves into his nostrils as possible. The hands clasping the mug of tea only trembled a bit, but he could explain that away as old age.

"Now you're settled, why don't you tell us who you are and why you're here."

Rhys glanced around for the other part of the 'us' the woman was referring to but there was no one there besides the two of them. Of course, that didn't mean no one was listening. He took a sip of tea to help gather his thoughts, watching her over the rim of his mug. She took her hair out of its tie and shook out the red curls. The orange from the forge fire backlit her cascade of tresses, and it appeared her hair was aflame. Rhys could appreciate her beauty from an aesthetic point of view.

He took another deep sip of the tea before speaking. "You're Finn, yes? Keagan's daughter."

"Mmm." The woman gave such a slight tilt of the head, it was hard to tell if she was agreeing or looking down her nose at him. Judging from the raised eyebrow, he went with the latter.

"I've worked with your father." He took another, deeper draught of tea, wishing he had a little something with which to fortify it, and himself.

"And who are you?"

"My name's Rhys."

The woman's eyes widened slightly. "*The* Rhys? The Librarian?"

"Mmm." It was his turn to tilt his head. "I usually don't refer to myself that way. But I can't imagine there's anyone else called the Librarian who runs in the same circles, as they say." He clasped the warm mug tightly in his hands and glanced around the forge, finally coming to land on the sketchbook she'd left open on the workbench. Obviously, Finn was more than just Keagan's daughter. Even without the ochre tattoos marking her place in the guild, it was clear she had a smith's skill. Looking at the project laid out in front of him, she was a downright engineer.

"So you'll want to be seeing my father then?" Her shoulders sank as she sighed.

"Not necessarily." Rhys stood and walked over to the workbench. He ran his hand over a page in the sketchbook — a linked chain, scythe on one end, mace on the other. "Maybe you can help." He pulled Jack's sketches out of his pocket. "I'm looking for something. I'd given Jack — you know Jack ...?" He could tell from her expression that indeed she did and there was a history there. "I gave him a printout, from a page that's disappeared off the internet. But now...well...."

"Jack's gone, so they say." She started to pull her flaming curls back into a bun but gave up, dropping her hands to the worktable.

"Mmm, yes." Rhys smoothed the pages from Jack's desk onto the workbench beside the sketchbook. She glanced at it, her eyes narrowing. He continued. "I was wondering if perhaps he'd shown it to you or your father the last time he was here, when he came for that thing." He nodded at her sketch.

"The kusarigama." Her voice was wistful, her eyes soft as she said it.

"Your work?" He could tell from her small smile that he'd guessed right. "You're very skilled. Beautiful in form and function."

Cocking her head, she turned her green eyes on him. "Thank you." Smiling, she added, "But flattery will get you nowhere." She turned to her sketchbook and flipped to the next page, this one covered with intricate drawings of mechanical or metal marvels. "Most folks don't see beyond my father's formidable presence." She looked at him with an arched eyebrow. Returning to the book, she flipped through a few more pages until she came to a folded piece of paper. Wrinkles traced lines across the parchment. She pulled it out, unfolded it and placed it beside the paper Rhys had taken from Jack's room.

"My father wanted nothing to do with it. I rescued it from the rubbish heap." She used one of the tools from the bench to flatten it even more then placed the two pieces of paper side by side, laying the tool across them both to weigh them down.

The breath caught in Rhys' throat, even though he was pretty sure what he'd see if he found the printout. Jack's drawing and the picture on the uncrinkled page were the same. A circle, or a hoop, empty in the middle, with etchings along its inner circumference.

"The Blade of the Sun," Finn said. She made a noise, as if to speak, then stopped. Rhys turned to her. She glanced at him, then back at the paper. "I might be able to help you find it. Well, part of it."

Crouched beside the tombstone in the cemetery, fractured scenes of the battle played through Mina's mind: Cam bent back over a tombstone, bleeding on the grey marble; Seema striding naked through the graves, a gleaming blade in her hand; Jack almost dying as he knelt in front of her, a crimson blade in his shoulder, before Lin and her creature carted him away. She lifted her muddy fingers to her lips. Breathing in deeply, she could almost taste Jack's blood in the dirt, even though it was long since washed away by the misting sleet that plagued the city.

She shivered, soaked through, her jeans tight and clammy against her skin. As a vampire, the cold bit less keenly but it still had teeth.

Seema, on the other hand, was a feline and a tropical one at that, regardless of what form she bore. Human at the moment, she stood with her arms hugging her torso. Despite her show of fury and force when she'd taken down Angelos, she seemed small now as she shivered under layers of scarves topped with a heavy wool coat that smelled like wet dog. The thought made Mina smile, given Seema's antipathy to the werewolves. Then she remembered the werewolf that had protected Lin's retreat on the night she'd taken Jack, and the smile fell.

"The trail's gone cold while we tended to your friend." Bee walked back along the path that had been Lin's escape route. Other than being tense, her tutor's expression was unreadable. With Dar dead and Jack gone, Bee had become the de facto leader of the conclave. "Hopefully the others have had more luck picking up his scent in the city."

An icy hand clenched at Mina's gut. The city was full of sounds and smells. And slush to mix it all together. There was little hope of finding Jack by tracking him, and no hope of helping Cam by crouching in a sodden graveyard. She pushed herself up, using the marble stone beside her to counteract the pull of lethargy that threatened to drag her down.

"We need to talk to them." Mina refused to look at Bee, and Bee said nothing.

"Them who?" Seema's teeth chattered as she spoke. Finally, Mina turned to Bee, and saw by the look in Bee's eyes that she knew exactly to whom Mina referred.

"No." Her teacher crossed her arms over her chest.

"It may be our only hope at getting Jack back." Mina mimicked Bee's stance. "And of finding out how to draw Cam out of wherever she's gone."

"Who might be our only hope?" Seema's accent seemed thicker in the cold air. "And why do you need Jack or Cam, anyway? Your priority should be to stop Night." She flicked her deep brown eyes between Bee and Mina. "Take out her army here on earth."

"The wolves?" Bee's eyebrow arched, her lips pulling into a deep frown, as she glared at the Were. "Don't tell me what my priority should be. Somehow I don't think genocide will deprive Night of anything." Despite the distrust and differences of opinion that plagued their relationship recently, Mina had to agree with her.

"The Necrophagus' mansion, then?" Mina tried to make it sound more like a statement.

"No." The word was clipped, Bee's jaw tense. "We find Jack through our normal means. Not by cozying up to the Necrophagus."

"It's not cozying up. It's conversing." Mina dropped her hands to her hips. "Matteo was a normal avenue for Dar."

34

"And now Dar is dead," Bee said in a whisper that hung heavy in the dark graveyard.

"Because he went off and did his own thing." Seema stared intently at a statue, her voice far away. Bee and Mina both looked sharply at her, and she turned her head slowly towards them. "He forgot the cardinal rule: the pride is stronger than the individual." She returned to her contemplation of the statue. "I should know."

Bee walked over to the woman, bringing her face to within inches. "Enough out of you. I'm letting you stay because a couple people I respect think you might be useful."

The woman shifted her eyes to peer at Bee. "Well, you shouldn't pay them any heed — they don't know what they're talking about." She stepped back, starting to amble away on the path out of the cemetery.

"Where are you going?" Mina canted her head sideways.

Seema glanced over her shoulder. "I might see what Rhys is up to." Her eyes flicked to Bee. "Since I imagine he's one of those people who think I might be useful." Turning back around, she continued her slow saunter towards the gate.

Bee's gaze tracked her for a few seconds before returning to Mina. "We meet up with the others. Then we decide what to do." She turned to follow the werecat.

Mina started to follow, one heavy step after the other, as she ran her fingertips over the tombstone that still smelled as if it were slick with blood. With a sigh, she turned away, pausing when a moaning tweaked her ears. Glancing around for the source, a glint of light caught her eye. Her eyebrows pulled together as she knelt down. With a gasp, she spotted what had drawn her attention.

"The Blade of Night." Her voice was barely audible even to herself, yet a shiver coursed along her spine at the words. She looked at the others meandering down the trail. Bee stopped, peering over her shoulder.

"Are you coming?" Bee said.

Mina nodded without fully taking her eyes off the blade. "Be right there." Using the scarf she had tucked in her pocket, she snatched up the obsidian dagger and slid it into her jacket, knowing the others couldn't hear its tortured song. Nausea heaved and sunk in her abdomen...she now had something Lin wanted. Could she trade it for Jack? Or the secret to save Cam?

As she started to jog towards them, a chill breeze skimmed the half-frozen grass, carrying with it a scent of...something familiar. Mina sniffed the air, but the breeze had carried it away. The scent was gone, but it left her unsettled. *I have the Blade of Night in my pocket*, she reminded herself, trying to chase the bogeymen away.

Mina hunched her shoulders against the wind and headed into the darkness, carrying the weight of a thousand souls in her jacket. And, once again, the scent of something tantalizingly, infuriatingly familiar, tickled her nose.

CHAPTER SEVEN

Rhys glanced up from the book he wasn't reading to check on Finn, who shivered beside him despite being nestled in the warmth of the small bookshop. Before leaving the forge, she'd layered herself in wool pants in a vivid plaid, a long turtleneck that fit snug against her neck to hide her unusual tattoos, and a puffy parka with a hood trimmed in fuchsia faux fur. Mitts covered the tattoos and burn marks on her hands.

Finn rubbed said mitts together then pulled the toque on her head lower. She nodded at the man who'd come into view, now that the crowd, mostly middle-aged women, had thinned. "That's him."

Rhys' lips pressed together as he peered at the man over his glasses. He appeared more rock star than serious purveyor of archaeology, with wavy brown hair tumbling over his forehead, not quite hiding the scar over one of his heavy eyebrows nor his dark eyes. An impression reinforced by his outfit of jeans and t-shirt, having stripped off his blazer, which hung over his shoulder from his crooked finger. "You sure? He doesn't look much like a professor."

"All I know is he's the author of this book." Finn shoved the book she'd kept tucked under her arm into his face, though he'd already seen it. A white stone building tinted orange by a setting sun took up most of the cover. But the title was broken by a symbol that looked an awful lot like the drawing of the Blade of the Sun.

Rhys frowned, knowing it was ridiculous. It was just a circle of gold. *But it isn't just.* He took the book and flipped through it again, reviewing the glossy pages tucked at intervals, which showed sketches of long-lost artifacts and pictures of ruins. There were characters that looked very much like the script that circumnavigated the blade in Jack's sketch, writing he hadn't yet been able to decipher. His nose wrinkled and eyebrows drew together. He may have misjudged the vampire. He'd always seen him as Dar's second, penitent for some crime Rhys never asked about, dedicated to the conclave and self improvement, but not terribly erudite. He tutted at himself for his own judgment as he turned the page...and stopped on a drawing he hadn't noticed before. Mina would have said it looked like a bat: the double-ended, crescent-shaped Blade of the Moon. He lifted his gaze from the page to the man: definitely not your average archaeologist. Turning to ask Finn how she'd come to know of the author, he found she was no longer next to him.

She wasn't hard to spot, even with her fiery hair half-hidden by her wool cap. Her physical presence — solid, tall, self-assured, socially obtuse — would have made her easy to pick out in a crowd, but at the moment she was the lone person still standing beside the archaeologist-cum-author, despite the shooing gestures of the store manager who stood behind the man. Rhys started towards her, ready to lend a hand. *Or drag her away*, he thought, hearing the heavy-handed flirtation she was laying on. The man was smiling, signing one last copy of his book for her, and actually seemed engaged by her questions. But as Rhys neared them, his eyes narrowed, and he wondered whether they might have more success convincing the man to join their cause if they'd brought young Sam along.

Besides, there was something about the man's expression — the pieces didn't quite fit together. His words were genial, but the smile didn't reach his eyes. *Sad eyes*, Rhys thought as the man shifted his gaze to him. Clearing his throat, he interrupted Finn's pointless flirtations. "Excuse me."

"The signing is over," the store manager said, the words short and clipped. "The store's closing."

"Yes, I'm sorry. But I'm such a fan." Rhys took Finn's book out from under his arm, ignoring her eyes as they bored into him at the interruption. "My niece wanted to be helpful, having you sign your book for me. She didn't realize I had my own copy." He placed the book down on the table in front of the man, hoping he'd be impressed by its well-read state, but not enough to start discussing its contents. "If you'd be so kind."

"Certainly. I appreciate you coming out on such a dismal night." His cadence carried a melange of his past, precise English infused by the rhythms of Hindi.

"I wouldn't have missed it. Are you in the city long?"

"I've actually started at the university campus downtown." The man handed the book back to Rhys.

"So I may get a chance to hear you speak? That would be grand." The archaeologist inclined his head and smiled, his eyes showing barely a spark. Rhys looked at the book jacket, running his thumb over the circle. He lifted his gaze. "I would love to have the chance to hear about this symbol on your cover."

The smile disappeared from the man's face as it shifted to neutral, and shutters fell in his eyes. "As the man says, the store is closing." He got up from the chair, not even taking his blazer, and headed towards the back of the store.

Rhys pulled an open-mouthed Finn in the opposite direction.

"Do you really think he has any idea what that is? That it's something more than an interesting picture from some history book?" Finn pulled her arm away, and Rhys glanced back.

The man was watching them. "Oh, he definitely knows something," he said as he pushed Finn out in front of him.

Unable to sleep, Mina sat in the chair in Cam's room, feet on the edge of the bed, sketchbook open on her lap as she absentmindedly drew the Cam she knew: smiling, mischievous, vivacious. Human. Not this wasted wreck of a vampire. She peered at Cam's face, half turned towards the wall, and her stomach twisted into knots at the dark shadows under her eyes and the twitch in the hand that lay limp across her stomach. Mina wracked her brain, trying to pinpoint the moment she'd exposed

Cam to the creatures of the netherworld and left her vulnerable to a vampire's bite. The only time she'd seen Cam since her own transformation was when they'd met in St. Frank's square, shortly before her first nightmare encounter with a gargoyle. Em and Ivan had come across them, but neither of them had turned Cam; Mina's blood told her so. Her eyebrows pulled together. Regardless, Cam should be awake. Turning hadn't been like this for her — she'd been in shock, she'd gotten angry, she'd been mortified at feeding on human blood — but she'd never been comatose.

"It has to be whatever Angelos did to you." Mina's voice was barely a whisper. "But what?"

Though she barely saw the page, she took to sketching again, the pencil scratching across the paper in jerky motions as she mulled over her dark thoughts. She drew Jack with his wolf's face and his monk's eyes and his penitent soul. She drew Dar, sketching a sadness she didn't remember seeing in life. She drew Bee, but couldn't tell whether the shuttered eyes spoke of distrust or self-doubt. Next, she started to sketch trees and grass and ended up with her parents' graves. More gravestones appeared beside them, with the names of Dale and Hana, Liam and Maggie. And finally Cam, throat slit by an obsidian blade.

Mina sat straighter, dropping the pencil and sketchbook on the floor as she wiped away the tear that trailed down her cheek. She glanced at her jacket, hanging on the door handle, and a sinuous whisper crept her way. She dropped her feet to the floor and stood up, drawn by the voices in the blade. With a gasp, she flopped back into the chair and returned her attention to her best friend. "I brought this on you, I'll take it away."

Leaning forward, she took the hand that lay by Cam's side, sensing the thready pulse under the cold skin. "I'm going to get you back. Even if I have to bargain with the devil."

The apartment door opened down the hall, and she cocked her head sideways: Brett, using the set of keys she gave him. She stared at Cam, dropping her voice to a whisper. "At least as much as I can. I can't change you being a vampire, but it's not

40

so bad. Though somehow, I think your medical career is over." She'd meant that as a joke, but her throat clenched around the words. Being a doctor had been Cam's focus for as long as Mina had known her. She still remembered the day Cam had taken pity on the too tall, too skinny, completely awkward new girl in high school. She wiped her face again as Brett came into the room.

When she turned her face to him, he stood in the doorway, eyes on Cam. Mina went to stand beside him. He slid his gaze to meet hers and took her hand in his.

"Thank you for watching her for me," she said, pulling the hand away and laying it on his chest. "Though you don't need to, if you have somewhere else to be." She stood on tiptoes to press her lips to his. He placed his free hand on her cheek for a second, then stepped past her into the room, coming to stand by the bed as he dropped his bag on the floor.

"I can study here as well as anywhere."

Mina canted her head as she peered at him. "Study?"

"Trying to better myself. Law school."

"Really?" A heaviness weighed down Mina's stomach at how little she really knew about him, and she vowed to rectify that.

"Really, I have nowhere better to be." He turned to her and gave a lopsided smile. "But shouldn't you be out saving the world or slaying dragons or something?"

She glanced at Cam again, then picked up her holster from the back of the chair. "Yeah, or something."

Sliding into her jacket, the weight of the black blade in the pocket reminded her she needed to deal with it as well. A weak thread of tortured music sang in her blood. Her heart skipped, and she blinked, trying to shut out the twisted melody.

Mina half-heartedly kicked the practice dummy in front of her. After leaving Cam in Brett's care, she'd returned to the

Sanctuary to arm up. Unsure how to go about bargaining for the life of her friend, she'd hung around, hoping being around the others, hearing their plans to find Jack, would spark some idea. But when she got home, it was still light out and the building was quiet as the grave, the others asleep, recharging from a fruitless night of searching for Jack. Without direction, she'd turned to meditation through physical activity, and had come down to the basement to practice and vent her frustration on the dummy. After her first few apathetic kicks and punches, it had been clear which of them would win this fight.

We've lost three people in short order, and yet they still slept like the dead. Though she knew that wasn't quite true: the sounds of life — the shifting and sighing and squirming of an uncomfortable conclave — echoed around her. She aimed a few more tepid blows at the dummy, and almost tripped on her own feet. With a growl, she threw another left hook at the dummy, but her lack of focus meant it went wild.

"Bugger."

As she rolled her shoulder, the music in her veins and the cat-like padding of a vampire's feet told her someone was coming her way, so she wasn't surprised when the door opened and closed behind her. *Bee*. Mina knew without turning around, and her hands clenched in her gloves.

Her jaw tensed. They'd lost three people, and all they had to show for it was her. She punched the form again, driving from her foot, through her hip, into her shoulder. She felt the sting this time. Shaking out her hand, she shifted her weight, getting set up to knee it in retaliation.

"I see the dummy is winning." Bee's voice was light, but Mina caught an undercurrent of tension.

"Would you cut me some slack?" She turned to Bee, deciding she wasn't in the mood for verbal sparring. But seeing the haggard aspect of the woman's face, Mina bit back the harangue building in her chest. Instead, she spun around, aiming another half-hearted kick higher up the form. The form didn't move, and the top of her foot stung.

"I thought we covered that in our first lesson: if I cut you some slack, you die."

Mina pivoted around to see Bee pulling on her gloves. "What's your problem?" Mina's hands came to her hips. "You're always riding me."

"My problem?" Bee's voice was even. "I've lost my mentor and my best friend since you came along. I've lost Jack and Astrid. Three members of my family. Four if we count Quinn." Gloves on, Bee clenched her hands into fists. "My life was ticking along just fine, almost normal. Then you came along, and everything went pear shaped."

Mina took a step towards her. "Guess what? So was mine." Bee peered at her as she sauntered closer. "I know others looked at my life and judged me a failure, a black sheep. But I liked my life. And it was mine." She tapped her chest as she got her face right up to Bee's. "I was happy," she snarled, baring her fangs.

Bee took a step back and sank into a ready position — fists loose but up, light on her toes, centre of gravity lowered. "I told you never to bare your fangs at me."

"Seriously?" Mina took a step back and turned away. "We have bigger things to worry about than—" Before she could finish, Mina found herself on the floor, wind knocked out of her and the words 'your pride' gone with it. She turned over to find Bee looking down at her. Mina scooted back, and half sat up, judging the reach of Bee's kick.

"I thought I taught you better. Never turn your back on your opponent." Bee held out her hand to help Mina up. "Obviously I've been remiss in my lessons."

"I thought we were allies, not opponents." Mina looked at the hand warily for a second, before taking hold of it. When she grasped it tight, she pulled back, using her body weight to drag

Bee down to the floor with her, wrapping her legs around the other woman's torso, and shifting so she was on top of her.

"I guess not so remiss after all," Bee grunted as she bucked to dislodge Mina. But Mina was having none of that. She squeezed her knees into Bee's sides and leaned forward to put her forearm on Bee's neck. She knew her grin was smug, but she couldn't help herself.

And then she found herself with her back on the mat and Bee looming over her. She brought her feet up as Bee came down, throwing the other woman over top her. But her teacher tucked and rolled back up to a ready posture, rocking back and forth. Flipping herself over, Mina mimicked the rocking, and the next time Bee took her down to the mat, she was ready. It still took a few long minutes of grappling before she had her legs scissored around Bee's shoulder, her tutor's arm locked and extended past the break point for most people. But Bee wasn't most people. Still, Mina was worried she'd have to let go or break the elbow, when Bee finally tapped the mat with her free hand.

"That's better. I've always said you were different. Different's not bad, but we need a warrior, not a whiner."

They both stilled as the door to the Sanctuary two floors above them opened and closed. No one was expected. They looked at each other and untangled, both reaching for bladed weapons before heading upstairs.

CHAPTER EIGHT

Rhys tugged the heavy door shut, left to close it himself as Finn forged pell mell into the converging conclave. He tsked as he turned and followed. She might be an ally, but they were still vampires. Emerging from the dark portal at the top of the stairs, Bee looked between him and Finn, a question on her face.

"Do we need to get this place blessed again?" she asked from behind the shirt she tugged over her tank top as she strode towards him. Mina followed behind her, similarly shrugging into outer layers. Given the disgruntled expression on both faces, he couldn't tell who'd won.

"It wouldn't do any good, as you well know." His gaze was drawn to the staircase again, where a pair of eyes near the floor flashed red before Seema the cat leapt out of the darkness and landed on fingers and toes as a woman. A naked woman. The Were cast her gaze around, obviously looking for something, and Rhys soon saw what as she bent to pick up a neatly folded pile of cloth. Her brown, wrinkled limbs moved fluidly as she wrapped it around herself. Turning to Bee, he added, "You could take away my key."

Bee grimaced but didn't ask him for it. Instead she scanned the conclave arrayed around him and Finn. Rhys followed her gaze, and had it brought home again how decimated the group was — so many had been lost in such a short time. Four since Mina was turned; he could understand how some might consider her bad luck. And those that remained were battered, bruised and broken. They may be vampires, but that only meant their physical wounds healed quickly. The raw emotional scars were plain to see, and with the undead those could last centuries. All their attention was now on Bee, and it was obvious she was uncomfortable with the shift. She hastily returned her scrutiny to him. "What's up?"

He paused before answering, catching Seema's sidelong assessment of Finn as the Smith unwrapped the scarf from around her neck, revealing the red ochre tattoos. Rhys followed Finn's lead, removing hat and scarf; it was a tad warm in the Sanctuary. Before he could finish and give a considered response to Bee's question, Finn piped up.

"We've found a clue," she said, her voice rushed, her cheeks flushed. Taking off her toque, her red hair tumbled over her shoulders.

"What Finn's saying is *she* found a clue." Rhys handed Bee the book. "I present to you the Blade of the Sun." He noted the reactions to the mention of the blade. Bee took the book from him, and Mina craned forward, her lips pressed tightly together, as if she was both curious and fearful. But it was the werecat's reaction that most interested him. First, she glowered at him, and he could almost hear an angry cat moan from her belly. She quickly masked that by peering at the book, but her nostrils twitched like she smelled something burning.

"It looks like a book." Bee turned the tome over, inspecting the back. "Nope, still a book." She passed the book to Mina, who opened it and scanned the inside flaps, then closed it to examine the front cover. Mina's lips opened, but Bee spoke before Mina had a chance to. "And it doesn't matter. We don't have time for reading or for magical blades. We need to rescue Jack. Every day that passes the more danger he's in."

"In danger of what?" Seema asked as she peered over Mina's shoulder, as Mina ran her thumb over the cover of the book. "If Lin wanted to kill him, she would have." Mina turned to scowl at the werecat, who looked back at her innocently, though Rhys saw a light in her eyes that belied the innocence. Mina handed her the book and shifted away.

"There are things worse than death, as you well know." He watched the barb hit home, then Seema's attention turned to the book, and his shoulders slumped as guilt at needling her settled in. They'd all suffered recently. In the end, it was Mina who replied, her tone soft.

"As you say. Which is why I need to get back to Cam, see if she's regained consciousness. And head to the Necrophagus' mansion to force them to help her if not."

"Are you kidding?" Finn stepped forward. "You're both being so...selfish." Her mittened hands clenched. "We bring you the weapon that could stop Night turning the world to a desolate wasteland and you're worried about one vampire, one person?"

"Night is *not* coming." Bee crossed her arms over her chest and glared at him, daring him to contradict her. They both were taken aback when Mina stalked towards the cupboards that held their day-to-day weapons.

"What are you doing?" Adeh asked, tracking her across the Sanctuary, but Mina didn't answer.

Finn followed, but Rhys stayed where he was. He watched Seema's intent examination of the book as she ran her fingers over the cover, tracing the image of the building, its intricate carvings and many storeys of windows. Then her finger traced the circle set in the middle of the title: the Blade of the Sun. *She knows what it is.* Next, she grazed the author's name, then opened the book, going straight to the back flap and the writer's picture. Her eyes narrowed.

"Something catch your eye?" Rhys asked, keeping his tone light. She snapped the cover shut and looked up. She shook her head and tried to hold the book casually, but her cheeks flushed.

Mina and Finn returned from the arcade, and the Smith's eyes were wide, shining. "Have you seen the weapons they have?" She came to stand beside him. "I can't believe Da made most of those."

Rhys was about to say something about a pen being better than a sword but stopped...the idea might not be appreciated by this crowd, especially given their current mood.

Bee repeated Adeh's question. "What are you doing?"

Mina glanced back at her as she shrugged into a shoulder holster. "Kitting up, what does it look like?"

She made a face. "You know what I mean, where are you going?"

Mina took her time pulling out a magazine. After loading her gun and chambering a round, she answered. "I already told you. Check on Cam. Then out, to find the Necrophagus...and whoever leads them now. Ask them what they did to Cam."

Bee strode over, stopping inches from Mina. "On and on about your friend," she said, her voice rising. "How many times do you need to be told—"

Mina spun to face Bee. "And Jack. Who do you think knows where he is?"

Rhys took a step back from the fire crackling between the two vampires. Seema stepped over to him and handed him the book, though she didn't quite let go and, for a few seconds, they both held the tome. She shifted to look him in the eyes, which reflected the light from the sconces.

"What clue?" Her voice was crisp and loud in the Sanctuary, caught in a lull between Mina and Bee's argument.

Rhys opened his mouth to answer but was interrupted.

"As I said before, she doesn't get a vote." Bee slid her gaze briefly to Seema, who looked ready to hiss. "The only reason you're even here is because you've lost everything and have nowhere to go."

Seema turned to her, hands on her hips. "As you say, I don't get a vote. However, I still have a voice."

"The man who wrote this —" Rhys started.

"An archaeologist," Finn added.

"The archaeologist who wrote this, well, he might have more information on the blade. I read the book while waiting for Finn. It's as if there is something missing from his tale. Something skirted around, left out on purpose." Rhys held the book up. "And you should have seen the expression on his face when I asked about the symbol."

"You mentioned the blade to him, a mere mortal?" Seema arched an eyebrow.

Rhys glanced at her but didn't answer. *She definitely knows something about the blade.*

"Mr. Devinder Rao was not happy." Finn smiled and rocked up onto her toes.

Seema's eyes went wide, and she snatched the book from Rhys. She ran a thumb over the author's name again before flipping to the back flap. Her eyes squinted and her lips moved.

"Are you sure there's nothing you want to say?" he asked. Her head jerked up, then she snapped the book shut and shoved it back at him.

"Nothing."

He didn't press her, instead turning back to Bee. "We need your help to find the Blade of the Sun. The riddles say—"

"I don't care what the riddles say." Bee held up her hand. "First priority is to help Jack."

Rhys cleared his throat and spoke. "Finn is right. More important than either of them is stopping Night." Both the battling vampires turned their glares to him. To his credit, he didn't flinch.

"I'm sorry." Mina went back to her weapons as she spoke. "That's not *my* priority right now." She pulled out a couple of daggers and a belt of throwing knives, cinching the latter around her waist. Spinning a pair of sai, she tested their weight before sliding them into the sheaths in her boots. Then she looked at Bee. "You know they have him." Mina turned towards the door, glancing over her shoulder before she opened it. "Or they know who does."

Bee didn't stop her as she headed into the night. Instead she turned her attention to Rhys and let out a heavy sigh. Her voice was back to normal when she spoke. "There's been no sign of Night. Without a clear and present danger, we have other priorities."

Rhys' shoulders slumped, and Finn's cheeks flushed. She seemed about to protest when Seema spoke up, sliding her gaze from him to Bee. "I'll go with them, help them in their hunt. Then their quest, however foolish it might be, need not impact the search for Jack."

"As you say, you have no vote, but you do have a voice. I'm not the boss of you." Bee turned on her heel and headed to the arcade holding their armoury. The rest of the conclave soon followed.

Rhys' lips thinned and he clutched the book tight as Seema turned to him. He caught a feral glint before a bland expression transformed her face. "So where do we start hunting this archaeologist?"

CHAPTER NINE

A question gnawed at the edges of her consciousness, eating away at the mind that imprisoned her. Something about the woman who came and went. This body still refused to listen to orders, which meant she couldn't open her eyes to see her, but the hum in her veins when the woman was near sounded familiar. *Maybe it's just that she hovers over me.* But as soon as that thought formed, she dismissed it. There was something else about her. Something ancient and powerful. Something hateful. As she imagined slicing the woman pubis to sternum, she swore her finger twitched again and her mind convulsed with the strength of her loathing.

Why do I hate her? With no answer forthcoming from the charcoal grey prison that held her, she returned to her present puzzle: there was something else she needed to do. Someone she needed to find if she was going to regain her strength and exact vengeance on those who'd stolen it from her back when she was Gabriel, then imprisoned her in that dungeon of emptiness. The last time she'd managed to escape, the Host and their Hunters had tracked her down and separated her from her few companions — they'd even taken away Angelos — leaving her with nothing but her own thoughts to keep her company over the centuries. The Host and their minions would pay, but to do that, she needed to be able to move. That single point of focus tugged her towards consciousness again. Slowly she became aware of her surroundings, even if she couldn't open her eyes or move her limbs. Her back ached and her shoulder blades throbbed. A rustling whisper tickled her ear.

The man watching her shifted, stopping his poetry reading. Wood creaked as he stood, and she sensed him moving away. Her teeth yearned to sink into him, and her gums ached with hunger for blood. So strong was the desire that her mouth almost opened. Almost. The hunger tugged at her gut. The strength of the longing startled her. Even though, she'd consumed flesh, she'd never needed it — or blood — to survive. She focused on the yearning as a jolt sent shivers across her skin. Her eyes fluttered open, and she gasped. He paused, turned towards her, and she watched through half-closed eyes, lying perfectly still. Her body craved his blood, but she'd learned patience in her cage of emptiness. He turned away again, and she exhaled slowly, tamping down the hunger that festered in her gut. Breathing in deeply, she tested the limits of these lungs, imagining the air reaching into the tips of her toes. When she couldn't get another iota of air in, she sighed, pausing at the end, not wanting to exhale the last bit of breath. She inhaled again, expanding her rib cage and diaphragm. She let it out through pursed lips as she examined the room around her through the slits of her eyelids. Not quite daring to open them all the way in case it was all a dream, instead she explored her other senses, testing whether she was truly awake. She wiggled her toes, flexed her fingers. She smelled the earthy scent of the man mingled with lavender and rosemary.

Alive. A breeze caressed her cheek as the man stepped back, sensing her movement. She went completely still as she rooted herself in this world. Starting with her unnatural hearing, she counted pounding pulses all around her: seven distinct beats, in the rooms above and below, each telling a unique story. And one next to her, loud and strong, though a tad off kilter. *But who can blame him, now that Night wakes.* She opened her ears to the distant sounds of a city: the traffic, the caterwauling, the heartbeats. All those souls to devour. Including the one beside her. She couldn't help herself — a smile twitched at the corners of her lips.

Night opened her eyes a little wider, letting in a speck more light, just enough to temper the darkness. She fluttered her lids, giving her vision time to adapt to this bright new world. *It won't be bright for long.* A sigh eased out of her, and she opened her eyes fully.

"I'm alive," she whispered, her voice husky, rough with disuse.

The man let out a small laugh. "Yeah, you're alive. It wasn't a sure thing."

She smiled to herself, her right cheek twitching with her constrained pleasure. "I'm free." She tilted her head to the side. The man with the smooth voice and earthly aroma looked down at her, a tentative smile on his lips. She took in his well-made form — broad shoulders, muscular torso, chiseled face — and decided she might not devour him yet.

"Cam?" he asked, his eyebrows pulling together. "How do you feel, other than alive?"

She ignored him. Sitting up, she lifted her hand, waving it slowing in front of her face, to and fro. Long, delicate fingers hinted at a fine bone structure. The tendons slid under her skin, and the muscles twitched. Turning the hand over, she inspected the lines of the palm, before closing her eyes and running the back of the hand along her cheek. It was soft, well cared for. This boded well. *Angelos chose well*. She stopped short at the thought and opened her eyes again, a frown furrowing the space between.

Angelos. She couldn't sense him anywhere near. She gasped, realizing where she'd last sensed traces of him. The woman. She'd had the sweet-spicy scent of Angelos' blood on her hands. *Has she killed him?* Night swallowed the burning in her throat. *Another person to add to the list of those who need to pay. But not yet*, another voice said.

She nodded half-heartedly as she ran her hands up her torso, across her breasts, over her face, through her hair. She ran her tongue over her lips and the nascent fangs as she gnawed over how to find the woman and tear her heart out. But there was something else she needed to do before she avenged Angelos. Something vital to her quest to get her power back. The image of a brilliant circle flashed in her mind's eye. As she clenched her right hand, she looked down at it, puzzled by its emptiness.

"Cam? Are you okay?" The man crouched in front of her, his hands on the bed on either side of her hips.

Peering into his worried face, her gut convulsed with hunger again, but she tamped it down with ferocity. This one had played his own part in Angelos' death, but she could use him before she punished him. "Cam," she whispered, testing the word out. Some creature deep inside tried to scurry towards the light at the word. She stabbed at it with an ice-cold, obsidian sliver of pain. She fixed a smile to her new face.

"I should call Mina. She's been worried." The man took some device out of his pocket. She grasped his wrist, a little too strongly.

Mina. Now she had a name to go with the hate. "Give me a hand...." She kept her voice weak, then paused, hoping he would fill in his name. She eased her grip; she didn't want him to run away, not until she was ready to give chase.

"Brett," he said, putting out his hand.

Nesting her hand in his, she placed one foot then the other, slowly, gently, on the floor. She wished she were outside, under the starlight, bathed by the moon, with wet moss between her toes. Leaning on the man more than she wanted to, she stood up.

She swayed slightly when she took her hand back, foreign muscles tense and tendons working to keep her upright.

"Are you okay?" The man's concern was written in the planes of his face. She lay a hand on his arm.

"I feel...alive," she said, her lips heavy with lust, though for what she couldn't pinpoint. She ran her hands over this new body, testing its response to her commands. There was a judder to the movement, but it became smoother as she moved fingers along her hips, across her abdomen, over her breasts. She tipped her head up to look at the man.

"I think..." She wanted to say she liked this new body Angelos had procured for her. "I want to go for a walk," she said instead. "Outside." She graced him with a crooked smile. "And get something to eat. I'm hungry."

Then I need to find the Collector. She stuttered and almost tripped at the thought. It came unbidden from some deep wells of knowledge she didn't know she had. Nonetheless, she knew it to be true. This was the thing she needed to do: Find the Collector and get the Blade of the Sun.

CHAPTER TEN

As Mina crept along the dark alley, stalking her prey, she glanced over her shoulder to check she hadn't become the hunted. The knot in her stomach wound tighter, and she wished she weren't so mule-headed and had asked for backup before leaving the Sanctuary. Turning forward again, she frowned. *Not that I would've gotten it.* As she peered into the darkness, the knot jumped into her throat: she couldn't see the shadow she was tracking. Reaching out with other senses, the catawampus flutes no longer resonated through her blood. She shook her head and chastised herself for being such a scaredy-cat. Pausing at every skitter of stone and splash of water, she'd let her quarry get too far ahead.

Mina took the next section of alley in a tiptoed run. If she lost Lin now, if Lin got to the security of the mansion, it might be weeks before Mina had her in her sights again. Mina didn't understand why Lin had stabbed Jack then turned around and spirited him away while leaving Angelos to die. From what little she'd gleaned, Lin and Jack's relationship was contentious.

But maybe I should focus on what to do with this cursed blade. Her hand crept to the left side of her jacket, where the obsidian dagger sat, wrapped in cloth. Why she hadn't left it at the Sanctuary, she didn't know.

Because we're not safe there. Even as she thought it, she knew it wasn't her voice speaking. Filled with equal parts longing and revulsion, she pulled her hand away.

Another drop of water fell from a line overhead, and a grumble rose from the rooftop over her left shoulder. Mina froze, pressing herself into the shadows as she considered pulling her gun from its holster. The sound rumbled again, and she realized it was just some rooftop mechanical box creaking into life. She let out the breath she'd been holding and continued down the alleyway towards the next junction.

"Yup, should have called for backup," she whispered, glancing over her shoulder again as a shadow fluttered overhead.

"Yes, you should have."

Mina spun around and leapt away from the sword that flashed inches from her face. "Lin. Just the woman I've been looking for."

Jack's maker cocked her head as she peered at Mina, letting her blade dip for a second before adjusting her posture and setting the short sword in the ready position: hilt at the waist, point aimed at Mina's chest. But that was enough time for Mina to draw the pair of sharpened sai from her boots. She lowered her centre of gravity and shifted her weight, imitating Lin's stance.

"I know. I've suffered your clumsy tracking for the past 10 minutes."

"Well, it was rude to keep me waiting then."

The blade arced towards her again, the breeze tickling her cheek as she turned sideways to avoid it. Stepping forward along the length of the blade, she tried to snare the sword in the side guards of a sai, but Lin knew her intention, and slipped back, drawing the sword up, out of danger. The move exposed her left torso, and Mina took the opportunity to drive the butt of the other sai into Lin's ribs. She made contact, but Lin was already dancing away, preparing for her next strike. Mina spun the sai around, pointy ends forward as she stepped in a circle around the pivot between them, trying to keep out of Lin's reach as she looked for an opening of her own.

Lin pulled the sword up and back while sliding her front foot forward, setting up to deliver a head-severing slice. In the moment before the downward arc, Mina lunged low, driving the sai in her right hand towards Lin's exposed belly, while lifting the other over head to block the impending strike. She braced herself for a bone-jarring blow, but she still wasn't ready for the impact when it came. Her arm vibrated and her teeth rattled, but she twisted the sai, torquing the blade out of Lin's grasp. The pressure pulled the sai from her hand. Lin arched herself away, and the other sai barely pricked her skin.

Even worse, Mina had overreached in her lunge, and was forced to place her empty hand on the asphalt to catch herself. She snarled as Lin spun away and slipped down to the ground to try to retrieve her sword. Mina kicked it out of reach and let a smile replace the snarl before she picked herself up. As she lifted herself, something contacted with her back and sent her sprawling. She didn't have time to chastise herself for losing focus: cold metal pressed against her throat and a weight dug into her back.

Lin's knee pushed against her spine while Mina's own lost sai was tight against her throat.

"Why were you following me?" Lin's knee sunk deeper, and Mina heard something a pop.

Mina coughed, unable to speak against the metal choking her. Instead of letting up, Lin tugged harder. Mina kicked out, but it didn't do anything to shift Lin, only stole air from her lungs.

Darkness filled Mina's vision. *I guess that answers my question: we do need air to survive.* She frowned, not wanting her last thought to be so random. Then the darkness shifted, and the pressure on her throat eased. The stolen sai clattered to the asphalt as the weight on her back disappeared. Coughing in air, she rolled to her side, looking back at a form swathed in black.

Lin lay sprawled sideways, rubbing her cheek. "Not very sportsmanlike, kicking a woman when she's down."

Mina gasped at the voice that responded.

"You weren't down, Mina was," Bee said. "And I might be more concerned if you fought fair." Before Lin could scoot away, Bee looped a silver lariat around her throat and pulled it taut, using her knee on Lin's back as leverage.

"And you speak of fair," Lin hissed, baring her fangs and kicking out her legs. Snarling, she clawed at the string of silver around her neck, drawing blood.

"I don't care about fair right now." Bee leaned over Lin as she spoke. "I care about Jack." She looked at Mina. "You all right?"

Mina nodded, rubbing her own throat, and decided not to mention her bruised pride. "What are you doing here?" she asked, her voice hoarse. She coughed again and crawled closer to the other two.

Bee shrugged. "We're family and I thought you could use some backup. Besides, you made a solid case, about her leading us to Jack...and Cam."

Catching Lin's expression change, Mina wished she hadn't asked, and Bee hadn't answered. Lin's scratching stopped and her kicking slowed. Her fangs were still bared, and she snarled, lip curled, but her eyes shone with a gleeful malice.

"You don't have to strangle Jack's whereabouts from me." Lin twisted her neck at an unnatural angle to look at Bee, who responded by shoving her knee further between Lin's shoulder blades. Lin hissed a breath in. "I'll give you a hint: somewhere six feet under." Her lips morphed into a sneer as she turned to Mina. "Or I could tell you what Cam...Camellia, right...what she's up to." She brought a finger to her mouth, using teeth and tongue to clean her own blood from underneath the nail. She did this for the remaining three fingers before returning her gaze to Mina. "Your choice."

A stone of ice dropped into Mina's stomach and travel through her abdomen. "What do you mean?"

"Nuhhuh." Lin shook her head, leaning forward against the silver lariat which had already left a red welt on her porcelain skin. "You didn't say the magic word."

"I don't need to." Mina smiled. "I know what she's up to."

"Really?" Lin arched at eyebrow at her and curled her lip.

"Yes," Mina said, though the knot in her stomach returned as she picked up the sai Lin had dropped and strode towards her. "Not much of anything, thanks to you lot."

"Oh no, not me. You have Night to thank for that." Lin's gaze slid from the sai to Mina's face, with a casualness that said she didn't believe her death was imminent. "And you're a little behind on news of what your friend is doing."

60

Hana crept along the rooftop, weaving her way between air conditioning units and abandoned antennae as she tracked the two vampires. The third had fled into the warren of alleys when Hana had startled a snoozing pigeon, drawing the attention of these two away. A frown furrowed her forehead. What she'd witnessed between the three vampires left her filled with confusion and questions.

Still doing her best to be a shadow, she kept her distance from the two she tracked. Though she was safe behind the noise of their petty squabbling, it meant she couldn't hear what they were saying, only that it hadn't gone to plan. Hana agreed: all three were still alive, relatively speaking, despite the thrashing Mina received from the one that got away. Her grandparents had taught her when the two vampire factions met, blood was shed. Of course, if she didn't have other priorities tonight, blood would already have been spilt. They would all be dead — three evil creatures removed from the world.

Including Mina Sun? she asked herself. But that was the puzzle she was there to solve, the conundrum that drew her onto the rooftops in the dark of night. Since when did vampires look out for each other? And, more importantly, when had Mina Sun become one?

Her foot splashed in a puddle, and she almost cursed out loud. Not because it was icy cold, even though it was, and not because it made her foot squelch in her shoe every time she took a step, even if it did. No, she cursed her carelessness. She'd let herself get distracted by the questions rattling around in her brain. Her teeth ground as her jaw clenched. *The only puzzle I need to solve is how to take down two vampires instead of one.*

The said vampires had stopped, the one grasping tightly onto Mina's arm. Hana inched closer to the edge of the roof, keeping low to eavesdrop on what they were saying without being seen, only her eyes and her black hood protruding over the ledge. She exhaled slowly, corralling her heartbeat to become a shadow again.

"What do you think you're doing?" the tall one said, jutting her chin at Mina, her dark skin luminous in the moonlight peeking through the clouds.

Mina pulled her arm away as she replied, saying something about Cam, a name Hana knew. Mina started moving again.

The other one let out a sigh, a huff really, loud enough it carried up to the rooftop. "What about Jack?"

Mina stopped and turned so her face was visible in a halo of light cast by the solitary working lamp along the entire side street. Her eyes glistened in the light, while damp hair stuck to her face, a bruise still mottling her cheek. "Without Lin, we have no hope of finding him. Not tonight." Mina's shoulders drooped. "She knows where he is."

"I know." The other vampire's frown deepened, and she rolled her shoulders.

Mina glanced up, and the shadow dropped down, missing what was said next. Hana breathed deeply to keep her pulse even, imagining herself like a torpid toad, barely alive. When no vampires appeared to rip her throat out, she let the air out in a slow, steady stream from her nostrils, then wiped her runny nose on her sleeve.

She gave it another second before tipping her head over the lip of the roof.

The vampires were gone. She cursed silently again as she dropped back down. The cold of the wet roof finally seeped through her pants, and her shoulders sank.

With a huff, she stood up and looked down. No point in hiding from prey that wasn't there. She'd let herself get distracted once again. And she'd lost. Again. She wasn't used to losing, and she didn't like it. She should have simply killed them and been done with it. *Even Mina?* Dale's face after his mother's funeral rose in her mind's eye. It was followed by his mother's face, etched with parental worry as she asked Hana to watch out for Mina, even though neither Mina nor Dale knew their mutual secret: that she and Hana were warriors in a hidden battle against ancient evils. Shaking her head, Hana glanced down at the desolate alley. *Yes, even Mina.* She nodded forcefully at the night. Better to amputate the diseased hand than lose the limb, her grandmother used to say.

She blinked at the memory, and looked up, using the light of the ringed moon that had appeared in a break in the clouds to staunch the tears. Noting its position, she pulled back the long, black sleeve on her tunic and pressed a button on her watch.

Halfway to sunrise. Time to return to home and hearth. And heart. Hana's heart clenched at the thought of breaking Dale's.

The light over Mina's head pulsed in a nauseating rhythm, even though it was new since she'd lived in the apartment.

"What did Lin mean about your friend?" Bee leaned against the wall beside the door, arms crossed.

Mina glared at her and decided not to tell her it was a bad idea to touch the walls. Instead her lips pressed tight together as she turned back to the door. Placing her hand on it, her mouth pulled into a frown. "Nothing, she said nothing that meant anything. Saying she could tell me what my friend's been up to...I know what she's been up to, lying in bed, comatose." But even as she said it, she knew it wasn't true. The apartment was empty. She took a deep breath, unlocked the door, and walked down the hall to Cam's room.

Bee followed, slowing as they neared the room. "Are you sure you want to go in there?"

"Why wouldn't I?" Mina stopped short in the dark hall. "It's not like she's in there."

"You don't know for sure. She could be..."

"Your senses tell you what mine do. She's not..." Realizing what Bee was implying, that Cam might be dead on the other side of the door, Mina's hand hovered over the doorknob. "She's not here."

"And neither is Brett," Bee said. "But that's not exactly what I meant." She placed her hand over Mina's. "Are you prepared for what you might find?"

She took a shuddering breath, staring at the door.

"Maybe I should go first." Bee's tone was gentle; Mina wasn't used to that from her.

She glanced at her tutor and sometimes adversary. "Thank you."

Bee turned the knob and inched open the door. No creature jumped out at them, and no corpse lay on the bed. The lamp on the bedside table was still on, casting a warm glow over the empty bed and disheveled closet. Mina stepped past Bee to said closet, while Bee went to the bed and the chair beside it.

"This isn't right." Mina looked at the mess that cascaded from the closet. "Something's wrong."

"I know," Bee said. "I feel it. Something wicked came this way."

Mina's brows drew together, not sure what Bee was referring to. "That's not what I meant. This closet. It's catastrophic."

Bee shrugged. "So?"

"It looks like mine. But Cam is a neat freak."

"She was in a hurry?" Bee came up beside her, dropping into a crouch. She picked up one of the pieces of clothing scattered on the floor — Cam's lab coat — and brought it to her nose. Taking a deep breath in, she ran it through her fingers before dropping it. Bee leaned into the dark recesses of the closet, digging around. "There's no sign of anyone other than the two of them, and yet —" Bee stood up and looked around, sniffing the air, mouth open. "There's a smell, a taste, of something foul."

Mina looked at her, eyebrow arched. "I don't smell anything. Maybe your vampiric nose is picking up some forgotten food in the fridge. Or Mrs. Munroe's cooking."

Bee peered at her for a second. "Whatever it is, they're not here. And we have higher priorities than your friend's whereabouts." She headed towards the door, pausing when Mina didn't follow. "What?"

"No." Mina shook her head, crossing her arms. "You have higher priorities." She sighed and turned her gaze to the floor. "I have conflicted ones."

Bee's hands went to her hips, and her legs went a little wider, as she took a half step forward. "You're a member of the conclave," Bee said. "It comes with protection, support, shelter. And responsibilities."

"But I still have other responsibilities. I haven't 'died' yet." Mina dropped her arms to her sides. "Jack was going to help me." She turned back to the picture. "Bloody hell, I had dinner with my family yesterday."

"The conclave is your family now."

"And what about Brett's whereabouts? Or is he not family because he's human?"

"Don't try to con me. If he's in danger, it's because you left him with your friend."

Mina searched for a retort, but the words tasted bitter. Instead she picked up the picture of her and Cam that sat on the desk. Taken at the beach, they each held a long piece of bull kelp they'd been jousting with. It was like she was there: the sound of the waves, the smell of the sea, the ache in her cheeks from laughing. Dale was behind the camera; in a big brother moment, he'd agree to take them to the beach for a day.

"How long have you been a vampire?" Mina turned to Bee. "Do you even remember what it was like? Leaving everything you know, everyone you love behind, surrounded by danger they don't even know exists?"

Bee looked away, at the picture of the Colosseum on the wall, taken by Cam on a trip to celebrate graduating first in her class. "I was far from all that when I was turned. It was easy for me to die."

Mina put the picture down and returned her gaze to Bee. "Cam is my family. Jack is my family." Using her jacket sleeve, she wiped at the tears that welled up. "I want to save them both."

Bee met her gaze, but when she spoke it wasn't the words Mina wanted to hear. "You might not be able to."

CHAPTER ELEVEN

Rhys flinched as a piece of wrought iron clattered to the floor and Finn slammed her hand down.

"I'm going!" She swiped her phone off the table and dropped it into the bag she clutched in her other hand.

"No, you're not!" Keagan's bellow echoed through the cavernous forge. The floor trembled as he stomped towards them, the muscles in his biceps twitching as he clenched his hands into fists like hammers. Rhys kept a wise distance away, suddenly regretting having involved Finn in his escapades. Seema, on the other hand, wandered aimlessly around the hearth, weaving amongst tools and half-finished projects, her swaying saunter feline even though she was human at the moment.

Finn stopped and glared at her father. Rhys followed her fierce gaze. "You don't get a say." Finn's hands came to her hips, and she tossed her head to the side in a failed attempt to get her hair out of her eyes. She huffed out. "In case you hadn't noticed, I'm an adult. Have been for years now. I can go where I please." She slapped the satchel into Rhys' unprepared arms. He fumbled and almost dropped it but managed to collect himself as she disappeared into a back room.

Keagan's face went a darker shade of red. Pivoting, he pointed a finger at Rhys, who pulled himself up, clutching Finn's bag in front of him, poor shield though it might be. "You." The Smith took a menacing step forward, which Rhys mirrored with a cautious step back. "You did this. You filled her head with fanciful notions of the world out there."

"I—" Rhys started, but stopped when Keagan waved his arm, considering for a moment the damage that meaty paw could do, though he'd never known the Smith to express himself through violence.

"You, bloody —" Keagan paused. "— gah, human!" The big man turned to Seema, who had paused at the last outburst.

She quirked an eyebrow at Rhys. "Pardon my French." The Smith lowered his voice and tipped his head at Seema.

"Don't mind me." Seema smiled at him. "I've heard a lot worse."

"A shame."

Finn reappeared, dressed in the clothes of a modern woman rather than a netherworld engineer. Looking at her father, she shook her head. "Fickle," she said with a small smile and an arch of an eyebrow. "What happened to not 'letting that thing in my forge'?"

Keagan cocked his head, a look of confusion passing across his face, morphing to suspicion as he glanced from Finn to Seema to Rhys. Rhys took the opportunity to step back and stay quiet.

"Father, meet Seema." Finn pulled a sweater over her head, tugging the loose turtleneck over her curls before nodding at Seema. "The werecat."

"The werecat." The big man's voice was quiet.

"Pleasure to meet you." Seema purred the words as she inclined her head at Keagan, her long lashes flicking lazily. His face went pale before blooming into an entirely new shade of red. Rhys pressed his lips together to avoid chuckling at the poor man's discomfort.

"I'm leaving." Finn's volume was normal this time as she took her bag back from Rhys. He felt a little more vulnerable without it. Slinging the bag over her shoulder, she turned to Seema. "You could stay and flirt with my father if you'd like. It's about time he had another woman in his life."

"I...." Keagan glanced from Seema to Finn. His face reddened under his beard then he pulled it into a scowl as he regarded her. "You're not going out dressed like that."

"As the woman says, you have no say," Seema said, her tone lyrical.

Keagan turned back to Rhys, away from both the women. "Did you mention to my daughter how dangerous it is out there?"

Rhys tried to speak, but was cut off by Finn, who came up to her father and placed a hand on his face, where the scowl had become a frown.

"I've been out there," Finn said, while Keagan stammered. "More than you lately. I know, 'beware the bogeymen and the ghosts'."

"And humans." Keagan's voice was suddenly quiet. "Especially the handsome ones."

"Yes." Seema's eyes narrowed. "Don't forget the humans."

They all looked at Rhys. "Oh yes, most especially the humans." He nodded as he glanced at them in turn.

"I know," Finn reiterated emphatically as she stood on tiptoes and planted a kiss on her father's forehead. "As if I could ever forget what the humans can do."

Rhys shifted, uncomfortable at witnessing whatever unshared story passed between them, though he had some idea. Then Finn broke away from her father and started up the stairs two at a time.

"I'm going. Who's coming with me?"

"I am." Rhys sidled cautiously past Keagan. "Just not that fast."

Outside, the warm, orange glow of the forge was quickly washed away. The day was a slate grey, and the rain had turned to slushy sleet. Rhys tucked his scarf into the nooks and crannies of his jacket collar, trying to block up all the little passages the wind and ice found their way down. Beside him, Seema shivered, a full body movement that was contagious. Glancing at her, he considered offering his jacket, but it would make little difference layered on top of the scarf, puffy parka and tall, clunky boots. And it wasn't even truly cold, just damp.

"So, where does this man reside?" Seema asked, then rubbed her runny nose on a mitten. "This archaeologist?" She enunciated the syllables as if the word were foreign to her lips.

"Here." Finn pointed to a mark on the map she held.

Rhys was surprised she didn't have some electronic device with a map; even he had that. He homed in on the spot she indicated, his eyebrows pulling together. Glancing from her to Seema, he saw the werecat recognized the location as well, even though Finn didn't seem to think it was anywhere special.

"Um, the museum?" he said, realizing perhaps Keagan was right — maybe Finn wasn't ready for the world at large if she believed the man lived in a museum. And their task was now that much more difficult — they'd planned to corner him at his residence, not barge into a public building. "Dear, I don't think he lives at the museum."

Finn swiveled her head to him and tipped her chin down. "Of course he doesn't live there." Finn started to walk down the street, looking back when they didn't follow. "But he's speaking there today. They have some special exhibit. All the way from India." Rhys flushed at having his assumptions so quickly turned around, and when neither he nor Seema followed, she pulled out her phone and opened some app. "I follow him online."

"Why?" Rhys asked as he walked over to peer at a website splashed with pictures of Devinder Rao.

"He's sexy and smart. Isn't that reason enough?"

"Huh." Seema peered over Rhys' shoulder. "I need to get me one of those." Then she turned away from Finn and started walking the opposite direction. Rhys' shoulders slumped as he wished Dar were there. He'd always been better at navigating interpersonal squabbles.

"Don't you believe me?" Finn strode up to Seema's back, placing a hand on her shoulder. The woman froze under the touch; even Rhys could see her muscles tense. Slowly Seema turned her head to glare at the offending hand. Finn let go and

Seema started walking again. "Or do you not trust me?" Finn shouted after her.

Rhys caught up and placed his hand on Finn's arm, his irritation and weariness colouring his tone despite his best efforts. "I think what Seema means to say, by not saying anything at all, is the museum is that way." He pointed at Seema's back, then turned to follow the werecat cocooned in her layers.

Rhys peered at Seema, who stood beside him in the vaulted hall, still shivering. She trembled even more inside than she had out. His eyebrows furrowed as he wracked his brain for Were diseases. Her arms hugged her chest, her hands rubbing opposite sides, as she stared at the painting in front of her. Rhys turned his attention to the large artwork. Men in jewel-toned jackets and feathered turbans sat on regal horses. Accompanied by elephants and leopards, they carried bows and arrows and brandished swords as they surrounded antlered animals in various stages of death.

Turning back to Seema, he noticed her face was a ghastly white, looking almost like she'd come down with a plague. Then he spotted the colour of her hair — no longer chocolate brown streaked liberally with grey, it was shifting instead towards gold and orange. Rhys swallowed hard and glanced around before returning to her face, where the lines seemed more angular than a minute ago.

He coughed to get her attention, to no avail. "Seema?" He lay a hand on her shoulder and she spun her head to glare at him. Her eyes flashed green and gold before settling into their more human brown. "Are you okay?"

The fire still in her eyes, she glanced sideways, not quite looking at the painting. "Fine," she said through tight lips before turning on her heels to follow the path Finn had taken into the theatre.

Rhys turned back to the painting, trying to decipher what had brought forth the feral cat. But it was like so many other paintings he'd seen in so many other styles, celebrating hunting prowess and casual death. Then he tipped his head sideways and squinted. It might just be the perspective, but the exceedingly large man looming at the left edge appeared to have tusks. And the snake-like creature in the background appeared to have breasts.

"It's astonishing, isn't it?"

Rhys spun his head to look at the person who'd snuck up on him. He hoped the archaeologist-turned-writer didn't notice the momentary widening of his eyes. "What's that?" he asked, turning back to the painting.

"That a painting about massacre can be this beautiful." Mr. Rao turned to him, the smile leaving his face as his eyes narrowed. "You're the man from the bookstore."

A statement, not a question. Rhys nodded. "Guilty as charged, Mr. Rao."

"Devinder." The man tipped his chin and brought a hand to his chest. "Call me Dev."

"Dev. I heard you were speaking today. It seems we share some common interests."

"Probably not so many. I know nothing of this...what was it you mentioned?" The man dismissed the idea with a disingenuous wave of his hand, then turned to leave.

"We missed — oh." Finn stopped on the stairs leading down from the theatre entrance. "— the talk." She waved at the archaeologist and smiled. "Hi."

Seema emerged out of the darkness behind the Smith like an apparition. If Rhys hadn't spent a lifetime observing people, he might have missed the slight tensing of her jaw as her gaze fell on the archaeologist. He swore her eyes flashed gold again. Then he was distracted by the archaeologist's reaction: he stared at Seema, frozen, his head tilted sideways, his mouth open without speaking. It was so blatant even Finn raised an eyebrow, a question on her face.

After a long pause, he glanced back at Rhys. "But if you all want to talk in person, the coffee shop is this way." He jerked his chin to his right shoulder.

Rhys held the cup in his hands, not drinking it, the tea no longer warm, let alone hot. Seema shivered beside him, while Finn absentmindedly sketched some contraption on a napkin.

"You're saying there is no Blade of the Sun?" Rhys asked, triple checking what the archaeologist had said.

The man shook his head. "There isn't. My family were Shields of the Sun for a millennium. Guardians." He brushed away the hair that had fallen in front of his face. "We failed."

"You betrayed." Seema's voice was quiet but thick with some unnamed emotion. These being the first words she'd spoken since the appearance of the archaeologist, they made Rhys even more curious. From her story, she couldn't have met Mr. Rao; she had been hiding in cat form since long before he was born. Still, her knuckles were white with tension as she clasped the empty cup in front of her. She stared at the dregs in the bottom of the cup, then slowly slid her eyes up to meet the archaeologist's. Rhys shifted from the intensity of her gaze, even though he wasn't the target of her ire.

The man took a ragged breath in. "Someone betrayed us, when we were too arrogant to think it possible." He ran a finger over the symbol woven into the title of his book, staring at it intently, as if it would reveal some secret, before looking up at Seema. "You are one of them, aren't you?" He didn't wait for an answer. "We thought you were all dead."

"We *are* all dead."

"What are you talking about?" Finn asked. "Is he referring to the fact you're a Were?" Seema hissed at the woman. Finn tipped back in her chair, crossing her arms over her chest, looking through long lashes at the archaeologist. "Because they're not all dead, as we know very well."

"The Bengali Were," Rhys said.

"Not just any Were," Dev said. "The kings and queens among cats."

"Cats your kin were sworn to protect." Seema pressed her palms into the table.

His cheeks flushed as he looked away across the coffee shop, running a hand through his hair before returning to fiddle with the mugs. "Well, my kin are all dead." He returned his attention to the cover of his book. "I'm also the last of my kind."

"Why are you here?" Rhys asked as he watched the pattern the man's finger traced. "I don't believe in coincidence." The man's finger faltered for a second before picking up its path once more. Again and again the same pattern, without deviation, without error. With a start, Rhys recognized it: an eye in a circle, symbol of the Watchers sworn to protect the Blade of the Sun. "There's something you're not telling us."

The man looked up at him, his lips rounding. His finger stopped its tracing but didn't leave the book. "You're right." His eyes narrowed at Rhys. He glanced at Finn and Seema, then returned to Rhys. "Come back tomorrow. There's something I need to show you."

CHAPTER TWELVE

Night snarled at the dog that barked at her, then swallowed hard against the desire to drag it from its owner, tear at its flesh and eat its heart. But that wouldn't go over well in this new world she found herself in and might break the tenuous hold she had on the man who walked behind her.

Brett. He was stronger than he should have been; in her experience, young, handsome men had the least resistance to her. Yet this one's subconscious fought as she visualized creeping, green tentacles weaving through his mind. Her snarling lips turned to a scowl for a second before she forced them into a smile.

The search for the Collector had been fruitless so far, which grated on her. She should be able to snap her fingers and draw him to her. But this world was a mystery to her, filled with metal and electricity, bright lights and voices in the air. Despite all of this noise, it gave up few clues to the location of kindred spirits. When she'd told Brett she needed to find a friend, he'd offered to use his gadgetry to help. But she didn't trust her hold over him, and the Collector was a creature of the shadows. Which meant she'd searched on foot, using what little magic she had to tease out his scent. Every once in a while, she thought she'd found his trail, only to have it dissipate when a truck thundered by.

They'd been out for hours, in the frigid drizzle and gloom, though she knew she should thank the unholy powers it was overcast, hiding the sun that had now set. As it was, she rubbed at her temples, trying to push the throbbing headache away.

"Are you okay?" Brett asked, a gentle hand landing on her shoulder. "Maybe we should go back?"

"No! I need to find the Collector," she snapped as she tore her shoulder from his grasp.

"The Collector?"

"My friend." She softened her voice, chastising herself at her lapse; she hadn't named who she was looking for. Shaking her head, she paused as sparks of light flickered in her vision. "Sorry, I need..."

"You need to feed."

She spun her head, setting off more sparks that forced her to grasp his arm. "What do you mean?"

He leaned in close. "You're a vampire. You need to feed." He stepped back, and her open lips reached for him. "I just don't know how to help you with that. We should get one of the others."

"Of course." Her lips tingled as she put a name to the aching gums and the burning thirst. Angelos had found her a vampire. Even though she'd been talking to herself, he took it as an answer.

"Let's go then." He lay a hand on her back, in that spot just above the sacrum. A little gasp escaped as she ran her tongue along her teeth, noticing the sharp canines.

"Just a little longer." Headache forgotten, she turned and walked towards the throbbing music up ahead — music meant people in whatever age she found herself. And people meant food. "I can manage this."

Night let the music wash over her, the beat throbbing through her bones. As it pulsed through her blood, it shoved aside the headache and pushed out the lassitude of a millennium of imprisonment. Even with her eyes closed, the lights sent flashes across her retinas. She breathed in deeply. Starved as she was, the mix of sweat and sex and freedom was intoxicating. She was almost afraid to feed: once she started, she might not be able to stop. A shiver down her spine. She exhaled with a soft sigh and opened her eyes. Her gums ached and her blood burned as the hunger coursed through her veins. The veritable buffet laid out all around almost left her paralyzed. Scanning the club, she sought her first mark. In the end her gaze fell on the man beside her. *Brett*. The man who'd read her stories. Whose heart beat a little off kilter. Who smelled faintly of death and blood and Angelos.

I need a replacement for Angelos. She willed him to look at her, and smiled to see him respond. His lopsided grin lifted, thinking her expression was for him. She peered into his eyes, trying to ignore the piercing flashes of light from the strobes in the club. *Maybe he'll do.*

"Let's dance," she said.

"I —"

She grabbed his hand and dragged him onto the floor, silencing his protest with her lips. Holding him close, heat emanated from him as she writhed around him, sinuous and sensual, channeling the soul of a lamia she'd consumed long ago. His heartbeat hiccoughed again, and knew it wasn't because of her. There was some defect in his body. Some weakness. Something she could exploit. She smiled at him, exposing her teeth, which were still the kitten fangs of this body. Her natural canines, long and strong, would take over in time. By then, her magic would be vigorous enough she could cast an impenetrable glamour. But once she was strong, she wouldn't need to.

"What do you want most in this world?" She ran her hand across his chest.

His eyebrow quirked as he peered into her eyes. "To grow old and grey with someone I love." His half smile was sad. "But that's not in the cards."

"I can give that to you." She returned his smile. "Let me give you what you want," she said, her voice rich with compulsion.

His eyes glazed over. "Want?"

"Would you prefer 'need'?" She held him close and ran one hand up his back, the other down his front. "I can give you what you need, if you want it badly enough."

"Whoa." His gaze snapped into focus again, and he backed away, his face serious, as she cupped his crotch. Her smile slipped, and he shook his head. "I need another heart; I don't think you can give me that."

Tamping down the acid that bubbled in her chest, she pitched her voice higher, more helpless kitten than predatory tigress. "And the vampires won't help you? Not even...Mina, is it?"

He looked down at her, the pain in his chest reflected in his eyes. "They don't know. She doesn't know."

"Do you really believe that?" she asked, a mask of concern on her face as she ran her hand up his torso to come to rest over his heart. "If I can hear your heart, so can they."

"They can't help because I won't let them." He pulled away. "And I don't want you to. Me getting a heart means someone else doesn't."

Fire ate at her gut at his resistance, but she kept her tone soft. "But I can give you what you want. Life everlasting. Without pain." She ran her fingers down his torso again, green threads of magic following in their wake. His muscles softened by fractions.

"How?" He didn't look at her as he spoke, but she brought her fingertips to his jaw to turn him towards her, and she saw the hunger in his eyes.

"You know how." She let a little iron into her voice. "You run with the vampires after all."

"Why would you do that?"

"Why wouldn't I? You have a good heart." Her voice deepened as she layered it with compelling magic. "It should be healthy. Don't you want that?"

"I —"

"Don't you want me?" she said. He paused at that, and she noticed the flush of his lips. "Come on, let's go somewhere a little quieter." She took his hand and led him outside, where the cool air hit her, easing the fire inside. She sucked it deep into her belly, like she hadn't breathed in a millennium. He raised his arm to hail a ride. She grabbed it. "Wait." She gave him a lopsided smile when he frowned. "We need someone else." Her voice was husky, this time from yearning rather than power. She left Brett standing off to one side as she sidled up to the group of clubbers who were negotiating how the five of them were all going to get into one cab. She leaned into one of the women. "I can give you a ride where you need to go." Her voice lured and her eyes compelled.

The young woman looked at her, barely turning her head back to her friends when she spoke. "She'll give me a ride home."

Her friends' looks of worry faded as Night stared at them. "Go home." She took the woman's hand and led her back to Brett.

Hana almost growled out loud, but she kept control this time. Even the dark turtleneck pulled up over her face wouldn't have muffled the sound of her frustration. She'd been tracking Mina for a couple of nights, trying to find out where the nest of vampires lived. Trying to catch Mina alone. *Trying to kill her?* asked a voice that sounded suspiciously like her grandmother's. Hana's neck tensed and her lips clenched. It didn't matter: Mina had slipped her tail. Again. And once again, Hana worried Mina had sensed her, that she'd lost her ability to become a shadow, so persistent was her sister-in-law's evasion.

But she had other methods of finding her prey besides tracking. Which was why she was downtown walking along the balance beam of a roof edge. She was searching the old-fashioned way, by visiting Mina's old stomping grounds. The apartment was empty. The tattoo shop closed. Instead, she wandered the neighbourhoods near where Mina lived, visiting the clubs where a vampire might find a meal. And after being jostled one too many times by people half her age, she'd come up to the rooftops, where she could be a shadow in peace.

Hana peered down at the clubgoers below, disappearing into and disgorging from dark doorways that spewed bass into the street. She caught glimpses of some netherworld creatures — a brownie, no need to tame her wild curls and sparkling eyes; a person possessed by a tanuki, fur tufting out the ears; even an incubus testing out his charms on the women and men around him. Normally, she'd have dealt with one or the other of them.

Maybe I should give up finding Mina and go after the incubus. Rain was starting to fall in heavy drops that bordered on snow. She pulled her turtleneck up and loosened her daggers in their sheathes. Then something threw her off balance, her soft-soled shoe almost slipping on the roof ledge. In the crowd outside one of the clubs, in the intermingling of those disgorging and those waiting to get in, a face appeared. A face she recognized: Mina's roommate, the one her sister-in-law had been worried about. The one she was searching for. "Cam." Hana's voice was barely a whisper, yet she chastised herself.

She hopped down onto the fire escape, half sliding down the handrails, then swung herself over the ledge on the bottom level, rather than making a racket lowering the ladder. She landed on the sidewalk with little more than a splash. Lowering her turtleneck slightly, so as to blend in with the other people, she tracked the woman. Her tumultuous curls were loose and bobbed as she strode down the far side of the road, followed by a man Hana felt she should recognize and a woman she was sure she didn't know.

She didn't look directly at them, and instead pretended to make her way along her own side of the street, casting sidelong glances every few light standards to make sure they hadn't seen her, and hadn't turned away. The woman still tracked ahead, eyes forward, pace steady, no question in her movements. Until she stopped. Until she turned a corner into a smaller side street. Hana waited a couple of heartbeats then crossed the road, dodging the scooter delivering takeout. Before reaching the other side, she had her course planned out: she hopped onto a newspaper box, leapt towards the building, and, hooking onto another fire escape, scrambled onto the roof.

She breathed deeply, bringing her shoulders down. Back in her element, she tugged her black toque down and her black turtleneck up, becoming a shadow once more.

Quiet as a mouse, she followed them across two more city blocks, picking her way easily across the roofs, only descending to cross the main roads. Peering into the side streets below, so focused on following them, she lost sight of where they were leading her. Only when she looked up and saw a swath of darkness did a flicker of fear travel through her gut: another fucking cemetery. Between her official job and moonlighting as a shadow, she kept tripping over death.

Exhaling slowly, she screwed her courage up and dropped down into the alley the threesome had vacated. Closing her eyes, she did a quick gut check and listened to any sounds of pursuit. But if there were any creatures following her, the rain muffled their sounds. Opening her eyes and pulling her shoulders back, she slunk across the quiet street.

CHAPTER THIRTEEN

The sounds of darkness swirled around Night. She cocked her head to listen. The whispering of wicked things in the breeze combined with the steady throb of the hungry things lurking below her feet reminded her of the rattle of desiccated bones around her neck as she rode to battle. These things that clung to the shadows, they were hers.

All except one. A pitter pat heartbeat to her left, behind her and just above. Her ear twitched as she tried to focus on it, but it came and went, as if the creature that owned it were blinking in and out of existence. But when the sound was there, it was the tick-tock of a very ordinary human heart.

She scowled, peering at the swath of trees and grass ahead, devoid of light in this over-bright city. Even though she'd never seen one exactly like this, she knew what it was: a home for the dead. The smell of ancient decay, glossed over by greenery and dirt. She sniffed at the wind, trying to tease apart the scents in the air. One caught her interest, and she open her mouth, drawing her lips taut over her teeth as she tugged at it like a strand of silk. Her mouth morphed into a snarl before she snapped her jaw shut: a Hunter. Her lips pressed into a tight line, as her eyebrows scrunched together...the pitter-pat might be human, but it was far from ordinary. A thousand years without light or dark or anything at all, and the Hunters were as much to blame as the Host. Night let her own pulse tick-tock in time with the traitor, imprinting the sound of the tracker's heartbeat in her very veins. Her mouth quirked into a smile — she would hunt the Hunter down and kill it. A cough sounded over her shoulder, reminding her she had a task tonight. The traitor could wait.

Night started across the street, holding the hand of the woman she'd picked up at the club, still in thrall, as Brett trailed behind. In her focus on the Hunter, her enchantment had slipped and, as they got closer, the woman slowed, as if sensing death approaching. Night clasped a little harder, forced a smile on her face and turned to the woman.

"It's a shortcut."

"It's a cemetery."

"Cemetery. Yes." Night glanced back, sensing Brett lagging behind. She marshaled her magic again. "You don't believe in ghosts, do you?" She softened her voice, adding a hint of mockery over top the enchantment. Arriving at the gateway, Night propelled the woman through, a hand on her mid-back, then stepped over the threshold herself, feeling a slight tug as she entered. Like all these places, it was semi-blessed, giving a slight resistance to her presence. But some of the spirits that haunted it welcomed her, and her skin tingled with their pleasure. As she fully entered the fenced grounds, she gasped.

"I've been here before." Her eyes narrowed in her effort to recall when and how and who, but all she remembered was piercing pain. With a sharp shake of her head, she dispelled the phantom pain, composing herself as Brett came up behind her and leaned over her shoulder.

"This is where we found you. Well, where Mina found you."

"Mina?" Night tipped her head sideways as a face flashed in her vision, her ear twitching at a sound behind them. The one whose blood held traces of Angelos. "Mina."

"Your roommate." He shifted from foot to foot, hands in his coat pockets, his forehead furrowed.

"I know." She smiled at him.

"So, what are we doing here?" he asked, his handsome face drawn down into a frown, his forehead furrowing in question. He had some inkling of what was to come, even if the thought hadn't surfaced to his conscious mind yet.

"I told you," she said, her voice hardening.

"No." He shook his head, as she watched the gears turning. "You didn't say."

"I can help you live." She placed her hand on his chest, where his broken heart beat off tempo then turned away.

He snorted beside her. "And how are you going to do that?"

"I'm not going to do anything." Tilting her head, she focused on the teetering, inebriated woman, who'd taken to hopping from headstone to headstone. She walked up to the girl, who looked at her and smiled when Night took her hand. "Come on down from there. The dead won't like that."

"I ain't afraid of no ghosts." The words came out slow and slurred. Nonetheless, she jumped down, forcing Night to catch her.

"You're drunk." Night kept the slight sneer from her lips but not her tone.

"No." The woman's head shook slowly. "Not even a little." She tottered and plopped down onto the wet ground. "Okay maybe just a bit."

Night frowned. She had no patience for inebriation. And she was unsure how the magic would work without a willing victim. "Do you want to live or not?" she asked, her voice like a whip, as Brett came up beside her.

"You're not Mina's roommate, are you?"

"That doesn't answer my question. I'll try again, how much do you want to live?"

He was silent for a minute, and she started to tap her fingers against her leg. Finally, he answered, slowly. "I became a familiar because I wanted to live. I would have died shortly after my brother if I hadn't become one."

"There, that wasn't so hard."

"But I don't want it this badly." He stepped back, and she had to grab his wrist, grasping harder than she should have. Thrall magic worked better when it was soft and coaxing.

Turning to him, she peered deep into his eyes, letting him catch a glimpse of the abyss in hers and giving him a second to drown in the dark wells of power she had access to. "What are you willing to do to live?" Her words came out one by one. She placed a hand on his chest, and his heart skipped a beat. She smiled when he shivered.

Then her fingers curled into claws as he shook his head, dislodging droplets from wet strands of hair that fell over his face. "Not this."

Unclenching her hands, she tried one more time, breathing deeply to marshal the strands of magic. "What will you do to help me help you?" He paused for a couple of catawampus beats of his heart, and her lips opened in expectation. She needed sacrifices and servants. She'd thought the girl would be the former, and he'd be the latter, but the reverse would work.

"What do you want me to do?" He glanced at the girl.

"That's not an answer," Night snapped. "It's a question. Enough."

With a vicious smile, she placed a hand behind his neck and pulled him towards her. His eyes widened, perhaps surprised by the strength of her grip. With a feral snarl, she tipped her head and clamped her lips on his neck, sinking the vampire fangs into flesh and sucking the life-blood out of him in great hungry gulps, drawing his soul down into the darkness with her — if he couldn't answer a simple question, she'd force him to. She gasped as she pulled her fangs out; she didn't want to but she needed to leave him enough life to choose and complete the ritual.

When he collapsed against her, clutching his neck, his skin was the grey of near death, and she dropped him onto the cold ground. She brought her fingertips to her wet lips; she'd never had a vampire's fangs before, and she'd never known how well the blood seasoned the taste of a soul. She glanced at the woman, who was staring at them, fixated, mouth half open in hunger. The woman didn't even recoil as Night turned her bloody visage towards her. "Come here." The woman did as commanded, stumbling to kneeling in front of her. Night reached a red hand down and stroked a damp strand of hair away from her face as eyes watched her reverently. Then Night turned back to Brett, who was on his knees now, gasping for air, trying to fill the void.

"Tell me what you will do to live," she commanded, her voice gravelly, as she grasped the woman's hair, forcing her head back. To punctuate the command, she sank her fangs into the woman's neck, savouring the spice of alcohol, before pulling out. "All you have to do is drink." Brett bent to do as he was told, the muscles in his jaw slack as his mouth dropped open, and Night smiled in victory. But then he stopped, his lips a hair's breadth from the skin and the artery that pulsed intoxicated blood over the woman's neck as she stared at Night with avid eyes. Night ground her teeth together, both out of frustration and to keep from sucking the life out of the woman herself.

Brett shook his head again and his jaw clenched as he broke away and fell back onto the ground, his skin a ghastly green-grey. "I can't."

"You won't, you mean." Night's lips sneered, and her words were crisp.

"If I do this, she dies." His words gasped out of lungs that couldn't get enough air, past a heart that couldn't beat enough blood, with the dark magic unfinished.

"If you don't, *you* die." Night stared at him. "Life and death are full of choices. What's yours?" Night saw in his eyes the moment he made the choice, before he even shook his head. She frowned and her nostrils flared. She cast her eyes around the not-quite-empty graveyard, then her gaze slid to the girl who still convulsed weakly and stared at her, glassy eyed, despite the blood pulsing down her neck. Kneeling beside her, Night ran a hand over the woman's cleavage, under which a strong heart ticked.

Night tipped her head to the side. "What about you? How much do you want to live?"

CHAPTER FOURTEEN

Jack pressed a hand to his shoulder. A dull ache persisted, even though the spot where Lin's sword had slid through was healed over, possibly helped along by the small feedings she brought him. His throat tightened at the thought of where that blood came from. But caught in an eddy of delirium and ravening hunger, and face with an anonymous source of blood, the hunger won out. The feedings might have kept him sane, but they left him haunted by visions from his early afterlife with Lin, when she kept him on a leash, half-crazed by hunger, half by lust.

And now Lin had him on a leash again, though tonight it was literal. As if she didn't trust him. Before they'd left the mansion, she'd laced a chain of silver around his neck. Even though he tried not to tense his neck muscles, it still burned where it touched, driving him to distraction. Delicate, barely a sliver of spider silk in the moonlight — he could probably have broken it, if he tried.

But he didn't try. Instead, he followed Lin like an obedient lapdog, tether or not. He needed to find out what she was up to and find the source of the dreams of a desolate, grey world inhabited by a haunting angel of darkness. It wasn't to save his own skin. And it certainly wasn't because he was falling under her spell again. He shook his head as if to emphasize the thought, catching Em's attention. Whatever Lin's plans for him were, Em would happily slit his throat with a silver blade and shove a stake of ash down it until it reached his heart, judging by the glower she alternated between him and Lin.

"Good night for a walk in the moonlight." He flashed a smile at her, then regretted it as Lin tugged on the silver chain.

"Hush, dog," Lin said, as she sashayed in front of him, lean dancer's limbs clad in skin-tight black leather. His body remembered what had drawn his human self to her in the first place, even if his mind wanted to forget. She cast a lascivious smile at him over her shoulder, as if hearing his thoughts, and he shook his head again to dislodge the images of those limbs naked in the moonlight.

Jack bit his tongue and bided his time. Pressing harder into his shoulder, he winced, letting the pain distract him as he probed it with his fingers. Deep within the wound, a poison still churned. Too distracted, he bumped into Lin when she stopped in front of him, and the old spark kindled as he breathed in the scent of her: orange blossoms and green tea. Swallowing, he glanced up to see the cemetery gates. He'd known where they were headed as soon as they'd turned the corner, even though Lin never said: he could smell the newly buried as well as any of the others. Maybe better than they could, given his half-starved state. The aroma of death, underlaid with blood, was almost suffocating. Its tendrils twisted unseen in the air, and his nostrils flared, causing the odor to burn his sinuses. His mouth dropped open.

"Something died here," Jack uttered without thinking. His fangs hurt and his gums ached, while at the same time he gagged. "Tonight. And it's unburied," he added when Lin slid her gaze his way.

"Death walks the night." Em's glower had faded, replaced by a curious reverence.

"I don't think Death had a part in this." Ivan brushed past Em.

"Trouble in the relationship?" Jack asked, prodding Em to distract himself, but he was once again rewarded by the sear of silver around his neck.

"Don't speak unless spoken to." Lin's lips were tight as she spoke. Despite the intervening centuries, he still knew her well enough to know she wasn't pleased by whatever had happened here. Which meant she was distracted. He noticed the little tick in her jaw as she ground her teeth together. Taking advantage of her distraction, he examined the cemetery with fresh eyes, even though he'd been through it hundreds of times before: how far away the fences were, what hiding places were available, and who was nearby to stop his escape.

Lin, but she was focused on whatever carnage they were approaching, still hidden from Jack by the other vampires.

Em, but she was intent on Lin, her hand on a knife at her hip as if preparing for a fight but just as easily plotting a coup.

Ivan, but he was even more taciturn than usual, wrapped up in thoughts too deep for the behemoth to wade.

Then they arrived at the place of bloodletting, and Jack couldn't think straight let alone plot an escape. He almost fainted at the reek of death mingled with the perfume of blood. Nudging himself into a gap in the line of Necrophagus, he lifted his head over the shoulders to peek at the scene. A woman stood in a puddle of darkness, only her head visible in a halo of light. A cascade of curls like dark chocolate set off the olive skin punctuated by rosy cheeks and red lips. A ghost of recognition passed through his brain, then she stepped fully into the harsh spotlight of the security lamp. Blood smeared down her neck and dripped from the fingers of her free hand. The other dragged something beside her. Jack forced himself to look.

A man. Or what used to be a man. A gash split his chest, and blood dripped onto the skiff of snow covering the ground. Pink blossoms bloomed as warm blood melted snow. A twinge of recognition ate at Jack's gut; there was something familiar underneath the gore.

"We killed him," a voice said, more curious than horrified.

Jack's head swiveled to see another woman kneeling where the man's body had obviously lain. Blood stained her face and neck, coating her jacket and the hands which held something that twitched. Bile rose in his throat as he recognized what it was in the split second before her teeth clamped down on the still beating heart. It throbbed in her grasp even though it should have stopped beating by now. He looked away, but that meant his vision filled with the man's body, heart carved out. Then, as he tore his eyes away from the sucking hole, his gaze fell on the face again, and the flutter of recognition turned to dread.

"Brett." His whisper was lost in the murmurs of the others as they homed in on the woman in the halo of the streetlamp. The harsh words of the vampires indicated they'd just had their world upended; they were used to ruling the night, and now something else did. Jack didn't know what they saw, but his own heart lurched. The part that told him to help Brett warred with the part that knew Brett was beyond help. In the end, he forced himself to be still and keep his eyes trained on the creature before them.

She tipped her head back to the other woman. Seeing what the woman was doing, she hissed and stalked over to her, tearing the bloody heart out of the woman's hands and throwing it in the dirt. "We didn't kill him, my dear. You did." Kneeling on the soft ground, beside Brett's body, she ran bloody fingers through the dirt, scraping up a fistful of mud from an icy puddle at her feet. As she formed it into a ball that shouldn't have held its shape, dirty streaks joined the rivulets of blood down her forearms. Once the ball was somewhat spherical, it began to throb. She knelt down and shoved it into the hole left in Brett's chest, plunging her hand deep in, unencumbered by skin or bone. Keeping her hand in the cavity, she leaned over the body, whispered her lips over Brett's then affixed her mouth to his. A small scream flew by Jack, and he turned to suss out its source, but it vanished in the dark. When he turned back, he stared in horror as Brett's legs kicked and his back arched; a spasm coursed through him as his blue lips in his pale face gasped for air. This was no mere necromancy; even the death dealers only dealt with the almost dead. No, this was a different kind of magic. The hole in Brett's chest glowed green as the woman chanted. Then the light disappeared so quickly Jack put it down to a fear-induced hallucination.

The creature let out a throaty laugh, her fingers clutching at the mud beside her. Brett's body jerked again then went still. Her laughter became a growl. She snarled and beat his chest with muddy hands. "No." Then she froze, only her eyes flicking sideways at them, before she flowed up to standing. In some small mercy, whatever magic she'd been working on Brett had failed: he would stay dead instead of rising as her minion.

Jack's fingers clenched into fists and his stomach churned as the beautiful creature turned to them. Her eyes were black from lid to lid, and glistened with chilling intensity, like orbs of obsidian. He knew those eyes. The angel from his dreams.

Night had arrived.

Night has come. Ivan's gut twisted as the woman paced back and forth through the salon of the mansion, her face blotchy with anger. Her eyes were still black orbs in their sockets, though green sparks flashed in them as she cast her gaze around. He certainly didn't expect Night to show up in the body of the vampire Matteo had made, not after the Herald had failed. But he knew without a sliver of a doubt what creature stood before him.

She spun to face them and spat her words out. "This is where you bring me?" She waved an arm wild, encompassing the room with its rare art and ornate furnishings, and her hand struck the woman she'd brought with her. The woman mewed, and blood welled up on her lips, joining the crimson from the familiar she'd killed. "You think that hurts?" Night pointed a long finger at the woman who peered at her with reverence. "I'll show you pain." Night drew her hand back, fingers splayed to claw at the woman's face.

He coughed, to relieve the tickle of bile in his throat, not being brave enough to intervene. The dark eyes turned on him, though the hand stayed poised to strike. "You have something to say?"

He swallowed as the thing beside her, her golem she'd called it, lifted its head. The woman couldn't have been more than 20, her red hair, so like little Katya's, hung in damp ringlets. It was as if she was staring at him with Katya's long-dead eyes. His skin crawled with a thousand spiders, and he fought a sudden urge to kill it and set fire to the corpse. But it was already dead, beyond the undeath of a vampire, and he'd be just as dead if he gave in to that impulse.

Instead, Ivan rocked back on his heels and shoved his hands in his pockets. Glancing at the poor woman, he shook his head, his gaze drawn back to Night. He'd spent hardly any time with the woman Cam when she'd been a dhamphir with Matteo looming over her, but it was clear that woman was good and gone when he looked into the abyssal eyes. Or rather, when they peered into him.

Their obsidian gleam had an undercoat of green that made him ill and pricked at his memory. He tore his gaze away, sure the spike of phantom pain the memory had tweaked was written on his face, but when he looked left and right, no one paid him any attention, and when he turned back to Night, her dark gaze had moved on.

Ivan considered the path of his undead life. The death of Katya and Maryska. The centuries of mercenary berserking, of fighting for whoever paid his minder the most, followed by slaughtering of Werefolk — fair or foul, he didn't care. Then came the necromancer's magic to form the wildness into something Matteo could control. And there was Em, who had never really cared for anyone but herself. Luca, the gargoyles, Angelos, they'd all been leading him to this.

To Night. His gaze shifted back to her. The guise was different, but the creature behind those eyes was the same: he'd met Night before. He swallowed against the hard stone in his throat; it dropped into his stomach with a terrible heaviness.

As he regarded her pale face and black gaze, her breathing changed to rasping gasps. Her eyes were wide and wild as they scanned the assembled vampires while she clutched her chest, before her attention settled on him for a second.

Her voice was hard and quiet when she spoke, her inhales and exhales even again. "You." Ivan held his breath, only releasing it as he followed her finger to see it point at Lin. "First, find

94

me a place to..." She paused, canting her head as if listening. "Rest." Night turned her neck at an awkward angle to look at Lin. "Then you'll take me to my gargoyles."

Ivan couldn't read Lin's expression, but he knew if he were in her place, he'd hope Night never woke. Given that all the gargoyles were dead save one.

C. René Astle

CHAPTER FIFTEEN

The next afternoon, Rhys and Finn found themselves back at the museum, waiting for Dev. They were without Seema, who had scampered off after they left the museum the day before, perhaps scared off by the archaeologist's keen interest in her and her kind. Or maybe still pursuing her vendetta against wolves, be they wicked or not.

Finn sat beside him, absorbed by weaving a piece of yarn in and out between her fingers. "Cat's cradle," she said without looking up.

"I thought that was a game played by two people. Two children."

"You were wrong." Her voice didn't change, and she stayed focused on her game. After a few seconds, Rhys went back to watching the birds. Finn had arrived at his place early that morning, flushed and flustered. As soon as he'd opened the door, she'd pushed past him, scooped up his cat, who'd shockingly not protested, and plopped herself down in the spare chair...but not before dropping a brown bag on his desk, which he soon discovered contained freshly baked scones. All of this when they weren't due to meet Dev until the afternoon. However, Finn was a fine guest, curling up with his cat, his books and a mug of his tea. He'd left her alone with her thoughts, and she'd done the same for him, until about an hour before it was time to meet Dev. At which point, she'd popped her head up from the book and spoken words after his own heart. "Roti for lunch?"

Rhys was just wiping the last bit of spicy sauce from the corner of his mouth when the archaeologist came up beside him.

The man stood in silence for a minute, peering at the museum, where a banner advertised the latest travelling exhibit: *Hidden Gems of India*. On loan from the collection of Sir Emmerson Windrow, Rhys read, his eyebrows tugging together, his lips sinking into a frown. He knew that name; he'd met the man in his youth, while still living in England, when he'd gone to study some of the man's eclectic collection of artifacts old and new. It had been impressive then and was rumoured to be even larger now, though no one knew exactly what he owned.

"Come on," Dev said, breaking the silence. "There's something you should see."

When they reached the door that led behind the magic curtain to the labs and offices, Rhys rehearsed his cover story, sure someone would stop them. That a guard would bar them from entering the inner sanctum, the holy of holies. Instead, Dev pulled out a plastic badge and waved it in front of a plastic box. With a beep and a flash of a green light, they were admitted. Though being admitted didn't mean they were welcome, judging by the glances Dev shot over his shoulder as he ushered Rhys and Finn through, into a dusky and hushed hallway.

"Ooomph." Rhys bumped into Finn, who'd stopped short. "What...." Then he saw what she was staring at. Row upon row of dead animals — skulls, skeletons and taxidermy specimens — watched them from the walls of the dim corridor, draped in ghostly cobwebs and disappearing into the darkness above.

"Some of the museum's overflow." Dev glanced at the objects of their attention then shut the door softly behind them. "Where's the cat?" he asked, careful to keep his voice neutral, but Rhys recognized the hunger of curiosity in the light tone.

Rhys stammered, trying to think of a good reason Seema wouldn't be here but that wouldn't make the archaeologist less keen to help. But Finn piped up before he could.

"She's probably playing hard to get." She flashed a smile at Dev. "You have something she wants...she has something you want."

Dev's thick eyebrows quirked at that, but he turned and led them through a maze of gloomy passageways, until Rhys was dizzy from turning. He almost expected a minotaur around the next corner, and knew he had no hope of finding his own way out. Then they turned another corner and he was confronted by an enormous set of horns connected to a massive skull. Despite himself, he let out a squeak.

I should have brought a string. He eyed the skeletal creature with suspicion as he followed Dev around another bend where he promptly bumped into him. The man was stopped at another door. Putting his finger to his lips, invoking silence, he cracked it open. He peered into the gloomy space beyond, then stepped through, apparently determining the coast was clear. Finn followed, and Rhys came through last, just as Dev found the light switch. A bank of muted lights flickered on. Rhys blinked, not because of the sudden brightness but the unexpected scene the lights revealed.

They were in a disordered exhibit room, clearly in the middle of being set up: the Hidden Gems of India. Dev's meandering path had probably taken them almost back to where they'd started. Rhys breathed in deeply, sucking in the heady mix of stale arsenic and dust. He was in heaven.

"It's wondrous." He cast his gaze around, not knowing where to focus.

Then he realized the other two were staring at the same thing, Finn with her mouth agape, her hand clutching Dev's.

Turning to look at the object of their intense focus, Rhys took a sharp intake of breath, and his hand went to his chest as his heartbeat tripped over itself. He spared a split second to think how ironic it would be if he keeled over from a heart attack, before moving his lips and trying to form words.

He didn't have much success. "I...It's...Is..."

"The Blade of the Sun." Dev's hushed voice still echoed in the large room, as if they were in a cathedral or an empty theatre. The man's shoulders sagged as he looked at the hand Finn had released, rubbing it with the fingers of the other. "Or part of it at least."

"It's broken." Finn stated what they could all see clearly. "Sundered."

Dev nodded, walking around the case. "Into at least two pieces. The one you see here, and the other half. Though that other half could be shattered into a hundred pieces for all I know."

"No, it's too well made. The break was deliberate. See the marks along that edge?" Finn reached out, moving to touch the glass, but Dev grasped her wrist, pulling her hand away.

"It's already alarmed. It came in that case, not to be taken out. A condition set by the man who owns the pieces in this exhibit."

"Emmerson Windrow." Rhys' hand clenched. "The family money industrialist-turned-venture capitalist-turned-philanthropist."

Dev nodded. "You know him?"

"Our paths crossed a long time ago. He's not a man you want to cross." He glanced around at the rest of the exhibit. "The other pieces aren't as well protected." He followed Dev over to another case, leaving Finn to circle the box that imprisoned the blade.

Dev ran his fingers over a case filled with normal blades, all vicious looking and deadly but ordinary in comparison to the fragments of the Blade of the Sun. "It's almost like he knows that one is special."

"From my limited interaction with the man, I expect he knows a thing or two about the provenance and power of that chunk of arcane weaponry." Rhys nodded over his shoulder at the golden arc. "He doesn't collect things without a purpose."

Dev glanced back at the object of interest, then spun on his heel and sprinted towards it. Rhys followed when he saw what had caught Dev's attention: Finn lying on the floor beside the case.

"Ms. Smith, are you alright?" Dev knelt beside her. Seeing her expression, Rhys knew the Smith wasn't hurt.

"I..."

Just then the door opened. Finn popped up as a large man in a too-tight black suit entered. "Mister Rao...what are you doing here?" The man clasped his hands in front of him, straining the shoulders of his suit jacket.

Dev motioned towards Rhys with a bobble of his head. When he spoke, he laid on an Anglo-Indian accent Rhys hadn't noticed in their previous conversations. "Just showing my old professor and his granddaughter the wonders of my home country." He brought his hands into prayer position in front of his chin.

"You're not allowed to be here without Mr. Windrow's representative."

Dev changed the movement of his head. "I know. He was so excited. I hated to make him wait until the exhibit opens. We are going now."

Rhys stepped towards the door as slowly and feebly as he could muster, Dev's hand on one elbow, Finn's on the other. "Thank you, Devinder. I hope I didn't get you in trouble, but I'm so glad I could see this collection before I die."

"Grandpa!" Finn exclaimed, playing granddaughter with relish. "Don't talk like that."

Dev paused to bow and nod to the goon before following them down the hall.

As Rhys and Finn came to the corner, she leaned towards him, her red curls brushing his cheek. "Do you think he believed us?" she asked, her voice dropping to a husky whisper.

Rhys paused, feigning a cough into his sleeve as he glanced back to see the man on his phone. He caught Dev's eye as he turned back around and kept walking. "I don't think so."

CHAPTER SIXTEEN

Mina's phone buzzed as she crept up the stairs, holding her boots rather than wearing them. Shifting to the left to avoid the creak in the third step, she kept quiet on her trek across the Sanctuary and out the door. Bee was still trying to give her orders, but Mina knew what she needed to do next: find Brett.

She pulled out her phone and swore under her breath when she saw it was another message from Mr. Whitaker. Of Whitaker, Whitaker and Lee. He'd already left one, wanting to set up another meeting to discuss her mother's estate. But Mina had blown him off; she was too busy saving Cam from the clutches of a possessed priest and rescuing Jack from his deranged maker.

Her shoulders drooped as she shuffled across the muted Sanctuary. She'd failed at both tasks. And now she'd lost Brett, her only ally in the conclave. She pressed her head against the door to the outside world, conflicted about whether to keep up her search for Cam, go after Jack or find Brett. *Jack can take care of himself*, she told to herself. *It doesn't matter that he's gravely injured?* another voice asked. "Brett's only human," she whispered to the door before pushing it open. She checked her phone again, but there was still no answer from Brett.

She stepped onto the portico into a drizzly, late winter afternoon, the shroud of clouds imbued with a ghastly pinkish orange. The rest of the conclave still slept — the sun might not kill them, but it certainly made them cranky, so she was glad to avoid them. The only person she usually encountered on these sleepless afternoons was Jack, doing some kata or other in the twilit space. Sitting on the stoop, she checked she had everything she needed. Phone...check. Gun...check. Daggers...check. Mina's hand grazed over her jacket pocket and twitched, almost as if jolted by an electric shock. Obsidian blade...check. She exhaled slowly, her breath forming contrails in the chilly air.

"I need to find a safe home for you." Her voice was quiet even to herself, and she swore the blade answered: *We're at home with you.* Mina swallowed, trying to block out its sibilant whispers. Even out of sight, with fabric between her skin and it, she still sensed the power of its tortured song. Why she hadn't given it to Rhys or Bee, she didn't know. *We want to be with you.*

Mina ignored it, sliding on her boots as she watched cat-clad Seema amble up the walkway to come sit beside her. As she laced her boots, she debated where to go.

"Where would a wayward familiar be on a grey afternoon?" She sighed heavily as she absentmindedly stroked the cat with one hand while spinning a dagger in the other. She cursed herself once again for not getting to know him better: she should know more than he worked in security, he cleaned up nice, and was great in bed.

"I suppose you're here to stop me going off on my own." Mina peered into the cat's golden eyes. Those eyes stared back at her for a second, then Seema turned her head to lick her paw. Mina ran her hand along the cat's back; even though Seema wasn't an actual cat, she seemed okay with it. "If not, maybe you can tell me what to do." The Werecat swished her tail and watched the traffic passing on the street, building to the evening rush hour.

Despite finding her inner human again, Seema still spent long hours in cat form, and Mina got the sense that as cat or human, she'd be happy to spend most of her days sitting on a sun-warmed stoop or curled up on a radiator. In either shape, she was silent more than not. Mina hadn't really sussed her out yet, other than she hated werewolves, and was happy Angelos was dead even though his death had added unpredictability to the prophecies of Night, a nebulous threat that continued to hang over them.

Mina empathized with the cat. They were both orphans, not quite belonging where they found themselves, not quite wanted or trusted. Tolerated, except by a few who might actually want her there, like Jack.

"Jack." Mina huffed, and the cat stopped scratching its ear to look at her. Mina dragged the tip of her dagger along the muddy ground, ignoring echoes of Bee in her mind enjoining her to take care of her blades. Her focus on finding Cam had masked the empty ache in her stomach at losing Jack. Her worry for him and what Lin might do to him came crashing back in tidal waves.

"Jack." Mina's voice softened as wires connected and a spark of an idea flared in her brain. Seema tipped her head, and Mina glanced at her before looking back at the mud in front of her. "Lin has Jack, right?" Seema stayed silent but her eyes were watchful as Mina drew lines in the mud. "And Lin was at the cemetery with Cam. And last I saw Brett, he was watching Cam at my behest. Maybe...." A hushed whisper of hope flittered through the dark despair in her chest. Mina turned to Seema, biting her lip before remembering her fangs. She licked her lips, tasting copper from the small wounds. "Maybe I need to find Jack after all. He might be the key." She sat up straight, then the wave of hope passed. Her shoulders slumped as she remembered the entire conclave had already been searching for Jack.

But Mina knew where he was. With a certainty that had no rational basis, she knew Lin had taken him to the Necrophagus' mansion. Bee agreed but she'd never investigated.

Mina slid her dagger into its sheath, stood up and jumped down the two steps, stopping and turning when she heard a mwrol. Seema peered at her. "Yeah, I know. Bee's said from the start we should focus on Jack. Don't tell her she might have been right." Mina turned back towards the gate, and her phone buzzed again as she reached the bottom step. Pulling it out, she noted the message from Mr. Whitaker had been joined by one from Dale. Mina huffed, then, looking at the time, slid the phone back into her left pocket, her lips lifting in a smile.

"Too late to meet them tonight."

"The squirrel says you can find Jack at Riverside Station."

Mina spun around to find human Seema, stark-naked in the setting sun, a squirming squirrel clutched in one hand. The feral look in her eyes fled as Mina peered at her in shock, still unused to seeing the Were as an unclad human of sagging skin, small breasts and luxurious hair. Seema bent over and let the squirrel go, which Mina suspected was not your garden variety bushy-tailed rat.

Mina waited for the Were to shift or move to get dressed. Instead she stared intently after the squirrel. "Are you going to join me?" Mina finally asked.

Slowly, Seema turned to peer at her, tipping her head sideways as her eyes narrowed. "I have my own ghosts to chase." With that, Seema morphed back to cat, a sight Mina hoped to never see again, all sticking out bones and stretched flesh. Then, with a swish of the tail, she went back inside.

"I take that as a no." Mina turned to the gate and the setting sun.

A wave of grief welled up in Jack's chest, and his throat tightened. He tried to let out the pain in a wail, but it came out as a muted sob. He blinked against the tears that threatened to fall, and the world around him resolved into a muddy grey. His heart clenched to find himself back in the greyscape. Eyes narrowing against the bright slate, he scanned the flat land, turning in a sluggish circle. His shoulder throbbed, and he brought his hand up to rub the ache away. An electric shock coursed down his arm when he touched his skin. Looking down, he saw he was naked, and a spider web of black lines radiated from where he'd been stabbed. He rolled his shoulders, trying to work out the ache. Then stopped.

Something wasn't right. An iridescent black caught his eye as he moved his shoulder again. As he tucked his chin to his shoulder and slid his eyes right, without twisting his torso, the ache moved to his heart. He'd thought it was the weight of this place that caused the heaviness when he moved his shoulder. But it was the heft of inky wings coming from out of his back.

A sharp scream rent the sky nearby, and Jack turned as fast as the thick air and awkward wings would allow. When he saw what had caused the otherworldly screech, he reached to his hip for a gun or a sword, forgetting he was naked.

A gargoyle stood nearby. It wasn't looking at him, even though he was the only other thing alive. Instead, it crouched over a hunk of grey rock. It shifted, and Jack saw the lump was one of its brethren, petrified. A ripple in the ground caused Jack to stumble, which drew the attention of the gargoyle. It howled again, turning away from the lump of stone to stalk towards him, its eyes burning and its teeth gnashing with equal measures rage and hunger.

Jack gasped, sucking in a lungful of air. Sitting upright in the dark room, he hissed in pain. Without thought, his hand came to his shoulder. Glancing down, there were no black lines crisscrossing his torso, though it was sheened with sweat. No wings fluttered from his back, though lethargy threatened to drag him down again. He kicked the sheet off, having had enough of dreams. It was time to get up anyway: the sun had set outside.

Getting dressed, he tested the door and was surprised to find it unlocked. *Lin's getting lazy.* It wasn't that she trusted him, no more than he would her if their positions were reversed. *Maybe it's a trap. Or a test.* Nonetheless, he took the chance presented and crept along the hall to the top of the staircase, where he stopped short. Down below, Lin conversed with Night, bobbing her head in agreement every few seconds. Jack's eyebrows pulled together at the sight of Lin being subservient.

Jack's gaze tracked Night when she strode to the door followed by her shambling golem. He shivered, watching the unfortunate woman. It was clear she was dead and still decomposing, albeit much more slowly than normal. Looking back at Lin, he caught the frown and wrinkling of the nose that told him she felt the same about the golem — vampires might be unnatural, but this thing was an abomination. At least he thought the look was for the golem; it could have been for Night.

Jack mustered up the will to go down and ask her, but she headed for the door herself. He paused for a second, unsure what to do, then he went down the stairs and out the door.

"Why do you haunt me?" Lin asked without turning, barely slowing as she neared the LRT station.

Jack stopped and tipped his head before answering, almost catching the heartbeat of whoever, whatever she was tracking, but it was carried away by the wind and the water. "I figured you'd want me to. I'm your lapdog after all."

There was a hiccough in her step, then she continued striding towards the stairs up to the platform. "When did you ever do what I wanted?" She took the stairs two at a time.

Jack followed her, mulling over his next words, casting his mind back to his heady first days as a vampire. "I did at first, as a dhamphir, new to the world of shadows." He stared at Lin's back, at the lithe limbs of a dancer clad in tight leather, at the smooth hair that shone like onyx, at her carefully crafted demeanor. He'd been entranced by her for a reason. He recalled that feeling now, rather than the image of her killing Dar. "You were my whole world. Its sun, its moon, its very heart." His voice became husky, thick with heated memory.

Her gaze slid sideways towards him, and he paused at the disturbing mix of excitement and hunger written on her face. It was like the expression she'd had when she killed Dar. Nausea crept in to mix with the sorrow as his blood rushed in his ears, drowning out the sounds around him. *How can I stand beside her again?* he asked himself. *Because Night changes everything.* He shifted, uncomfortable with the answer.

"Leave the riddles to me," Lin scoffed, casting her gaze along the track as the station started to vibrate with an inbound train.

Jack scanned the platform. There was only one other person there, bundled up in a worn jacket and a toque pulled low over his ears. Turning back to Lin, he continued. "Your riddles ensnared me."

She snorted as she craned her head, as if looking for something above them. All Jack saw was a glass ceiling covered in bird crap and caked-on dust. "I was your heart." Her lips formed a sneer as she turned to him. "Until you decided you'd had enough of me. And then you tried to kill your sun, slay your moon, cut out your heart." Lin's voice became a thin hiss.

"I'd had enough of killing. Enough of death." He took a step towards her. "But not enough of you."

Lin barked a sharp laugh. "A vampire who's had too much blood. You need to get your head out of the dark place it's in and get real." The train pulled in, squealing to a stop. Lin glanced overhead again before getting on. She didn't speak to him, but neither did she shoo him away.

As he entered, he stepped up close behind her. "I know." He pitched his voice low, his lips whispering over the skin of her neck. With the night dark outside, now the sun had set, he caught her gaze reflected in the train window. She was silent on the trip across the river, and Jack had no desire to speak, his stomach churning. On the other side, the train descended underground, and he wondered where she was leading him.

He didn't have long to wonder; she got off at the first stop in an area between the noisy club district and the shrouded neighbourhood of palatial, old homes. Lin strode ahead of him, and he had to jog to keep up. As they surfaced into a clear, icy night, she paused and tilted her head, as if listening, then turned the corner into an alleyway. Jack followed.

And stopped short at the person they found there. "Mina." Jack's heart stopped for a second as Mina's mouth opened with a gasp. She started to speak then the space between her eyes wrinkled in question.

"Mina?" Lin's eyes narrowed, and a half smile twisted her lips as she looked from Jack to Mina. "Ah, she is the one."

"What?"

"The one who made you smile."

Jack forced himself to look away from Mina to Lin. "I don't know what you mean. She's Luca's rebellion against Matteo. Just a stupid dhamphir." He spat out the last few words, his eyes sliding towards Mina. He imagined ice and stone when he looked at her. Her head tilted, her eyes furrowed, and her lips parted in an unasked question.

"But she's the one who makes your heart skip a beat nowadays." Lin lay her hand on Jack's chest as she turned to Mina, who still stared at him, as if Lin hadn't spoken. "And she's not a dhamphir anymore. She's dracul."

"We've been looking everywhere for you." Mina stepped towards him, shying away from Lin. "We thought you were dead, or as near as."

Jack took a deep breath, forcing the words out on the exhale, forcing his posture to be casual, his arms going wide. "Here I am."

"As you can see, he's fine." Lin's voice dripped with venom. "And free. He could return to you any time he wanted to." Lin pushed past Mina, walking down the alley as if to test him.

"Is that true?" Mina looked at him.

"Which part?" He looked away.

"Both, I guess." She ground a heel into the sidewalk.

Jack swallowed passed the lump in his throat. "Yes."

Mina spared a backward glance at Lin, her lips closing into a tight line, then returned her attention to Jack. Her hand lifted, her fingers coming to his chest before dropping again. "The conclave needs you." She paused. "I need you."

Jack's gut twisted. "As you can see, I don't need them. Or you." He stepped past her to follow Lin then stopped, almost turning, at Mina's intake of breath.

There was silence for a second then she spoke. "I miss you. I miss the brooding, I miss the angst. Heck, I even miss the riddles."

His chin dipped down, but he didn't turn, forcing his eyes to stay on Lin as she sashayed down the alley. "I don't." As he started forward again, leaving Mina behind, he didn't dare look back. Instead he focused on Lin and a too-fast heartbeat.

When he caught up to Lin, she turned her head to the side. "Good boy. But if you want me to trust you and your treacherous heart, you're going to have to earn it." She shifted to face the street but kept her eyes to the asphalt. "Do you hear that person on the roof behind us?" Her gaze slid to Jack and she placed a hand on his chest. Her touch was cold through his shirt. His unnatural ears picked up the tick-tick-tock but he didn't move, not looking anywhere but at her ear. "Imprint the heartbeat in your blood," she said as Jack started to shake his head.

"Why?" His heart raced.

She turned fully to face him. Jack almost recoiled at the ferocity in her gaze. "Because I say so. Dredge up the hunter buried in your soul. Track that heartbeat. Find it."

"Do you want me to kill it?" he asked, anticipating and dreading the answer.

"No. Leave the killing to me."

That answer terrified Jack even more, and he racked his brain for excuses.

C. René Astle

CHAPTER SEVENTEEN

A searing pain coursed from Night's back through her entire body. For a terrible moment, she was locked in rigour surrounded by a void. Without light...without darkness. Her body frozen, all except her eyes, which flew open as she tried to banish the emptiness and the sensation of power being ripped from her nerves, like a thousand red-hot needles being shot through her body. She drew a ragged breath in and let it out with a shudder.

Wiggling a toe, she found she could move, and sat up, running her hands over her abdomen. Her back ached, and she wanted to blame the overly soft bed. But oily black, phantom feathers fluttered at the edge of her vision. Her eyes slid a millimetre to the right, but so did the flicker. They weren't real. She let out a slow sigh. Not anymore. Eons ago, they'd been very real and a key that unlocked a well of power. Like the legend of Samson and his hair, except her strength had been in those wings. And the Host had sliced them from her using a blade of pure light wielded in pure hate. The severing had torn the magic from her in long silver filaments. Punishment for joining her lover in his rebellion, and then killing him when he betrayed their common cause: freedom from the Host and their rigid rules. Thinking on it now, she didn't know what irked the Host more — her rebellion against them or her loyalty to the cause.

Either way they'd stolen her wings from her, severing her from the deepest wells of power, in an age before time. She'd been trying to get back that power ever since. And if not that, then to make the Host pay for what they'd done.

She hadn't wanted to sleep, fearful of being locked in the abyss again. But the voices of the dead called to, a weight on her chest, like a millstone pressing the air from her lung. And when the dead had something to say, it was wise to listen.

And they had shared a secret. It wasn't the Collector she needed, but something in his collection. A blade of pure light to wield in pure hate. With it, she could avenge her loss, and maybe, just maybe, get back what was stolen from her. The excitement trilled through her veins like an electric shock.

Canting her head, Night huffed. Even though she couldn't see the sun, she knew it was still day outside. She picked up the book that lay on the bedside table — a hefty tome the previous occupant had been reading — and threw it against the wall, barely missing her golem, who lay curled by the door. The girl's head popped up, her eyes shining in hope as they looked at Night.

A green spark flashed as Night flicked a finger, and the girl yelped. She smiled; she couldn't yet access the darkest magics, but she has some. Kicking off the covers, she strode naked across the room and pulled on the clothes she'd worn the previous night.

She held up the shirt and scowled. "I hate the mundane details of humanity." The garment was plain and drab, and smelt of decay, but it would do for now. She certainly wasn't wasting precious magic on making it shimmer. Not when she had a much more important mission.

"I need to find the blade of light."

What unmakes can make again. Besides, she could always make herself shimmer the old-fashioned way: slaughter a lamia and make a coat.

Ivan hung back, staying away from the front line of the phalanx of vampires, who were all grim as if heading to battle. Or execution. He stared at the back of Night's head. He maintained a distance where he was out of sword's reach but close enough to watch her. Just to be sure he was right. Lin flanked on the left, returned from whatever errand she and Jack had gone on; her golem was on the right. Every now and then Night glanced at the creature, and her fingernails tapped her thigh. As he inhaled, Ivan suspected she sensed what he did: the woman was rotting. Neither alive nor undead, whatever magic Night had wrought had gone wrong. Her grey pallor was pasty even in the dim light, her red curls limp and plastered to her head, like Katya after she was killed. An ache settled above his stomach, and he shifted his gaze back to Night, not wanting to be reminded of his dead daughter, but the ache turned to a burn.

Night cast her gaze sidelong over her shoulder, and Ivan glanced away, not wanting to be caught thinking. Thinking got you killed. His pulse quickened at the idea that she could detect dissension in his heartbeat. When he looked back, she'd turned her attention towards the river and the dark bulk of empty warehouses. Her creature glanced around, and as her eyes grazed over him, they were glassy, milky almost. He shivered, and looked at Em, who sulked behind the A-list, alternating between glaring daggers at Lin and sliding surreptitious glances at Night. Clad in black leathers, head to toe, she was ready for the prowl — or a fight — yet she was consigned to being a lackey. They all were. *Cannon fodder.*

Night ran her hands over her body, through her hair, across her lips as she walked. Every now and then her limbs went herky-jerky, like a tendon had caught on bone, as if her bits and pieces didn't quite fit together. But these became less and less as she made her way towards the target warehouse. No one had told her yet what she would find. Ivan slowed even more. Her neck cracked as she tilted her head one way then the other, appearing to listen to some unheard sound. She stopped, and the phalanx halted as well. Vampires glanced nervously at each other then at the dim surroundings, searching for a threat. But she just reached up, grabbing at the air as if to pluck a star out of the sky.

Ivan flexed his shoulders and turned his head side to side, trying to crack the tension out of his own neck. As they started walking again, he peered along the canyons of containers to his left that led towards the dark river. He was a creature of the steppe. The gentle bobbing of the ocean put him in mind of waves of grass, and the rush of the surf, the rustle of grass. But this sluggish, murky meander of water looked like oozing tar in the dark, waiting to drag him down, and if he watched it too long, the bloodthirsty creature inside him rebelled, causing him to become unbalanced, nauseous. Whatever made vampires what they were hated water.

Night slowed as they arrived at the door, its shiny chain and oiled padlock the only sign of care in the long line of abandoned warehouses. Her limbs became still, and even her hair didn't seem to move in the breeze off the water.

"Where are my gargoyles?" she asked, staring steadfastly at the door, her voice even as ice.

Lin glanced back, possibly looking for an ally in this nest of vipers...or a patsy. Ivan didn't need to read minds to know what was going through hers: she didn't want to be the one to tell Night her royal guard of gargoyles had been reduced to one raving specimen. But whatever excuse Lin had planned was interrupted by something slamming into the other side of the door. They all jumped back, almost in unison, even Night.

Lin stepped towards the door, making a cooing sound deep in her throat. The door groaned as a mass hit it again, pushing Lin away, a pained expression cracking her normally serene visage. The phalanx edge back. All except Night, who flew at the door and started tearing at the chain with her fingers. The door rattled again, the hinges squealing, as a mass of muscle pounded into it.

"Stop!" Lin said, then froze as Night twisted her head around, lips thin and cheeks flushed, to peer at Lin. A taut silence filled the darkness. Lin's breath misted the air. "I meant the gargoyle. That it shouldn't attack."

"Of course it should." Night's face, normally a tanned olive, was a pale grey in the low light of the city reflected off the clouds. "You don't keep a lion in a cage and not expect it to turn on its keeper." She looked like she would channel the gargoyle's fury at Lin, a green miasma forming around her. Then a snarl sounded from the shadows to Ivan's left. Spinning, lowering his centre of gravity, he prepared to be pounced on. He'd almost forgotten about the werewolves Lin had bargained with to guard this particular cage.

Night didn't even look at the werewolf, keeping her back to the creature that sprang out of the darkness, as she continued to stare at Lin. "Why do I only hear one heartbeat on the other side of the door?" she asked, her lips tense. The werewolf changed tactics mid-leap and landed on all fours, coming to kneel before Night. Caught mid-transformation, it was even more horrific than it would have been as a wolf.

Casually, Night turned to the beast. Its shoulders heaved, and its bristly skin glistened with sweat.

"Majesty." The word was mauled by its still long snout.

She laid a hand on its head, in between tufted ears, then crouched before it, sliding her hand down its jaw. It shivered and looked at the ground between her feet. Placing her fingertips on its chin, below its retreating canines, she lifted its head up, forcing it to look at her. "You'll be honest with me, right, dog?" The wolf huffed, then nodded its head. "What's happened to my gargoyles?"

"One gargoyle." The half-transitioned maw chewed the word. "The others are dead," it slurred, looking away. *Casting an accusatory eye at the vampires*, Ivan thought. Night used her fingernails to drag the now mostly human Were up. The wolf tilted her head down but lifted her eyes up to Night. "But one beast survives." The werewolf's words became clearer as her transition continued. She couldn't keep a toothy smile from her face. The look sent a river of ice through Ivan's veins. "And were there's one...."

Night finished the wolf's statement. "I can make more." The thing on the other side of the door rammed it again, causing the door to bulge. Ivan jumped back, and reached one hand for his blade, the other for his gun. He swallowed hard as the wolf handed Night the key to the padlock. "I suppose I won't kill you then." Her gaze slid to Lin. "At least not tonight."

A pair of eyes glistened in the dark of the warehouse. Catching what little light came in from outside, the orbs turned into two iridescent beetles. As Night waited at the threshold, it sniffed her, as if it were unsure of what to do with this new thing invading its nest. But it was her beast. It would learn to bow before her. Or it would die.

Night stepped towards it, holding out a hand to keep the others back, though they seemed disinclined to come in anyway. *Cowards.* She picked her way over bones and gristle, keeping to the arrow of moonlight let in by the open door. A low growl rose from the creature as it lowered to a crouch that could have been preparation either to kneel or to attack. She paused, narrowing her eyes, lifting her chin, trying to remember how to treat injured animals, besides killing them. All things considered, she'd rather not kill it — it was her last gargoyle after all. The thought still caused acid to burn in her chest. Lin had finally spat out the truth: she'd let those meddlesome Athanatos kill all but one. Breathing into her back, Night reminded herself where there was one, there could be more. With her hand out, palm forward, she stepped forward another pace then stopped and waited. *Let it come to me.* Ignoring the impatient shifting and sibilant whispers behind her, she waited.

The scent of its tension joined the odors in the rank air of the warehouse, creeping in underneath the reek of rancid meat and decomposition mixed with urine and feces. Crouching down to its level, she spoke in an even voice. "I'll make them pay — both those that killed your brethren and those who kept you caged like an animal. But you need to come with me." A hard core of steel entered her voice. "Now."

There was silence in the corner. No movement but also no more growling. The beetle eyes stared then blinked. She stared back, her patience wearing thin. "If you don't move, you die," she said through a clenched jaw. "I can't have malingerers in my army." A murmur rose behind her, and she turned to hiss them into silence. That's when the creature moved. Shifting with subtle

118

speed, it came right up to her hand, sniffing with its mouth open, its head inching into the light. But it didn't attack.

Carefully, hair by hair, Night moved her hand to stroke the creature's head. It had the glorious grey skin she remembered. She ran her hand down its back, causing it to coo, until her fingers came to its back. Leathery wings flapped lazily, and acid burned in her throat at the sight. It had wings while hers had been severed from her. Her hand clenched, her nails digging into her palm. The creature hopped back, and she noticed the battered state of its wings. She breathed deeply, forcing her fingers to release. "My poor, sweet thing. I'm sorry if I frightened you."

She held her hand out. It shuffled forward again, and she brought her fingertips to its face, which was not so beastly. Almost human, in fact. She canted her head, her eyes narrowing as she peered at it. "What are you?" It was similar to the gargoyles she'd had when the world was young, but not the same. The creature churred, opening its lips in a semblance of a smile. That's when she saw the fangs, not quite the canines of a Wolf, but neither the even serrated maw of a gargoyle. "Oh, I like you," she whispered as the fangs grew a little bit longer.

She stopped her stroking, placed her hands on her knees, and stood up. Striding to the door, she stopped just outside the warehouse. The others shifted back and into a fighting stance, as the creature followed her. She glanced sideways at a tickle on her hand. The gargoyle, squatted beside her, had sent a probing tongue out, like a snake, to taste the air, to find her fingers. At her other side, her golem crouched and hissed at it. She swatted the golem, drawing blood with her sharp nails, and the woman scurried back. She let the gargoyle lick the blood from her nails then pet its hairless head. A skitter to her left drew her gaze to the roof of a nearby warehouse.

She closed her eyes and found a familiar heartbeat. Sniffing the air, she tasted a familiar scent. The shadow that had plagued her steps last night was back.

"Lin," she said, her voice quiet. Her old servant came to kneel in front of her. "Get up. No need for ceremony."

Lin stood, but Night noted the shake in her hands, the flutter in her heart, the quaver of her lips. *She's afraid. Good.*

"Come closer," she whispered. Lin leaned towards her without actually stepping forward. Night moved her lips over Lin's cheek as her fingers wrapped around her arm. "Do you hear that person over there?" Lin's mouth opened, but Night cut her off. "The one who dares stalk me?" Lin nodded, her head shifting sideways to look at her. Night dug her fingernails into the vampire's arm. "I told you to find it and kill it." Lin nodded sharply, but Night tipped her head as a different idea formed. "Don't. Instead, find who it loves and kill them...no, bring whoever that is to me." Lin stepped back and nodded again.

Pointing at Em, she said, "You will tell me how this beautiful creature was made." She placed her hand gently on the creature's head again, and it churred in response.

CHAPTER EIGHTEEN

Ivan stood in the grey afternoon, ignoring the big, fluffy flakes of snow that fell and melted as soon as they landed on his face. It wasn't really snow until it was up to his knees, or he couldn't see a hand held in front of his face. He was supposed to be hunting for a man Night sought but gave few details on. Instead, he stared at the tattoo shop across the street, without really seeing it. People walking by flowed around him as they rushed about; every once in a while, one would glance at his face before shying away a bit more. Maybe sensing the steel of his resolve if not the horror of the things he'd done.

But he barely registered any of it. His head was full of other sights, other sounds...other times. He relived another day, also on the edge of winter. On the cusp between day and night.

The cars honking as they slushed through the wet streets became the clang of metal on metal and the whinny of nervous horses. The murmur of passersby was the roar of battle rage in his ears. The pounding of hooves reverberated through the ground, up his legs, and into his chest. The temperature dropped as darkness descended, and he continued to stare.

Smoke and water swirled in his vision as he fought his way through the tide of people, the tugging undertow of battle. He shouldn't be out there, sword and axe in hand. He should have been nestled under furs with Maryska, his wife, her body softer, more malleable, more beautiful after having borne and birthed their only child. He loved to run his lips along her stretch marks while cupping her breasts in his calloused hands. Those moments were precious, captured between the responsibilities of leadership and the demands of little Katya's curiosity about the world. Katya, his angel of russet curls and bright smiles.

That's why he fought the flow of people. She and Maryska were out there somewhere on the other side of this melee. His wife could take care of herself, a warrior in her own right before bearing Katya. But their daughter, she'd barely picked up a toy bow.

The strangers had come as night fell, a small group led by a man too smooth to be the traveller he claimed. Too clean for Ivan's liking. But the dictates of hospitality demanded Ivan share their fire. The travellers had refused any of the food and drink they were offered, a refusal that spat on the clan's generosity. They didn't want to impose, the slick man said after glancing at his companions. They had their own food, and were only seeking the safety of company, he added, his words punctuated by the howl of wolves.

They'd sat around the fire for an hour, the clan asking for news of the wider world, the strangers dropping small gems of information. The unmarried women of the clan had smiled behind hands at the close-shaven, slim men in the party. Then the pair of female travellers had asked for a place to clean the road off, even though they were cleaner than the women of the clan. His wife, being first among the women, had shown them to the river, glancing his way as she left the fire, her eyes reflecting the unease in his chest. Then she'd walked away, Katya half asleep on her hip, followed by a handful of others curious about the strange women, with their dark hair that shone in the moonlight and their black eyes that ate the stars.

Shortly after that, more strangers arrived, embracing those already there. That was when the clan members who still sat around the fire started to shift, edging away from the strangers. Their movements showed they shared Ivan's unease: these folks were too polished and too clean to have come from these harsh trails. The strangers kept up their banter, as if oblivious to the change in the air.

Ivan moved further away from the group, on the pretense of getting more food, noting his warriors were doing the same. He waited until he was out of the circle of light cast by the fire and his eyes adjusted to the darkness before he hastened his pace to retrieve his weaponry.

122

He was in his tent, one hand closing around the hilt of his sword, axe already in the other, when the first scream pierced the night. A crystal-clear shard of noise that was abruptly cut off.

That's when he headed towards the river. Towards Katya and Maryska. The fire at the centre of the camp smoldered, as if it had been doused with water, cloaking the encampment in a shroud of smoke that burned his throat. Ivan sensed rather than saw the form appear to his left. He spun towards it, swinging his sword in an arc as he turned. The blade cut through the man's torso from shoulder to waist.

Correction. Not a man. Ivan didn't know what the thing was, but it certainly wasn't human. The shriek it made as its insides spilled out caused his guts to liquefy. Whatever it was, it wasn't getting up soon, and there were likely more of them in the dark haze. He yanked at his sword, the tip wedged into the ground from the force of his follow-through. Pulling it free, he turned and continued his push towards the river through acrid, blinding smoke.

Another scream split the night, and Ivan broke into a run. He passed the fire, now a heap of ash. Just beyond, a small form lay on the ground, a fiery halo around its head. Her head. Something inside him convulsed and died.

"Katya!" Ivan powered through the last few steps and slid to a stop, sinking to his knees, dropping his sword and axe. Gently, tentatively, he turned the limp body over.

"Katya," he whispered, cradling his daughter in his arms, brushing curls from her face, his hands covered with the blood that seeped from the wound in her neck.

He howled, raising his head to a sky he couldn't see, his pain blocking out the melee around him. An inhuman howl answered him back. He didn't care. He dropped his chin to his chest. As he moved, he saw a cascade of copper in his peripheral vision.

Maryska. A form crouched over her. Neither man nor beast, it held her almost as he held Katya, and its long, dark hair mingled with his wife's.

Then it raised its head. A woman. His wife's blood dripped from her teeth, surely his daughter's blood on her lips. She, it, stared at him with shining eyes that ate the stars. That and a howl of empty rage were all Ivan remembered before something hit his head and his world went black.

And he'd remained in darkness ever since. Until Night rose again. Now, he was awake, and the pain speared his chest.

A car screeched to a stop nearby. Ivan blinked. Back in the present, he lifted his head, and peered in through the tattoo shop window. It was empty except for the man behind the counter. Lips pulled into a severe frown, Ivan considered his next move as he watched the man oblivious to the beast on his doorstep. He couldn't remember crossing the street. All he remembered were those eyes — she wore a different cloak now, but the eyes were the same. Eyes that ate the stars. There was no doubt: Ivan had met Night before.

Mina sat in the near darkness, surrounded by lifeless dummies and unmoving pommel horses, tossing star after star into the torso of a man-shaped target. She tried to make sense of Jack turning her away. They'd faced down a gargoyle. Together they could certainly take on Lin. Unless he didn't want to. *Unless he wants to be with her.*

"Why do I always pick the broken ones?" The dummies and pommel horses didn't offer their opinion. She cursed as her finger slipped and the blade nicked her. Sucking at the wound, her stomach twitched, reminding her she needed to feed. It had been days and the creature in her blood gnawed at her insides. Normally she'd turn to Brett but he was still MIA.

The corner of her lip quirked up. "Brett's not broken." Then her heart sank again. He was another person she'd lost and couldn't find. And Jack, the one she'd found, didn't want to be.

Despite the constant twilight inside the bowels of the Sanctuary, she knew the day outside was almost done, which meant she hadn't slept and wouldn't get to. She rubbed the space where her eyebrows met her nose. She hadn't really noticed much difference between being a dhamphir and a dracul yet except the headaches she got if she was outside too long during the day — no mad fighting skills, no new unnatural music in her veins, no greater hunger. Her stomach tweaked again, and Mina leaned her head back against the pommel horse she'd sat down beside. A slithering, sinuous sound grew softly around her, and her hand went to her jacket pocket, to the blade she'd yet to find a home for. It was still there, but even through the fabric, she knew the sound wasn't coming from it. The dagger was quiet, recalcitrant even.

Without shifting anything but her head, and barely that, she scanned the dim room. She didn't see anything, but there was a subtle shift in the air. Something was there in the darkness with her. Her stomach fluttered and her fingers reached towards the abandoned stars beside her. Then she saw a golden pair of eyes staring back at her and she retracted her hand, leaving the star behind. The werecat sauntered over and jumped onto her legs.

"Do you know how close you came to having a blade embedded in your head?" The cat turned a circle in response, then settled down to knead her stomach, a soft purr vibrating through its body into its paws. Mina lifted her empty hand to stroke the cat's head. Despite having seen the transition herself, she had a hard time connecting this cat with the woman it shifted into. It didn't help that Seema was cat more often than not, even though she'd found her human form again.

"I'm not really up for company right now." Mina gave up the effort of petting the cat, her hand flopping back down to the floor. The cat ignored her, instead jumping off her and nipping her hand almost hard enough to draw blood. "Hey!" she said. The cat danced back, jumping up onto a pommel horse. Mina glowered at her. "What's gotten into you?"

In answer, the cat jumped off the horse and shifted, mid-air, into a naked Seema, long wavy hair covering her small breasts. "Stop feeling sorry for yourself." She peered at Mina with serious brown eyes, flecked with gold.

"I'm not." Her voice lifted in indignation she didn't really feel.

"You feel sorry you can't save everyone. I know what that's like." Seema's voice was soft and lyrical.

"No, you don't." Mina scowled.

"And I know sitting here in the dark won't help anyone."

Mina's anger flared. "Says the woman who hid for a lifetime then spun around to avenge Mike's death, heedless of the consequences. Like bringing about the descent of Night." She stopped herself, hand coming to her mouth, shocked at her own words. "I'm sorry."

Seema's eyes narrowed. "Being sorry doesn't change it, though you might be right." A shoulder moved under the cascade of hair. "But guilt and self-pity won't help either." She quirked an eyebrow. "I know."

"It might help me."

"From my experience, that's unlikely." There was silence from Seema for a minute, and Mina let it grow, until the woman stepped forward. "What I do know is Sam called with some big news."

"What big news?" Mina frowned, wondering why he hadn't shared with her.

Seema shrugged a bony shoulder. "He's asked Bee to meet him at his shop."

"Bee?" Mina stared at the floor in front of Seema's bare feet. "She told you this?"

"Not exactly. But people don't always notice a cat curled up in the corner." Seema padded past her, heading towards the door, but Mina heard her stop. "I think you should be there," she added.

"Why?" Mina asked, but then she felt a whisper of air and knew she was alone again. She shifted her gaze to the impaled target and weighed her options. With Jack rejecting her, Cam gone and Brett missing, she really didn't have any. She wiped away the tears that threatened and swallowed away the lump in her throat.

With a huff, she got up and tromped up the stairs in her shit-kicking biker boots. It had been a while — a week, at least — since she'd seen Sam. Time to haunt his doorstep again.

CHAPTER NINETEEN

Mina watched from the corner as Sam shifted and twitched behind the counter of his own shop, every once in a while glancing sidelong at Rhys in between staring at Ivan. She was curious about what was making self-possessed Sam so uncomfortable in his own domain. It wasn't the behemoth — Ivan might be a mountain with a shaved, tattooed head bedazzled by piercings, but that was nothing Sam hadn't seen before, and Sam seemed fine gawping openly at him. It wasn't Bee either, even though she was the one interrogating the behemoth; Sam mostly ignored her. Instead, his gaze kept flicking back to Rhys. Her head tipped sideways as she peered at Rhys herself, trying to understand what about the old bookworm unsettled Sam.

"Why shouldn't I just kill you?" Bee stood pillar straight, facing Ivan, her hands on her hips, fingertips inches from multiple weapons. Seema, who'd told Mina about this meeting she wasn't invited to, was nowhere to be found, even in curled-up cat form.

"I think we should at least listen to what he has to say." Rhys stepped forward, laying a hand on Bee's arm. *A braver soul than I*, Mina thought.

"Why?" Bee turned to glare at him, slicing her hand through the air to point at Ivan, who leaned against the concrete support post at the end of the counter. "He's killed more than a few of us over the years."

"And yet here he is, at your mercy. Surrounded by enemies. Why would he do that, if not for a good reason?"

"Maybe he's a spy." Bee quirked an eyebrow at him, demanding a response.

Rhys stepped back, his gaze sliding to Ivan. "At least listen to him before you kill him." Ivan shifted at that but stayed silent, perhaps not as dumb as people took him for. "Besides, we need all the help we can get."

"Why, what can he possibly help us with?" Bee crossed her arms over her chest.

Mina mimicked her posture, then dropped her hands to her hips a second later when she realized what she was doing. "Can he help us get Jack back?" She frowned; even her tone copied Bee's in its strident accusation.

Rhys ran his hands over Sam's counter, breathing deeply, as if he was preparing to explain good behaviour to a child. Mina saw Bee's lips press together. "Night," he said when he finally spoke. "Maybe he can help us defeat Night." This time Ivan opened his mouth to speak but Bee cut him short.

"Not this again." Her voice got louder.

Rhys' rose to match her. "Yes, this." Mina took a breath, wanting to bring the conversation back to Cam and Jack and Brett.

"Night *has not* come." Bee's hands went to her hips. Ivan made a sound but was quelled by her glare.

"What about the sickness, the disease, the Blade of the Sun?"

"It's all hearsay, rumours, arcane riddles."

"Like the Blade of Night?" Mina added, her eyebrow arched but her voice quiet. The blade, still in her jacket pocket, seemed to sing at the mentioned of its name. Bee turned her fiery gaze on her before returning her attention to Ivan.

"Why didn't you come directly to us?" she asked. "Why involve Sam?"

Ivan continued to lean on the support post, arms crossed over his chest. "Somehow I didn't think you'd invite me in." He nodded at Sam. "Him I knew where to find, and this isn't holy ground."

"So you threaten our man to get us here?"

"To get you to listen." Ivan scuffed his shoe along the floor. "And there was no threat." He nodded at Sam. "Ask him."

Bee turned her glower on Sam. He cringed, and Mina sympathized.

"I..." Sam started, shifting his gaze to Mina. She gave him a shrug and a half smile. "No, there was no threat." He stood up straighter, glancing at Rhys before returning to face Bee.

130

"You believe him?" Bee asked, eyebrow arched.

"Not my stage, not my drama." He raised his hands beside his head.

"What the hell does that mean?"

"I neither believe nor disbelieve." Sam shrugged, shoulders falling a little bit further on the release. "I'm just the messenger. Please don't shoot me." He looked away, picking up a pen to sketch on his scratch pad.

"Hmm, I've heard that before." Bee returned her penetrating gaze to Ivan. "Why do this? Why now?"

Ivan looked at a spot between Mina and Bee, but his unfocused eyes saw something much further away. "Because, as your man says, Night has returned." He returned to the present and nodded at Rhys.

"Enough about Night." Bee sighed. Mina leaned forward to speak, and watched Rhys do the same, but Ivan beat them to it.

"I've seen her. I've seen bits of what she can do, weak as she is." He looked at the floor. "And it's made me finally come to my senses after taking leave of them so many years ago."

"Why should we believe you?" Mina asked, her voice even.

He shook his head slightly, the muscles in his neck flexing. "You shouldn't. I wouldn't if I were you." He released his hands from across his chest and stood up to his full, overshadowing height. "But you can test me." He took a step towards Bee. Her response was subtle, a shift of this joint, a twitch of that muscle, but Mina saw her teacher prepare to fight. Ivan stopped in the middle of the shop.

"Bring us Jack," Bee said.

Ivan paused, his mouth hanging open for a few moments before speaking. "I can't bring him if he doesn't want to come."

Mina came to stand shoulder to shoulder beside Bee, intentionally mimicking the hands on the hips this time. "Fine. Find Brett and bring him safely home."

Ivan's brow furrowed. "Your familiar?" Mina nodded. Her stomach fell as Ivan's expression did. "I can't. He's dead."

"How do you know that?" Bee's voice was quiet.

Ivan held his hands up in peace. "I wasn't there. I came after she killed him."

"Who?" Mina spat the word out.

"I can take you to her."

"To who?" Sam asked, not looking up from his doodle.

"To Night, of course." Ivan cast his gaze around the small assembly.

"I don't understand," Dev said. The archaeologist leaned over Sam's shoulder to stab a finger at the screen Rhys had open on his laptop. The three of them were the only ones left in Sam's shop. The vampires had cleared out, taking the behemoth with them. Presumably to interrogate him in ways they felt humans were too delicate to witness. Rhys was fine with that. Dev had shown up as they were leaving, at Rhys' behest: he wanted to get the scholar's opinion on the webpage he'd found.

"It's a computer...you can't actually touch the paper." Dev didn't respond, aiming a rattling cough into his sleeve instead, but Sam pulled a face on the archaeologist's behalf. Rhys ignored him and used a corner of his sleeve to wipe away the fingerprint that sat on top the scanned image of a very sketchy sketch, a circle with some poorly delineated writing beside it. He presumed it was the Blade of the Sun, as did Dev, but the archaeologist could make no more sense of the writing than he could.

"Neither of you can read that?" Sam asked in between sips of his coffee. He'd deigned to make Rhys a mug of tea, though Dev had declined either brew.

"Oh, I can read it." Rhys swivelled the bar stool to face them, mug in hand.

"But it still makes no sense." Dev finished Rhys' thought, gesturing at the computer as if it were at fault, then a sneeze followed the cough. This time, he aimed it into his tweed jacket.

"What does it say? Can you translate?" Sam's eyebrows pulled together as he handed Dev a tissue. The archaeologist tipped his head in thanks.

"Same old." Rhys took a sip of tea, and huffed, causing his glasses to steam up. It was some epicurean blend; not his comfortable Earl Grey. "It speaks of the Blade of the Sun being the key to destroying Night. For once and for all."

"Not exactly." Dev rubbed his temples, his eyes squinting as he looked at the image. Leaning forward again, he skimmed over a line, keeping his finger off the screen this time. "It says it was the key to destroying Night. Past." He stepped back, turning away and swallowing before looking at them again. "But that isn't possible. Night walks."

"Are you certain you're okay?" Sam asked. "Sure you don't want some tea?"

"I'm fine. Thank you. Just adjusting to a new city. Maybe still jet lag?"

"Jet lag doesn't give you a fever." Sipping his tea, Rhys mulled over the image and Dev's translation. "But what I really don't get is this bit." He tracked a faint line, almost an afterthought, with his finger. "As the Moon cannot shine if severed from the Sun, Night has no power if severed from the Dark. The Sun is a blade of light."

"That seems obvious enough. Slice up Night with this sunny blade, and poof." Sam made a motion with his free hand. "No more Night."

"Okay, but what about the rest?"

Dev took up the recitation. "What the Sun takes can be taken again. But the Dark reaches ever on, grasping for what was stolen by the morning light."

Rhys put his mug down on the counter beside his computer. "Not enough context."

"No, not enough English." Sam cocked his head and peered over Rhys' shoulder, causing Rhys to turn to look at the door, but there was no one there. Returning his gaze to flick between Rhys and Dev, Sam continued, his tone curious but his expression grave. "What if what the sun takes can be taken back again?"

"Yes, that's what it says."

"No, I mean what if Night can take back what was taken if she takes back the Blade of the Sun." He shook his head and smiled then. "No, that's silly." His face scrunched up, his glasses lifting before he let out a sneeze into his shirt sleeve. "Sorry."

"No, I'm sorry if I made you ill." Dev gave Sam a small smile.

Rhys smiled to see he'd been right about Dev. After a minute of Dev and Sam's sideways glances and shy grins, he cleared his throat. "You might be onto something, Sam."

CHAPTER TWENTY

Night brooded on the throne of bones. The space between her eyebrows scrunched tight, and a scowl carved lines into the planes of her face, despite her efforts to turn that frown upside down. Once she wrested her full power back from those who'd stolen it, she'd forestall aging, slowing down cellular damage and decay — or trade this body in for a newer model. But for now, this shell was all she had, and it was still fragile, as was her hold on it.

She shifted in the uncomfortable atrocity of a chair, disgruntled at the former owner's choice of decor. She appreciated the aesthetics, with its carvings of righteous creatures contorted in agony, being punished for their judgment of the wicked, but the execution was lacking finesse. The contours bordered on self-castigation. And this body's posterior was bonier than she was used to. She rolled her shoulders back — the space between her shoulder blades ached, though she wasn't sure if it was because of the effort of sitting upright or a phantom pain from wings severed long ago.

Cloaked in cantankerousness, she debated what to do with her meager resources: one broken, mutant gargoyle; a decaying golem; a pack of snipping werewolves; and a handful of untrustworthy vampires. She scanned the room through narrowed eyes. *Not much of an army.* She tapped a finger on the armrest. A nose nudged at her fingers. Sliding her gaze sideways, she stroked the gargoyle's head. *I need a bigger army to regain my power. And to control that army, I need more magic.* Night growled at the vicious circle. *I need to find the Collector.* The man had some artifact, some weapon she could wield to seize what was hers. Or so said the whispers in the void. Her stomach ached with the yearning that the whispers were true.

Her new pet, her golem, shifted at her other side, trying to rub her chin against Night's hand again. She slapped the woman's face, using her fingernails to draw a line of welts across her cheek that soon welled up with blood. The girl touched her hand to her face then looked at the blood on her fingers with glassy eyes. She brought her fingers to her lips and licked the crimson liquid off them slowly, one by one. Night shivered, and let a low growl reverberate in her throat, but the woman barely paused.

Night flicked her fingers in annoyance, sending sparks of magic from her fingertips at the pixie unlucky enough to have gotten in her way, and the creature jerked, a marionette on her sinister strings. The frown carved deeper into her face. There was something off with her magic in this world, and it wasn't just that she was newly awakened. It tasted off, smelt off.

At that moment, Em sidled through the door, and Night's gaze swivelled from the pixie's contortions to her. The blonde vampire froze, as if pinned in place like a bug, and Night almost sent tendrils of purulent magic to twist around the woman's throat. But something in the woman's expression made her pause. Em apparently marshalled her courage, as she pulled her shoulders back and strode across the room, sinking to kneel in front of her.

"What is it?"

"I..." Em stared at the floor.

"Look at me." Night reached down, digging her fingernails into the skin under the woman's chin. "And don't stammer."

Em's eyes lifted, coming to Night's face for a second before sliding over her shoulder. She looked about to speak, then closed her mouth again.

"You disturbed me for a reason. Spit it out or get out."

There was a flash in Em's eyes as they flicked to her face again. "A hobgoblin came by." Em's nose wrinkled, but she reached a paper towards Night, her hand remarkably steady. "Said you'd be interested in this."

Night took the burnt piece of parchment between her fingertips. "Did you test it?" she asked, her eyes sliding to Em's face. The vampire's eyes widened for a moment.

"I...no."

136

With a flick of the wrist, Night presented the paper to her. "You open it then."

Em took the paper back, holding it away from her as she carefully unfolded it. No screaming curse or whispered hex emerged, though that didn't mean there wasn't something more insidious woven into the fibres, the ink and the words. The vampire's hair cascaded over her shoulder when she tipped her head to read the paper, eyebrows pulling together.

"What is it?" Night snatched the sheet away.

"It's a map, with some squiggles."

The drawing meant nothing to Night, but the squiggles took her breath away. She couldn't believe it. She didn't have to find the Collector. He'd found her. "It's a name," she said, not really speaking to anyone but herself.

Absentmindedly, she tapped the armrest before sending another cold spark at the pixie, who whimpered when it hit his bare chest. A copper tang bloomed in the stuffy room as magic broke skin. Her golem shifted again, sniffing the air, glazed eyes watching the pixie twist and contort. Night slid her gaze sideways, her shoulders drooping as she sighed. The golem was no replacement for Angelos, her mind and soul bound to her only by magic rather than by will.

"What time is it?" she asked Em, even though she knew the sun hadn't set.

The woman looked at some contraption. Her eyes flicked to Night's face then over her shoulder once again before she responded. "Two hours until sunset."

Like most creatures of shadow, the sunlight weakened her, burnt exposed skin, and pierced into her skull like a spear of light. But for her, it also revealed her true, inhuman form to those with the Eye. She could blind them and drive them mad before they raised the alarm...if she were strong enough. But if she were strong enough, she wouldn't need to.

Once the Blade of the Sun was hers, it would all change. She'd bleed power from the day itself. And the Host would never sever her from the dark wells of her own power again. Once she had the blade, she'd reign over both dark and light, day and night.

She slammed her palm down on the armrest, causing her tiresome golem to flinch. "Close enough," she said through tight lips. "Take me to this place." She held the parchment for Em to see, and the woman glanced at her then gave a sharp nod.

"You, come." Night beckoned Lin with a crooked finger. The vampire's jaw ticked with tension, but she complied, stepping carefully around the golem, her nose wrinkled. "This is the place?" Night asked. "You're sure?"

They stood on the stairs of a brick building, elaborate knocker on the green door and a glistening set of numbers on a plaque matching those on the sheet of paper. Lin's eyes slid to Em, and Night's gaze followed before returning to Lin. The animosity between the two vampires amused her, and she relished making Lin confirm the information Em had provided.

"It's what the paper says." Lin's eyes flickered over her face before turning to stare at the door. Night could see the woman knew the consequences of making a mistake.

"Knock." She jerked her hand to indicate she should rap the knocker. Lin did, and started to step back. "Where do you think you're going?" Lin froze. "You're my shield."

Lin returned to the door, her hand reaching behind her back to rest on the hilt of the short blade she had nestled there.

The knob rattled, and Night took a breath in. She coiled what magic she had, letting it writhe in her abdomen and wriggle through her limbs. Her shoulders tensed as she readied for battle. But when the door opened, it revealed a dour-faced woman. Salt-and-pepper hair marshalled into a severe bun tugged her face in one direction while her deep frown pulled the other. Black eyes stared at them from behind tortoise-shell glasses.

138

When the woman spoke, her voice was precise and imperious, but not hostile. And betrayed no power beyond that of a woman of wealth and means. "What can I do for you?"

Pushing past Lin to stand in the doorway, Night drew her shoulders back and pulled herself tall, stopping inches from the woman to loom over her. She twitched an eyebrow when the woman didn't step away. "I'm here for the Collector."

The woman's eyelids narrowed, then she turned away. "I'm afraid I have no idea what you're talking about." Her accent was crisp, cultured English.

Like a viper snatching its prey, Night's hand lashed out and grasped the woman's neck, fingernails digging into flesh, while her other hand pressed into the space between the woman's shoulder blades. The woman gasped and clawed at Night's fingers as tendrils of green pulsed from the hand between her shoulders, spearing into her and wrapping around like an octopus. Veins bulged under the woman's skin, the same lime green. Behind her, Night sensed the vampires shift, as if not wanting to be touched by her magic.

"I am really not in the mood for prevarication and obfuscation." Night raised her voice until it echoed through the foyer, ricocheting off the marble floors and up the wooden staircase. A man in a suit appeared in an entry across the space, gun raised. He fired a shot, almost by accident, as his eyes bulged wide at the scene. The gun wavered, and Night spoke again. "You're not the Collector. Get him. Now."

The distraction was enough to cause an ebb in her magic, and the woman thrashed, the heel of her left shoe making contact with Night's shin. In a second, the world dimmed, going a shade of drab olive. She lifted the woman with a strength her borrowed body didn't possess and tossed her, as if she were no more than a doll, onto the marble. With a sharp thud, like the crack of a watermelon, blood started seeping from the woman's skull onto the tile. A creak sounded from the stairs and Night snapped her head around to glare at the creature who stood at the top.

"Welcome to my parlour," the ruddy-cheeked man said, with a nauseating smile on his face and a British accent that was too posh to be fake. At first, he seemed unbothered by the woman bleeding on the marble tiles. Then he glanced at her, his eyebrows raising. "Or I should say welcome to dear Gretchen's parlour." Mincing down the stairs, he tiptoed around the spreading pool of crimson. "How sad." He picked up his cane, keeping it from touching the blood. "A good co-conspirator is hard to find."

"You're the Collector." Small drops of blood dripped from Night's fingernails to the floor, and her golem crouched beside her, straining her head towards the dying woman.

The man tipped his head, a double-chin forming. He wasn't overweight, but he was soft, doughy. He even smelled yeasty, like sour milk instead of rising bread. "Some call me that. But you can call me Mr. Windrow." His nose wrinkled as he looked down at Gretchen, a handkerchief to his face. "Could you ask her not to do that? It's unseemly."

Night's gaze flashed to the floor. Her golem had started licking at the crimson pool seeping across the tiles. She hissed and the woman crept back to her side, pressing her bloody face into her palm. Night pulled away, bringing the hand up to tuck a curl behind her ear, smearing blood across her own face.

"Where is it, Collector?"

"Where is what?" The man tapped a long fingernail against the head of his cane, which pulsed with a pale, orange light.

"Don't be coy with me. You see what happens when you do." Night jerked her chin at the dead woman. Green magic oozed from her fingertips again, and she smiled as her strength grew. Her smile turned to a frown as wispy tendrils of fire snaked between the Collector's fingers.

The orange tendrils dissipated. "Of course. What else could you be asking after but the blade of light itself?"

"I want it. It's mine."

"Of course, but it's not here."

Night stepped up to the Collector, whose face turned a shade similar to the green miasma swirling around her. "Were you not listening? Don't lie to me."

"I am not lying, my dear." The Collector's face paled when Night growled. Then he continued, feigning nonchalance as he peered at the handle of his cane. "It is not here, but I know where it is." His gaze returned to her face. "And I can help you get it."

CHAPTER TWENTY-ONE

Jack turned over in the overly soft bed. When Lin had first brought him back to the mansion, he'd been thrown in a cell in the basement. Delirious with silver poisoning, he'd been bound and caged, until Lin let him out with no explanation. Flipping onto his other side, he almost wished he were in that cell again. The cot had been hard but more comfortable than this bed, and he'd been blissfully ignorant of Night and her putrescent magic.

He'd woken up when a gang of vampires had left with Night earlier, and couldn't get back to sleep. He flopped onto his back, throwing an arm over his head.

Where did they go? And what are they up to?

Breathing into his diaphragm, he rubbed his shoulder, which was still sore even though the necromancer had pronounced him healed. But Lin had finagled the man into treating him, so his opinion might be suspect. Jack held his breath then exhaled slowly, trying to force his body into a sleep state. He repeated the long, slow inhale, envisioning it going all the way to his toes, then let it out again.

This room was next to the one Lin had procured, ignoring the protests of the former occupant. Jack's ear twitched. She'd left with Night, leaving him behind, and hadn't returned. Turning over, he stared at the wall separating the rooms and images of the night before rose in his brain. His eyebrows pulled together, not wanting to go back any further. That would take him to when Night murdered Brett. Instead, he thought of Mina, painful in its own way.

Was it really only yesterday? The image of Mina's face when he told her he didn't need her, didn't miss her, flashed in his mind. He rubbed his shoulder again, trying to push away the ache. After that encounter, Lin set him free, sort of, sending him to track some quarry. And he was a hunter — he found the mark. A woman who worked at the hospital. Jack pressed his thumb hard into his shoulder until a stab of pain shot down his arm and across his back. He gasped with the shock of it.

He'd followed the mark all the way home, where a cold chill had spread through him that had nothing to do with the lingering clutches of winter. It was a place he recognized. A home, where he'd found Mina once, watching a family through the window. Her brother's house.

When he'd returned to the mansion, Lin grilled him. *I lost her*, he'd said, commenting on how hard it was to follow the thread of a single heartbeat in an overcrowded city. Lin's lips had pressed together, but she didn't call him a liar.

Does she know what I did? Jack had no idea if she believed him when he recounted the meandering path the mark had led him on, through the club district then the night market. *Or was it a test? Did she follow me?* A cold hand squeezed his heart, but he shook his head. *No, I was always the better hunter.*

Jack flipped over to his other side, causing a jolt of pain where the wound had been. He huffed it out, leaving a dull ache. Turning onto his back again, he searched the ceiling for answers as he contemplated the mess he found himself in.

Can I get out alive? Maybe if I get up and sneak downstairs, I can slip out, away from this ridiculous espionage. He sat up, ran his hands through his hair, then hung his head and stared at the floor. He couldn't leave now, any more than he could last night. Something was happening. Something bad. And he needed to be there for it.

Lifting his head, he peered at the door. Downstairs, the dull thud of the great doors closing rumbled through the foyer. They'd returned. As if on cue, the rest of the house started to stir.

Jack ran his hands through his hair again. All he wanted was to stay in this room for the night with the book he'd found in the surprisingly well-stocked library. Looking in the gilt-framed mirror that hung over the ornate dresser, he ran his knuckles across his stubble. The unkempt look might project the right state of mind: slightly wild and rabid. Sniffing as he pulled on his one shirt, he vowed to find some new clothes and figure out where the showers were in this place. The shirt had been laundered while he was semi-conscious, and mended to seal up the tear where the knife had sliced through to pierce his shoulder, but it was still in a state. He was surprised Lin hadn't thrown him in the river last night, given a vampire's heightened sense of smell. But she wanted him alive for some reason.

Kitted out and cleaned up as much as he cared, Jack cocked his head to the side as a bright tap-tap-tap-tap-TAP-TAP sounded on his door. He tipped his head towards the door and closed his eyes.

"Em," he said to himself. She'd been disturbingly chipper in her interactions with him, possibly biding her time until she was given the freedom to torture him. Though he doubted Lin would allow it — that was her prerogative — and she wasn't disposed to make Em happy. He rose and walked to the door as it opened, and his guess was confirmed: Em stood there grinning.

"Rise and shine, sleepy head. We have a date with Night."

Jack didn't reply. Instead he took his sweet time grabbing his jacket before leaving the room to follow her downstairs. On the main floor, Em led him into the room with the grisly throne.

An itch crawled up Jack's spine as he took in the scene: Night sitting on the throne with Lin kneeling before her. Lin didn't bow to anyone. As they entered, Night stood, and the chair creaked. "Rise," she said, her fingers under Lin's chin. "You did well." Her eyes flashed a dull green in the unlit room.

Jack pressed against the wall, trying to be inconspicuous and fade into the shadows. Unfortunately, the shadows didn't phase Night. They attracted her.

She glanced his way at his slight shift, and stepped down from the dais, her movements like a snake. Lin rose and followed her. Night's eyes fixed on him, pinning him like those needles used to stick insects in a display. He pressed further into the wall, but there was nowhere to go. Em sighed beside him, and Night's attention turned sharply to her.

"Where's your partner?" she asked, her tone flat.

Em didn't answer right away, instead glancing around the space, her eyebrows twitching. "I...Ivan?" She gave a barely perceptible shrug of her shoulder, looking at Night before turning her eyes to the floor. "I don't know."

Jack let his gaze trawl the motley collection of individuals arrayed around the room, but his attention was drawn forward again as Night slunk another step closer. She stopped and half turned her torso to Lin, keeping her eyes focused on Jack.

"I want him." She stepped up to him, and Jack's skin crawled with a nauseating mixture of dread and anticipation. "He should come with us. Learn what it means to be a creature of Night."

"He should." Lin's nostrils flared, and Jack watched some calculation flicker over her face before she spoke again. "But he's untrustworthy."

"And yet, you have him here." Night's eyes barely flicked towards Lin before returning to him. Jack swallowed.

"He can be broken." A smile slid over Lin's face.

"But not yet." Night mimicked Lin's smile, and Jack squirmed, wanting to go with them to see what they were up to but wanting nothing more than to be left behind. "Fine. He can stay and wait for the behemoth, while you and I run our errand. Em, go with Kian." Night pointed at the werewolf. "Find your friend."

"He's not..." Em's eyes went wide as Night homed in on her. Jack almost felt sorry for her. Almost.

"I don't care. Find him." Em snapped her jaw shut and did as she was told, eying the werewolf as it eyed her.

Night crooked her finger at Lin. "You're with me. Let's get this over with." Lin strode towards the door, and Night spun on her heels and followed.

A knot formed in Jack's stomach. "I need to go," he said to the empty foyer. *Warn the mark.* Then he watched as a fluorescent green ward pulsed through the door. He wasn't going anywhere.

146

"You're sure?" Night perched on the edge of the rooftop, damp curls drooping in front of her eyes as she watched the couple below. She canted her head, exposing her face to the slushy raindrops, so she could better catch the syncopated beat of their hearts, one slightly faster than the other. They kissed again, a last lingering goodbye, and Night's fingers tensed around the handle of the dagger. An ordinary blade, if extraordinarily sharp. A more magical weapon would help channel the chaotic powers flowing through her. But the Collector said he couldn't get her the blade until tomorrow. She didn't trust him, but now she had a mark on him, so he couldn't run away before he gave it to her. Her fingers tingled with anticipation, but she now had enough self-control that magic didn't spark between them like little bolts of lightning to give away her position. She breathed deeply, dampening the fire in her blood, and shifted her attention to Lin, who crouched beside her and peered down at the couple. "This is not something you want to get wrong." She saw Lin stiffen and heard the moment of hesitation before she answered.

"I'm sure." Another pause, and a nod of the head. "That's your stalker."

Turning back to the street below, she saw the couple had parted, the woman walking away down the street and the man watching her go. Night's own gaze followed the woman.

"She doesn't look like much, does she?" Though even as she said it, Night saw what Lin had: the Hunter training infused her every movement, even the tilt of her head as she glanced back at the man before rounding the corner.

"Looks can be deceiving as they say." Lin still didn't look at her.

"Too true." She hopped up onto the roof edge, then turned to Lin, who glanced over her shoulder instead of jumping to do as she was told. "Let's go." There was no one else on the rooftop, save the grey bulk of her sole remaining gargoyle, hanging back, perhaps still mourning the loss of its wings. Her lips thinned, and her cheeks flushed as she peered at Lin.

"If I lose him, it's on your head," Night added before stepping off the roof, not waiting for an answer. But a satisfying thump sounded on the pavement behind her and gave a silent nod of her head — Lin might actually learn the lesson she herself had all those years ago, that the crown comes to those who seize it. A soft sound broke her reflection and she snapped her head up to glare over her shoulder. The wingless gargoyle watched from the rooftop.

Night smiled then turned and stalked down the street after the man. Her fingers tapped against her leg, playing out the rhythm of the heartbeats around her on her thigh. The rain seeped through her pants and trickled through her hair, but her focus was so keen she barely noticed. She hardly even noticed Lin pacing behind her. Not until she spoke.

"Shouldn't we be following the woman?" Lin asked.

Night's lips pressed together. "No." This was another lesson she'd learned early, at the same time she'd learned not to love anyone or anything. "Lesson one: find what your enemy loves and exploit it or destroy it. Or both." Lin was silent. *Thinking. A dangerous thing for her to do right now.* Night turned to her. "Where should we take him?"

"What?" Lin's eyebrows wormed in confusion.

Night narrowed her eyes, her lips pressing together as she huffed out a breath. She annunciated her words when she spoke again. "Which way should we nudge him? Somewhere quiet, where we're not likely to be disturbed. Or disturb anyone else. The last thing I need is some hero showing up."

A light of understanding sparked in Lin's eyes, and she looked down at the gadget in her hand, its bright light offending Night's sensibilities. Glancing around, Lin pointed left. "Their home is that way." She shifted her stance, keeping the gadget in front of her. "The park is up ahead, empty at this hour except for rats and the indigent." She looked back down at the phone. "Or the warehouses to our right."

Night smiled, glancing up and to her right, where her gargoyle stalked them, a shadow in the back of her mind. "The warehouses." She paused, focusing her will on this one idea, not even sparing energy to breathe: turn right. At the next corner the man paused, and looked both ways, hesitating at the crossroads. Then turned left. Night let a low growl rumble in the back of her throat, and her nostrils flared. "Home it is."

The street was dark and deserted. Just as she liked it. Maybe 'home' wasn't so bad after all, though she sensed an imp in the shrubbery of a house they passed, but it was wisely feigning sleep. A light came on as the man neared the door of a little house half a block down. Night quickened her pace. She didn't want to break a nail breaking into the house. She whispered to the shadows, asking for a delay, and the man fumbled his keys, dropping them at the dark base of a planter.

"What did you say his name was?" Night asked over her shoulder, her voice low.

"I..." Lin started then stopped. Night glanced at her, and she could see the splotches of red on Lin's cheeks.

"Oh right, you didn't." She let her voice go hard and brittle as ice. But as she turned away, the name came to her. As if by magic. She smiled.

"Dale."

The man started, standing up straight and almost tripping over the step as he edged back. Then he paused, tilted his head sideways, his mouth half open. "Cam?"

Night moved her head, almost like a nod. It was the name Brett had called her. The man knew this body, if not the soul inside it. She filed that fact away as he stepped forward, almost into the halo cast by the streetlight. She moved towards him, edging him back into darkness again.

"What are you doing here?" he asked. "Has something happened to Mina?"

"Mina?" Lin's voice was sharp, and Night swiveled her head around to glare at the woman. Lin pressed her lips together and took a step back.

Dale's gaze slid sideways, eyebrows pulling together, before returning to Night. "She's been looking for you."

As Night inched forward, a soft whoop sounded from above, and she tipped her head up to gaze at her beautiful gargoyle, which was perched on the roof of the house. Her gaze dropped as the man's drifted up, craning his neck to look.

"No, I'm not here about Mina." Night stabbed her dagger into the man's chest with one hand, pressing him back into the door and covering his lips with the other, all in one fluid movement. She stepped back, bloody hand grasping the slick dagger, red drops falling onto wet concrete, and let him slide onto the stoop.

Her gargoyle made a mewling sound, quietly keening its hunger. She glanced up at it, its lips drawn back over enormous canines that were neither gargoyle nor vampire, and knew what it wanted. "Sorry, sweetmeat. I need this one."

Blood gurgled from the man's lips as she knelt by him and drove her dagger into the torso once more, slicing it open enough that she could reach her hand inside. Green magic throbbed from her fingertips, and she shoved her hand into the chest. She sighed and closed her eyes when her fingers wrapped around his heart, cradling it for the last few pathetic beats. Then she yanked it out, carving it away.

She turned to Lin, who stood agog at the edge of the step, and barked at her. "Help me get him on the dirt. I need to send him to the underworld creatures for safekeeping."

CHAPTER TWENTY-TWO

Mina waited in the lobby of Whitaker, Whitaker and Lee, rocking up onto her toes and back down again, rubbing her stomach as if that would get rid of the knot. Before leaving the Sanctuary that morning, she and Bee had fought again; Bee repeating her usual mantra that the conclave was Mina's family now, and Mina replying with her usual retort that her family was still her family.

She was here to meet Dale and Mr. Whitaker about some new issue with their mother's estate. Mr. Whitaker hadn't said much when he called, only that he needed to speak to them. Mina looked at her phone. Dale hadn't responded to her text, and he was now 15 minutes late.

A cough drew her head up. *Mr. Whitaker.* The sudden movement made her dizzy, and her ears buzzed. She needed to feed, and soon.

"Still nothing from Mr. Sun?"

Mina shook her head, her eyebrows pulling together. "Sorry. He's usually so punctual."

The lawyer reached a hand towards her. "It's all right. We can discuss the issue and follow up with him later." Mr. Whitaker looked over her shoulder as the elevator chimed. Mina turned, slowly, but when the doors opened, it wasn't Dale. She caught a glimpse of two burly men in suits and sunglasses before Mr. Whitaker hustled her down the hall.

Once in his office, Mina's new dracul senses picked up things she hadn't the previous times she'd visited. The room was humid, but the tropical plants were wilting. His heart beat a little too fast. Whether or not that was normal for him, the bags under his eyes and the pastiness to his skin were new.

"Are you all right, Mr. Whitaker?"

"What?" He snapped his head around to look at her, then nodded and gave her a small smile. "Yes. Just busy around the office." Mina started to drop into one of the chairs beside the table where they usually signed paperwork. "Nothing to sign today Ms. Sun." He went over to the wall, and shifting a portion of the bookcase, revealed a safe. He punched in some numbers Mina tried hard not to memorize: 9742.

Her forehead tightened as she watched him. "Maybe we should wait for Dale."

He shook his head but didn't look at her. "No, that would not be wise." Reaching into the safe, he pulled out a small box. "Your mother left you a very special bequest. A family heirloom." He turned and held the box almost reverently in both hands. "She left it to my discretion as to when I should give it to you and your brother." His eyes flicked up to her face, before returning to the box as he reached forward. "The time has come." A crash sounded from the direction of the lobby.

"What..." Mina stopped when she found the box shoved into her hands.

"Take it. Use it wisely."

"What is it?" She started to open the lid and found Mr. Whitaker's hands clutched around hers.

"Now is not the time." He glanced over her shoulder. "Come, let me show you out."

"I know the way." Mina scrunched her eyebrows together, searching the lawyer's face for signs of mental illness. She might have to get in touch with the other Whitaker or Lee. She tucked the box into her pocket, the left one, since the right still held the bloody obsidian blade. But instead of leading her back the way they'd come, he took her through the door on the far side of his office and hustled her along a winding route to a service elevator. He pressed the button to call the car, and she inhaled deeply, thankful for a pause to ask him what had gotten into him. But as she opened her mouth, the door slid open and he nudged her inside, his hand on her shoulder, while he stayed outside.

"Take care, Ms. Sun." He pressed a button, the doors closed, and the knot in Mina's stomach tightened as the elevator descended.

152

It wasn't until Mina was in the subway, on her way back to the Sanctuary, that she opened the box. Looking at the contents, she tipped her head to the side, but that didn't change what lay inside. "A necklace?" She peered at the twisted piece of bright orange metal hanging from a delicate strand of the same. "An ugly necklace."

She'd never seen her mother wear it, and couldn't reconcile the rustic lines with her mother's polished style. Her head tilted the other way as her left eyebrow went up. "Use it wisely?" Her lips twisted into a grimace as she snapped the box shut. "Yeah, keep it in the box."

The knot in Mina's stomach became a gnawing as she sat on the concrete ledge in St. Frank's square, watching from behind her dark sunglasses as the mid-morning pedestrians scurry to and fro. She ran her fingers over the necklace clenched in her right hand, having taken it out of the box again. Her eyebrows pulled together as she inspected it, the twisted metal tugging at some stubborn memory. Dropping it in the box again, she unzipped her pocket and shoved the necklace in. Her fingers brushed the obsidian blade. With a gasp, she withdrew her hand. More carefully, she tucked the box into the inside pocket of her jacket. I really need to get rid of that thing, she thought as a wail of voices echoed in her blood.

She reached into her other pocket, intent on checking her phone again, even though it hadn't chimed. She'd called Dale after leaving Mr. Whitaker...maybe he knew something about the necklace and the lawyer's weird cloak and dagger routine. But there'd been no answer. She'd waited patiently then tried again. Then she texted. Then she called Hana. All to no avail. Mina brought a fingernail to her lip as she moved to put the phone away.

It rang, and she fumbled, almost dropping it in shock. The ache in her stomach eased, replaced by a flutter of butterflies when she recognized the ring. *Aunt June.*

"Yoboseyo." *Hello.*

"You need to come to Dale's. Now." Mina opened her mouth to ask what was wrong, but the call was cut off before she could get a word out. She pulled the phone away from her head and stared at it, and the gnawing became a pit. She considered calling June back to ask for more information. Instead she sprinted out of the square and hailed a cab.

As the cab pulled into Dale's street, red lights strobed the street. The pit in Mina's stomach opened into a dark abyss. When the cab couldn't get any closer, between ambulance, police car and nosy neighbours, Mina got out, fumbling with her wallet to throw some money at the protesting cab driver. The EMT was shutting the door on the ambulance, and she caught a glimpse of a white tarp-like thing inside. Her vision blurred as the silence made itself known — there were no sirens. The abyss turned to icy stone. Mina started to run, only to be grabbed as she ran between the ambulance and police car.

"Whoa, watch where you're going," the policeman said.

She scowled at him, his words taking a few seconds to process: the ambulance had almost run her over. *I'm a vampire; I'll heal.*

"My brother." Mina pushed against the officer. He didn't budge, and she had lost her unnatural strength. "Dale. He lives here." But she knew that was no longer true, the cold realization confirmed when the police officer looked at her with soft brown eyes, and his face, weathered and erose like the bark of a tree, pulled down into a sad frown.

"Dale Sun?"

Mina nodded, her voice failing her as her legs wobbled and her knees buckled. She lay a hand on his arm, leaning forward, trying to catch her breath but it felt like she'd been punched in the stomach. Her knees fell to the ground and her hands planted themselves on the wet asphalt as she gave up her fight to stay upright, her stomach heaving. Luckily it was empty so there was no bloody liquid to disgorge onto his shoes. The man was trying to say something to her, but she barely heard him over the rush in her ears and the buzz in her blood...*heart attack*. Through watery eyes, she stared at her fingers in the mud as she sniffed back tears. Then something tickled her nose.

Blood. A hot ember formed in that pit in her stomach. "Heart attack." Her voice was quiet. She swallowed but the buzzing remained — something wicked had passed this way. As if compelled by magic, she stood up and pushed past the police officer with a snarl that must have shocked him, since he made no move to follow. Sprinting, she made it up the stairs and through the open door before she was stopped again, this time by a compact Latina, who stood like a rock in the hallway of Dale's home.

"Oomph." The impact was compounded by Mina's momentum and she fell to her hands and knees again, coughing, trying to get her lungs working.

"And who are you?" the woman asked.

"I...." Mina shook her head to clear away the stars and the odor of bloody death. She jerked her head upright. "Dale?"

The woman crouched to look her in the face. "You the sister?"

Mina nodded and wiped the tears from her cheeks.

"I'm Inspector Guerra. Come." The woman led her down the hallway, glancing over her shoulder a few times to peer at Mina, leaving her with the impression the woman was weighing her soul like Anubis. And Mina was found wanting.

Mina surreptitiously glanced into the rooms they passed, looking for signs of blood, but there was nothing. Surprisingly, the scent of death dissipated as they went further into the house.

When she entered the kitchen, she was confronted by a tearful June, a sobbing Maggie, a quiet Liam who seemed to not quite know what was happening, and an angry Hana, who stood up and strode over to Mina with short steps.

"What are you doing here?" she snapped, her words short and clipped and cold.

Feeling like she'd been slapped, Mina took a step back from the fire in Hana's eyes and aggression in her stance. She breathed in through her nose, out through her mouth and re-minded herself that Hana didn't have the same experience with death, for all she was a pathologist. "I...Dale and I were supposed to meet Mr. Whitaker this morning. When he —"

"When he was dying? Alone? What happened to him?"

"I —" The gears in Mina's brain turned slowly, trying to process Hana's questions. Mina shook her head. "They said Dale died of a heart attack." Hana's lips pressed together but she didn't say anything, so Mina filled the silence. "When he didn't show, I pinged. He didn't answer. I wanted to ask him about something Mr. Whitaker—" Mina looked from Hana to June, glancing over the kids' heads before returning to Guerra. "...said. How? He was young, healthy."

"Yes, he was." Hana turned away, going back to Maggie and Liam.

The inspector stepped up beside Mina. "Since he died alone, we'll confirm cause of death. But all indicators point to —"

"Evil." June's voice was quiet, but it silenced everyone, in-cluding the police officer. Mina looked at her aunt's pale face ...stony, tearless. It wasn't the expression of stoicism June and her mother had shared. No, this time, June's eyes were haunted, re-flecting a horror she couldn't unsee.

"The initial examine indicates a heart attack." Guerra's tone was calm but it tipped up at the end, almost turning her statement to a question.

"Heart attack?" The words came out slow and plodding, as the stone of fire in Mina's gut turned to worms of ice spreading through her veins. "But what about...." Her brain caught up with her mouth and she stopped herself from asking about the blood.

The inspector's eyebrows scrunched together as she peered at Mina. "What?"

Mina looked over her shoulder, down the hallway to the front door. "Nothing." She turned back to Guerra with a shrug.

"Hana, if there's nothing more, I should be going," the inspector said as she glanced at the other officer, who'd come to stand quietly by the door, and gave a barely perceptible jerk of her head. "I'll be in touch." Guerra headed down the hallway, glancing back once at the kitchen door.

Mina walked over to June, wrapping her arms around her, trying to channel her mother in those moments when she'd been Mom, rather than Mother — a full body embrace that encompassed the whole world. "I'll find this thing," she whispered. "I'll kill it." Aunt June returned the hug briefly then Hana laid a hand on her shoulder and pulled her away, yanking her halfway back to the kitchen door with a fierce strength Mina was shocked to find her sister-in-law possessed.

"Stay away from us," Hana hissed. "Stay away from my children." Turning to the policeman at the door, she said, "Get her out of here."

Stunned by Hana's reaction, Mina let herself be led away down the long corridor to the front door. As she reached the door, she saw the inspector standing on the lawn, looking at the grass as she talked on her phone. As the officer stepped past her, the air in the entryway eddied about them, and Mina was overwhelmed by the scent of blood, her knees almost collapsing underneath her again. But under the blood, there was another smell, a fragrance she recognized.

Rosemary and lavender.

Cam. Her lips moved but her throat tightened around the sound. She breathed deeply, trembling hands on shaking knees. *If she was here when Dale was murdered, she's in danger.*

As she stepped outside, Inspector Guerra looked up, her eyes narrowing as they homed in on her. Mina swallowed. *I wonder if she realizes this isn't just a heart attack.* Mina wasn't sure that made her feel any better. She turned away, imagining herself an unimportant shadow as she walked away from the house. She glanced back to find the inspector's gaze trained on her. Her breath caught in her throat, and she forced herself to turn away and keep walking.

CHAPTER TWENTY-THREE

Mina stumbled up the stairs to the Sanctuary. After fighting with the door, she slunk in, finding it hushed and blessedly empty. She plodded through the dappled light cast by sun through stained glass, and slumped down the stairs, her knees weak and muscles twitching the whole way. The corridor was dark, without even any light peeking out from under doors. The conclave was either empty or asleep. Or decimated. At the moment, she didn't care which.

In her room, she kicked off her boots, sending them against the wardrobe with a thunk. Then she collapsed on her bed and waited for the oblivion of day-sleep to take her, welcoming it. But, however tight she shut her eyes, sleep refused to take her away. Instead, she replayed the scene at Dale's house on a never-ending loop in her brain. She pulled out the necklace Mr. Whitaker had given her, trying once again to puzzle out what was so special about it that her mother had left it with him. And why he had acted so strange when she'd seen him. But the answer didn't come, no matter how hard she grasped the pendant.

She flopped onto her back and stared at the ceiling, fighting the onslaught of tears. Her sore throat clenched around the sob, and she swallowed against it. A creak sounded from the hallway, but she ignored it. She was numb to her very soul. Her eyes slid sideways as her door moved. A shadow she recognized filled the doorway, and Mina turned to the wall. The shadow didn't move, nor did it speak.

"I want to be alone." Mina sniffed back tears.

"No, you don't." The air moved as Seema stepped into the room.

Mina turned to glare at her. "Don't tell me what I want or don't want." The knot in her throat got tighter. "My brother is dead. I certainly don't need another lecture from you."

"I know what loss is. My family is dead. The human who saved me from myself is dead."

Mina huffed then turned back to the wall and waited for Seema to leave, closing her eyes against the tears. There was silence, and she thought, despite the evidence of her senses, that she was alone. Then the bed shifted. Opening her eyes, a golden pair stared back at her. Mina stared at the cat for a second before lifting a heavy hand to stroke the cat's head.

"But this is *my* fault," she said, her voice husky. The cat rubbed her face with its jaw. "I brought this evil into his life." The cat brought its paw close to her cheek, claws retracted. "But it is. He'd be safe, at home with his family, if it weren't for me." Mina peered into the cat's eyes, then turned to stare at the ceiling again as the cat turned in a circle before settling beside her. Kneading her stomach, the cat's purr vibrated through its body into its paws and into her as she sobbed.

"I tell you, I can do this." Finn picked up the mug in front of her, brought it to her lips. She peered into the empty vessel in consternation. It was a sentiment Rhys understood — the bottom of a cup of tea was a terrible thing. Especially at times like this. He pondered getting up and making some more but the kitchen seemed so far today. He was bone tired.

"There's no way." Dev ran one hand through his mane of tousled hair while the other held his own cup of tea.

Rhys slowly turned his mug around in both hands. "When did breaking into security systems become part of a Smith's skill set?" He watched her fingers fly over the keyboard of his laptop, mug abandoned, as she uncovered secret scent trails of information, unlocking doors he hadn't even known existed.

"Since me."

"Am I going to get a visit from the authorities for anything you're doing over there?" She ignored his question and furiously scrolled down a screen filled with letters and numbers.

"Why learn to break into computer systems when you can make mechanical marvels and wondrous weapons?" Dev asked.

She quirked an eyebrow at him. "Let's just say I saw the future." Punching in a key combination, she spun the screen to face Rhys and Dev. An etching of the Blade of the Sun appeared, line by agonizing line, on his screen, so detailed he saw additional scripting along the edge. Taking back the computer, she poked at a key with vigour. "Arg! How do you work on this thing? It shouldn't even be used for a doorstop."

With that, she slammed the case shut, or so it seemed to his ears. She picked up her mug, then, judging by the look on her face, realized, once again, that it was empty. Putting it down, she opened the laptop again, caressing the lid with her hand. "Do you know what it's like being trapped in that forge with my father all the time?" With her other hand, she stroked Grey, who traitorously sat in her lap, purring away. "I love him, but, well, one goes looking for something to break the monotony of living and working with the same person, day in, day out. Especially one who frets over you, even though you're old enough to have a family of your own. It was either this or alcohol. And bending technology to my will seemed a perfect counterbalance to a father who wants to protect me from the world."

"Maybe he wants to protect the world from you." Dev gave her an arch smile as he watched her pull up another trove of information, this one showing all three blades - Night, Moon and Sun.

She ignored the jibe. "I just happen to have developed a knack for hacking, as well as safe cracking, if it comes to that. Not that it will." Finn's fingers travelled over the keyboard again, running through code while images came and went in another window.

Rhys took another sip of tea, getting dizzy trying to track the carousel of images.

"I —" Dev started as he cocked his head and peered at the screen.

Rhys sat up straighter at what had appeared: the plans for the new headquarters of the Brothers of Light, including expanded laboratories where they could experiment on netherworld creatures, living and dead, so the rumours said. Something a curious archaeologist with a keen interest in werecats didn't need to see. "And you think you can break into the security at the museum?" Rhys asked to draw attention away from the screen, uncomfortable with Dev's curiosity.

"It's not so much breaking in, as bypassing." Finn switched to another screen.

Rhys slumped back. "Whatever the details, you can really do it?" Dev shook his head, his lips tense, as he focused on a spot over Finn's head.

"Yes." Finn turned away from the computer. "Step one: relieve this odious hoarder of cultural treasures of his half of the blade. That I can do." She looked down at Grey and nodded. "And step three: find the other half and join them together."

"What about step two?" Dev asked, sipping his tea.

Finn paused to stare at her hands on the keyboard then sighed. "That's a little more difficult: convince my father to help us."

CHAPTER TWENTY-FOUR

Jack threw the pointed stars at the juicy bits, or what would have been if the target were a real person. He'd always been a good shot, but tonight even when he tried to miss, he hit his target. In his mind's eye he saw the target as a person, lacerated by the delicate blades, blood seeping over the body, and he struck over and over again with unsettling accuracy. As he pictured the scene, the saliva in his mouth grew. He shook his head, but that did nothing to quell the thirst. He swallowed. *Maybe Lin's micro-feedings are getting to me?* He had no choice but to let her feed him if he wanted to stay, and he had no choice but to stay. *Do you even want a choice?* a seductive voice whispered from the back of his mind.

Sitting cross-legged in the practice room of the Necrophagus' mansion, he reached for another star, only to find he'd used them all. He stared at the star-spangled target for a long minute, the silver projectiles mapping out arteries and veins, before getting up and collecting the stars.

He returned to sitting cross-legged, absentmindedly tossing the projectiles at the target, unerringly hitting the tender bits. His blood told him it was day outside, despite being shuttered in the shadowed mansion. Still, he couldn't sleep. Every time he closed his eyes, he felt seasick, like the world had tipped sideways and he was trying to find his feet in a mire of blood and grey mud. He couldn't escape the feeling, only block it out by keeping his mind busy on other tasks. Like throwing stars at a target. He homed in on said target again.

"I know you, Jack."

Finally, one of the stars went off course, skittering across the concrete floor until it hit the wall.

"What do you want, Em?" he asked without turning, instead picking up the next spiked projectile to throw.

She sat down beside him, her arms hugging her knees. She bumped her shoulder into his, as if they were friends having a heart-to-heart. "I know you, even if Lin doesn't. And I call bull-shit."

He turned to look at her. The eyes that met his shone like a junkie's, and her lips had red streaks in their fine lines from a recent feeding. But he still saw how he'd been taken by her — intelligence and beauty masking a rotten core. He was ashamed at how long it had taken him to learn that old lesson: don't judge a book by its cover. "And I ask again, what do you want?"

Her lips morphed from the false smile she had painted on her face into a thin line as she pressed them together. She lashed out and grasped the wrist of his throwing hand, wrapping her fingers around it, her grip tightening like a boa. "I want to know what game you're playing. Are you slipping notes out the window to some Athanatos spy?" She dug her nails into his flesh, and her voice turned to a hiss, her eyes almost snake-like to match. "I haven't seen it, but I know you are not on my side. You're too tortured by the pathetic suffering of others. That's what you could never get: I don't care that they suffer, as long as I don't, ever again."

He tore his eyes from her gaze and turned back to the target. "I don't play games. That's your forte." Yanking his wrist from her hand with a little more force than was needed, he sent another star flying. "Maybe I'm tired of caring," he added, half wondering if it were the truth. The idea settled in his stomach, a burning ember: life would be easier if he didn't care. Pressing his lips tight, he continued throwing until she got bored and left. Then he stopped, lay back on the concrete floor and closed his eyes. Only to open them again as the heaving nausea and the sensation of bloody worms crawling on his skin returned.

The deep clang of the doorbell resonated through the mansion, as Night hurled another vase. It splintered into a thousand pieces as it slammed into the wall. Inches from the head of her festering corpse of a golem, the shrapnel lacerated the woman's face and brown blood seeped from a constellation of wounds.

Night scowled. If only it had smashed the woman's head like a rotten gourd, it would have taken care of the small problem of ridding herself of the creature. The golem's eyes grew wide, and a simper formed in its throat. Night's scowl deepened as her eyes narrowed, then a shuffling caused her to spin around, homing in on a new target for her wrath.

Lin paused in the shadows by the door. Dull magic crackled along the lines of Night's palms. She let it build as she regarded the vampire. Something tickled her fingers, and she jerked her hand back, turning to glare at whatever had dared touch her. The gargoyle shied away, cowering from her. Her purulent magic dissipated, and her wrath turned to a burning acid in her stomach.

"I'm sorry, pet." Her voice was soft and coaxing. "I would never hurt you." She reached out her fingertips, so recently tainted by angry magic, for it to sniff. Tentative at first, the gargoyle craned its neck and huffed, then sidled towards her, finally letting her fingers scratch behind its ears. "I'm angry at myself, not you." And she was. She'd taken such pleasure in killing the man. Dale. It was only after he was already dead that she discovered his secret: he was a Watcher. She'd found the tattoo when she went after his heart: a circle of fire filled with an eye. The sigil of those who protected the blade — from her — had remained unchanged for thousands of years, though she hadn't seen it imprinted on flesh before. Even now, her clenched fist throbbed with the strength of her anger and her frustration that she'd been so close. Opening her hand, she looked at it. Her nails had drawn blood.

She stared at her blood-smeared palm, already healing. *Maybe it's a coincidence.* Even as the words flowed through her mind, she doubted them. Unfortunately, her power wasn't strong enough to resurrect him to a state where she'd get useful information out of him. She slid her eyes sideways, towards her golem. A throbbing miasma of magic started to pulse in her palm again as her anger built. A nudge at her fingers drew her eyes back the gargoyle as it sniffed her bloody hand. She stroked its head.

The tak-tak of Lin's shoes drew her attention, but she didn't turn her face to her, keeping her gaze trained on the gargoyle until Lin stopped on its far side, and mimicked her petting. Finally, she glanced up at the woman, who kept her head bowed, focusing on the grey beast between them.

"What do you want?"

Lin's eyebrow arched, though she kept her gaze on the gargoyle. "This man...the Collector is here to see you." She scritched it under its chin, and Night scowled when the creature responded to Lin's ministrations.

"Do you have the weapon?" She raised her chin to peer down her nose at the Collector. He stood in front of her examining the head of his walking stick. An ochre patina over a beige base suggested it was made out of the bones of some creature, though she couldn't tell if the shaft and the head were from the same beast or not. His thumb caressed the head, but he didn't answer. Her magic simmered in her gut as she waited. Flowing through her veins, it infused her with its venom. "You don't have it, do you?"

The Collector glanced up at her. "It's a delicate matter. It's safe in the museum for now." His words were crisp, and he looked back at his walking stick before he continued. "Are you sure you want it?"

"I want to destroy it." She arched an eyebrow. "No one should have that much power."

He looked her full in the face then, clearly sensing the lie. "Destroy that beautiful piece of magic?" With his mouth agog and his free hand clutching his chest, she could almost believe he was genuine. She almost asked what he would do if faced with some weapon that could destroy him utterly, but she was saved from that slip when he continued. "You know —" His eyes peered at his ringed fingers, eyebrows raising. "—what can kill can also resurrect."

Her eyes narrowed, and she let the silence grow until he nervously flicked his gaze at her. "What do you mean?" she asked, her tone flat.

"I know what they took from you. And what the blade has severed, maybe it can join again." He tilted his head sideways, looking sidelong at her. "It is magic after all."

She considered the Collector again, seeing him in a new light. "You know a few things about magic blades, do you?"

"Just bits and pieces collected along the way."

"Why are you here if you don't have it?" The words were strangled through her tight lips.

"Because you told me to come, and I do as you command." He tipped his head forward and gave half a curtsy.

She frowned. "When?"

"Tomorrow night at the latest."

She tipped her head in a slight nod, an indication he was dismissed. She watched him walk out of the room, not using the stick at all. "Where's your behemoth?" she asked without looking at Lin.

"My...you mean Ivan?" Lin shifted beside her. "He's not mine."

"You mean you don't know."

"Why do you want him?"

"We might have to break into a museum. Or break a Collector."

CHAPTER TWENTY-FIVE

Her tears run dry, Mina lay in bed and stared at the wall, trying to push out images of an angry Hana and desolate Liam and Maggie. Purring stopped, the werecat still lay nestled against her stomach. Soft steps along the hall, followed by a thump and a muted curse, caused the cat's ears to twitch. The footsteps stopped outside Mina's door, and after a short pause, there was a quiet knock. She ignored it. It sounded again, and she continued to inspect the wall as the cat twitched beside her, craning to stare at the door. A squeal of hinges and Seema's ears coming forward told her the person was entering, invited or not. Funny how one of the main rules of the vampire world didn't apply at a personal level.

She closed her eyes and breathed deeply: cinnamon and vanilla. "Go away, Nicole." Opening her eyes again, she didn't turn over, instead glancing down as Seema padded to the end of the bed. Nicole came to stand at the edge and ran her fingers, nails painted a sparkling black, under the cat's chin.

Mina flopped onto her back. "I'm not really up for company right now."

"Yeah, I heard." Nicole shrugged a shoulder, then looked at her, sadness in her black-rimmed eyes. "Vampires are horrible gossips."

Mina arched an eyebrow, and almost smiled in spite of her mood. "So I've been told."

Nicole peered at her for a second, her kohl-rimmed eyes scrunching. "You're pale." She sat on the edge of the bed, still lavishing attention on the werecat as it craned its neck. "Even for a vampire."

"My brother's dead." Mina swallowed as the knot in her throat returned. "Because of me."

Nicole shook her head with intent, her red lips pressing together, as the cat's golden eyes turned to Mina again. "No, not because of you. Because of evil."

"Evil I brought into his life!" Mina's voice rose and grew louder to fill the room. She brought the back of her hand to wipe at the itchy trail of dried tears, and pressed it to her nose, which was threatening to run.

"No." Nicole placed a hand on Mina's leg, causing the cat to scurry up the bed. Mina didn't say anything, stunned by the conviction in that one word. There was a crack in Nicole's voice when she continued. "Evil is all around us. Paranormal and mundane."

"What do you know?" Mina turned her head to the wall, only to find the werecat staring at her with its golden eyes. Then, without warning, it used her stomach as a trampoline to launch itself off the bed. Mid-air, the cat shifted into the woman, naked with long, wavy hair covering her small breasts. Mina wondered if she'd ever get used to the transformation. Seema seemed to have become quite comfortable standing around half naked, though she was still cat most of the time.

Seema the woman stared at Mina with serious brown eyes, flecked with gold. Her eyebrows lifted when she finally spoke. "You should listen to her." Seema glanced at Nicole. "I suspect she knows a thing or two about evil."

Before Mina could gather her thoughts enough to chastise her for judging Nicole by how she looked and to inform her the woman was a doctor in training, Seema had spun on her heels and left the room.

Mina turned towards the wall. "Seriously, what do you know about some dark magic killing your brother?" Nicole shifted, moving from the end of the bed and coming to sit in the crook of her back.

"True. I never had a brother." Her voice was quiet, forestalling Mina's retort. "Maybe my parents would have had a son if they weren't murdered when I was a child."

Mina blinked at the wall, then slowly turned over onto her back. Nicole's gaze shifted from a pendant on the necklace she was fiddling with to meet hers.

"I'm sorry." Mina meant it in all the ways she could think of: for Nicole's loss, for her assumption the young woman didn't know grief like hers, for Dale's death and his family's pain. She placed a hand on Nicole's knee.

"I know." Nicole looked at the pendant again before dropping it and returning her attention to Mina. "The killer was an ordinary person capable of extraordinary evil. For some unknown reason, he decided my parents needed to die." She reached her arm over Mina to place it on the other side of her shoulder so she could pin Mina with a fierce gaze. "Wallowing in grief won't bring them back. Just like lying here won't help find out what happened to your brother."

"It might help me."

Nicole's black hair tickled Mina's nose as she shook her head. "No, it won't. And it won't stop the darkness descending." A tear trickled out the corner of Mina's eye, tracking down her temple and into her hair. She opened her mouth to protest again, but Nicole's finger pressed to her lips. "Seriously, you're looking pale." She tipped her head to the side, flipping her hair back to expose her neck as she leaned in close. "A good meal always helps *me* put things into perspective."

M ina stretched like a cat, deep and full-bodied and accompanied by a soft moan. Nicole had left in the early hours of the afternoon, claiming she had somewhere to be. Mina didn't argue. The goth-familiar-PreMed had been right: she felt better having fed. Jack was still a turncoat; Cam was still missing; her brother and Brett both still dead. But her course was clear. Find this creature called Night and get revenge for the pain it had caused.

Her ears twitched as the rustle of waking vampires disturbed the blanket of silence that hung over the residential level of the Sanctuary. Bee came up the stairs from the training rooms, her blood song of rain on metal giving her away. Mina shifted onto her back and peered at the ceiling. Bee wouldn't like her plan. A tromping of boots followed Bee, intermingled with another song: a flute, high and crisp.

Ivan. Not what she would have pegged him as; she'd have gone more with drums. Mina frowned and squinted at a spider crawling across the ceiling. Ivan had said he could take them to Night. Bee had nixed the idea, and Mina had agreed, Ivan being suspect. But that was before Dale had died.

Everything was different now. Mina flung the covers off and kicked her feet up to propel herself out of bed. Pulling on the same clothes she'd been wearing before Nicole arrived, she grabbed her jacket and a pair of shit-kicking boots from the bottom of the wardrobe, and then jogged up stairs to join the gathering conclave.

They all turned and stared as she entered the vast space. She paused, frowning to see Rhys was there with Sam beside him. It was like Sam had adopted the old man. Turning away, she bent over to pull on one of her boots. Footsteps came over, and a hand landed gently on her shoulder.

"You okay?" Bee asked, her voice quiet.

Mina nodded brusquely before focusing on her other boot. "Evil doesn't stop because someone dies."

There was silence for a second, then Bee spoke. "No, it just gets stronger."

Mina stood up straight, glancing at Bee before striding over to the small circle. She noted the two vampires who flanked Ivan — Adeh and Tana — had left a little more space between themselves and him. Surprised to see he wasn't in chains, magical or mundane, she jerked her chin at him. "Should he be allowed to wander free?"

Bee crossed her arms over her chest and arched an eyebrow. "Rhys?"

"I..."

"There are few chains that can hold me." Ivan shrugged a shoulder. "You can bind me in silver, but then you wouldn't get the information you need. You trust me or you cast me out."

Rhys cleared his throat and continued. "I think Ivan's tale of having met Night before is true. Or at least, it could be true." A few people interjected at once.

"It lines up with the last time Night stalked the earth." Sam's deep voice was quiet, but it still stopped the squabbling.

"How do *you* know?" Mina's eyebrows pulled together as she tried to reconcile this Sam with the one who had been her boss for the past few years.

"I have interests outside of work." He peered at her for a second then rolled his eyes. "And I was watching over Rhys' shoulder as he researched. It's fascinating the stuff he—"

Bee held up a hand. "Not the time for an exposition of the Librarian's methods." She turned to Ivan. "Where is she then?"

"I can't just tell you." He made a small sound in his throat as Bee took a menacing step forward. "I know what she looks like and the places she's likely to be. She was after some —" He stopped and glanced at Mina, a flick of the eyes that was barely perceptible. "— one." He shook his head. "I don't know why."

But Mina knew who. As soon as Ivan looked at her, she knew Night had been hunting Dale. Dale was dead and Night had killed him. A fiery lance stabbed into her chest, replacing the ache, and she realized there was a big difference between suspecting and knowing.

Another person Night had taken from her. Whatever Bee did, Mina was going with Ivan to find Night. To kill Night. She didn't even try to tell herself it was to stop Night from hurting anyone else. The burning in her stomach told her clearly that it was to avenge what this creature had done to her. And maybe exorcise the pain of Dale's death.

Mina shifted, surprising herself when she spoke. "We should go with him. Stop her before she kills again." She gestured towards the door. "Maybe even get Jack back."

"I thought Jack was lost to us, as the cat said." Rhys glanced down at his hands as he spoke. Both Mina and Bee ignored him.

Bee stared at her for a second, her eyes shuttered, her head tipping. "We can't just go after Night." Bee used her hands to punctuate her words. "We have no weapon that will kill her." She turned her palm to the sky as she looked at Ivan.

Ivan met Bee's gaze. "*How* is not my problem."

Bee turned back to her. "So how?" Her eyebrows knit together, and her lips pulled into a frown. Rhys coughed beside her, and she cast a sharp glance at him before returning to Mina. "How do you reckon we take down this supposed demi-god that spreads death with a breath? Unless you know something you're not sharing?"

Mina shrugged. "I took down Luca?"

"And that turned out so well." Bee's tone was baiting. "However shadow-haunted he was, he was just a vampire, a dracul at that." Bee crossed her arms, looking down her nose at Mina. "Not so hard to kill."

"We've killed gargoyles." Mina glared at Rhys when he coughed, though her immediate annoyance was tempered by the fact that he did, indeed, look ill. "*I've* killed them, on my own, when I was nothing but a dhamphir."

Bee didn't say anything. Instead she walked a circle around Mina, sizing her up. "True, you got lucky," she said, when she was facing her again. "*After* we knew what would kill them."

Mina glanced at Rhys, hoping he'd provide some backup, but he stared at her, his mouth opened as if to speak, his eyes narrowed. But he remained silent, and his expression was mimicked by Ivan, who looked at her with a question on his face. Out-numbered, Mina's cheeks flushed. She wanted to kick something. Or someone. Instead, she slouched, her shoulders slumping.

Then Rhys finally broke the silence. "Maybe if we had the Blade of the Sun," he said, still staring at her. "The one weapon the legends say can take her down."

174

"But we don't have it, do we?" Bee said. "We have no idea where it is, or whether it will even help."

"Maybe we have more than we think." Rhys glanced at Ivan. "I'd like to show you something."

Out on the street, Mina canted her head as she shuffled behind Rhys and Bee as they debated, while Sam tried — and failed — to act as peacemaker. Rhys hadn't revealed where he was taking them, relishing the surprise, but Bee didn't seem to like surprises. Part of her hoped Rhys would tell them what he was doing, but the other part slowed her pace and shortened her stride. She dropped back. Beside her, Ivan mimicked her movements. None of the others seemed to notice when the two of them slipped back a bit more.

"Would you take me there?" Mina tipped her chin down and to the side, keeping her voice down, pitching it low.

"Can you really kill her?" Ivan kept looking straight ahead.

Mina was quiet, weighing the probability of her killing Night versus ending up dead herself. But seeing their opportunity to slip away up ahead, she answered. "Yes."

CHAPTER TWENTY-SIX

Mina's stomach clenched as she passed the sign: 'Future home of the Albright Institute for Human Development'. She knew where she and Ivan were: the old warehouses where Dar met his end.

"You're sure about this?" She slowed down, dropping back.

Ivan peered at her, his face unreadable, though she noticed he'd loosened the daggers at his hips. He nodded. "Are you?"

Mina felt queasy as she drew her gun. "Why here?"

Ivan shrugged, staring at the water. "She's taken with it. Less history than the mansion maybe. Less traffic than the cemetery, but just as drenched in death." He stopped, glancing sideways at her. "More so, since Dar's death was recent and bloody." He started walking forward again.

"How did she even come across this place?"

There was a hiccough in Ivan's gait. He didn't turn, but looked at her over his shoulder, a look that made her downright ill. "I should warn you," he said. "One of the gargoyles survived."

"I know. I've seen it." Her eyes stung at the memory of Jack being carted off after Seema killed Angelos.

"The gargoyle...." He stopped.

"What?" Her voice came out as a whisper even to her.

"Night's taken it under her wing, so to speak."

Since nothing else was forthcoming, Mina repeated what she'd said to Bee. "That's fine, I've faced gargoyles before, and beaten them."

Ivan's neck twitched, and he started walking again. "Not like this one."

"What are you on about?" Mina sighed, realizing she was tired of the caginess that plagued vampires. She cast her eyes over her left shoulder to the flickering lights of the city on the other side of the river, then arced her gaze above to the twinkling lights of a clear, cold night sky, before landing in front of her on the consuming darkness of the abandoned warehouses.

"There's something different about this one. It's not pure gargoyle. It's...smarter."

"What's that supposed to mean?" She plodded forward as a heavy feeling took hold of her gut. When Ivan didn't answer, she swallowed down her nerves, compressing them into a nauseous ball in the pit of her stomach, and caught up with him. As they got closer to the third warehouse on the left, Mina saw there was actually some faint light spilling out. It gave her comfort, that this creature called Night still needed illumination.

That was until the shriek shot through the air like lightning. Mina started toward the warehouse at a run. Ivan swore but joined her, following at a more plodding pace. She sprinted up the stairs to the open loading dock door. Then skidded to a halt just before she ran out of shadow to hide in.

A creature unlike any she'd ever seen was crouched in a halo of light, its face covered with blood and bits of gory flesh. It had the form of a gargoyle: ashen skin covering wiry sinew, accented by velociraptor talons and beetle black eyes. Its wings were tattered and torn — battle-scarred — but the edges had patches of pink and soft fuzz. They were regrowing. Its flesh was more rose grey than slate grey, and its face was longer, fuller, more human. But it still had a gargoyle's usual set of sharp, serrated teeth...except for the enormous canines. Those were new. This one sunk those canines into the creature at its feet, piercing through bone with a crunch. It used a long, forked tongue to lap up the blood that flowed before tearing out a chunk of flesh. The poor creature that was its meal was not quite dead, nor was it quite human. A shifter of some kind, it was stuck in a perpetual loop of terrified change: one part smooth flesh became brown fur became bloodied flesh. Vomit and bile burned at Mina's throat, but she swallowed and forced herself to stay frozen in the shadows.

Around this spectacle, a handful of figures were arrayed. Mina recognized the one on the left as a werewolf by her unique musty smell. The faces of the others were either lost in shadow, or, like the person right in front of her, facing away despite being so close she could almost touch the cascade of dark curls.

"Do you have the information you need? Can I kill it now?" said a sad wreck of a woman, crouching beside the gargoyle thing. The skin of her face was a sickly sandstone and covered in seeping sores.

Again, Mina tamped down the bile. Ivan stepped up beside her, his chest rising and falling as he tried to mute his breath. She loosened her blades in their sheathes then raised her gun before taking a soft step into the warehouse, still keeping to the circle of shadows around the edge.

"Not yet," another voice said, coming from the person directly in front of her, the tones smooth like liquid chocolate. "I want to see what it does. I want to see what the gargoyle becomes next." The voice sent a shiver down Mina's spine, and her eyebrows scrunched together. It was familiar, like an animated character voiced by some actor she should know. "But first, we should welcome our unexpected guests." The figure turned around, and Mina's stomach heaved, as her arms drooped. Somehow she managed to keep hold of her gun.

"Cam?" But Mina knew there was someone else in control of her friend's body.

A shot cracked the sudden silence in the warehouse. The creature that had taken up residence in Cam's body looked down to where a viscous liquid, the colour of a starless sky, oozed out of a hole in Cam's chest. For a second Cam's eyes flashed across Mina's face before glaring over her shoulder at Ivan as they turned a solid black, like blots of India ink.

"That wasn't very nice." The words sounded like they were coming through some auto-tune filter, layering a multitude of voices into one. It laid Cam's hand over the wound and paused. Its lips snarled. "It stings. What poison did you try to use against me?" She brought an inky finger to her lips and licked. "Silver." The creature stepped forward, putting a sneer onto Cam's face. "I like the sting of silver."

Ivan pulled at Mina's arm, dragging her away, back into the night.

She struggled against his grasp, pulling her arm free and heading back towards the warehouse.

"What are you doing?" Ivan hissed.

Mina looked at him, gesturing with her gun. "My friend..." She looked back at the warehouse.

"You mean Night? If that was your friend, she's dead."

There was a skitter of noise behind them, as she turned so her back was against Ivan's.

"Wolves." The word escaping the warehouse was soft, almost seductive in the auto-tune voice. But the next was sharp and ricocheted through the warehouse. "Attack!"

Mina never knew a single word could drip with so much malevolent delight.

Hana crouched lower on the warehouse rooftop, careful to avoid the gaping holes and the puddled water, her heart tripping as howls ripped through the night. She pressed against the low wall at the edge of the roof, but not too hard since she didn't trust anything to stay intact in this neglected block of warehouses, then she slid up to peek over the edge and watch the scene below unfold. Her eyes narrowed and her cheeks flushed as the female who'd tumbled out of the warehouse spun around to face the encircling werewolves.

Mina.

Hana frowned. Mina was a vampire. When, how, why. None of it mattered...her sister-in-law brought darkness down on the family. She knew in her bones Mina was involved somehow in Dale's death...why else would he be targeted. Hana's throat closed, cutting off the sob that threatened to escape. She pushed it deep into her stomach, to deal with later, after she found Dale's killer. It had been clear to her as soon as she'd arrived home that Dale hadn't died of a heart attack.

Hana squinted at the scene below as another figure fled the warehouse. Another vampire, one she recognized. When she tracked Mina before, she'd acted adversarial with the Necrophagus, and yet the muscle-bound vampire was one of them. Not that it mattered. Vampires were vampires; they were all evil and needed to be wiped from the face of the earth. That's what her grandparents had taught her. And that's what their bloody deaths had etched into her soul. Still, a worm of doubt worked its way through Hana's abdomen. Mina was family; she had been good people. *Maybe I can save her, exorcise the vampire from her. One last gift to Dale.* But another little voice reminded her that was impossible: once a vampire, always a vampire, until it was slain.

Hana drew the long silver sword from the sheath strapped to her back. Below, her actions were mimicked by Mina, who now held a short sword in one hand, gun in the other, while her back was pressed against that of the other vampire.

Above the black scarf pulled up over her nose, Hana's eyebrows drew together. *Mina is in league with the Necrophagus after all, no matter how unfriendly they say they are.*

Though, as a couple more vampires emerged from the warehouse, joining the menagerie of creatures encircling Mina and her companion, Hana admitted she'd missed some nuance in vampire politics. There was more going on down there than she realized.

As the wolves closed in around Mina, Hana made a decision, one that surprised her. She stood up, stepped onto the parapet, and dropped in behind the werewolves. When her toes touched the ground, she relaxed into the impact, tucking into a roll. Halfway through the roll, she coiled her muscles, ready to spring into action. Year after year of training from her grandmother had toned her mental and muscle memory so finely she could come out of a fall ready to fight. She slid her sword through the torso of the nearest wolf, before it could even howl in outrage. She drew her shorter sword and spun to meet the next, driving the blade through its eye, into its brain, just as it started to realize there was some shadow it should pay attention to.

An eddy in the air marked the location of her next target, then hot breath caressed the back of her neck as it closed in for the kill. Hana dropped to one knee, tipping her torso forward, her neck out of reach, as she drove her long sword up behind her between arm and torso. Judging from the howl and the resistant tug on the blade as she drew it back, she knew she'd hit her mark.

Between Hana's blows and the shots fired by Mina and her vampire associate, the wolves started to hesitate, to draw back out of sword's reach, into the shadows. However, the howls of the injured had drawn more spectators to the warehouse door, including a woman Hana thought she recognized. And the woman was livid. Hana ducked as a blade came towards her head from the side, hitting air instead of its target. She turned to glare at the wielder: the big vampire.

"I just saved your skin, you pestilent tick," she hissed as she grabbed Mina's arm. "Come on!"

Mina scowled and pulled her arm away and started to turn back to the warehouse. Hana pulled her scarf down, revealing her face.

"Hana?" Mina whispered, her mouth dropping open.

Hana pointed the tip of her sword at the vampires spilling out of the warehouse. "They will kill us if we don't leave now." She turned and ran into the darkness, towards the bridge, not looking back to see if Mina followed.

CHAPTER TWENTY-SEVEN

Mina ran after Hana. Quiet, solid Hana, who should have been an anchor of normality in her world. Instead, the appearance of her sister-in-law at the abandoned warehouses, decked out like a cat burglar and wielding a pair of swords, sent her head spinning again. But she couldn't figure out how this piece of the puzzle fit in to the picture while fighting gargoyles and fleeing werewolves.

So she followed Hana, who ran full tilt towards the concrete piles that marked the start of the bridge.

"Where are we going?" Ivan asked between breaths.

"Forward," Hana said without even a backward glance or a hiccough in her pace. Only 'forward' was cut off by a deep ditch, the bottom filled with stagnant water and scum of unknown origin. Hana ran full speed across a rickety piece of wood that wobbled even under her light step. Not quick enough to change course towards the plank, Mina called on her minimal high school track experience and managed to pull off the hop-skip-fling of a long jump to propel herself across. The splash and swearing behind her told her Ivan hadn't quite made it.

"Hana," Mina shouted through her raspy throat. "Slow up."

Hana stopped, turning around to glare at her. Mina slowed to a jog. Joining her sister-in-law, she turned and spared a glance backward. Ivan had clambered out of the ditch.

"Where are we going?" Mina panted, as Ivan joined them, his face towards the river.

"There," Hana pointed to a black car Mina hadn't seen, parked on the far side of the on-ramp.

A splash behind them drew Mina's attention back to the ditch, and to the werewolf scrambling out of it. Its brethren had learned from its misstep and were crouching down to leap over the gap.

"Come on." Hana sprinted the last few metres to the car.

"This isn't your car." Mina's gaze travelled over the sleek lines and shining chrome as Hana unlocked the doors.

"Seriously? That's what you focus on?" Hana disappeared into the driver's side. Mina accepted that with a tilt of her head, and slid in beside her, forcing Ivan to cram himself into the back.

Putting the car into reverse, Hana tore away from the wolves, backing the car all the way up the on-ramp to the bridge before spinning it around to point the nose in the direction they wanted to go: over the water.

Mina buckled her seatbelt, staring at her sister-in-law with wide eyes as Hana accelerated across the bridge, swerving sideways to avoid rear-ending the one car dawdling its way across. As they reached the other side, a rumbling rose all around Mina.

She twisted her torso around to look out the back window, searching for the source. Shoving Ivan's head aside, she peered out the slit of glass that made up the window, her mouth dropping. A phalanx of werewolves on motorcycles was gaining on them.

"There are wolves on motorbikes."

"You didn't think they ran everywhere, did you?" Ivan poked his head between the seats.

"Well, kinda." Mina turned back around, just in time to see another squad of wolves blocking the exit from the bridge.

"Hold on." Hana downshifted and stepped on the gas. The car shot forward, towards the wall of werewolves.

Even with her seatbelt on, Mina responded to her knee-jerk reaction to brace herself as best as possible against the dashboard.

A yelp sounded as Hana plowed through the werewolves without slowing down. This was followed by a screech as claw tore through metal. Hana fishtailed the car, trying to dislodge the wolf, but the next thing Mina heard was a pop-and-squeal as one of the car's tires was shot out. The car swerved sideways with a shudder before Hana corrected it.

"Fuck!"

Mina glanced at her sister-in-law. Hana never swore.

"We need to ditch the car." Hana took her foot off the gas and spun them sideways around a corner.

"We need to get to Sanctuary."

"If you know somewhere safe...."

"Somewhere they can't follow." Mina nodded.

"It's too far." Ivan shifted his bulk in the back seat. "The church is closer."

"St. Frank's? But Father Pietro is dead."

"It's still holy ground."

"But you're not—"

"Good enough." Hana careened the car around another corner then slammed on the brakes. "I need to get something out of the trunk. Then get ready to run."

Mina sprinted into the square in front of St. Frank's — St. Francis' — Cathedral. The square where she and Cam often sat and people-watched. The church where Jack found her, introducing her to her undead life. It was dark, likely deserted at this time of night. As she ran, the edges of her vision blurred and her breathing became heavy. Her legs were sluggish, as if filled with wet concrete, and she had to force every step. A yelp echoed off the glass and steel, she glanced back to check that Ivan and Hana still followed her.

Her eyes went wide and she almost fell. A black mist shot through with snot-green filaments was enveloping the square. The miasma sent tendrils along the ground, and the nearest wormed around her feet. She grabbed Hana's arm and propelled her forward. About halfway across the square, she was shocked to see the door open and a warm light spill down the steps. The sight gave her hope, and she surged forward. Reaching the steps, Hana took them two at a time, and Mina prepared to do the same. A

185

second later, she was on her back on the cobblestones of the square, the wind knocked out of her, and a beneficent face peering down at her.

"Holy ground, vampire." The woman's smile filled her face, crinkling crow's feet into the corner of her eyes.

Ivan's hand grabbed her arm and hauled her up. "Apparently you've been uninvited."

"What's the hold up?" Hana asked from the stairs, backlit by the light from the still-open door.

"New priest, new blessing." The woman stood up, making room for Mina. The movement revealed the white patch of a clerical collar at her neck.

Nausea swept over Mina, undercut by gnawing dread as a baying echoed around them. "Can you invite us in?"

"Oh my." The woman peered over Mina's shoulder at the magic looming behind her, a frown finally replacing the smile. She gave Mina a sad look. "I'm afraid I can't. Not my church."

"No, it's mine." A young man stood at the top of the stairs, his arms crossed as he peered down at Ivan and Mina.

"Father, will you give us sanctuary?" Mina stepped up to the very foot of the stairs, forcing herself to look at him rather than at whatever was snaking around her legs. Judging by his accent, he wasn't local, but his olive skin gave few hints to where he hailed from. Neither did his frown. Ivan stepped up beside her, and the priest's eyes flicked to him before looking past them both.

"Father Luiz?" the woman said.

He looked sidelong at her then dropped his arms. "All right then, you'd better come in."

Mina glanced at Ivan then ran up the stairs, followed by the woman with the clerical collar.

The sound of the door echoed through the space as it slammed shut behind them. They continued forward and only stopped once they were in the sanctuary proper. Then they all turned around and faced the two clergy.

"What a day for an interfaith meeting." The woman's face beamed with a smile. "I'm so glad I came. I get to meet not one, but two vampires, a Hunter, and quite possibly the beginning of the end."

"These are not things to joke about, Reverend Margaret." The priest's frown was as deep as the woman's smile was broad.

"Forgive the Father. He's only recently been made aware of the existence of creatures such as yourselves. He's still adjusting to the idea that there might be such a thing as a good vampire."

"I'm not good." Ivan glanced around the church.

"Good-ish then, if you're running from whatever is out there. Best any of us can hope for." Despite it not being her church, the woman walked down the aisle like she owned it. "Come on then, might as well get comfortable. You might be here for a while." Ivan followed her, trailed by the priest.

Hana hung back, wrapping her fingers around Mina's arm to the point of bruising. *I'm a vampire. I'll heal.* But there were some wounds she wouldn't heal from. And she saw one of them when she looked in Hana's eyes, which reflected the pain of her brother's death back at her.

"You know." Hana's tone was flat but hard. A howl sounded outside, and the windows rattled, and Hana's arm dropped to her side, to the hilt of her short sword.

"We should join the others." Mina started walking towards them, noting the old woman had her hand on Ivan's shoulder. Hana's fingers tightened around her forearm again, to the point of pain, making her stop. She looked in her sister-in-law's eyes and nodded.

"It's your fault my husband's dead."

Silence fell as the other three stopped their quiet conversation. "He was my brother too."

"Just because she's a vampire doesn't make it her fault." The reverend stepped closer, and Hana shot her a glare full of venom. The woman just graced her with a sad smile.

"Why do you think it's Mina's fault?" Ivan came to stand behind the reverend, almost using her as a shield against Hana's anger. "You were at the warehouse. What other evil have you been hunting?"

"You're not helping." Mina's cheeks blazed with a mix of anger, frustration and guilt. She shifted her gaze between Ivan and the woman until they backed off a few paces, then she turned back to Hana. She opened her mouth to apologize but was cut off.

"Promise me." Hana stared at her, hands on her hips, though some of the ire had left her gaze. "Promise me you'll help me find the creature that took Dale from me and his children. And help me kill it."

Mina stood in a state of shock. The cascade of revelation after revelation was too much to process. But Hana demanded an answer, and Mina had little doubt what Hana would have done if it had been her. "I promise."

Hana nodded, then walked away, finding a pew to lie down on while they waited for the maelstrom outside to dissipate.

CHAPTER TWENTY-EIGHT

Snarls and yips were punctuated by sirens and Mina spun, sure the werewolves that still prowled the pre-dawn streets had found them again. Instead a sound closer by drew her attention back to the Sanctuary. Her Sanctuary.

"Where've you been?" Bee's voice was flat, the words spit out between tense lips. A cat, Seema, bounded down the stairs then skidded to a stop and hissed. Rhys rounded out the group at the top of the stairs, a glass of what looked like whiskey in his hand.

Mina tried to formulate an answer. "I —"

"And what's *that* doing here?" Bee looked past Mina's shoulder, her gaze hard and sharp like broken glass.

"I thought you'd decided to invite him into our home." Mina glanced over her shoulder, her eyes pulling together when she saw Hana's hand on the hilt of a short sword. The hairs on the nape of Mina's neck rose, and she gave a sharp shake of her head that Hana ignored. She turned back to Bee, who'd pulled out her own weapon.

"Not Ivan. The Hunter." Bee's eyes flicked back to Hana.

"The what?" Mina turned around again to examine her sister-in-law more closely.

"Oh my, mythical creatures abound." Rhys beamed at her. "Might as well invite them all in. The more magical beasts, the merrier," he added, before taking another sip from his glass.

Her sword sheathed, Hana pushed past Mina, pausing to respond to Rhys. "I'm human. Unlike you lot."

"I'm human too, my dear. Doesn't make me any less of a legend." He looked at Mina, a half smile brightening his face, as his eyebrows waggled.

Hana ignored him. Instead she walked to the foot of the stairs, causing Seema to hiss again as she got close. A howl rose from a road nearby, accompanied by the wail of a siren.

Bee glanced back at Ivan, Mina following her gaze. "He's invited." She turned back to Hana. "You're tolerated, but not welcome. Don't get comfortable."

Hana snorted. "I have no intention to. Besides, I don't need to be invited." She sauntered up the stairs, past Bee, and through the large doors. Bee frowned at Mina, then turned and followed, accompanied by Rhys and Ivan. Mina slowly brought up the rear, walking backwards as she scanned the street for movement. Feeling something sharp against her skin, she looked down to find Seema pawing her leg, her golden eyes staring at her. Another howl, closer this time, followed by a snarl, snaked through the night towards their patch of blessed earth.

Glancing back up, Seema shift beside her.

"We should join the others," the woman's voice sagged, heavy with misgiving. Mina turned her head to look at the woman's profile. Her jaw was tense and her eyes scanned the street, seemingly unconcerned about her nakedness. Slowly she turned, her eyes catching Mina's gaze, before slinking up the steps. Mina followed the shifter into the building.

"I told you I knew where Night was." Ivan's voice raised to be heard over the general cacophony of a debating conclave. The voices ebbed, which left space for the yips and yowls outside. In the silence, Mina also heard a familiar heartbeat. She glanced towards the arcade but couldn't see Sam, despite her vampire vision.

"And now where do you think she is?" Bee stood, hands on hips, her chin jutting out as she spoke. "Because you two decided to go off on your own, she's probably gone into hiding somewhere."

"No." Hana's voice was completely normal, not raised, not angry, not challenging. "This creature won't go into hiding.

She'll hurt and maim and kill —" She swallowed then continued. "And kill until she has what she wants, or she's killed."

"And what do you know, Hunter?" Bee strode up to Hana, coming face to face. "Moving in and out of the shadows, killing without conscience or consequence. Because you deem something evil, and *you* judge that it should die."

Mina came to stand beside Hana. "That's my family you're talking about."

Adeh was quiet when he spoke. "How many times do you need to hear it before you understand?" He peered at her, forcing her to meet his gaze. "We're your family now." Mina sighed, her chest heavy with the impossible tug of war between her human family, the conclave, Jack and Cam. She opened her mouth to say something. Another howl reverberated outside the stone walls.

Bee pointed a finger at her face. "You knew about this...that you were bringing a Hunter here?" She nodded her chin at Hana.

Mina shook her head. "No, I still don't know what's going on. I don't know why you call her 'Hunter'. I don't know why she's dressed up like a ninja. I don't know why she rescued a pair of hapless vampires. But that doesn't change the fact that she did indeed save my life. And Ivan's."

Bee didn't answer, just scowled. Instead it was Rhys that spoke. "What do you know, Hunter?"

"Why do they keep calling you that?" Mina turned her head sideways.

Her sister-in-law looked at the floor instead of at her. "Because I hunt your kind. Their kind. The werewolves and the cats." She slid her eyes over in Seema's direction. "The pixies and the lamia. All of them. It's what I was born — and raised — to do: kill any and all of the unholy creatures that bedevil humankind."

"You think I'm evil?"

Hana finally looked at her, her eyes shining, her shoulders slumped. "It's in your blood. The vampire strain always takes over. But —" She looked back at the floor. Mina wanted to reach out, but she couldn't break through her guilt at Dale's death.

After an uncomfortable silence, Hana shifted, stood up straight, and looked at Bee. "All I know is this new creature, the one the Herald woke...call her what you will, she kills without compunction, without any more reason than someone steps in front of her on the street. We need to kill her before she kills us."

"The first thing a Hunter's ever said that made any sense." Seema stood, arms crossed over her still-naked chest, leaning against a pillar, long hair flowing Godiva-like over her shoulders, around her hips.

Hana turned her head towards Seema, then returned to examining the floor. When she spoke, her voice was quiet. "And she killed my husband."

"What?" Mina turned to look at Hana again. "No. It wasn't her." But Mina remember the scent, underneath the stench of blood and death: rosemary and lavender. "No," she repeated, but there was no strength in the word. Cam had been there when her brother died. She took a step forward, but her knees felt like they would give way if she attempted another. Instead she shook her head. "Cam's possessed. We need to get this thing out of her, then kill it."

"Cam?" Sam spoke for the first time, stepping out of the shadows. "What does she have to do with this?"

"Who's Cam?" Bee asked.

"My roommate." Mina didn't want to elaborate, but the silence required it. "The one we brought back from the cemetery."

Bee stepped closer. Mina didn't move. "The one who went missing? Along with Brett?"

Mina's stomach clenched. It finally hit her, what had likely happened to Brett. Her knees went weak, and she lay a hand on the pillar beside her. Her eyes darted from Bee's face to the floor. "Yes." Her voice rose at the end, even though it wasn't a question.

In a flash Bee stepped right up to her. Looking sidelong at her, Mina saw the muscle in the side of her neck tense and her jaw clench. And when she looked in her eyes, she saw Bee had reached the same conclusion about Brett.

"That's why you went off with Ivan, isn't it? To try to rescue your friend?" Bee paced across the rough circle formed by the members of the conclave. "Do you realize you've put us all in danger?" Her hand gestured towards the door. "All of *them* in danger? The humans know nothing about vampires or gargoyles or the descent of Night. And we're supposed to keep it that way."

Hana shifted, catching Mina's attention, and causing all the members of the conclave to scramble.

"What are you doing, Hunter?" Bee's hand went to her gun. Tension strained the air in the Sanctuary, punctuated by yips and growls of werewolves, though they sounded farther away now.

"I've had enough of your squabbles." Hana glanced at the door nonetheless. "I need to get back to Liam and Maggie."

Mina's eyes went wide. "Are they at home?" If Night had killed Dale, it meant she knew where Hana lived.

Hana shook her head sharply. "With June." She looked at the others, taking her hand off the sword hilt, now that it was slung over her shoulder again. "My children."

"They might be safer if you didn't return." Bee's hand was still on her gun.

"Is that a threat?"

Bee shook her head, as another howl ricocheted through the night. "Just saying."

Rhys stepped close to Hana, placing his hand on her forearm. "She might be right, at least for tonight." His words were underscored by a siren screaming by.

Hana pulled her arm away and sent the palm into the pillar nearest her, as Mina wondered what the denizens of downtown thought was happening out there.

"Call and see if they're okay," Mina said. "If so, stay here tonight. If not, I'll go with you."

"So the Hunter knows nothing," Bee said, the anger having left her voice. "Mina and Ivan have tipped Night to the fact we know about her. Meaning we're back where we started."

"Not necessarily." Rhys stepped forward, his glass having disappeared. "Mina might be on to something, about freeing her friend from this creature. Or freeing this creature from her friend. Finn and I have been searching for the Blade of the Sun."

Adeh scoffed. "Magical weapons won't help us."

"What, you mean like how silver and lead don't do any more damage than steel and iron?"

Adeh's jaw snapped shut, biting back any response.

Rhys glanced at Seema. "We think we've found it. Or half of it anyway."

"Locked away behind high-tech security." Seema stepped away from the pillar, reaching down to pick up the cloth at her feet and wrap it around herself.

"Hmm, good thing we have a hacker Smith on our side." Rhys looked at his empty glass. "Speaking of, I should get back to her."

"If it's not safe for her —" Ivan nodded at Hana "— it's not safe for you."

Bee frowned, then huffed. "At least wait until sunrise."

Mina swiveled her head to stare at Rhys as he clapped his hands together.

"Then we can all go to our Sam's and hear Finn's plan," he said.

CHAPTER TWENTY-NINE

Rhys sat on a stool in front of the counter in Sam's kitchen. He ran a hand over the polished concrete, as Sam dug around in a cupboard for a dusty, old tin of tea. He knew Dar had a special relationship with Sam; it was strange that didn't bother him more. He liked Sam. The man was good people under all the tattoos.

While the water for tea boiled, Sam made coffee for himself and Finn, using some contraption with levers and knobs and pressure gauges. Rhys wiggled his nose; tea was much simpler. Finn wandered the apartment, looking at the artwork — watercolour cityscapes Rhys suspected were Sam's own. Ivan stood sentinel by the door, though Rhys was unsure whether that was to protect them or because he felt unwelcome. *Or he doesn't trust us.* Rhys ignored that inner voice, and turned to look at Mina, who was slumped into a chair beside the window, where she'd dropped herself after saying something along the lines of vampires still needing sleep. Given that the couch in the centre of the room, away from the rising sun, would have made a more comfortable bed, he doubted sleep was the reason she was curled into a ball in the corner. He hadn't corrected her that it was the thing inside her, the one that made her a vampire, that needed to recharge; vampires didn't like being reminded they had some evil, life-sucking symbiont living inside. The other members of the conclave had stayed at the Sanctuary, apparently deciding his and Finn's quest for the blade wasn't important. But for some reason Mina had come to Sam's, even though she clearly needed rest. And feeding.

The kettle whistled, and Rhys turned around, expecting Sam to pour scalding water over delicate tea. But Sam didn't, instead putting the kettle down on another burner, while he finished up with the coffee. It was almost like he knew what he was doing.

"Coffee's on." Without turning around, Sam finally poured the water over the tea as Finn made her way to the counter, taking a seat on the end. Turning around, Sam picked up an oven mitt from the counter and threw it at Mina. "Wake up, sleepy head."

A grumble arose from under the blanket that covered her head. Pulling it down, she said, "I'm not sleepy, I'm catatonic." She curled back into a ball and buried her head again.

Sam send a potholder to follow the mitt. "Shift it. We have scheming to do."

Shooting him a scowl, Mina got up and came to join them, sliding onto the stool beside Rhys. He'd never seen a vampire so rumpled.

"You should go home and get some sleep," he said.

She turned to him, the weariness of the last few weeks showing in the dark circles under her eyes. "I'm fine." She gave him a wan smile. "You heard him...we must plot." Sam grimaced at her as he handed a mug of coffee to Finn. Mina stared at the cup like it was a chalice of blood.

"You think Night is after the blade in the museum?" Sam asked over his shoulder as he cleaned the coffee contraption.

"Half a blade," Finn corrected.

"Still a powerful half." Rhys wished the tea was a hearty black; he needed all the fortification he could get. "If Sir Windrow is after it, it can't be good."

"So what do we do?" Mina lay her head on the countertop.

Finn placed her cup on the table, freeing her to use her hands when she spoke. "We need to get the blade before Night does. And find out what this collector knows."

Rhys nodded. "Yes."

"Maybe he doesn't know anything." Sam wet a cloth to wipe down the counter.

"He knows something," Rhys said.

Ivan shifted from his pillar, though his arms stayed crossed. "Why do you say that?"

"Do you think he doesn't?" Rhys raised an eyebrow.

"I have no opinion." Ivan leaned on the pillar again, approximating casual but Rhys didn't buy it. "I'm just wondering why you think that."

Mina looked sideways at Ivan before turning her attention to Rhys. "I can't imagine with his interest in, uh, legendary artifacts that he doesn't know something more than he's said."

"Which is nothing," Finn said.

"True." Rhys reached out for the cup of tea Sam passed him like it was water in the Sahara. He paused, taking a careful sip before continuing. "But he's the kind of man who would seek out an object of awesome evil potential."

Sam stopped running a cloth over the counter to look at Rhys' face. "You never did mention how you know him."

"And it's too long a tale for today." Rhys took a sip of tea. "I don't really know him. We crossed paths when I became a bit of a gnat in his peripheral vision."

Sam finally picked up his own coffee, turning to lean against the far counter. Rhys could appreciate what Dar had seen in him: chiseled features, an inquisitive mind, and caring concern for his friends. "Meaning if he remembers you, it's not fondly?"

"Not likely, no." A twitter travelled through Rhys' stomach, as his mind cast back to that encounter a lifetime ago.

"So you're not the one to try to find out what he knows." Sighing, Mina ran her hands on her pants. "Fine, I'll go."

"No." Rhys put his mug down.

"Excuse me?" She arched an eyebrow at him.

Rhys shook his head. "I don't think that's a good idea. You're just the kind of unusual artifact Emmerson Windrow would like to collect."

"I'll go." Finn peered into her coffee, hardly touched, as she turned the cup around in her hands. She looked up at them finally, when no one responded. "It just makes sense."

Rhys frowned at her. "No, it doesn't. Why you?"

"We've gone through the list of possibilities. There's no one else."

"I can go." Sam leaned against the counter behind him and crossed his arms over his chest.

Finn shook her head. "No, no one else will know the questions to ask."

Ivan stepped forward from where he'd been leaning, taciturn, against the wall. "I can go with you."

Sam glanced at the big man and stood up straight. "How about we three go?"

"Why don't we all go?" Mina slid off the stool. "It's been a while since I scoped out a magic blade at the museum."

"I don't like this." Rhys ran his hands over the countertop, as if trying to smooth it.

"Like I say to my father, you don't have to like it." Finn got up from the stool. "Shall we?"

Rhys sighed, realizing he'd lost a fight he hadn't even known he was fighting.

The ticket taker at the museum was new, and looked askance at the odd assortment of people who tumbled up to her to be let in. Mina understood her chagrin: a tattooed slacker (herself); a freckled, fiery red head (tattoos hidden except for the bits not quite covered by Finn's cuffs); a muscle-bound mountain of a man in motorcycle boots and a leather jacket; and a distinguished gentleman not obviously related to any of them. Oh, and Sam had joined them, apparently having nothing better to do with the shop closed. So a dapper, spectacled gentlemen with tattoos up to his ears.

Finn threaded her arm around Rhys' elbow. "*Granddad*, what's this amazing thing you wanted to show us?" She smiled and handed her ticket to the woman, followed by Ivan and Sam.

Mina brought up the rear, giving the woman a big smile, noticing the tattoos that peeked out above the woman's collar when she turned to stare at Ivan. "She'll do anything for her grandpa, including dragging us all to the museum for the afternoon." Mina rolled her eyes, before turning to follow the others, taking the escalator steps two at a time until she'd caught up with them.

"Where to now?" She glanced around the atrium, searching for signs of a magical weapon. Tapping her fingers in a random rhythm on her thigh, she asked herself again why she was there. The Blade of the Sun wouldn't help her rescue Cam from the beast that held her, nor keep her promise to Hana. Mina's stomach dropped at the reminder of her promise to avenge Dale, though she couldn't quite say why. She'd killed before, for less reason.

"We need to find Dev." Rhys looked at his phone. "He mentioned he'd be at the museum today."

"Check that broom closet they've stuck their visiting expert in?" Finn glanced at Rhys with the look of a doting granddaughter, a look Rhys responded to with relish.

He smiled, shrugging. "Sounds as good a plan as any." He stepped off the escalator and leaned in to whisper to the group. "Though I don't imagine we can get access to that broom cupboard."

"You do have the technology to ask him to come to us," Mina suggested, glancing at the phone that was still in Rhys' hand.

"That I do." When Rhys started pecking out a message, Mina was half tempted to tear the phone away and do it herself. Instead she sighed and turned to lean on the banister overlooking the atrium

"You too?"

"What?" Mina half-glanced at Ivan as he came to lean beside her.

"Need to work on your patience?"

"I —" She turned to him, to find Sam looking at her with an arched eyebrow and half-cocked smile.

"No comment," he said.

"What, I never did take a boot to Paul's head, did I?" Mina smirked as an image of her aiming a roundhouse kick at her former, pig of a coworker's head popped into her brain.

Sam shrugged. "I suppose not. More's the pity."

Mina was about to respond when Sam's attention was drawn to something over her shoulder. Following his gaze, she saw an Indian Adonis striding towards them. His mane of wavy hair fluttered as if there were a breeze, and his luscious lips pulled down in a frown. He cast his rich brown eyes from left to right, glancing back the way he'd come.

Coming up to them, he leaned towards Rhys. "What are you doing here?" he hissed, taking in the ragtag group. "You can't all be here." His tongue clicked against his teeth.

"Why? You said we should come visit. I wanted to introduce you to some friends." Rhys turned towards them. "Friends, this is Dev. Dev, this —"

"The owner is here to check on his collection." Dev looked down into the atrium, his brown eyes shining.

"Oh." Rhys' smile fell.

"Yes, oh." Dev's hands clasped together, but that didn't stop him from fidgeting.

"Maybe we shouldn't all be here," Rhys said. "Maybe we shouldn't be here at all."

"Why?" Mina asked.

"The owner of the collection is...well —" Dev inspected his palms.

"A rather peculiar man," Rhys finished. "I doubt he would react well to any unusual interest in his collection."

Mina nodded slowly. "Such as a Smith, a familiar, two vampires and their known associate, the Librarian, stopping by to chat with the visiting expert."

"Something like that," Rhys said as Dev's gaze moved between her, Ivan and Sam.

"Vampires?" the man said, his fidgeting calming as he eyed them.

200

"Something like that," Mina said.

Dev huffed, glancing around again. "Come to my broom closet."

"It's crazy," Dev said, after listening to Finn and Rhys explain their plan to liberate the blade from the collection, and Mina couldn't argue with him. "There's no way you can bypass his security."

Finn sat on a wobbly chair in front of the table that served as the archaeologist's desk, one end piled with papers and books, his laptop on the other. Rhys was in the only other chair in the space. Ivan and Sam leaned against jambs on either side of the door, while Mina squatted on the floor with the dust bunnies. Dev paced across the centre of the small room, if it can be called pacing when you can only take a step and a half in any direction.

"Your computer's connected to the museum network, yes?" Finn waved her hand at the laptop.

Dev paused for a second, coming to a stop in front of Sam, who stood up a little straighter, then turned to Finn. "Yeah. So?"

"So..." Finn pressed a key. "Trojan horse deployed. Greeks awaiting orders."

"What?"

"I added a little file. A backdoor, if you will."

"Really? Just now?"

Finn scowled then her face lit with a smile. "Beware of Smiths bearing gifts."

"Without asking? What if it's found?" Dev's voice rose.

"It won't be found." Her smile was dampened by the shake of Dev's head.

"I'm sorry to have to tell you this, but it still won't work."

"What do you mean?"

"My computer is on the museum network. The one controlling the security for the exhibit is not. Another thing the owner of the collection insisted on: an air gap." Mina didn't understand what he was talking about but presumed it wasn't good. She had to admit her curiosity about the blade had been piqued after listening to the others talk about it with awe and trepidation.

"Oh, bugger." Finn closed the lid of the laptop.

"Where is it?" Mina asked, drawing herself up to standing.

"What?"

"The computer?" She looked at Finn. "If you got access to it, could you put your little horse on it?"

"I might need more than my little horse, but yes." Her smiled returned, and Mina saw the cogs working in the Smith's brain.

Dev glanced around the room, then back at Mina. "It's in the server room."

"Could you get Finn in there?"

Dev was silent, then shook his head. "Not until the owner leaves."

"But it's possible?" Sam asked.

Dev tipped his head, looking sideways at Sam. "Possible. Not easy, but possible." He sighed. "And not until tonight."

"Well, gives me time to work on step 2 then." The smile disappeared from Finn's face.

"Step 2?" Sam asked.

Finn looked at him. "Convincing my father to help repair the blade."

"He doesn't want to?"

Finn tilted her head sideways, looking at the floor. "I haven't actually mentioned it to him yet. But he's not going to like it."

Mina stepped up beside Dev. "I'd suggest you get on that then. Do you need any help?"

Finn's lips moved, but no words came out.

"I can go with you," a deep voice said. Everyone turned to look at Ivan. "I've always wanted to see inside the forge." He focused on Finn and shrugged his shoulder. "Come on, this room is getting stuffy."

Finn didn't need anymore of an invitation and followed Ivan out the door.

"I should get home to feed Grey," Rhys said, but made no move to get up.

"I'll walk with you on my way to the Sanctuary. I have to patrol tonight, and I should get some sleep." Mina eyes slid sideways: it wasn't a total lie.

"Anything I can do?" Sam asked.

Mina raised an eyebrow at him. "You could help Dev figure out how to get us into that server room."

"Um, ok."

"Sam knows something about computers?" Rhys asked as she headed with him towards the escalator, punctuating his question with a cough into his sleeve.

"No." Mina slowed her pace to match his, which was slower than normal.

"Security systems then?" The phlegm rumbled in his throat.

"No." She glanced sideways at Rhys, eying him suspiciously before continuing. "I just figured he could use a man in his life."

Rhys' mouth opened as he looked at her, his eyebrows pulled into a question. That turned into a smile as he stepped onto the escalator. "This patrolling you have to do?"

Mina turned away, focusing on the approaching floor below. "Yes?"

"I'm pretty sure Bee would understand if you took a few nights off. Given the circumstances." His voice softened, became quieter, but Mina ignored the sympathy.

Instead, she fixed her gaze on the tall man coming through the entrance as her stomach rolled with nausea. His white, three-piece suit was pristine, despite the weather outside. His blond hair was slicked back from a sharp widow's peak in the front. He exuded an aura of control and...something else she couldn't put a pin in. "Mmm," she mumbled. "We're so short-handed, I'm sure she'll welcome any help she can get. Even mine." Her eyebrows pulled together and her head tilted as they neared the bottom.

Stepping off the escalator, she stopped.

Rhys managed to stop before bumping into her. "You know she's hard on you because she sees your potential?"

"I know no such thing." Mina's words were rote, vacant of meaning, as she tracked the gaggle of men in black coats surrounding the man in white she'd seen from above. The black mass parted for a second, and she heard a gasp beside her. Turning to Rhys, she saw him staring at the same man. Then the circle closed and the man in white was gone.

Rhys pushed her forward, propelling her to the door. "We need to get out of here now."

"I know," she said. He looked at her quizzically but now was not the time to explain.

"**N**ow that we're speaking again, why did you want to leave the museum so quickly?" Rhys poured himself a cup of tea from the steaming pot.

Mina stood in the corner, hands in her pockets, having a staring contest with Grey, who'd claimed the other seat. She glanced at him, which Grey took to mean she conceded defeat as he set to cleaning himself.

"Why did you?" she asked. She hadn't taken her coat off; she didn't intend to stay, though she also wasn't planning to head out on patrol, regardless of what she told Rhys. She had a promise to keep.

"Fair enough. I'd met Mr. Windrow, the owner of the collection, before. It was not a friendly parting."

"That's cagey." She shifted to lean against the arch that led into the living room.

"I took something from him that he wanted. Your turn — what about him set you on edge?"

She scowled but didn't comment on how that didn't provide any new information. "That was him, in the atrium?" Her voice rose slightly at the end, though it wasn't really a question.

Nonetheless, Rhys nodded as he took a sip of tea.

"He's not human." She paused as Rhys coughed, apparently having swallowed some tea the wrong way. She took a step into the room, opened a random book, closed it, then glanced back at him as the coughing subsided.

He peered at her, as Grey jumped down from the chair and into his lap. "I don't suppose you know what he is then, if he's not human?"

It was Mina's turn to shake her head. She plopped down into the chair. "Nothing good, that's all I'm sure of. It's like there was this pus yellow miasma surrounding him. A sepsis of the soul."

She examined her right palm, feeling him stare at her. She knew she was strange, and seeing auras probably wasn't any more normal for a vampire than hearing a particular tune in a vampire's blood.

Rhys turned his attention to Grey, stroking the cat's head as it kneaded his stomach. "That sounds about right." He lifted his cup to his lips, and apparently discovered it was empty, since he put it right back down and stood up instead, dislodging Grey with a disgruntled yowl. He was quiet as he poured himself another cup.

"You know I need try to save her." She ran her left thumb along the lines of her right palm.

Rhys turned to consider her, and finally she looked up at him. Putting his mug down, he stepped over to her, and laid his hand on her shoulder. "I know, though I fear nothing good will come of it. Despite what I said, I believe your friend is lost." She watched as he inhaled deeply and heard a little rattle on the exhale. "Go home. Rest up before your go hunting. And feed before you pass out."

Mina nodded and stood up, her bones aching. "You should take your own advice. You sound as worn down as I feel."

"I will. I just have a bit more research to do." With that, Rhys turned to his computer and the pile of books beside it. Mina frowned at him, then turned away and headed out into a bright afternoon where the sun stabbed into the space between eye and nose.

CHAPTER THIRTY

A roar of fire and brimstone rose behind Ivan. He froze, grasping one of the tools he'd been randomly picking up and putting down as he waited for Finn to reappear from wherever she'd disappeared to. Poker in hand, he turned to meet the beast attacking him.

Metal rang on metal, echoing through the cavernous forge, as he ducked and prepared for the follow-through attack. A breeze whispered over the hairs on his neck as a hammer narrowly missed cracking his skull. He drove his shoulder into the torso coming towards him, at the same time swinging the poker around to take out the beast's feet. His attacker fell sideways onto the floor but had enough wherewithal to bring the pincers he held in one hand down hard onto Ivan's shoulder, with all the downward force of a falling bear. There was a dizzying crunch as he landed hard on one knee.

"Da! Enough!" Finn's voice filled the forge.

Ivan scooted back. "Da?" He took his first good look at the creature that had attacked him: a man in a leather apron, arms the size of an elephant's leg, a torso broader than Ivan's own, topped with a square head sporting red hair and a beard neatly trimmed into mutton chops. Ivan stood up, rubbing his knee, and placed the poker back on the table. He held a hand out to help up Keagan, the Smith. Keagan didn't take it.

Ivan wiped his hand on his pants instead. "Sorry, I just reacted to being charged. I didn't realize who you were."

Keagan eyed him as he rose, changing his focus to his daughter as she came to stand beside Ivan. "What's he doing here?"

"I invited him."

"You're just letting anyone in nowadays, aren't you?"

Ivan bristled and made to step between Finn and Keagan. "I weaseled my way in. I wanted to see this place with my own eyes."

Finn laid a hand on his arm. "There's no need to protect me." She let go, pushing her way past him, towards her father. "Neither of you." Ivan looked down at the spot where her hand had been but said nothing.

"Where have you been?" Keagan laid the hammer down on the nearby anvil, propping the pincers up beside it.

"Out there." She nodded her head up.

"You'll get yourself killed." Keagan busied himself at the table, shifting instruments, much as Ivan himself had done.

"You can't escape what's coming by hiding down here." Ivan leaned against the workbench, arms across his chest.

Keagan didn't look at him when he spoke. "I wasn't talking to you, Necrophagus." He glanced sideways at his daughter as she grabbed his arm. "You do know what he is, don't you?"

Finn glanced at him, the brown in her green eyes sparking with light to match the fire in her hair. "All I know is he's helping us."

Keagan's face went red. "Us who? You and the vampires who use you? They're our patrons, not our friends."

"That's not what you taught me. Not what Mom taught me." Finn paced back and forth, hands on her hips as she continued. "And I quote, 'We have a sacred duty to the Good, bound in iron, seared in flesh, passed down from our ancestors' ancestors, into time immemorial'. Or were those just words?"

"I repeat, you'll die out there."

"Just because Mom did doesn't mean I will."

Ivan jumped as Keagan's palm crashed down on the table.

Finn sighed and looked from her father to him. "See, what did I say — the hardest part."

"What are you talking about, child?" Keagan's face now rested in his palm.

"Convincing you to help us. To show me how to repair the Blade of the Sun."

Keagan looked at her, the colour draining from his face. "That's a myth."

"And you're a legend. Heir to Hephaestus, ancestor of Vulcan. I'll try to do it with or without you, but I know there's some metal magic you've held back."

"Dark magic." Keagan's big shoulders slumped.

"These are dark times." Ivan stepped away from the wall.

Keagan slid down to sit on the stairs behind him, dropping his head into his hands, and Ivan saw a man who'd been broken in ways he recognized. "I can't help you." Keagan lifted his head. Finn's hands came back to her hips as she inhaled, getting ready to harangue her father again.

Ivan placed a hand on her shoulder, and she turned to scowl at him. "Maybe if we get him the blade, he'll change his mind," he said, recognizing the resolve in Keagan's eyes and the set of his jaw. Finn looked at him for a second, then turned and snatched up her bag before walking in silence past her father to head up the stairs, taking them at a jog. Ivan followed, stopping beside Keagan. "I may have been a Necrophagus. But Night has returned, and that changes everything." Ivan looked at Keagan, before turning to track Finn's path up to the door. "I intend to be on the right side this time, even if I have to die to get there."

L urking at the periphery of the museum cafe, Ivan stood watch over Finn as she sat, exposed, at a table, waiting for the collector. A twitter of some unnamed emotion flittered through his stomach. He couldn't quite place it. Perhaps this was fear.

She had a notepad out in front of her, posing as a reporter who wanted to do a social interest piece about the man's philanthropy and one-of-a-kind collection. He doubted her cover or her chosen pseudonym — Ms. Margie Mason — would fool the man, but she'd stubbornly insisted on this plan.

Ivan looked at the time on his phone: the man was late. The museum would close soon. He huffed and looked back at Finn. He knew this lure wasn't going to work. They should have just charged in on the man and beaten him until he talked or was unable to.

"Stop fidgeting," Sam said at the next table over, from behind his newspaper, not looking up. He crossed one leg covered in grey tweed over the other and turned the page. "You look like you're watching her."

"That's what we're *supposed* to be doing." Ivan shifted so he wasn't directly facing her.

"Yes, but we're not supposed to look like it." Sam rustled his newspaper again.

"He's not coming," Ivan mumbled.

"Not if he thinks it's a trap." Sam turned another page, an eyebrow raising at whatever he read there. "Stop staring at me."

Ivan stepped away from the wall, going over to the next table to sit down. He looked at his arms folded over his chest, away from Sam, then glanced at Finn and almost stood back up.

"Stay down!" Sam hissed. His paper was folded on the table in front of him, the pen in his hand not actually touching the crossword. His head looked like he was concentrating on the puzzle, but Ivan knew what he was really focused on.

The collector. He'd finally arrived, coming to a stop beside Finn's table. Smiling, he told her to stay seated when she made to get up. She held out her hand for him to shake, making Ivan nauseous. The collector sat down across from Finn, clasping his hands on the tabletop, his rings glinting in the light. Being a vampire, Ivan could hear almost every word.

"Thank you for taking time to talk to me, Mr. Windrow."

"My dear Ms. Mason, let's skip the pleasantries, shall we? I'm a busy man." Despite his words, the man's smile stayed in place. Ivan's jaw clenched, and his mind filled with visions of ways to teach him some manners.

Finn stammered and looked down at the notebook, no doubt searching for the next point in her script. "I...of course." Ivan sensed her heart trip, before she recovered. "It is just such a pleasure to meet you." She brought out her cell phone. "I hope you don't mind if I record this. I want to make sure I get all the details." She flashed him a smile, and he gave a patronizing nod.

Finn started by asking him questions about himself, his business, why he'd chosen to collect such rare things when he was so busy.

"Because I can. My wealth comes with responsibility to care for these artifacts and keep them from those who can't understand them." He fiddled with the white fedora he'd placed on the table. "And I'm in a position where I can take what I want."

Finn didn't appear fazed by that response, even though it left the taste of bile in Ivan's throat, and she moved on to her questions about other items in the collection. *Why was he drawn to this? Where did he find that? The Blade of the Sun was so stunning — what was it made of?*

The man tensed. Finn didn't seem to sense it, but Ivan did. The narrowing of the blood vessels, the shift in his heartbeat. Finn carried on with her questions, asking about some sculpture or other. The collector gave brusque answers, his eyes not leaving Finn as she looked down at her paper. *How did he choose which items to acquire? Did he really seek out all the items himself, surely he sent others to do it for him? Where in the world did he find something like the Blade of the Sun?*

At that, the man stilled, his fake smile disappearing as he stared at Finn.

"You might want to practice your spiel a bit more, Ms ...Smith, did you say?"

Ivan's intestines went liquid: Finn hadn't given her name as Smith. Finn went a paler shade of white, her cheeks flaring red under the freckles. Beside him, Sam seemed to sense the shift.

"What's wrong?" he asked, having abandoned any pretense of doing the puzzle. Ivan waved a hand to hush him.

The collector continued. "Nowhere in the exhibit text is the object you're so interested in referred to as the Blade of the Sun." The man stood up, looked directly at Ivan despite the people in between. A jolt punched Ivan in his chest: this thing was not a man, though he had no idea what it was. Its eyes flashed, the blue too bright, then he turned back to Finn. "This interview is over."

Finn stood up, her cheeks red, her jaw set. "I'm just interested in unique artifacts like yourself, Mr. Windrow." She swiped her phone with her thumb then slipped it into her pocket. "I do hope we can talk again."

"If we meet again, Ms. Finnegan, I doubt there will be much talking." The man placed his hat on his head. He brought his fingers to the brim and tipped it towards her. "Good day."

Finn watched him walk out, before striding over to Ivan and Sam, fire in her eyes. "I think we need some backup. I'm getting that bastard's blade."

CHAPTER THIRTY-ONE

The Collector's young assistant punched in the numbers that unlocked the door, then turned to gawp at her. Night noted that the Collector stood to the side, handkerchief to his face, his white coat flecked with red. *A ludicrous colour to wear to a robbery.* She herself was dressed head to toe in red leather. She sighed and ran her fingertips lightly down her torso, over the slick spots where blood had spattered. Bringing a finger to her lips, she licked it clean. The assistant's eyes went so wide, she thought they'd fall out. She gave him a predatory smile, and he swallowed.

Lin's boot heels clacked along the empty hallway as she jogged towards them. Night turned her head to the vampire, who gave her a crisp nod, as blood from the pair of daggers in her hands dripped onto the tile floors. Lin looked like a wraith, an angel of death decked in black from neck to heel.

"Open it." Night jerked her chin towards the now unlocked door. She still didn't trust this collector of things he shouldn't have. He wasn't entirely human, but she couldn't suss out his true nature. Glancing sideways at him, magic tingled over her fingers. She probed his truthfulness, but all she got was an orange haze and shadows. Following him as he opened the door, she entered the room.

Her breath caught in her throat. The blade glowed like a beacon in the dark, lit by some hidden light in its cage of glass. A stab of pain shot through her chest into her shoulder blades. She brought a hand to her heart, trying to catch her breath, then took another step into the room. A clacking sounded overhead, and she froze for a second. Composing herself, she turned towards the Collector, poised to strike him from the earth for his treachery, but then lights started to come on. Starting at the perimeter and moving to the centre, they illuminated the room in tempo with the clacking. She eyed them suspiciously for a second, before moving towards the blade again. She stopped inches from its cage, her hands coming up of their own accord, wanting to touch.

"Don't."

She twisted her head around to peer at the man, her lips pressed into a severe line.

He swallowed hard enough for her to hear, his pulse pounding in his neck. "If you disturb the glass, the alarm will sound."

"So?" She looked back at the blade, her fingertips hovering over the glass. "All the guards are dead."

"This alarm will alert the police."

She turned to him again, stepping up to him and staring into his cold eyes. "You said you'd lead me to the blade so I could take back what's mine."

He wiped sweat from his forehead with the well-used handkerchief. "And I meant it." He put the handkerchief back in his pocket, taking out a phone instead. "I just need to call my security. Tell them to disable the alarm."

"So do it." She arched an eyebrow before turning back to the blade.

The man cleared his throat. She ignored him. He tried again. "Before I do, perhaps...."

Night spun to face him. "Perhaps what?" Lin stepped up beside her, slender stiletto dagger in hand, and peered at the man as she ran a finger up and down the length of the blade. "Perhaps Lin can show you how she can fillet a man while he's still alive?"

The man's eyes flicked over to Lin before returned to Night.

"Or perhaps I can show you how I can disembowel a man with my bare hands?" She smiled at the sultriness of the words as she spoke, almost like she was talking to a lover.

"No, perhaps...perhaps I should just call." He turned his attention to the phone.

The smile fell from Night's face. "Perhaps you should."

214

He started talking to whoever was on the other end, but Night paid no attention to the words, instead focusing on her objective: the blade and how to use it to get all her power back.

"It's done." The man slid the phone into his pocket then looked her in the eye, seemingly unbowed. Sweat trickled down his neck, thick with the scent of fear, but he made no move to wipe it away.

Night pulled out the small steel punch meant to break glass. She paused, laying her free hand on the glass. "You know what will happen if you've betrayed me?"

He nodded. "You'll kill me." His voice surprisingly even, given the threat of death.

"No, I'll kill you *slowly*." Night swung the punch at the glass, stopping in the moment of contact. Fragments flew, and her cheek stung as one sliced the skin. She smiled. A small, shy smile like a woman at a new lover. Tipping her head to the side, she heard no alarm, but then she might not in this new-fangled world.

"I don't care," she said to no one in particular. Now that she had the blade, let them try to take it from her. She glanced up at Lin who stared at her, eyes shining, then at the Collector who stared at the blade with a similar rapt expression. Night reached amongst the shards of glass to claim her prize, stopping just shy of touching it as her fingertips tingled. The thought that this half circle might not really be a piece of the Blade of the Sun, that it might be an elaborate trap, perpetrated by countless generations, flickered through her brain. She peered at the golden crescent, but it was inscrutable, offering no answers. "I don't care," she said to it.

Her hand clasped onto it. "Ow!"

Lin gasped, and the Collector went a shade of lizard belly white-green.

A line of red welled up on Night's palm; the frailty of this form always caught her off guard. But she looked up at Lin and smiled a crooked smile. "It's just whetting its appetite." She reached out again, more carefully this time, and grasped the half circle, avoiding the honed edge, still so sharp after millennia of neglect. She turned it one way, her head going the opposite direction. "Now it needs a blood sacrifice to really get it going." Not looking, she sent her arm out to her right, slicing through the neck of the Collector's assistant, her body flowing around on the follow through until she was facing him again.

"Gargh, gak." He grasped his neck with his hands, but blood spurted out between his fingers and onto the Collector, further staining the man's white suit. The Collector's pale face turned fish-belly white as he stared at the dying young man.

He turned to her, the question in his eyes before he spoke. "Now why did you have to go and do that? Good help is so hard to find."

She stepped up to the Collector, dripping half-blade in hand. "You needed to learn a lesson: don't try to negotiate with the devil."

She wiped the blade on his white suit then strode out of the room, leaving the death and destruction behind her. She wanted to wallow in triumph, but she knew she still had the other half of the blade to find.

CHAPTER THIRTY-TWO

"What are we doing out here?" Mina alternated her scowl between Ivan and Sam as slush fell from the sky and pooled at her feet. It dripped from her hair, down her neck, over her nose. At some point it would turn to big fluffy flakes, creating a winter wonderland tomorrow. But not tonight.

Tonight, she was soaked to the bone, lurking in the cold and dark as she stood amongst the trees bordering the park beside the museum. But at least she wasn't alone in her misery. Half the remaining members of the conclave fanned out beside her, while the others approached from the opposite side of the square. At this hour, the only people in the park were up to no good or had nowhere else to go. Tonight, it was empty, except for them.

After following Hana to make sure she got home safely, even if she had no interest in Mina's protection, she'd joined the reconnaissance at the museum. Afterward, she'd gone back to the Sanctuary, planning to feed. Instead, she'd lain down — just to rest her eyes — and only woke when Bee came knocking, telling her to get ready to rumble. Though those weren't the words Bee had used.

Waves of dizziness plagued her, and hunger gnawed at her insides. She needed to feed: the beast inside was ravenous. But not yet. She had something more important to do...Sam had called, asking for help: he never asked for help, having survived on his own since his parents kicked him out at sixteen. So she stood in the icy precipitation, waiting for him or Ivan to tell her why. While she waited, her mind wandered.

Maybe it is me. Scenes of all the bad things that had happened since Luca made her a vampire flashed through her brain: Cam disappearing, Jack getting taken, the deaths of Dar, Brett and Dale. All connected to her. *Maybe I'm cursed, or I am a curse.* Despite Rhys' whispering, Mina knew what he'd said about Luca: the man played with arcane magic before turning her, and he'd had a purpose for her besides thumbing his nose at his father's rules. She glanced at the vampire on her right. Bee shifted and peered back at her. *My maker meddled with dark forces. Perhaps I'm one of them.* She looked away, breaking contact, shifting to watch the others approach. Her eyebrows pulled together.

"Why are we all here?" She glanced back at Bee.

"Sam asked for help. He's a familiar. Family." Bee quirked an eyebrow. "He says Finn has some information."

"Don't you have more important things to be doing?"

"Like?"

"You've been saying we need to get Jack back."

"The cat might be right. Jack's lost."

Mina's head snapped around to glare at Bee. "You believe that?"

Bee shrugged. "You don't?"

Mina opened her mouth to speak but had no answer. Instead she turned to Sam and asked him. "Why are we here?"

Sam stuffed his hands in his coat pockets. "I...."

"We should let Finn tell you." Ivan jerked his chin towards the group approaching them. Finn, her red hair flaming out around her, strode in front of the others.

Finn glanced between her and Bee before looking to Ivan. "This collector knows we know the Blade of the Sun isn't your average ancient artifact."

"Seriously?" Bee scoffed. "That's why you called the conclave together?" She shifted, putting weapons away and zipping up her jacket. "To hunt after a weapon to fight a creature that's shown no signs of causing trouble."

The falling slush muted any sounds from the trees around them, and the space between Mina's shoulder blades itched, like something watched her. Her ear twitched at a snap to her left. She tuned out Bee and Finn as they continued to bicker, her attention focused instead on the museum.

She tipped her head sideways as figures emerged from the side door. Figures heading their way. "Um," she said. She wanted to believe they were museum employees, working late, but the symphony in her veins told her vampires approached.

Sam stepped up beside her. "Incoming." The bickering behind them quieted.

"What?" Bee came to stand on her other side. "Oh." The others pulled further back into the shadows of the trees.

Mina froze, unmoving, until a hand dragged her back. As the Necrophagus neared, the jangle of wind chimes underpinned by a deep cello thrummed through her blood: Cam's blood song. She wanted to be happy Cam was there, but her heart sank into her stomach. *Night's song.*

Cam spoke, the words unintelligible except for their harshness, as she peered at someone over her shoulder. *Lin. And Jack.* Her hands moved, animating what she was saying — just like the Cam Mina knew. Her heart rose again at that; maybe Cam was still in there somewhere.

But the words became clearer as the group came closer: plague, wroth, and vengeance. Those weren't Cam's words. But it was Cam's hand that moved to punctuate the violence being spouted, hints of green and gold flashing in the air.

Lin strode beside her, and spoke, her words carrying across the diminishing distance. "You're wise, as always." Her words were toadying but her voice tense.

Cam spun around and slashed Jack with her fingernails, glaring at Lin as she did. His hand went to his face, where blood quickly welled up in lines across his cheek. Cam's other hand came up, ready to strike again. It glinted as light hit metal. Mina's ear twitched at an intake of breath from someone beside her.

"She has the blade." Ivan's whisper was barely audible, but Cam stilled, hands coming to her sides, though she didn't turn around.

"My wisdom isn't important." It was Cam's voice, but not her tone, laced with venom as it was. "Only my desire. And right now, I desire that the vampires hiding in the trees like cockroaches show themselves." Slowly, the eyes moving last, her face turned from Jack to them. A small gasp escaped Mina's lips when she saw the eyes were fully black, like two puddles of ink. "Come. Stand by my side to greet them."

Jack's expression was flat as he obeyed the order. *Maybe Seema is right.* Mina's chest tightened. She stepped from the trees, ignoring Adeh's hand on her arm.

"Cam, stop this." The two ink wells peered at her from Cam's face, no white visible. "I know you're in there. You can fight her." Movement on the right side of the square caught her eye. Bee emerged out of the shadows and sidled towards Jack.

The creature in front of her barely shifted to acknowledge the vampires appearing out of the woods behind her. Instead she focused all her attention on Mina, her head tipping to the side.

"Cam?" The voice reflected uncertainty, the brows above the black eyes pulling together. "Cam. And Mina." The black eyes became richer, shifting towards brown. Then Bee attacked from the side.

Night spun to meet her, but there was no need. A pair of vampires blocked Bee's advance. Jack drew a sword but didn't move to help Bee.

Then Mina's attention was drawn to her right. A werewolf slunk out of the trees, and she spun to protect herself, drawing her gun, aimed and firing all in one fluid movement. The wolf yelped and leapt sideways, bleeding from its right flank. A clash of swords caused her to glance left, where Bee and Adeh stood like a shield in front of Finn. All three were hemmed in by a pair of Necrophagus on one side and a werewolf on the other. Nearby Ivan had found a pair of daggers and was using them to great effect against another creature, all pointy bits but neither wolf nor vampire. Mina's mouth dropped open, shocked at the agility and speed the muscular vampire possessed. A snarl sounded behind her and she turned, expecting another wolf. Instead, it was a woman, who stood in a half crouch, as if preparing to lunge. Her eyes were cloudy, and her lips twisted into a rabid grimace. Mina took a step back before recovering herself and preparing to shoot.

220

"Enough!" Night snarled, no longer sounding like Cam at all. Her hand clenched around the blade's sharp edges. Blood dripped from between Cam's fingers. Then Cam's body dropped, one knee coming to the ground, driving the golden blade into the frozen dirt. She dropped both palms onto the earth beside it, her fingers lost in the blanket of pine needles. Mina was so shocked she jumped back a space.

"Mina. And Dale." The eyes, back to black, shone as they peered at her. Night flipped her hands over, turning her palms to face the sky. Then she rose, moving inch by inch, straining, as if gravity was somehow stronger around her.

Below Mina's feet, the ground shifted, and the frozen mud liquefied. She fought to maintain her balance as the earth in front of her swirled and heaved. She took a few steps back, seeking solid footing.

Night crouched again, like a cat ready to pounce, but all she did was retrieve the blade before taking large steps backward, towards the cover of the trees. Mina made to go after her, but between her and Night, the mud became a pillar. And the pillar morphed into a man. A tendril of fear mixed with revulsion travelled Mina's blood. When the features were fully formed, her heart turned over in her chest. Although still the colour of dirt and decomposing leaves, the face was one she recognized.

"Dale." Mina heard her short sword drop into the slushy mud, though she hadn't felt it leave her fingers. She braced herself for attack, but the figure didn't lunge at her. Instead, it advanced towards Sam. "Cam, stop it."

Night stopped, turning to look at her amidst the whirl of battle around them. "Oh, I don't think so. If you want to stop it, you have to kill it." She pivoted away and strode towards the park.

Jack paused, his gaze flicking between Mina and the mud man, his eyes unreadable. His lips opened and closed, as if he wanted to speak but couldn't.

"Come, dog." Night didn't even turn around, and no crackling power or tendrils of magic emanated from her. Still, Jack's face hardened, and he spun on his heels and did as he was told.

And Mina was forced to face her dead brother.

The thing in front of Mina made a sucking, moaning noise as a blade formed at the end of its right arm. It lumbered forward and swung. Numbed by shock, she barely stepped back in time to avoid a blade embedded in her torso. Still, it sliced through her pant leg, despite being made of mud, and her thigh stung as a line of flesh opened up. She staggered back.

She gaped at the simulation of her brother's face, but a snarl behind her drew her attention around. The large wolf she'd shot dragged himself forward. Half human, half animal, his hindquarters bled profusely from the wound she'd given him. A pang stabbed at that spot where rib cage gave way to abdomen, reminding her she wielded real weapons and could deal death. The pang passed as his jaws snapped towards her arm. She jumped sideways, out of reach of the werewolf, but not of the creature of mud.

She ducked when the blade came towards her again, with more speed this time as the creature found its feet. Seeing that it was going to cut straight down, she tucked and rolled. The blade slammed into the ground where she'd been a second ago, the rocky soil trembling with the impact. Mina grasped at the muddy ground, trying to grab the sword she'd dropped earlier. As she rolled to standing, her fingers found the hilt. Weapon in hand, she turned to stare at the murky copy of Dale's face. But without the smile at the corner of the lips or the laugh lines around the eyes.

The simulated blade cut an arc through the air, low this time, an extension of the creature's arm, with all the force of its weight behind the swing. Jumping over the weapon, Mina spun and prepared to be attacked again. Instead, the creature once again stepped towards Sam, bringing its weapon up, readying to hew him from shoulder to hip. Sam didn't move, eyes wide in shock.

Mina lunged at the Dale-shaped form and drove her sword into its belly from behind. Drawing her blade out as she retreated, a tide of viscous black liquid followed. It looked like tar but smelled of rot and decay and feces.

As the liquid left the creature, it started to melt. Mina jumped back, out of reach of the vile fluid. The flood was so quick that within seconds the creature had all but disappeared, though Mina caught a last look of Dale's features melting back into the earth, the mouth open in a wordless scream.

She wanted to scream herself, to let her pain out in a howl of rage. A snarl and a whimper behind her caught her attention. The werewolf was back to mostly wolf, and trying to drag itself into the woods, likely to die alone. Mina strode up to it. Her nostrils flaring, she glared down at its heaving chest. Then drove her tarry blade into its torso, pulled it out and stabbed again, until the heart popped under the tip of her sword.

Ice cold to the bone, she watched the red and black rivulets drip from her blade in the slushy rain. Then she turned back to the others. Night and the Necrophagus had fled.

Sam stared at her, the look of shock replaced by a mixture of disappointment, sadness and anger. She looked down at her sword again, as heat washed over her cheeks.

"What the hell was that?" Sam's voice was quiet, almost inaudible above the splat of sleet on the slushy ground. Mina made no reply. Instead she cleaned her sword. Again and again. She swore the blade was tarnished after being coated in the black ooze from the mud man and the blood of the werewolf. It gleamed when she held it up to the streetlamp, but she still wasn't satisfied.

Seema stalked past Sam, over to the spot on the ground where the werewolf had been, bones now. Her fingers tapped a discordant rhythm on her thigh. She strode back to Mina. Mina concentrated on her sword for a few seconds longer before finally raising her eyes to look at Seema, ignoring Sam. The cold had raised red blotches on the woman's cheeks and the end of her nose. Mina's eyes teared in the wind that had risen while they fought, driving pinpoints of sleet into her skin.

"I have no idea." Mina stared at the patch of dirt that had been the Dale-shaped creature. "Some soulless thing called up from the earth." She looked back at Seema. "Maybe Rhys can tell us."

Seema's eyes narrowed, her brow furrowed. "What are you talking about?"

"The mud man. What are you talking about?"

"You know what I'm talking about. The werewolf." Seema gestured to where the bones were returning to the earth. "You killed it."

"It was a battle."

"No, you walked up to it, looked down on it then just killed it." Seema frowned. "I know the look you had on your face."

"You hate the wolves." Mina focused on sliding the sword into its sheath and pulling out her gun, trying to hide her flushed cheeks. "To quote: 'I want to wipe them from the earth'." Seema's only response to having her words thrown back at her was to deepen her frown and glance sideways, so Mina went on. "Well, maybe so do I. To avenge my friend's abduction. To exact payment for Jack betraying me...us." Mina swallowed back tears. "And I want to make Night pay the price for killing my brother. And what other price can there be but death?"

"An eye for an eye?" Sam's voice was low and his tone flat. She didn't need to look at him to know the expression of disappointment was still there.

"A life for a life." Mina pulled out a fresh magazine and slid it into the gun. She glanced up in time to see him shake his head and turn away, going to join Finn and Ivan.

"And what happens when someone comes to collect on your life?" Seema stalked off without waiting for an answer.

"I pay my debt," Mina whispered, holstering her gun.

"Where's she off to?" Bee asked, stepping up beside her and gesturing towards Seema's retreating back.

Mina stared at the werewolf bones dissolving as if they'd been doused in acid. "I don't know."

"She seems in a snit."

Mina nodded. "Yup."

"Any idea why?"

Mina shook her head. "Nope. Cats?" Bee shifted, and there was silence for a long minute. Mina finally lifted her head to find Bee staring at her.

"We need help," Bee said. "We've lost too many people."

Mina nodded but didn't say anything, not sure where Bee was going with this.

"Jack's a lost cause," Bee continued.

A part of Mina still rebelled at that thought, but she squashed it; he could have saved her brother or helped free Cam. But he didn't. "What are you getting at?" Mina asked.

"Will your sister-in-law help?"

"If by *help* you mean lodge a silver bullet in my heart and rid you of my troublesome nature, then yes, I think she'll help." Mina shook her head, dislodging icy drops. "She wants my head on a stake." *And my help avenging Dale's death.* Mina flicked her gaze over Bee's shoulder.

"Can you at least ask?"

"No."

"Seriously? You're so afraid of her that you won't even ask?"

Mina glanced at the ground, where the monster Dale had risen then melted away. "I'm not afraid *of* her. I'm afraid *for* her."

She didn't mention the promise she'd made to Hana to help her kill Dale's killer. She looked at where the werewolf had died — to where she'd killed it — and her stomach heaved.

CHAPTER THIRTY-THREE

Mina trudged along the path towards the Sanctuary, the imposing building she now called home. Her gaze travelled from the dome, down the columns to the top of the stoop, where Seema waited in human form, a frown pulling her face down.

"Where are the others?" Seema asked, her fingers tapping against her thigh in a nervous tic Mina recognized from herself.

"Here, I imagine, given the time of day." She slid her eyes sideways to indicate the morning sun, in no mood for twenty questions. She'd been wandering around since last night, seeking solitude and solace and finding neither.

"Not the vampires. Rhys, Finn. The prying archaeologist."

"I don't know. Maybe they've gone after the Blade of the Sun. The other half, that Night doesn't have." Mina waved a hand; at the moment it wasn't important, since she struggled even to lift her feet up the stairs. Seema hissed, though Mina couldn't tell what had upset her the most. The Were scanned the street as if looking for something, but she didn't move out of Mina's way.

"You look like shit," Seema said, looking back at her.

Mina shouldered past her into the Sanctuary. "Sorry. I haven't kept up with my normal beauty routine, what with my brother being murdered and all."

"You're not the only one who's lost someone." Seema followed her inside.

Mina spun around. "Really? And who have you lost? A mouse?"

Seema took a step back, her eyes going wide and her lip tightening into a thin line. "Who have I lost? You can ask me that?" She walked around the pillar, putting it between them, something Mina was glad of given the fire that flared in Seema's eyes, and the tension drawn in her every movement. A cat preparing to pounce.

Then it dawned on Mina. "Mike. Right, I forgot about him."

Seema's stance softened a fraction, and she looked at the pillar, running a finger along its grooves. "Most people did. He saved me when I didn't want saving." Seema turned back to her, the hardness returning to her face. "But that's not who I'm talking about. Rhys mentioned it, but you were too absorbed in yourself to realize what it meant. I am the last of the Bengali werecats. But I didn't spawn out of water and muck." Mina flinched, Dale's muddy face rising in her mind's eyes, but she stayed silent. "I had a family once. Cousins upon cousins. Friends. Now I am the last of my kind. The last of that family, those friends." She stepped out from behind the pillar and sidled closer to Mina. "But that was not the last of my enemies."

Mina's head spun as she took a step back, rebuffed by the fierceness in her quiet voice. "I'm sorry. I wasn't —"

Seema continued as if Mina hadn't spoken, her voice sounding far away. "They slaughtered my family from the grand old toms to the little kits. And I thought I was dead too." Seema stared at a space between them, before turning her eyes to Mina, though Mina couldn't be sure she actually saw her. "I wanted to be dead. I retreated into my feline form, got into any fights I could find. Until Mike found me, scratched and bleeding, on a stinking pier, ready to throw myself into the water if I hadn't been too weak." Seema came back to the present, her eyes clearly seeing Mina, though her voice still sounded trapped in memory. "By the time I was strong enough, I'd decided he needed me more than Death."

"If you'd told me..." Mina couldn't compose the rest of that sentence as Seema blurred in her vision.

"If you'd only opened your eyes." Seema stepped towards her as she swept her arm out. "What about Rhys losing Dar, the love of his life?" Seema dropped her arm and lowered her voice. "What about Bee losing him and Jack, and her friends all those years ago? Every vampire loses everyone they love."

"I..." Mina peered at Seema, trying to fix on the face that wavered in front of her, then she caught a glimpse of a star-filled sky before everything went black.

Dale peered at Mina with a question on his face, his eyebrows pulling together, his lips slightly open, his head tilting to the side. Then he looked down at his stomach, where his intestines spilled into his hands, tumbling through his fingers.

Mina tried to scream, but her voice was stolen as the figure beside Dale, a shadow with a cascade of brown curls, turned to face her. One hand held a golden half circle, dripping blood and bits of Dale's insides onto the ground. The face was a void, like empty space except for two bits of onyx where the eyes should be. A sound like rusting metal hinges rose from the shadow, and its visage morphed into a skull. Tendons were painted onto bone then muscles oozed into place. Finally flesh appeared, moist and red like an open sore, before turning to pale olive skin. Cam's face looked back at her, though the eyes were still two hard stones glinting in the harsh moonlight.

Mina's hands clenched in frustration, and pain shot up her right arm. Looking down, she saw the obsidian dagger clasped in her hand. Her fingers opened to expose her bloody palm. Then the blood was gone, sucked up into the blade. She gasped but found she couldn't breathe. As she fell to her knees, Cam reached towards her. Towards the blade.

"I'll take that," her former roommate said, her voice fading as the roar of souls trapped in the blade filled Mina's ears. Something pressed down on her, an oppressive weight pushing her away from Cam and Dale, as if she were under the earth, in her own grave. Unable to breathe, Mina choked on the lump in her throat.

"It's okay," a disembodied voice told her.

Mina wanted to say it was *not* okay. Nothing was okay.

"You're safe."

She pushed against the weight holding her down, and kicked at the darkness, flailing arms and legs. She lashed out at the creature that had taken her friend and her brother.

The weight left her, and she sat upright, a snarl on her lips. Her eyes flew open, squinting as they were flooded with light. She was in her bed. In the Sanctuary. There was no Dale, no Night, no Cam.

Only Nicole.

"You were dreaming." Nicole sat on the edge of her bed, eying her. "Well, having a nightmare."

Mina breathed deeply, slowly, in, out, trying to calm her trip-hopping heart. She blinked, getting her bearings.

"Are you okay?" Nicole shifted closer, running a finger down Mina's nose. "Did you want to talk about anything?"

Mina shook her head, more to rid herself of the vestiges of the dream than in response to Nicole's question. "I'm okay. Thanks though. I...just...." Mina stopped as her throat tightened.

"Yeah, I know. I'm sorry, you know, about —"

"Thanks." Mina didn't really want condolences at the moment, as close to tears as she was. But then she remembered Nicole had familiarity with loss. She reached a hand to Nicole's cheek, trying to wipe away the worry that still clouded the familiar's face. She shivered, and wrapped her arms around herself, rubbing her biceps. Her eyebrows pulled together — she was in her tank top and underwear under the blanket, nothing else. "What happened? Last I remember is talking to Seema about...." Mina looked down at her hands.

"What?" Nicole tipped her head to the side, sending her black hair over her shoulder, exposing the familiar tattoo on her neck.

"Nothing."

Nicole laid her own hand on Mina's. "You're trembling."

"I'm cold." Mina looked up into Nicole's eyes.

"You're lying." She nonetheless pulled the blanket around Mina's shoulders, leaning forward so her exposed neck was inches from Mina's lips. Mina smelled the blood flowing beneath the skin, under the scent of talc and antiseptic. Nicole sat down again, closer this time. "You passed out. You're starving."

Mina didn't say anything, just swallowed as her stomach rumbled.

"You know you need to feed." Nicole leaned closer, her lips by Mina's cheek. "Otherwise you're a danger to yourself and everyone around you."

Of its own volition, Mina's hand wound around the back of Nicole's neck. The throb of the familiar's blood caused Mina's head to spin. She made to pull her arm back, but Nicole grasped her wrist.

Nicole sighed and tipped her head forward, so her lips brushed Mina's ear. "If you bite me, I promise it'll be good for you too."

Mina's fangs sunk into the skin of Nicole's neck, and she shuddered as the metallic tang of blood filled her mouth before flowing over her tongue and down her throat. The beast inside sighed with satisfaction.

Mina crouched in front of her wardrobe, clad in underwear and a tank top, her jacket in one hand and the obsidian blade wrapped in a scarf in the other. At a shuffle of fabric behind her, she shoved the blade into the drawer at the bottom, half hidden by her tangle of footwear, then turned around and crawled back onto the bed, where Nicole lay, eyes unfocused.

"There really is no feeling like it. It's a high unlike any other."

"Is that why you do it?" Mina watched the last blood seep from the pinpricks on Nicole's neck. She shifted forward to lick the wound before settling onto her elbows, back arched.

Nicole shook her head slowly. "No. It's my Gran."

"Your Gran? I thought she was dead." Mina paused at her own abruptness. "Sorry."

"It's okay." Nicole sat up and crossed her legs into half lotus. "My Gran was a phenomenal woman. Smart as a tack, adventurous. She was my hero. And then it all changed, as a monster ate away at her brain. She was unrecognizable when she died."

"I'm sorry," Mina said, though she wondered what this had to do with Nicole being a familiar.

"Runs in families." Nicole played with a piece of fluff on Mina's blanket. "Well, my family. My Grandma took care of me, from when I was little." The fluff seemed to be the most interesting thing in Nicole's world. "After my parents were murdered."

"Right." Mina shook her head, a movement that was part sympathy and part castigation that she knew so little about the members of her new family.

"I assumed she was crazy when she started talking about vampires. But apparently my ancestors have been bitten before. She would have lost herself sooner if she hadn't been a familiar." Nicole looked up at her with shining eyes. "The thing that makes you a vampire...well, it has some unusual benefits for the people you feed off of. One of them being protection from certain diseases, if you're bitten regularly." Nicole formed her lips into a crooked smile, then uncrossed her legs and started to clamber out of bed.

Mina grabbed her wrist. "Thank you. For sharing that with me."

Nicole shrugged but didn't say anything. Mina loosened her grip on her wrist, noting the time on Nicole's watch as she did.

"Shit!" She threw off the covers.

"What?"

Mina paused, lips parted, staring at Nicole. "My brother's funeral."

Nicole shifted her hand to take hold of Mina's fingers. "Did you want some company?" She stood and spread her arms wide, displaying her black outfit. "I'm always dressed for a funeral."

CHAPTER THIRTY-FOUR

Mina was fine, swallowing back all her tears. Until the final song, which played while pictures flickered by on the screen at the front of the church. Of Dale as a child with her parents, running towards the camera; of him with her as a baby in his lap, a bright smile lighting his face; of him with a newborn Maggie in his arms; of him beside Maggie, with Liam in her arms, the same beaming smile on her face. Mina choked a sob back, and Nicole's hand moved from hers to around her shoulder.

Mina glanced over at the remaining members of her family. Maggie and Liam both gave small, sobbing cries. She wondered if they really understood what this meant. She'd been a few years older than Maggie when her own father had died. Aunt June wiped tears away, and the salt-and-pepper man put his arm around her shoulder. *Ren, his name is Ren.* There was no point in committing it to memory though — she still planned to die. Causing more pain with her 'death' tore at her gut, but they would be safer if they had no contact with her. Her eyes moved to Hana, who stared at the front, though Mina wasn't sure she actually saw anything. Her face was flat, stony, without a tear.

As people left the church, and Mina breathed deeply, forcing her shoulders down. Aunt June served as the family representative, shaking hands, receiving the murmur of kind words from the last of the attendees, with Ren and the priest beside her. Nicole was telling Maggie and Liam a story, leaving Hana free to kneel beside the casket. Her hands rested on the polished wood, her forehead on top of her hands.

Mina stepped towards the front of the church when fingers touched her shoulder. Her head spun around to glare at the offender. Mr. Whitaker took a step back, and Mina rearranged her face into a less feral expression.

"Mr. Whitaker. Good of you to come."

"I'm terribly—"

Mina lifted a hand. "I've had my fill of condolences today, if it's all the same to you."

Mr. Whitaker tipped his head in a nod of acknowledgment, then his eyebrows pulled together as he looked at her chest. She was about to snap at him when he spoke. "You're not wearing your mother's necklace."

Mina blinked in surprise, her hand coming to her throat. "No, not really my style."

Mr. Whitaker's eyes opened wide again as his gaze returned to her face. "It's a precious heirloom."

"It's somewhere safe." The necklace was nestled beside the obsidian blade, but she decided that was a detail he didn't need to know, given her suspicions that he wasn't quite human. "If you'll excuse me." She waved her hand in Hana's general direction.

"Of course," he said, though he didn't move for a second, his gaze returning to her throat. Then with a crisp nod, he walked towards the back of the church, where Aunt June stood.

Mina turned towards Hana, hearing her whispers but not the words she said. As she stepped closer, she felt wrong at intruding on her sister-in-law's grief.

Hana stilled, went quiet, and lifted her head, though she didn't look at Mina. "What do you want?"

"I..." Mina paused at the question: what did she want? She wasn't sure anymore. She'd made a pact with Hana to wipe Night and her accomplices off the face of the earth. But in that moment, Mina realized she didn't care about vengeance anymore. "I want you and Maggie and Liam to be safe." She started to kneel but stopped when Hana stood up. Mina glanced over Hana's shoulder at Nicole and the kids. Hana tracked her gaze, her eyes narrowing, lips tightening. "I want my friends to be safe," Mina continued.

"You want your blood-sucking coven to be safe?" Hana spat, her voice a little too loud in the empty space. The priest glanced at them, before turning to take the hand of a congregant. "You want your murderous monsters to be safe?" Her voice rose again.

Mina shook her head. "They're not all like that."

"What, you're saying you don't need to siphon life from the living to feed yourself?"

"I don't kill the people I feed from." Mina arched an eyebrow. "You said you'd help me fight Night. Will you still?"

Hana turned back to the casket, running her hands over the warm, brown wood. "You and I have different memories of our conversation. You said you'd help me avenge Dale's death. I don't care about one creature of the night. I want them all: the werewolves and the golems and the gargoyles."

"And the Athanatos?"

"I expect you to keep your promise." Hana turned away. "Tomorrow night." She stared at Mina over her shoulder before going to collect Maggie and Liam without another word. Mina didn't follow; she wouldn't be welcome at the graveside.

Nicole came to stand beside her, watching them walk away. "After my Gran's funeral, I ate a bucket of ice cream sprinkled with chopped chocolate bars. Not so much an option for you." Nicole turn her head towards Mina. "What do you want to do?"

"I want to go home." Mina threaded her arm through Nicole's and together they walked down the aisle before heading back to the Sanctuary.

Mina stepped into the hush of the Sanctuary, shaking droplets of melting snow from her hair. In the end, she'd dropped Nicole at her own place before coming home.

Home. She stood in the entryway, looking through the arch into the Sanctuary proper. The light from the sconces cast a warm glow into the room, almost like candlelight. Plenty bright enough for a vampire. Tana and Simon were sparring, bare knuckles, smiles on their faces as they flowed through capoeira-like movements. Off to the side Sha and Adeh played a video game, watched by Ivan, Finn and Sam. Adeh was clearly winning, but Sha might have been letting him.

She wiped her shoes on the mat and stepped into the space. Everything went still. The sparring stopped; the suddenly forgotten video game made unhappy sounds. Everyone looked at her. The circle of people closed like a noose, and Mina fought the urge to flee. She stood her ground and told that voice to be quiet. Sam broke the circle and stepped towards her. He didn't say anything, just looked at her for a second before wrapping his arms around her and pulling her close.

Mina tensed, a voice whispering about the danger of getting too close, then she told that voice it could also shut up, and leaned into the hug, sending her arms around Sam.

"I'm so sorry," he whispered in her ear before letting her go. His action propelled the others, and each in their turn came to give her a hug, or pat her shoulder, or squeeze her hand. She took it all in the spirit it was intended. Finally, Bee stood in front of her, eyes glistening. Her arms circled Mina's shoulders and pulled her into a fierce hug.

"I know what it's like to lose a sibling." She let go and placed a hand on either side of Mina's face. She peered into her eyes, not letting her break the gaze. "And what it's like to think it's my fault, even when it isn't."

Mina nodded, not ready to face that thought, and looked over Bee's shoulder to where a shadow slunk between pillars.

Seema the woman emerged from behind a pillar, wrapped in a length of white cloth. She walked up to Mina, raising her hands to her eyes before lowering them into namaste. Mina pulled away, unsure what Seema's actions meant.

"I'm sorry," Seema said. "I was harsh with you earlier."

Mina shook her head. "No, you were right. We've all lost people. I don't want us to lose anymore." She stepped back, looking at the tiles. "At least not to this monster."

The door opened, a draught of air fleeing across the Sanctuary to some unseen exit on the other side. Rhys tumbled in, followed shortly by Dev, who shoved the door shut against the growing wind. They stomped and shook the weather off them then joined the group gathered under the stained-glass sky. High above, Mina heard the plink of icy rain pelting the panes.

Sam walked over to the new arrivals, taking Rhys' coat and hanging it behind the door. Dev shook his head, dislodging icy droplets from his curls, then glanced around at the assembled conclave as if unsure about entering into the circle of vampires. But apparently his duty or his curiosity won out as he followed Rhys into their midst.

"What did you learn?" Rhys asked as he homed in on Finn.

Finn opened her mouth, then closed it again, tipping her head as she glanced at Sam and Ivan. Her cheeks flushed, and Mina noticed the graze on her jaw.

"What happened?" She lifted her hand towards Finn, who pulled her head away.

"Nothing."

"Not nothing," Ivan said.

"The collector isn't quite human." Sam looked down at the floor, shifting nervously. Mina frowned; that was uncharacteristic for him, then she saw the bandage around his arm.

"We knew that already," Bee said. "Anything else?"

"Your wolf allies —" Sam glanced at Seema "— their fur falls out and they scratch their skin raw. The incubi and succubi who fight alongside you wake up covered in boils. Pixies appear, damaged and deranged. And they all rave about a beautiful evil spreading plague with a whisper. It's Night." His eyes were sad when they looked at her, then he grimaced, clutching his arm. "And the Collector is helping her."

Mina struggled to form her thoughts into questions, but Dev took up the tale. "The witches and warlocks are doing brisk business in protective potions and wards. Even the imps are buying."

"That doesn't explain what happened with the collector? Or what happened to your arm?" Mina nodded at Sam, but it was Finn who spoke.

"We tried asking him a few questions. I was nice about it, but he didn't want to answer." Finn crossed her arms over her chest.

"He took his anger out on me when we followed him to see where he went next. The human, the easy target. But Finn and Ivan had my back." Sam's left eyebrow lifted as he looked at her. Mina bit her tongue, keeping back the comment that he shouldn't be chasing these creatures at all.

"Any idea yet what he is?" Rhys asked.

"Isn't that your area of expertise?" A smile played at Sam's lips despite the seriousness of their conversation. Rhys just rolled his eyes at him.

"He knew I was there." Ivan shifted, taking his jacket off to reveal a short-sleeved T-shirt, his only other layer despite the cold. "I don't know if he knew what I was, or who I was, but he knew I wasn't human."

"No idea what he is?" Mina asked, repeating Rhys' question. She'd never seen Ivan without his jacket. Without it, he looked less like a bouncer for a biker bar and more like a linesman for a university football team.

Ivan shook his head. "But he seems familiar somehow." His eyebrows pulled together, and he crossed his arms over his chest. "Not him, exactly, but you know when you smell one rose, and then you smell another one, you know it's a rose?"

Mina didn't know, but saw others nodding their heads. Silence descended for a minute as the assembled motley crew turned inward.

Finally, Bee stepped forward, assuming a power pose, hands on hips, legs apart. "What about you two?" She nodded at Rhys and Dev. "What did you find?"

"We found..." Dev started but seemed unsure what to say next. Mina's jaw tightened as she fought the impulse to tell him to spit it out.

"A tale of rebellion and retribution." Rhys' gaze travelled the group. "Death and despair. Of power taken and a quest to get it back."

"That...doesn't really tell us anything useful," Mina said.

"No, but this might be useful: this is not the first time Night has returned." Dev shifted back as attention turned to him.

"I told you that already," Ivan said.

Dev tipped his head. "Yes, but each time, she's sought the blade. And each time, she's come up empty."

"Until now." Bee's arms crossed over her chest.

"Until now," Dev repeated.

"What does that mean for us?" Sam asked.

"Death and despair." Dev's tone was matter-of-fact. "If she gets the blade, makes it whole, she'll get most of her power back."

"Not necessarily." Rhys shook his head. "What giveth can also taketh away. Magical artifacts, including arcane weapons, often aren't evil in and of themselves. It's how they're used, and who wields them." His hand waved in Mina's direction, but when his head turned, he looked at Seema standing beside her. "Seema wielded the Blade of the Moon."

"You say 'most of her power'?" Bee turned to look at Dev. "But not all?"

Dev shrugged. "We think some of her power was in the weapons she used."

"The Blade of the Moon," Seema said. "And the Blade of Night." Dev tipped his head in acknowledgment. Mina squinted, as the lights from the sconces seemed suddenly brighter.

"What do we do now then?" Sha asked, turning to Bee.

Bee was quiet for a moment, her jaw clenched. Then she looked up, glancing around the assembly. "Keep the Blade of the Moon safe." Mina nodded, even though she knew Hana would be upset about not getting her family heirloom back. She jerked her head up, finally connect the dots: Hana had the blade because she was this hunter. She shelved the thought as Bee continued. "Steal back the Blade of Night from Lin." Mina opened her mouth to say she had the obsidian weapon, but she was interrupted when the doors thumped and the glass overhead rattled as a gust of wind slammed into them. "And find the other half of the blade before Night does."

"If we can stay alive long enough." Ivan glanced up, his eyes scrunched with suspicion, before turning his gaze to Bee. "She knows we're coming after her."

Bee ignored him, turning to Rhys instead. "Anything in your research tell you how to fix this blade?"

Rhys shook his head then turned to look at Finn. "She's the one you should ask. Magic weapons are her area of expertise."

Finn's lips formed a thin line. "I need some tools from the forge. And my father has a book...."

"Mina."

Mina was startled out of her own reveries, filled with inky blades and crimson blood. "Yeah?" she asked as cat-Seema twined through her ankles; she shook her head, having missed the transition.

"Go with Finn. Watch her back as she gets what she needs." Bee nodded at Ivan. "You too."

Mina had other plans but the best way to accomplish them was to go along.

CHAPTER THIRTY-FIVE

"Where is the other half?" Green tendrils crept from Night's fingertips, undulating through the air before twisting around the Collector's neck. He made some indistinct sound, and she realized he might not be able to answer. She pulled the magic tighter and smiled as his face turned red. Lesions seeped on his cheeks, and boils erupted on the hands that clawed at her tentacles of fluorescent green. His eyes bulged, and she sighed, loosening her grip.

"I swear I don't know," he croaked.

She frowned at the fight that still sparked in his eyes. "Can't your magic ferret out its location?" A smirk twisted her lips; she'd seen no sign of his magic since their first meeting. He'd learned to keep it reigned in around her.

"I...." He rubbed his throat. "I can't tell, not exactly. All I know is it's close." He glanced to her left. Night's gaze followed to see Lin standing beside the gargoyle, petting its head. Her mouth pressed into a thin line to see her grey warrior treated like a dog. And enjoying it.

Ropes of magic snaked along the floor, black this time instead of green, and grabbed Lin's neck. Night dragged her forward, bringing her inches from her face. "Who in this city would know about an arcane blade?"

Lin's nostrils flared, and her mouth stayed shut and her eyes flicked over Night's face.

"What about the Smith?" Em stepped from the shadows beside the door.

"The Smith." Night tracked the woman's languid approach, seething with impatience.

When Em stood beside Lin, she slid her gaze sideways then back to Night. She nodded her head once, slowly. Night let her magic go, and Lin sunk to the floor, gasping, before turning to stare daggers at Em. "I know how to get to the forge."

"The Smith doesn't know anything." The Collector's snort of derision stopped short at Night's sharp look. "He's a shell of a man, broken by life."

Night tipped her head one way then the other, cracking her neck, her gaze moving between Lin and the Collector before settling on Em. "Take me."

"I don't think so," Night said when Em stepped aside to let her go first.

"I, I can't open it." Em waved her hand at the lock beneath a dark, metal knocker forged into a dragon's head, holding a heavy ring in its mouth. Night stared at the knocker. Running her fingers over it lightly, they tingled at the magic. *Forged in dragon's fire*. She raised an eyebrow. Still it was no match for her power, weak though it was. Breathing deeply, she sent green spider webs under the knocker, and into the lock on the door. With a crackle, the lock clicked open.

"Lead the way." She peered at Em, who paused a second before entering the hallway. Night sent the Collector after her. Lin and her pet vampire took the rear. Jack. Night scrunched her nose. She'd hoped he might be a replacement for Angelos, but he slunk around, hands in his pockets, morose and melancholy. Lacking all the bloodlust Angelos had.

A rhythmic pinging intruded on her pondering. It got louder as they came to a set of stairs and started down...they hadn't alerted the Smith to their approach. She ran her fingers along the bricks and the webs of magic hiding this place from the top-side world. The warmth grew as they descended, and the pinging changed tempo before stopping. Another sound reached her ears, a murmur like a burbling river. It took her a minute to realize the man was speaking.

Em slowed at the front of the line, and Night did the same. With only their breathing in the passageway, she caught the man's words.

"Go lie down. You're just underfoot at the moment." His deep voice rumbled along the brick. "Good dog." The pinging started up again.

"Oh, he has a pet. How adorable." Night caught the glint of Em's eyes peering at her. "Go on. Unless you're afraid of a dog."

"A forge dog," the Collector mumbled but followed after Em. They stepped onto a landing in the middle of a large staircase that rose into darkness in one direction and descended into hell in the other. Below them the Smith hammered a piece of metal he held in a gloved hand.

Finally, Night stepped out in front of the others, clenching her hands, priming her power. She strode down the stairs, sensing the slight hesitation before the others followed.

The Smith stopped hammering to turn the piece of metal on the anvil. "Whatever you want, I don't have it," he said without up.

She was silent for a minute, waiting for him to look at her. When he didn't, she spoke. "I want information. Surely you have that?"

Finally, he lifted his head, his gaze flicking left and right, taking in the others over her shoulder, before returning to her. "Not for you I don't." He returned his attention to whatever he was working on.

Night repressed the urge to snarl. Instead, she took a step forward as she scanned the forge. She saw no signs of the dog he'd been talking to. She paused at a workbench, hefting a long sword in her hand. Peering down the blade towards the Smith, she ran her palm along the flat. "You really do beautiful work."

"I know."

Continuing towards him, she dragged the sword behind her along the stone floor.

"I'd appreciate it if you wouldn't do that," the Smith said without looking up. "A lot of work went into it."

"What are you doing?" Jack asked. "You can't get anything out of him if he's dead."

She turned her head slowly to stare at him. "Search the place. Make sure there's nothing here." The others did as she bid, but Jack stayed where he was, his eyebrows scrunched in consternation. *He thinks too much.*

Night turned back to the Smith, sending green threads of energy down the length of the sword. "Look at me, Smith." Surprisingly, he did as she asked. "I want the other half of the Sun." Her hand went to her hip, where the golden half circle was lashed to her belt. His eyes flicked to her hand, and his lips pressed together before he caught himself. He definitely knew what she was talking about.

"I don't know what you're talking about." He stepped away from the anvil, leaving the half-wrought piece of metal, but keeping hold of his hammer.

Night huffed. "I'm tired of all the lies and prevaricating and misdirection." Her voice rose to echo off the forge walls. Green lightning crackled along the length of the sword. "I want to know what you know, or I'll burn this place down with you in it."

"Attack." The Smith's voice was calm and level when he spoke. Night drew her eyebrows together, then there was a flash and a wave of heat to her right. She spun her head. A creature of flame snarled at her, small flames dropping from its snapping jaw.

She turned back to the Smith so fast it made her dizzy. "You have a hell hound?" She stared at him, her eyes wide, before turning her body to face the beast, the magic-imbued sword between her and it as she inched away.

"There's been a lot of unsavoury folk around lately." The Smith flicked his gaze to where the Collector rummaged through books on a shelf, putting one on a pile behind him. "Seemed a good time to get a guard dog."

"A hell hound is not a guard dog." Her voice was rough, and she hated herself for it. The dog jumped up on the workbench to her right, and the flames dripping from its jaw fell to the wooden surface, catching the paper that lay scattered there. "It's going to burn your forge down."

The Smith shrugged and hefted his hammer up. "It was either you or it." He took a step towards her on the left while the hell hound paced closer on the right.

"What—?" Lin stumbled into her, coming through the door over her left shoulder. "What is that thing?"

"Death." With her free hand, Night unlashed the Blade of the Sun from her hip. "But not if I kill its master." She spun towards the Smith, lifting the sword that pulse with angry magic to cut across his torso. But her strike was thwarted by a pair of tongs bashing into her arm. The sword clattered to the floor.

"Jack, don't." The Smith lunged forward, raising his hammer.

"Jack." She hissed at him, then raised her hand to the Smith, sending needles of green fire into his torso. A crackle sounded to her left, followed by the snapping of jaws. The hell hound was down on the ground sniffing the Smith. It turned its gaze to her and opened its mouth to form an unholy howl. It was time to run. Turning on the balls of her feet, she faced Jack again, who was staring at the Smith. Heat flushed her skin, and she drove the Blade of the Sun into his abdomen.

"I can't stand traitors." His eyes fell from her face to his bleeding belly. "Angelos would never have betrayed me."

Drawing out the blade, she fled into the far room, where a current of fresh air flowed. She didn't look to see if the others followed.

CHAPTER THIRTY-SIX

Ivan's steps slowed, his strides shortening as they neared the forge. This path was different from the last one they'd taken — Finn led them deep underground, along a route neither he nor Mina had been down before — but the rising temperature told him they were getting close. His shirt stuck to his back, though approaching Keagan might have contributed to the sweat that sheened his forehead. He knew people called him 'behemoth' and 'mammoth', but he didn't have Keagan's fiery temper. Or his hammer.

Finn strode more quickly along the narrow corridor, and Ivan sped up to keep with her. They turned another corner, one just like all the others. But as he squinted into the gloom ahead, something glittered, as if in defiance of the shadows. He peered at it as he passed: a small anvil. As they moved through the next passageway, he saw another one marking the next turn, and the one after that. At this point, Finn was downright sprinting, and Ivan ran to catch up, until he found her stopped in front of a door marked with a hammer and an anvil.

"No," Finn whispered. The door was ajar. Light from the forge fire seeped into the tunnel, along with waves of heat. Ivan's hand went to his holster before remembering they hadn't trusted him with a gun. He growled deep in his throat, then placed his hand on Finn's shoulder to prevent her from pushing her way into the room.

She looked at him with wrathful eyes that shone with defiance, and pulled her arm away, causing the flame tattoos peeking up above her collar to dance.

"We don't know what's in there." He pitched his voice low, trying not to alert anything lurking on the other side of the door to their presence.

"My father's in there," Finn hissed, but let him press past her. He leaned an ear towards the door and sniffed the air. Looking at Mina, he could tell she was doing some assessment of her own, though he noticed her right hand didn't hold a gun. Instead, it tapped some unheard tempo on her thigh. She turned to him, her lips mouthing the word 'anything'. A question. He shook his head in response.

Mina laid her hand on the door, then pulled back, clenching and opening her fist. "It's hot." She didn't bother to keep her voice down.

It obviously wasn't so hot she couldn't touch it, since she proceeded to push it open. Flames leapt from small fires that danced around the forge.

Finn pushed past them and ran down the stairs, two at a time. Mina followed her. Ivan glanced over the rail at the uneven ground below and decided discretion was better than broken bones, even if he would heal. He followed the other two down the steps, causing the staircase to rattle and groan.

"Dad's books!" Finn stopped in front of the first fire. "All his sketches, his drawings." She spun around, casting her eyes over the forge. "Dad?" she shouted.

"Keagan?" Mina ran into the room Ivan recognized as Finn's, remembering her sashaying out of it in defiance of her father.

"Smith!" He sprinted into the other room and slid to a stop. Keagan lay on the floor, blood from his head congealing around his face. "In here!" He knelt beside the Smith, taking the man's meaty paw in his own, lifting it from the box the man clutched to his chest. He closed his eyes and tuned into his vampire senses, shutting out the roaring fire and the acrid smoke. A thready pulse rewarded his efforts.

"Dad!" Finn cried as she came into the room, clutching a pair of lightly charred books to her chest, a satchel slung over her shoulder. She fell to her knees beside her father. "Da?" All she got in response was a crash from the room behind them.

Mina flew into the room. "Oh!" She stopped short at the scene in front of her.

"He's still alive." Ivan looked down at the Smith. "Barely."

Another crash sounded from the other room.

"Finn, is there another way out?" Mina looked over her shoulder at a scene Ivan couldn't see.

Finn didn't answer. Instead she got up, went over to the shelf and picked up something. Ivan recognized it immediately as a weapon, though it wasn't like any he'd used before: on an arm's span of wood sat a metal head clearly meant to maim before it killed, as it sported an axe on one side, a mallet on the other, and a mean looking pike shooting out the top.

"Finnegan." The word was barely audible, but it captured everyone's attention. The Smith's eyes fluttered open, then shut again.

"Da!" Finn dropped down beside her father again, her face once again settling into a steely mask.

"Finn." Mina placed her hand on the woman's shoulder. "We need another way out."

Finn turned to Mina, but Ivan continued to look down at the Smith and the box he'd been clutching. A bloody handprint highlighted the golden symbol inlaid on the seamless side: the Blade of the Sun.

A groan of metal shuddered through the forge. "Mina," Ivan said calmly. "Grab the box." He raised an eyebrow as he looked at her. Her gaze went to the box before flicking back to meet his, then she snatched it up and clutched it to her chest.

Once she had it, he picked up the mountain that was Keagan, and then turned to Finn, who reluctantly turned away from her father to lead them into another hidden tunnel.

In front of Mina, Ivan stumbled under Keagan's dead weight. She smelled the blood that seeped from the wound on the Smith's head, even though it was congealing and starting to dry at the edges. *He's still alive.*

Ivan recovered and took another step, then went down, landing hard on one knee. Mina winced, as if it were her knee crashing into the hard floor of the tunnel. She opened her mouth to call out to Finn to wait but saw she had already stopped, her silhouette clear to Mina's vampire eyes despite the weak lights strung far apart.

Mina's vampire senses went on high alert — they weren't the first to pass this way tonight. The tunnel was redolent with the scents of a variety of creatures, and she couldn't tease them apart. She sidled past Ivan, shifting the awkward box into her other hand and pulling out her gun as she did so. Some dark shape coated with the aroma of blood staggered towards them out of the shadows. Finn's free hand clenched into a fist, as Mina's mouth dropped open, her gun forgotten. She'd let her fear blind her, deafen her, but now she heard what she should have before: woodwinds and brass.

"Jack," Mina uttered.

"Jack." From Finn's tense lips the name was a harsh, explosive curse.

Jack reeled towards them, weaving back and forth, catching himself on the wall of the narrow corridor. Mina sniffed — the blood was his own. *Not Keagan's*. She sighed, some bit of her relaxing at that realization.

In that moment, Finn's fist slammed into Jack's face. He slumped against the wall, shaking his head. Finn drew her foot back to kick him. His arms crossed in front of his face, so Finn's foot connected with his forearm rather than his cheekbone. Finally processing the scene, Mina dropped the box, holstered her gun and wrapped her arms around Finn, dragging her away from Jack as Ivan came up beside them, sans Keagan.

"Jack." That was all Ivan said as Jack lowered his arms.

"Let me go!" Finn twisted and writhed in Mina's embrace, the axe side of the weapon slung across her back threatening to cut Mina's nose off.

"No." Mina cinched her arms tighter as the Smith struggled. Because of her profession, Finn was strong. But Mina was a vampire. She was stronger.

"I'll kill him for what he did to my father." Finn sent the heel of her boot into Mina's arch. Mina cursed but didn't let go.

"I..." Jack shook his head again as if clearing away the stars.

"He didn't hurt your father," Mina said.

This did nothing to stop Finn's struggles. "Then why is he here?"

"I came with them." Jack pulled himself up, using one hand against the tunnel wall, while keeping out of range of Finn's appendages. Now that he was standing in the light, Mina could see where the blood was coming from. A gash in his head still seeped copious amounts, and a slice on his arm shed droplets onto the tunnel floor. More worrisome was the wound in his stomach, which he pressed with his hand in an effort to staunch the bleeding.

"You've been shot." Mina looked from his hand, covered in blood, to his face.

"Them?" Ivan said at the same time.

"Night. And a man. Slick hair. Too white suit."

"The Collector." Finn stopped struggling but Mina didn't let go.

"They came about the blade." He glanced at Finn. "Your father wouldn't help them."

"Of course not," Finn snorted. "But you—" Mina was sure the Smith would have pointed an accusatory finger at him if her arms hadn't been trapped by Mina.

"No." Jack shook his head. "I spied. But when...." He looked down at his hands and blinked. "When she went into a rage, set on Keagan, the time for watching was over. Time to save Keagan." Jack coughed, and his shoulder slumped. "But I failed. I tried to go after them but...I failed." He peered up at the three of them, his eyes glistening with unshed tears.

"What?" Finn said as Mina finally released her.

"I was too late for Keagan." Jack weaved to the side but stayed upright, reaching a bloody hand to the wall. "I'm sorry." He fixed his eyes on Finn.

"No, he's just back there, still alive." Ivan stepped back, revealing the pile of blood and leather that was the Smith. "You're a vampire, you should be able to smell him."

"I..." Jack slumped against the tunnel wall again, his eyes blinking rapidly.

"There was silver in that bullet," Mina stated. "You need to stop getting poisoned."

"Blade."

"What?"

Jack's voice was quiet and hoarse. "Blade. Not a bullet."

Ivan came up beside them, Keagan's still breathing form over his shoulder again. "Whatever it was, we'd best get you both out of here."

"No." Jack shook his head. "There's something—" His head lolled back.

"Hush. You can tell us later." Mina stepped up to Jack and slung his arm over her shoulder, her arm around his waist. Finn took the lead again, book and box now clutched in her arms. Ivan followed, Keagan's unconscious form bumping against his back. Mina and Jack took up the rear as they made their way out of the dark tunnel, into the grey night.

CHAPTER THIRTY-SEVEN

Mina slumped deeper into the chair beside the bed, watching Jack's chest rise and fall. There was a bandage around his abdomen, a dark spot indicating where the blood would soon seep through. She ignored the restraints around his wrists and ankles.

"He's not healing like he should." Bee stood in the doorway, her face scrunched in an expression that could be worry or suspicion.

"He mentioned something," Mina said, not taking her eyes off him. "Maybe it wasn't silver on the blade. Can thyme poison vampires?"

"Thyme?" Seema stood in the hall, just behind Bee.

"It sounded like thigh or tie." Mina scrunched her lips. "But obviously that wasn't it. So thyme?" Bee just shook her head.

"Titan arum?" Seema offered.

"No." Mina's left eyebrow lifted. "What the heck is that?"

"The corpse flower."

"No," a voice said from behind the werecat. A human Mina had never seen, dressed in a black and white frock, almost like a priest, nudged past the women. "Doesn't harm vampires." He placed the basin of water he carried on the book that sat on the night table. The thought that Jack wouldn't like his precious book to be treated that way flitted through Mina's mind, then a rattling moan rose from his chest to remind her he might never know.

The man's lips pressed together when he lifted the bandage to examine the wound underneath, then he looked at Bee. "I don't know what else to do. I've tried all the antidotes to silver, as well as the other vampire poisons." He took the cloth from the basin and wrung it out, sending droplets onto the book cover, then he wiped Jack's forehead, his torso, his arms. After sniffing the cloth, he placed it back in the bowl, then he took one of Jack's hands and inspected the fingernails. Picking up the basin, he stepped to the end of the bed, looking back at Jack. "It may be

255

magic itself that poisons him." He turned to Bee again. "If he's not strong enough to fight it, or if the caster is not found and forced to undo...." The man's lips pressed tight again, then he bowed his head to Bee and shuffled out of the room.

After he left, Bee spoke. "We're meeting upstairs in 15." Bee turned to Seema. "You too." Spinning on her heels, she followed the healer down the hall.

Seema looked from Jack to Mina. "Timothy?"

Mina's eyebrows drew together. "What?"

"The word."

When Mina shook her head again, Seema also left. Alone with Jack, Mina leaned forward, placing her chin in her hands.

"What have you been up to?"

Jack chose that moment to murmur something, his eyeballs racing under closed eyelids. Mina startled, pushing back into the chair. He continued to mumble, without moving. Mina shifted forward again, tipping her ear to his lips. This time, all she could make out was something that sounded like 'I sun-dried', repeated.

"What does that have to do with anything?" Mina sighed, annoyed at herself for snapping at him. Standing up, her joints ached and her back protested at having sat for hours. "I'm a vampire," she said to herself as she headed to her room to change out of her bloody, grimy clothes. "This was not in the brochure."

After she was washed and changed, she stopped at Dar's room, where Keagan lay on Dar's old bed, russet chest hair peeking out from under the sheet covering him. Finn's head lay on the bed, her hair covering her face. Mina jumped at the whisper of sound to her right when she stepped into the room.

"Ivan." She nodded at the former Necrophagus. The rest of the conclave likely had little to do with him; she herself was still suspicious of his change in allegiance but there was nothing to be gained by ignoring him. He nodded back at her, and she returned her attention to Keagan. His skin was ghostly, with a green cast, and she could smell the edge of sepsis in his sweat even from her place in the doorway. But this wasn't some unknown poison. It was simply injuries he couldn't heal from.

She turned back to Ivan. "They're having a meeting upstairs. Figuring out what to do next...if you wanted to join us."

"Yes."

Mina startled at the raw voice from the bed, thinking Keagan had suddenly awoken. But it was Finn that looked at her with puffy, red eyes.

"You heard her." Ivan stared at Mina. "Yes."

Stopping in the shadows at the top of the stairs, Mina watched Bee and Seema spar. They fought hand-to-hand, using long, low movements that put her in mind of two tigers circling each other. Most of the conclave was already gathered, whispering to each other as they watched the two women. Whether they were placing bets, or remarking on what they'd do differently, Mina couldn't tell. She squinted, trying to figure out where she'd place her wager, but decided she was too smart to bet against either of them. Propelled by a noise behind her, she stepped into the sanctuary and moved to one side.

Ivan and Finn entered the large space, causing the fight to stop and the watchers to turn. Finn walked to the circle, clutching the few possessions she'd rescued from the forge: a satchel of tools and the box. The awkward load obviously had some weight, causing the muscles of her neck to tense with the effort. Either that, or she was just tense. Mina noted she'd let Ivan carry the book, though she wasn't letting it out of her sight.

Bee bent down to pick up her hoodie, keeping her eyes on Ivan. "I don't remember inviting you."

"That makes two of us." Ivan frowned and lodged himself against a pillar.

"He stays." Finn stood up straighter.

Bee stared at Finn. "I don't recall anyone giving you a vote either. Unless someone made you a vampire, and I missed it."

"Nope, still a Smith." Finn stared back.

"So you're our guest, and you have a say only so far as we say you do." Bee shrugged into her fleece. "But given your expertise and what's happened to your father, you should have your say." Her gaze slid back to Ivan. "And I don't have a problem if he stays. Anyone else?"

No one else in the conclave spoke up in contradiction, though it seemed to Mina they all shifted a little further away from Ivan, and from Finn and her cargo.

Simon, normally quiet, hugged his left arm to his side as he spoke. "So, what do we do?"

"If I might make a suggestion." Seema stepped forward, hands together at her chest. "It's sometimes useful to review what we know, when faced with a mystery for example. Or before a battle."

Mina moved to join the others, opening her mouth to say they didn't know much. But the door opened before she had a chance to be a smart aleck.

Bee strode towards the entry, towards Rhys who was shaking out his coat to hang on the hooks beside the door.

"You really should knock, you know."

Rhys didn't respond right away, instead putting his hat to join his coat. "I'm sorry," he said. "I just feel so welcome." Mina smiled at the sparkle in his eyes.

"Hmm, it's unwise to enter the home of a nest of vampires unannounced."

"I thought you called yourselves a 'conclave'."

"Not the point." Bee sighed and followed him back to the centre of the Sanctuary.

Rhys barely spared a glance for the assemblage of vampires, instead walking straight up to Finn, placing his hands on her shoulders. "How is he?"

Bee answered for her. "He's alive, but it's still not a sure thing."

"And Jack? Has he told you anything of his time behind enemy lines?"

Bee shook her head. "Not really. He's tied up downstairs, still trapped in delirium.

"Tied up?"

Mina glanced at Bee before answering Rhys. "They're not sure he isn't the enemy."

"Our Jack? Preposterous."

"Really?" Bee arched an eyebrow. "You weren't saying that before."

"But that was before Jack came back." Rhys produced a handkerchief, took off his glasses and proceeded to dry the rain off them. "Really, Jack's told you nothing?"

Mina finally stepped forward. "He did say something."

"The poison?" Seema asked.

"Poison?" Rhys turned to her, his left eyebrow raising.

"I think he was cut with a poisoned blade," Mina replied.

"Likely a bad reaction to silver," Bee said. "He's gotten himself stabbed a lot lately."

Seema tipped her head as she peered at Mina. "You said you can't remember what he said."

"No, I didn't quite catch it...thyme or time." Mina shook her head. "But that's not what I'm talking about. Just now, he was mumbling again."

Bee looked at her with suspicion, Seema like she thought her mad, Rhys with pity.

"I know you were close," Rhys said. "Are close."

"You shouldn't get your hopes up," Seema said. "If we can't figure out what it was...."

"I wasn't imagining it. Trust me, I would have come up with something better. Not 'I'm sun-dried'." She glanced at the others, stopping on Rhys, whose eyes were wide.

"Could it have been 'I'm sundered'?" Rhys' voice was hushed. "Though that makes no sense."

"It could have been a lot of things."

"This is important." He came up to her, grabbing her arm.

She pulled away. "Everything is important right now. People are dying." She stopped herself from hissing and baring her fangs, recognizing they were all on edge.

"And I'm sorry. But Dev and I did some research. He has access to some interesting material, though he's still cagey about how he came by it." Rhys waved his hand. "But that's not important." He paced back and forth, from one side of the rough ellipse formed by the group to the other, looking at the floor, starting to speak then abandoning what he was going to say. He finally came to a stop at a pair of bare feet. He looked up into Seema's face. The lines around her eyes got a little deeper, her frown a little sadder. "One of the scrolls, in ancient Sanskrit, it talked about the sundered blade. The blade of opposites. The sun and the moon. Day and night. Heaven and hell." Rhys didn't move and didn't look away from Seema. "And its Keepers."

The cat stared at him, her eyes glistening. A single tear rolled down her cheek.

"What?" Bee took a step towards them, then stopped.

Rhys turned his head to her. "The sundered blade — the Blade of the Sun — can be used to shield or to slaughter. It's been used for both. Many years ago, the Keepers of the blade realized neither man nor beast should have that kind of power. They broke it into halves, so it was truly sundered. Sent to the far ends of the earth. No one should know where they are."

"I told no one." Seema's eyes were fixed on Rhys' torso. "I couldn't, I was a cat."

"You know what he means by all this?" Mina shifted her gaze between Rhys and Seema before catching Bee's eye and raising an eyebrow.

"My family were the Keepers." Seema slowly turned her head towards Mina. "They were slaughtered because they wouldn't reveal where the boxes were."

"That's why the archaeologist was so interested in you." Finn cocked her head. "Not because you're Were, but because you're a Keeper."

"Was a Keeper." Seema tugged the cloth around her shoulders tighter.

Rhys flicked his gaze from Finn to her before he continued, a slight disapproval in his tone. "One box stayed in India, hidden away with its key."

"How do you know that?" Seema's voice was a rough whisper.

Rhys shrugged. "They don't call me the Librarian for nothing. Dev and I think that's the one in the museum."

Seema's jaw clenched, her eyes fiery, but she gave a crisp nod. "We kept one box. One key. The other box and its key were sent in opposite directions."

"The key ended up in the land of the rising sun. Japan, we think."

"And the other box?" Mina asked.

"Western Europe somewhere. Basque country, maybe ...Languedoc...Ireland?"

CHAPTER THIRTY-EIGHT

A gasp, so quiet he almost didn't notice it, shifted Ivan's attention from Rhys' tale back to Finn.

She stared at the box in her arms, no longer clutching it as tightly. Without warning, it dropped to the hard floor with a resounding thud. Looking at the box sideways, she took a step back, then apparently changed her mind, and came to kneel beside it instead. Running her hands over the lid, she opened her mouth to speak then closed it again.

"What is it?" Ivan knelt beside her, conscious of the others staring at her. "What's wrong?"

"It's the box."

"Yes, it is a box." He looked at the rich brown wood, undamaged by its fall to the hard floor. Even the tiles in the lid were all still intact, except for the one already missing.

"No." Finn turned to look at him with her green eyes. "It's *the* box." Her voice grew louder, and she cast her gaze around at the others. "It went to Ireland. This box holds the other half of the blade." She turned back to it, and slammed her palm into the lid, before running her hand gently over it again. Ivan realized she was looking for the hasp. "If I can ever get it open."

Movement caught his attention, and he tracked Bee until she disappeared into the arcade. He turned back to the box, to find Seema and Mina kneeling on the other side.

"Maybe if you push one of the tiles." Mina prodded the lid.

"That won't work," Seema said.

"You know the secret?" Ivan asked.

"No, it was legend long before I was born, the details scoured away by the sands of time."

"How do you know it won't work then?"

Before Seema could answer, a shuffling behind drew his attention over his shoulder. Shock and fear coursed through him when he turned his head. Without thought, he shoved Finn out of the way as an axe came down onto the hard wood. And skittered off.

"Whoa! You could have killed us." He glared at Bee.

"Sorry." She shrugged. "I really thought that would work."

Ivan looked down at the box. "It's magicked." He ran his hands over the lid. "There's not a scratch."

"Maybe if we can't get in, neither can Night?" Bee suggested.

"Someone got the other one open," Mina said. "Assuming the other half was packed in a magic box."

"Not necessarily a safe assumption." Rhys peered over her shoulder.

As Ivan ran his fingers over the tiles, they shifted slightly. "It's not impervious to damage. It's lost a tile already, and some of these are loose." He tried to pry one free with his thumb, without luck. He pulled a knife out of his boot.

"Hey!" Bee exclaimed. "I thought the rules were clear. No weapons for you until I'm sure I can trust you."

He peered at her. "Will you ever be sure?" He didn't wait for a response. Instead he turned back to the box and dug the point of the knife under the edge of a tile. The knife slipped and stabbed his finger. "Bugger!" He sucked the blood away.

"Stop." Finn placed her hand on his. "It's not working. And I don't want to damage it anymore than it already is. It's all I have left of my mother."

Looking at her hand, Ivan set the knife aside. He turned the box around, spinning it so the tiles that had been nearest him were further away. He tilted his head as a ghost of an idea lodged itself in his mind. "Maybe it's not damaged. Maybe all the tiles are there."

"What?" Finn looked from him to the box. "But you can see as well as I can there's one missing."

He turned to look into her green eyes, tearing his gaze away before he lost his train of thought. "Not all gaps are missing pieces. Some are just spaces for creating something new."

He felt Finn's gaze on him. Thankfully Rhys tore her attention away.

"It's a tile puzzle."

"A what?"

"You slide the tiles to make a picture." Ivan placed his hand on hers and slid it, along with the tile under it, into the empty space. Finn stared at the box.

"A puzzle? Damn it. I hate puzzles." Her lips contorted into a grimace. "Maybe I can take a torch to it instead."

"You saw what happened with the axe." Bee stared at them, her hands resting on the butt of the axe handle. "Don't burn our home down." The wind buffeting the windows punctuated her words, and the door rattled.

"What's going on out there?" Seema pulled her wrap more tightly around her shoulders. "You'd think the end of the..." The Were stopped mid-sentence as the door rattled again.

"I think there's actually someone out there." Ivan nodded towards the door. Bee shifted the axe handle towards him, and he took it from her — apparently she didn't count it as a weapon — before she ambled over to the door. On opening it, Sam and the archaeologist tumbled in. It took the three of them to press the door closed and shut out the wintry night.

"What brings you here?" Bee asked, running her hands over her hair to dislodge water.

"The pox," Dev said.

"The plague," Sam added. "It's getting worse."

Hana shivered as the cemetery descended deeper into winter. The wind picked up and the soft snow became needles of ice. Still she knelt in front of Dale's plaque, waiting for Mina. Running her thumb over his name, written in English and Hangeul, she dusted off the snow.

A noise to her left caused her ear to twitch. Breathing deeply, she stayed calm and slowly turned her head. A crow sat in the tree beside the columbarium wall, staring at her with its beady, black eyes.

"Shoo." The word hung in a cloud of frost before dissipating. She scanned the ghostly graveyard. With the city lights partially blocked by the spindly firs and skeletal branches of naked deciduous trees, the near-full moon cast a blue hue over everything, and the headstones glowed.

The crow cawed and flapped its wings in a furious response, but then settled on another branch, higher up. For a second it appeared to have three legs, but when she blinked, the extra leg was a branch the creature was pulling apart for some purpose. Another of its kind cackled nearby, unseen, and she tried to remember the riddle about crows: one for sorrow, two for.... A shiver travelled down her spine again.

"Enough of this." She glared at the crow as she pulled out her phone. Finding Mina's number, she dialed. "Enough waiting."

She was about to give up when Mina finally answered. "Yoboseyo?"

Hana gave a small smile. Dale always made Mina try to use Korean. "Where are you?" Hana asked in English.

"What do you mean? I'm at the Sanctuary. Where are you?"

Hana sighed. "I'm at the cemetery."

There was a second of silence on the other end; she could almost see Mina's eyebrows draw together in a question.

"Fuck! Sorry, I forgot."

"No shit."

"There's been a lot happening, people injured, seriously. Someone...some people I care about."

"Don't you care about me? About Liam and Maggie?" Her voice was loud in the deserted cemetery, and the crow cawed its perturbation. "Dale?" There was no answer from the other end. Hana went on. "When can you get here?"

More silence. "Um, well, we're in the middle of trying to, kind of, crack a safe. Solving a puzzle that might reveal the answers we've been seeking."

"God, you've spent too much time around those creatures, with their pointless riddles and malevolent magic." Hana rubbed her temple, trying to prevent it from ticking her irritation.

After the tick of a heartbeat, Mina spoke, her voice serious. "I can leave now, if you need me tonight."

It was Hana's turn leave a pregnant pause. "Never mind," she said finally. "You'd just better not be reneging on our agreement." She hung up before Mina could respond.

Then she wished she hadn't hung up so quickly as a twig snapped behind her. Spinning around, she saw a face warping between wolf and woman. Adrenalin shot through her system and she reached for her gun, but strong arms wrapped around her from behind, a hairy hand clasping over her mouth.

"Come along quietly, pretty thing, and I won't have to let the wolf out to play," a man's voice growled in her ear.

She didn't scream, but she did drive her foot back into a naked knee and, shifting her head, sunk her teeth into a juicy finger. In response, the werewolf tightened the arm around her throat until her world went black.

CHAPTER THIRTY-NINE

Night peered out the broken window of the warehouse at the sluggish, tarry water beyond. It made her queasy, but she kept staring at the river as the creature beside her nattered away. The squirrel, little more than a rat with a bushy tail, claimed to have a secret. It had seen something that would interest her. She slid her gaze sideways, watching as the Were rubbed its dirty little paws together. It wanted to share the information with her if she would give it something.

Her arm flashed out, and her fingers wrapped around its midsection. The squirrel made a noise like a vomiting chicken being strangled, even though she'd barely applied any pressure. Its legs kicked at her hand, drawing blood, but she didn't let go. She drew it close and stared into its beady eyes. It stilled and started to tremble.

"Silly little rat. If you tell me, I'll give you your life." The fur around her fingers started to fall out. She blew it off her hand. "How's that for a deal?"

Its delicate paws rubbed together, and it nodded. In its quiet chitter, the creature told her of a box. A special box. A magic box marked with a golden circle, smelling of smoke, that had been taken into the home of the Athanatos. It told her of a mountain of a man carrying a boulder of a man, a woman with hair of fire, and a vampire with black hair and red lips helping a wounded warrior.

Night's blood boiled. The box had been at the forge all along. Her fingers clenched into fists. A squeal drew her attention. The squirrel squirmed in her tightening grasp. She tipped her head to look at the creature. It had started to turn a greener shade of grey. It peered back at her with its black eyes, like pinpoints of onyx. "You've learned a valuable lesson, Squirrel. Don't bargain with Night." She released her fingers one by one. "Next time you have information I want, run as fast as your legs will carry you to give it to me."

When she let the thing down, it tore across the floor, almost flying out the door.

"Do you think it's wise to let it go?" Lin asked, coming up behind her. "What if it runs and tells them where you are?"

Night snapped her head around, eyebrow raised. "You question my actions?"

"I...."

Night smiled. "I'm hoping it does."

The Collector's cane tapped on the floor as he stepped out from behind a column. "If it tells them where she is, they'll bring the blade to her."

She pressed her lips together. The man was too smart for his own good. "Something like that."

"The squirrel says there's a werecat. And not any old dame — a Bengali." The Collector's eyes shone as he spoke. "Maybe she'll come. I could find room for a creature like that in my menagerie."

Night tipped her head, turning to glare at him. "You'd better not touch any of my creatures."

He clasped a hand to his chest. "I wouldn't dream of it."

She was certain that was exactly what he dreamt of, but if he was so smart, he knew how quickly it would become a nightmare if he did.

Night looked back at the inky water for a minute, and as she stared, the surface churned and bubbled. She smiled as the first of the arachnoid bodies twitched its way out of the water, its movements jerky until it found its legs. Another followed it, and another, and a wave of spidery bodies started to tiptoe towards the warehouse. She tore her gaze away and turned her attention to the other two occupants of the room. Em, and beside her the Hunter, bound to a chair and already bleeding.

"Now, what shall you and I do to pass the time?"

CHAPTER FORTY

Ivan sat in the kitchen of the Sanctuary, surrounded by the daytime hush of vampires sleeping. The room was a puzzle to him. The mansion probably had something similar, but he'd never been in it during all his long years of living there. Staring into the dying flames in the fireplace across the room, he spared a thought for what Em was doing now. Certainly not thinking of him.

Rhys sat in the chair nearest the fire, an empty scotch glass on the side table next to him, his head turned to the side, snoring quietly. Mina lay on the floor in front of the fire, absentmindedly stroking Seema, who was being a cat in more ways than just form, baring her belly for Mina to scratch. Ivan couldn't wrap his head around the idea of petting a Were-anything. Dev and Sam had found some other nook of the building to curl up for a few hours. All of them found sanctuary in the Sanctuary from whatever raged outside. Disease, they'd said, that was now spreading like wildfire. Netherworld creatures turning up dead, or wishing they were. Humans filling hospitals to overflowing, with symptoms that stymied the doctors. Because modern medicine had no way to diagnose a magical malady.

A soft snort brought his gaze back to the form beside him. Finn. Her face peeked out from a halo of red hair that had sprung free from the braid she'd tried to tame it into while they'd put their heads together over the puzzle of the box. Her head rested in the crook of her elbow, sleeves rolled up while they'd worked. He looked at her face, away from the wrist where her pulse beat. The Smiths weren't entirely human, but they weren't inhuman either: best not to dwell on how hungry he was, even though he hadn't fed since coming to the Athanatos. Her eyelids flickered, and Ivan wondered what she dreamed about. A soft, pained gasp came from her lips. Maybe not a dream after all.

He turned back to the box and absentmindedly slid the tiles along their tracks. He was sure he was right: the picture unlocked the box. If only he knew the picture it was supposed to form. But the black lines, swoops and whorls could form a thousand shapes.

"What is it?" Finn raised her head a few inches and looked at him with bleary eyes.

"What?"

"You growled." A crooked smile formed on her lips.

He blinked and shook his head. "No."

"Yes, you did," Mina offered from her spot in front of the fireplace without shifting her attention from the cat.

He glared at Mina's back then turned to Finn. "Sorry, I didn't mean to wake you."

"It's okay." She placed her palm on the back of his hand. "It's time I check on Pa anyway." She put her hand on his shoulder to help herself up, then started to walk away when he grabbed her wrist.

"Hey!" She made to pull away, but he wouldn't let go. Drawn by the exclamation, Mina came to the table, disturbing Rhys' fitful slumber.

Ivan turned Finn's arm over, exposing the vulnerable inside of the wrist. Her heart beat faster in her chest. His did as well but for a different reason. He slid her sleeve back up over her elbow, once again exposing the tattoo at the crook.

"What's this?" he asked, running a thumb along the swooping lines of a tattoo. It stood out starkly against the ochre flames that covered the rest of her arm. Black lines interwove to form a cross-like shape, except the top was a flattened circle. And in the centre of that oval, an eye stared at him.

She looked at him, her head tilted. "Nothing. Just a tattoo my mom gave me."

He stroked the flames the covered her forearm. "These are the marks of the Smiths, yes?"

She nodded, no longer pulling her arm away.

He moved his thumb back up to the other tattoo. "One of these things is not like the others."

272

Finn pulled her arm away and looked more closely at the tattoo, showing it to Mina, Rhys and the now-human but still naked Seema, while Ivan pulled the box closer.

He slid the tiles along their tracks, the movements and sequence clear now that he knew what the final image was supposed to be, shuffling them in and out of the empty block. He barely registered the others turning to watch his fingers move over the wood, until the last tile was ready to be shifted into place. Even without the last tile set, the shape was clear — the tattoo from Finn's elbow, complete with the eye in the middle. He looked up at her.

"Do you want to do the honours?" he asked Finn. "It is your box."

She glanced from the box to him. Taking a half step back, she shook her head. So Ivan moved the last tile into place, then lifted his hands away.

Nothing.

"It should open." He cast his eyes over the box, ran his hands along the sides, looking for a latch they hadn't found the first one hundred times they examined it. He looked back at the others. "Right? It should open."

"No." They all turned to the source of the word. Jack stood in the doorway, his skin an abnormal shade of grey-green. Then he slumped to the floor.

CHAPTER FORTY-ONE

$\mathbf{M}$ina lay beside Jack in his narrow bed. Turning onto her side, she propped herself up on her arm. Ivan had carried Jack downstairs again after he passed out. They hadn't bound him this time, perhaps thinking he was so near death that he wasn't a threat.

Bee and Rhys had stood in the doorway for a bit, while Mina had stationed herself at the end of the bed, listening as they talked in hushed tones about Jack's prognosis and Finn's box, lowering their voices even further after glancing back at Dar's room where Keagan still slept, and where Finn had disappeared to. Bee had decided to do nothing during the day. Instead, they would wait until nightfall, then try to track down the source of the pestilence that stalked the streets. Not try to find what poisoned Jack. Eventually, they slipped away, and Mina offered Ivan her room if he wanted to get some sleep.

Shortly after that, the healer had also left, perhaps seeing there was nothing he could do, and having another patient to attend to. That's when Mina had lain down beside Jack.

With the fingers of the arm she lay on, she played with his hair. It was already longer than when she last lay beside him. Her other hand fiddled with her mother's necklace. She'd taken to wearing it, hideous as it might be.

He murmured, shifting his head slightly, so he was in half profile. His face was flushed and his skin hot. She dropped the pendant and brought her fingers to his forehead, running a thumb over his eyebrow, down his nose, across his lips. She placed her hand on his chest, which still rose and fell, though his pulse was thready, and a sheen of sweat coated his skin.

"I wish...." She stopped, unsure of the words. "I wish I'd gotten to know you better, before Night changed everything. Until she took everything, everyone, away." She lay her head on his chest, her ear over his heart.

Mina woke to the sound of her phone. It rang and vibrated against Jack's bedside table. Reaching to grab it, she saw an earlier missed call from Aunt June that had somehow not woken her despite its sharp trill. Flicking away the missed call notification, there was also a mittful of unread messages. All from Aunt June. Her stomach fluttered as she sat up and opened the first — asking if she'd seen Hana, she hadn't come home — then flipped through them, the flutter in her stomach turning to a knot that got tighter and tighter as the messages became more and more frantic. Her phone pinged, indicating a voicemail. With trepidation, she accessed the message. Aunt June's distraught voice filled her head, asking the same things as the texts until it finally came to something new.

'Are *you* alive?' Her aunt's voice turned tearful before the message cut off.

Mina rang her aunt.

'OhmygodImsogladtoknowyourealive' was followed by some Korean words she never expected to come from her aunt. "Why didn't you answer?"

"Sorry." Mina felt the word to the tips of her toes. "I...my phone was turned off." She couldn't say she was dead asleep on a man's chest. "Hana didn't come home?" Mina's mind flashed back to her last conversation with her sister-in-law: she'd abandoned Hana, leaving her to face the dangers of the night alone.

But Hana was a fighter, with some secret mad skills Mina was only beginning to learn about. She could protect herself as well as Mina could...unless she was distracted by thoughts of Dale and a burning hunger for revenge.

Mina sighed. She knew vengeance was an unquenchable thirst. She tuned back into what June was saying. Something about calling the police. She shook her head, glad her aunt couldn't see her. "Are you okay taking care of Maggie and Liam? I'll talk to the police." She knew there was nothing they could do; they didn't even realize things like Mina and Night, even people like Hana, existed. "I'll figure it out."

A Spell of Death

I just don't know how. She hung up before June started again. Retracing her steps, she puzzled over where to look for Hana. She went back to Angelos' death, to Luca and the gargoyles, to her own rebirth. She dismissed the usual haunts: the cemetery was neutral ground, with no protection for Hana or for Night. And Mina had no doubt about who had taken her sister-in-law: she was looking for Night. She couldn't get into the Necrophagus' mansion, and Night hadn't shown any love for Matteo's Baroque home anyway. No, when they'd searched for Night before, that's not where they found her.

"The warehouse." Mina looked back at Jack, imagining what he would say. *Don't be rash.* She leaned over and kissed him lightly, her pendant falling at the divot between his collarbones. "I know, but they're family." She lifted the necklace off and placed it over his head instead. "I'll get it when I come back. If I come back."

If you *come back.* a voice whispered. Mina glanced over her shoulder even though she knew they were still alone. Her forehead scrunched as she peered at the door. She needed an edge, something she could fight with...or trade for Hana's life.

"The obsidian blade."

Mina cursed when she opened the door to her room: a big vampire filled her bed. She forgot she'd offered it to Ivan. Inching the door the rest of the way open, she tiptoed into the room. A snort from Ivan caused her to freeze, only moving again when the snort turned into a whiffling snore. She walked the few steps to her wardrobe, her calves on fire from trying to keep her heels from contacting the cement. Slowly, she opened the door, lifting as she pulled to try to stop the usual squeal.

I should oil the hinges one of these days. Mina snorted at the thought, knowing she wouldn't, then glanced at the bed to check that she hadn't woken Ivan. His chest still rose and fell rhythmically. Reaching for the drawer in the bottom, careful to not cause an avalanche of the jumbled shoes and boots, she opened it halfway, enough to retrieve the black shard of a dagger. Remembering its voices and their dirge, she pulled her sleeve down so she didn't touch it with bare skin. Still, when she turned it in the dim light, it glinted. Hungry. *Thirsty.*

Mina slid it into her pocket before she got sucked into its depths, then slowly retraced her steps out of the room and down the dark hallway to the stairs.

Slinking up the stairs to the Sanctuary, she was glad to find it empty, hoping to slide out the door without any questions asked. She didn't dare stop to armour up or replenish bullets, so she only had the ammo in the clip in her gun and the long dagger she always kept with her nowadays.

She was almost at the inner doors when an English voice piped up. "Where are you off to?"

Mina shifted her gaze sideways to where Rhys sat in an overstuffed chair with a closed book on one armrest, an empty scotch glass on the other. She never used the little reading nook up here, preferring solitude when she was deep in a book. She'd actually never seen any of the vampires use it, not even Jack, and wondered if Dar set it up especially for Rhys.

He arched an eyebrow at her silence. She shook her head.

"Sorry, just lost in my head."

"It can sometimes be a great place to get lost."

"And sometimes not." Mina's phone vibrated, and she pulled it out, realizing she had the perfect excuse. "I'm heading out to meet Hana, to ask if she'll help our cause." They wanted her sister-in-law's help; let them believe she could get it for them.

"Really?" Rhys picked up his whiskey glass and stared at the empty bottom. "Good luck with that."

She paused for a second, waiting for him to say something more, then nodded and left.

Outside, she zipped her jacket up all the way and wished she'd worn more sensible boots. Checking her wallet, she sighed when she saw it was empty except for an ill-used credit card, then she looked up. She wasn't dead yet — she still technically had the money from her mother's estate. She raised her hand, and soon was in a relatively warm, foggy cab.

"That is not a safe place for a young woman, a young man even, with night falling," the cab driver protested again. She could count the distance either by the ticker at the front or by the number of times he mentioned how sketchy her destination was.

"Nonetheless, it's where I want to go." Looking over the side of the bridge, a dark void in the city lights demarcated the abandoned warehouses.

He slowed as they left the bridge. "Really, I can't possibly drop you off there, all alone. As a father, I'd never forgive myself." He waved a hand at the picture tucked into his visor, a boy and a girl.

Mina saw the turnoff up ahead. She pulled out her gun to check how many bullets she had. "I can take care of myself."

The driver looked at her in the rear-view mirror, his eyes wide. His voice was flat when he spoke again. "I can't go in there then. I'm a father, with kids to go home to."

Mina leaned over and dropped the money for the fare plus a decent tip onto the passenger side seat. "You can let me out here then."

The driver pulled over right then and there. Luckily the road was empty, the workday traffic having disappeared. She slid the gun back into its holster as she jaywalked across the deserted street, cursing her choice of footwear when she sploshed her foot into a slushy puddle.

Mina wended her way through the buildings, trying to remember which one it was. But as she got closer to the water, she didn't have to wonder. The smell of blood and decay and death oozed from one particular building. She paused, breathing deeply to open her senses and calm her heartbeat. Then she continued forward, inch by cautious inch, until she started to see some light escaping through chinks and cracks. She moved forward, each step careful, until she heard voices.

Then Mina stopped. "Hana."

The rain started to fall, its pitter-pat masking the sound of any threats. Pressing her lips together and pulling her shoulders back, Mina continued to creep forward. Once she got to the building, even though she was already soaked through, she ducked under an overhang by a side door. Shifting, sliding along the wall, she peeked inside.

CHAPTER FORTY-TWO

Jack stumbled down the hallway, barely able to see. Blinded by fire, smoke, and the haze of pain from the stab wound. Night had driven the blade, searing hot, into his abdomen, furious at his treachery for defending Keagan. He took another step forward, amazed he wasn't dead. It was an arcane, magical blade after all. *A fragment of the blade,* he reminded himself.

Pausing, he propped himself up with one hand on the wall while the other probed the spot with tentative fingers. The wound still burned, but it was the visions in his mind's eye that left him cold. It was like the blade had sent a spike into his brain and left behind washed-out brightness splattered with crimson. Like the greyscape, sere and desolate, but drenched in blood.

They called to him, the blade and the blood. And they were both near. His stomach clenched, and he swallowed, clamping his lips together. Ahead, a soft light spilled from the kitchen. *It was there: the blade, or part of it. And food.* His gums ached as his fangs yearned to sink into flesh. He shook his head to clear it. Still half in the greyscape, the scent of blood clung to his nostrils, and the starved creature inside him convulsed. He knew he couldn't feed. Not yet...it didn't want blood; it wanted death, and he refused to give it that.

He started walking again. As he stumbled, an annoying tingle spread from the space between his collarbones. Catching himself on the door jamb, he scratched at the spot, finding a necklace that wasn't his. Lifting the golden pendant up, he tipped his head to the side. It was hideous. Grasping it in his hand, his palm started to itch, and he opened his hand again. It was almost like a cross, or an ankh, except the post was round and the top circle flattened into an oval. He closed his fingers around it again, intent on ripping it off. But as he did, a fragment of scent snaked into his nostrils amongst the odor of blood: Mina.

He let the pendant drop as he lifted his head, his attention drawn to a voice he didn't know.

"Maybe there's a code word?" The man who spoke stood in profile, his face masked by wild, brown curls. Given how close Sam stood beside him, the man obviously wasn't a stranger. Rhys sat at the opposite end of the table, while Ivan was between them on the far side. *It's true*. He did defect. In front of Jack, Finn's halo of fiery curls was unmistakable. They all seemed to accept the strange man's presence.

"No." Jack swallowed, trying to lubricate his parched throat. He pushed away thoughts of the thing that would quench his thirst, and spoke again, louder. "No."

Finn spun around as the others turned to him. "Jack! You're back." She came up, a broad smile on her face, their past forgotten, if not forgiven, at least temporarily. She threw her arms around him and squeezed, giving a big, Smith bear hug. He brought his arms between them and pushed her away, though he was too weak to do much. She backed off when he gasped. "Sorry."

Dropping his hand down, he clutched at his side, pretending it was the pain that made him gasp, not the sweet aroma of her blood so close to his lips. He forced himself to give her a small smile. "It's okay. I'm okay." He turned to the others, looking down at the box. Tipping his head to the side, he swore the thing had a heartbeat. "We need to destroy it."

"We can't even open it," Ivan said. "We don't know for sure what's in there."

"I do." Jack stared at the wood, examining the tessellated picture on the top. He squinted at the image they formed — that was new.

"We need to find the other half of the blade." Bee stepped up behind him, and he cursed himself for not knowing she was there.

He shook his head. "No." His voice was weak. "If she gets it, she destroys everything."

"If we can fuse the pieces, we can use it to destroy her." Finn's tone was lecturing as her hand came to rest on his forearm. He pulled away and reeled towards the box.

Bee grabbed him in time to stop him falling. "You should still be in bed."

"I'm okay." He waved her off as he flopped with a thump into the nearest chair. "Really." His eyes were drawn to the image on the box again, and his forehead furrowed. He brought a hand to his throat and swallowed. "We have to destroy it. It holds too much power. Her power."

"And we will," Bee said. "After we fix the blade and use it to stop Night — send her back to her prison, kill her if we have to — then we can destroy it. No one will have that power again."

He shook his head, then placed a steadying hand on the table as he threatened to topple over. "If we don't destroy it now, she will find it. Getting her power back is her consuming passion." He shifted his gaze to Finn and Ivan. "We should destroy the box too." His voice grew stronger as he felt weaker. "Any clue as to where it was and what happened to it. If we leave so much as a hint, she can torture the information out of us. You don't know what she'll do with the blade. I do. I've seen it." He went cold as visions of a blood-drenched wasteland filled his mind's eye again. Then he flushed, seeing the pitying looks of the others. All except Finn. She glared at him, her jaw set, arms crossed over her chest.

"Does that include destroying me? I know how to fuse the halves."

Jack let his mouth hang open, unsure how to answer. He was saved from answering by the uproar her statement caused.

"What?" Ivan asked. "Why didn't you say?"

"When did you figure it out?" Rhys asked, without waiting for an answer.

"You know?" Finn's hands dropped to her hips as she turned her angry eyes on Rhys.

He shrugged over his tea. "I read your father's book while you were sleeping." He took a sip from his mug. "I have to admit I don't quite understand the details."

Finn slumped down beside Jack. "It still doesn't do any good if we can't get this damned, cursed box open."

"Maybe the vampire has a point?" said the Indian man beside Sam. "Destroy it." He jerked his chin towards the fire. "Wood burns."

"The name's Jack, not vampire." Jack reached his hand, the one not clutching his side, towards the man.

"Dev."

"I don't think we need to do that." Ivan's voice was quiet but clear when he spoke, forcing those at the table to look at him. His eyes pinned Jack to his seat as he leaned over the table, reaching a hand toward him. Jack instinctively jerked away, and Ivan froze for a second, then looked him in the eyes again as his fingers lifted Mina's pendant from Jack's torso. He let it drop as Jack locked eyes with him.

"What does this god-awful thing have to do with anything?" Jack's words were slow and measured, and he peered at Ivan to see if he saw what Jack did: a round peg topped with a flattened circle, very similar to the image on the box. All it lacked was the eye.

Finn ran her fingertips over the pendant. "Where did you get that?"

"Mina." He scanned the group. "Where is she?"

"Gone." The word from Rhys turned into a cough.

"What do you mean, gone?" Bee asked. "Gone where?"

"She didn't say."

"You didn't stop her?" Bee's voice and Rhys' response — something about him being an old man and Mina a young vampire — faded into the background as Jack lifted the necklace over his head. With a strength he didn't know he had, he pulled the box towards him.

"Stop." Finn's wide eyes met his, and the argument between Bee and Rhys went silent.

"You're the one who wants to find out what's in here."

"And you wanted to destroy it, unopened. What's changed?"

"Maybe I decided you're right." He blinked slowly and shrugged, unwilling to face the real reason himself. But Finn had no problems cutting to the quick.

"It's Mina. She's gone, in danger. And you want to save her."

"She's probably just gone to her family again." Bee stood beside him, hands on her hips, but her expression made it clear she didn't believe her own words. "Or still trying to save her friend."

"Her friend." He locked Bee's gaze with his own. "The one who's body was stolen by Night."

Bee's mouth was already open, but whatever she planned to say turned into a small gasp. "She's gone after Night."

"Alone."

Jack slid the key into the pupil of the eye on the box's lid and turned.

The box clicked, and Ivan forced himself to exhale when no vile magic oozed out the sides.

Jack placed his fingers gently on the sides then looked up at Finn. "Your box, you should do the honours." He shifted it towards her.

"Right." She arched an eyebrow. "You just think it's booby trapped."

"I—"

Finn's full-bellied laugh almost brought a smile to Ivan's face before she turned her attention to the box. She ran her fingers lightly over the top then along the sides before lifting up. Nothing happened. She let out a growl. "Infernal contraption!"

"I think it's brilliant." Seema stepped forward from where she'd been lurking by the fire. Coming to stand beside Finn, she placed her hands on the lid, running her fingers over the lines of the image, until her thumbs rested at either side of the eye. Then she pushed. With a soft pop and a light sigh, the box cracked open, letting out a hiss of stale air. "The eye. That's what Jack said."

The room was silent for a long minute, the only sound the crackling of the fire. Then Finn lifted the lid back in one swift move, exposing the contents. Bright flashes dazzled Ivan. Instinctively his eyes squeezed shut. When nothing happened, he opened his eyes again. It was only the kitchen lights hitting the golden metal inside: the other half of the Blade of the Sun. It had kept a keen edge hidden away in the cursed box.

"Magical," Finn whispered, almost as if reading his thoughts. But her eyes were focused on the pieces in the box, her fingertips hovering over them.

"What do you need to fuse the blade?" Bee asked, her eyes narrowing as they homed in on Finn. Ivan stepped up behind the Smith, crossing his arms over his chest so his biceps flexed tight in his shirt. Bee flicked her gaze at him but seemed unfazed.

"I..." Finn stammered. "I need my father."

Ivan paced back and forth down the hall, accompanied by the werecat, its...her tail twitching. He strode from Bee, who squatted at the foot of the stairs, to Jack, who sat slumped against the wall across from the room Keagan was in. Turning on his heels, he faced Sam and the archaeologist, who stood on either side of the door, looking in. Rhys stood at the end of the bed, as Finn sat down beside her father. Keagan hadn't stirred at all.

Ivan paced the hall again, then stopped, irritated with himself for being so agitated. He stepped into the room. Finn talked to Keagan, saying in soothing tones that he needed to wake up. She took his large hand in hers and squeezed. "What am I supposed to do?"

"You know what you need to do." Rhys stood beside Finn. "It's in your father's book."

Finn turned to glare at Rhys, and Ivan followed her gaze. He stayed silent but went to stand beside her.

"There's nothing there." She turned back to her father as the healer wiped Keagan's forehead with a damp cloth. "It says to magic the magic blade. I can't."

"Yes, you can."

"I don't have the skills." Finn stood up as the werecat jumped up on the bed.

"It's not about skills." Rhys stroked the cat's head.

"Fine, I don't have the power." Finn strode towards Rhys, her hands clenched. For a second, Ivan thought she was going to hit the old man, but she turned to pace the small room. "I'm not magical. Why do you think I tinker like I do? Why I learned to hack into computers? I don't have the Smith magic my father has."

"That's the lie he told you?"

Finn's lips pressed together. "It's not a lie. I can feel it."

"I'm not sure you can feel a lack of magic."

She glared at him. "And what do you know, human?"

The healer gasped, jumping back as far as she could with her wrist caught in the strong grip of a Smith. Ivan's gaze went from her face to Keagan's, as the man's wild eyes roved the room. Landing on the healer's frightened face, the Smith let go of the wrist. She scooted back so fast she knocked over the bowl of water on the nightstand, then fled the room.

Finn slid into the chair beside the bed again, and Keagan's eyes came to rest on her, settling there. "Be one."

Ivan took a step forward, worried about the wildness that still clouded Keagan's vision, and placed his hand on Finn's shoulder.

"I know." Finn leaned toward Keagan. "We need to make the blade one." Her shoulders came to scrunch up by her ears. Ivan squeezed her shoulder and they relaxed as she let out her breath. "But I don't know how."

"No, you don't." Keagan struggled with every word, as if relearning what each one meant and how to string them together to express as thought.

"I heard he's awake." Bee skidded into the room followed by the healer, who'd gotten over her initial fright.

Ivan nodded. "Not making much sense." Keagan's lips pursed as he glanced at Ivan. Apparently, his listening comprehension was fine.

"You don't need to know." Keagan's voice was raspy.

"We do." Bee came to stand at his other side. "We're facing disease and death."

Keagan shook his head. "Don't need to know." He lifted a shaking finger to Finn's forehead. "Just do."

"But I don't have the power to do," Finn said. "I don't have the magic. I'm just a regular smith, however much I've been your apprentice since, well, since Mom passed."

Keagan scrunched his eyes shut as a coughing fit took hold, then opened them again. "You do." Finn started to protest. Keagan placed his large hand on hers, which was almost as large.

"Let him speak." Ivan leaned closer to Finn's ear.

Keagan glanced at him, his expression unreadable. "You're a Smith. Have more power." Finn began to pull away, but he gripped her hand. "Unity. It wants to be one. Bring the pieces together." He took a deep shuddering. "It will heal itself in your hands."

"That's it?" Finn said. "But that's...."

"Magic," Bee said.

"But I don't have...."

Keagan shook his head slowly, his eyelids fluttering. Then he collapsed back on the bed, eyes closed.

"Da!" Finn stood up to lean over him but was pushed away by the diminutive healer.

"He's fine," the healer said. "Just sleeping now."

Seema jumped off the bed and morphed into a woman, a process Ivan still couldn't bear to watch, with bones moving under skin and flesh reforming itself.

"What next?" Seema asked.

"The same as before," Bee said. "We wrest the other half of the blade from Night, bring the pieces together with magic Finn doesn't think she possesses, destroy Night. Then make it so no one can use the blade to bring her back again."

"Sounds simple," Dev said as he stepped over the threshold. "Do we have any idea where Night is?"

"Where's Mina?" Seema asked. "If she's gone after Night...." She shrugged.

"Certainly not where she said she was going," Rhys said.

"The warehouse."

Ivan spun around at hearing his own thoughts echoed in Jack's voice. He was a sickly pale green, but was dressed in street clothes, a gun on his hip. "The warehouse."

Bee looked up from her phone and huffed. "The warehouse. Over the river."

CHAPTER FORTY-THREE

Mina breathed in deeply, her back pressed against the damp concrete wall of the warehouse. Drawing her gun and trying to keep her twitchy finger away from the trigger, she slid up to peer through the corner of the window. Hana hadn't spoken for...too long. As she'd crept around the building, trying to suss out the best way into the warehouse without getting them both killed, her sister-in-law had kept up a steady stream of Korean curses Mina was shocked the woman knew. Finally, Mina found this door held slightly ajar by a severed, decaying hand that had gotten in the way. She swallowed back the bile and avoided looking down, instead turning her head to the small window. But she couldn't really make out what was going on through all the grime.

Once again, she checked her phone, which she'd muted entirely, to see if Bee had replied to her bat signal. Nothing. Mina started entering another message but stopped. If Bee hadn't responded to the previous ones, another one wouldn't do any good. She slipped her phone back into her pocket and grasped her gun with both hands.

Once again, she wished she'd come better armed. She only had the one gun, loaded with silver rounds with no lead bullets to take down gargoyles, and a couple of blades tucked into her boots. And the obsidian blade in her pocket that she planned to trade for Hana's life. Her hand fell to her right side; it suddenly seemed an unwise bargain.

Breathing deeply, Mina prepared to charge into the open space when an inhuman howl sounded, stopping her mid-movement. Her heart racing in her ears, it took her a second to realize the sound came from Hana. The noise propelled her forward, through the door and into a scene she couldn't compute.

A werewolf snarled, another whimpered. A gargoyle limped in a wary circle. Night, still looking like Cam, bled from a cut across her cheek. Hana rocked from foot to foot in a half-crouch in the centre of the circle, a thin stiletto in one hand, a short dagger in the other. Both were bloody.

"Who's next?" Her lip curled, and she shuffled in a small arc to face her attackers, favouring her right leg. A dark spot on her thigh smelled like blood. Mina shoved the door open and ran up beside her, coming to a teetering stop as Hana swung towards her.

"Whoa!" Mina caught a glimpse of the large abrasion on Hana's chin and the bruise on her cheek, before she spun around to face the other creatures emerging from the shadows, some the likes of which Mina had never even imagined. The most numerous were spider-like, their carapaces a gleaming slate grey and their many legs ending in sharp points. She pressed her back to Hana's. "I'm here to rescue you."

"I could have used that an hour ago," Hana stated. "Now I could use the cavalry. I don't suppose you have backup lurking outside."

Mina shook her head as Hana's back pressed against her. "Nope, it's up to us to save the world."

"I'd settle for ourselves tonight," Hana said. "Live to fight another day and all."

Mina couldn't really argue. Death loomed over them as more creatures emerged, encircling them in an ever-tightening noose.

A number of the beasts were also crowding around Night, weaving in front of her, forming an undulating shield. A pit formed in Mina's stomach. She knew what she had to do: kill Night even if it meant killing Cam.

She raised her gun and took a couple of pot shots at a creature and its friends that were slinking towards them along the rafters up above, then she lowered it, taking the fraction of a second necessary to aim and relax the tension in her torso. Then she pulled the trigger.

At least that's what she intended to do, but she paused when she saw Cam's face peer at her with an expression of hurt and confusion through the shield of creatures. It took her a second to remember appearances were deceiving, and this creature wore Cam's face like a mask. A wicked smile, ripe with the promise of pain and eventual death, cracked open the facade. Eyes, all black, stared at her from Cam's face. Mina raised the gun again and took aim. Her finger twitched to squeeze the trigger, just as one of the creatures dropped down on her from above.

Hana shouted, then howled another Korean curse, but her sister-in-law was no longer against her back. Instead, long, sharp fingernails raked her face as the thing that had fallen on her reached around to scratch her eyes out. Mina pressed her eyes tightly closed, dropped down into a somersault, and rolled over the creature that didn't want to let go. At least not until all her weight landed on it.

Mina continued her somersault, ignoring the angry claws that scrambled at her flesh, popping up with her gun held steady in both hands, aimed at Night. This time she squeezed the trigger without hesitation. The sound of the gun was followed by a blinding flash of light and pinging. When Mina blinked, Night was a few steps closer, her head tilted and right eyebrow up, peering at the golden half-blade in her right hand. It took Mina a fraction of a second to figure out that Night had somehow deflected the bullet with the blade. A nanosecond later, Mina took advantage of Night's distraction and fired again.

She squeezed the trigger. More light, more zinging, but this time Mina watched Night flick the blade to match where the bullet was going to impact. Again, she fired. Again, Night twitched, and the blade became a shield.

Again and again. Each time with the same result. It was Mina's growl that filled the warehouse this time as her fangs came out. Night sidled closer with each shot, a smile in her eyes that didn't reach her lips.

Mina squeezed the trigger again, thinking at this short distance Night might not have a chance to react. The gun clicked.

Jack kept close to Bee as they crept up to the warehouse. Somewhere in the dark, in feline form, Seema scampered, checking out scent trails. But Jack didn't need a cat's nose to know they were surrounded by wolves. And he didn't need a cat's eyes to see there was a battle raging in the warehouse. Mina was in trouble.

Bee stopped and he moved to push past her.

"What do you think you're doing?" she hissed.

"Going to help." He took another step forward.

Bee stopped him with a hand on his wrist. "And just how are you going to do that? You can barely stand upright."

Jack paused but didn't protest. Bee took the lead, going a few steps further before stopping again, her hand coming to his chest.

"Do you see that?" She turned to look at him. "Those things?"

Jack peered into the light of the open bay door on the warehouse loading dock. "The spidery things?"

Bee nodded. "What in holy hell are they?"

"Does it matter?"

Bee looked from him to the scene before them. "No. She's family, even if she doesn't want to be."

"It's not that she doesn't want to be. It's just...she still has another family."

Bee's voice was sad when she spoke. "She needs to die."

"She knows. But hopefully not tonight." He sighed. "Right now, we —" He stopped and spun around when a pebble rolled behind them. A human Seema morphed out of the darkness. Bee tossed a bag at her, out of which she drew a black catsuit and slipped it on.

"We need a plan." Seema barely even lowered her voice. If she had, he wouldn't have heard her over the noise from the warehouse. A Korean curse filled the air.

"That's what I was about to say." Bee turned back to face the warehouse.

"Were you also about to say the place is infested with koemijari?" Seema wrapped her long hair up into a bun on the top of her head and fastened it with some mechanism he couldn't see.

"That's what those things are?" Bee drew her gun and nodded at something over Jack's shoulder. He turned to check out what she was looking at as he drew his own weapon. Finn, Ivan, Dev and Sam strode up through the darkness, with something wrapped in a scarf in Finn's hand.

"Is that what I think it is?" Seema stepped up to Finn. "Let's see."

Fin clutched it to her chest. "I'm the Smith," she hissed. "I'm the one with the power to unite the pieces. Or so my fever-addled father says."

"Sorry." Seema took a step back. "I just wanted to take a look. My family were its guardians for centuries."

Finn peered at Seema before sliding down behind the concrete dock and unwinding the scarf.

They all ducked to join her as a bullet came flying past them, hitting the ground a few feet away.

Then the shots stopped. Jack inched his head above the dock to peek into the warehouse. His heart skipped a beat then dropped into his stomach.

CHAPTER FORTY-FOUR

"**B**ugger." Mina looked at the gun, then threw it since she didn't have any ammo to reload, beaning one of the arachnoid creatures that flanked Night.

"Mina, tuck and roll." She heard Hana's shout, but knew her sister-in-law had no better weapons than she did. Instead of ducking properly, she moved to draw the blades out of her boots. But Night was too fast. With moves that certainly weren't Cam's, Night kicked the daggers out of her hands before she got a good grip on them. Spinning around to face her attacker, Mina remembered she still had one weapon left: the blade of Night, which she'd planned to trade for Hana's life. Her hand slipped into her pocket and her fingers curled around the obsidian shard. The wail of voices rang through her blood as she brought it out into the light of the warehouse. Its facets glinted sharply, and a trill travelled through her stomach at the raw avarice on Night's face.

"How thoughtful." An eyebrow arched. "You brought me my blade." Night took a casual step back, arms opening.

Mina lunged, and a creature dropped onto her head, trying to stab glistening fangs through the leather of her jacket. She shook the arm in an attempt to fling it off, but, cat-like, it landed on its feet and scurried towards her. Without thinking, she dropped to a knee and drove the obsidian blade through its carapace.

Green liquid oozed out, bubbling around the dagger. The voices of the souls in the weapon quelled at that, but Mina didn't have time to consider why. She had barely pulled the dagger out when a golden half-blade connected with the flesh of her throat. It didn't break the skin. Instead Night applied upward pressure, scraping the keen edge along Mina's neck like a razor until the flat was touching her chin. Her skin tingled where it touched.

"Stand up." Night's voice was reminiscent of Cam's, but with too many sounds layered on top, as if echoed through a poor, mixed up phone connection.

Mina swallowed, the skin of her throat moving over the blade. She debated telling Night what she could go do with herself but decided against it.

That's the old Mina. This *Mina needs to figure a way out of this*. At the edge of her senses, there was music, and she blinked, not believing her ears. Woodwinds and brass. Jack. And where there was Jack, the rest of the conclave was likely not far away. If she closed her eyes, she thought she could pick out Bee's song: a metallic tick-tack. But she snapped them open again. She needed to end this before they charged into a massacre.

"What shall I do with you, thorn in my side?" Her adversary walked slowly around her, trailing the blade a hair's breadth above her skin.

"Let me go?" Mina arched an eyebrow. Night stepped in front of her, shifting her grip to keep the blade close to Mina's neck and its arteries.

"Do you really think flippancy is what's called for?" Night leaned close, her voice whispering over the hairs on Mina's neck, her breath holding a tinge of sickly sweet decay. "Give it to me and I'll let them live."

Mina clenched her jaw to keep herself from giving a flippant retort in response. She didn't need to ask what Night meant by *it*. At a scream to her left, her head turned involuntarily. Hana was held down by a triad of arachnoid beasts, her feet kicking, restrained but not subdued. A scattering of throwing stars glittered around her — maybe Hana had been better armed than Mina realized. Then Mina saw the pointed appendage driven into Hana's shoulder.

"Eyes front."

Mina flicked her gaze back to Night, debating what to do. If she didn't give Night the blade, she and Hana would both die, and Hana's death would be painful. If she gave Night the blade, they were both still dead, as were thousands of others.

Out the corners of her eyes, she cast around for some weapon she could use if she gave up the black blade, remembering Bee's lesson that sometimes all you have is a stick. But there was nothing, not even a stone. Her own daggers had disappeared amongst the scrabble of pointed legs. The only weapons were those Night herself wore strapped around her waist — she wasn't relying on the Blade of the Sun alone. But she was being very good at keeping Mina at arms length. Well, arms length plus a blade.

"I don't like to ask twice." This time Hana's cry ricocheted off the rafters, and, glancing her way again, Mina saw green ooze dripping from the fangs of one of the creatures, poised over Hana's belly.

"Let her go." Mina stalled for time to come up with a plan.

"Why would I do that?"

"A sign of good faith?" Mina looked up into eyes that were oily black, tinged with swirls of green. "You have me at the knife's edge." Mina shivered then narrowed her eyes and steeled her spine. "You're not going to spare me either way."

"I might." Night dragged the blade a little further up Mina's neck, forcing her to stand tall. "If you bow down before me."

"Kind of hard to do with a knife at my neck." The sharp edge moved away from her neck by the merest fraction, but Mina still didn't breathe deeply. "I'd rather die than bow down before someone who enjoys torture and making the powerless squirm before murdering them."

The knife twitched, and a sharp pain blossomed as it nicked Mina's throat. She gasped, her body taking an involuntary breath at the sensation. Night drew a line of blood around Mina's throat as she walked behind her. Mina's eyes narrowed as movement caught her attention, but then she was distracted as Night leaned close to whisper in her ear.

"Then you'll —" Night was stopped short, distracted from what she planned to say, though Mina was pretty sure she could guess.

Hana froze when she saw the knife at Mina's throat. A part of her wanted to hurt Mina, to make her pay for the pain she'd brought to the children, herself, to Dale, by bringing this evil into their lives. But she didn't want Night to win. And she certainly didn't want Mina to die.

The Necrophagus, the arachnoid creatures — koemijari, she recalled from her grandfather's lessons — and the sibilant, scaly lamia all focused on Night. A thousand eyes gleamed with hunger. Hana shifted a step to her right, then another, pausing between each step to reset the tableau for anyone who might glance her way: let them think she'd always been standing where she was now. She shifted again, ending up behind the vampire Lin. Flowing down to the floor, she disturbed the dust, and a sneeze grew in her sinuses. Pursing her lips, she looked up into the light, trying to squash the sneeze.

A pair of multi-faceted eyes peered down at her from the rafters. She slid her hand along the concrete floor, inch by inch, as she watched the creature to see what it would do. It turned its head. She wrapped her fingers around the object of her quest: one of her throwing stars, littered around Lin's feet. The creature overhead tipped its head the other way. She inched back, flicking her eyes between it and the tableau at the centre of the scene.

Once she was out from under the creature, she would have to shift her attention entirely. But she only needed a few seconds. She focused on Mina. In that moment, Mina's eyes homed in on her before looking away, shifting her weight away from Hana's position.

That slight movement was a bonus, opening up a larger target area. Hana sent the star spinning. It lodged in Night's forehead. Thick, crimson blood welled up from the wound and dripped down her face.

Night tried to look at the weapon, eyes crossing and eyebrows pulling together as if she couldn't quite believe it, and Hana waited for the woman to fall. Instead, she took the Blade of the Sun into her right hand, still pressing it tight to Mina's throat, and reached up with her other hand to pull the star out. She held it up to her face, turning it in the light.

Then she looked at Hana, tipping her head. "You. Meddling Hunter." Her eyes narrowed. "You're persistent. I thought I got rid of your interference when I killed your husband."

Hana froze again. Her brain struggled to catch up with what her heart knew in that instant: Dale was dead because of her. Her hands went to her knees as she doubled over, wanting to retch, but all that came up were dribbles of bile. Luckily, she knew she wouldn't have long to suffer in the knowledge that she'd been the one to lead Night to Dale, not Mina.

With Night's focus elsewhere, Mina took her chance. Mimicking Hana's movement, she started to flow down to the ground, as if she were fainting. On her way down, she grabbed the arm around her neck and shifted into a sideways step, pulling the arm back, twisting the hand around. Night turned from Hana to her, the smile on her face fading, replaced by fury. In her eyes, Mina saw death and destruction.

Mina didn't hesitate. She tore the golden blade from Night's grasp and, before she had a chance to call on any hellish magic or mundane reinforcements, Mina flung the weapon away, a Hail Mary with no one to catch it. Following the momentum of her turn, Mina found herself face-to-face with Lin, whose expression shifted from a snarl of anger to confusion and back.

"This is death, then?" Mina held her hands up, palms forward, and waited for the bite of Lin's katana through her torso. Lin took a step towards her, the katana going further back, preparing to strike.

Mina closed her eyes, then opened them, realizing she wanted to face death. As Lin's sword descended, Mina was yanked backwards. She had a split second of hope that someone had pulled her to safety before she noticed the tendrils of magic around her waist. *This is new.* In front of her, frustration warped Lin's face, obviously unhappy about having her coup de grâce stolen from her. Behind Mina, Night pulled her tight into her chest.

"You think I have no more weapons?" Night's voice rasped over the hairs by her ear and her fingers wrapped around Mina's throat. "What happens when a dracul is bitten by a demon? By *the* demon?"

Mina's eyes widened in a moment of comprehension a second before the teeth sunk into her neck. She let out a soft mew of shock, mixed with pain. Night's teeth were not like a vampire's. Though she couldn't see them, with Night behind her, they felt longer, wider.

Somewhere off to the side, someone spoke her name and her eyebrows pulled together: it sounded like her brother. But he was dead. *So this is death?* Her lips moved to form Dale's name but no sound came. Grey crept into the edge of her vision. She focused on the only things she could see: Lin, and Hana behind her, eyes wet with unshed tears.

Lin's face was a mask of ivory as she stepped forward. "Guess what, you don't turn into a nosferatu. You turn into something much worse." She glanced quickly away from Mina's face, over her shoulder. "Much better."

Mina's knees went weak, and her free hand clutched at the arm around her neck. The fingers of her other hand, sticky with blood, clutched something. Even in her fogged state, she recognized it: the obsidian blade, eater of sacrificed souls. Still, she clung to it, something solid in the encroaching grey void. In the end it wasn't enough.

She heard her name again as she slid to the ground, landing on her side. Then all sound stopped. Jack's face, contorted in pain and rage, stared at her. *How did he get here?* The scene behind him crystallized: the conclave fighting for their lives.

"No," she whispered, a tear falling from the corner of her eye. "Why did you come?"

Then Night leaned over her, blocking the others from her view. Shoved onto her back, Mina looked over Night's shoulder, peering out the window at the purpled sky of the pre-dawn. She opened her mouth to speak, but then her back arched and her world went black.

CHAPTER FORTY-FIVE

Ivan spun around, searching for something to use as a weapon in the melee around him, even just a stick. They were happy to bring him to battle but still not willing to give him a gun. To his right, Jack battled like a berserker. To his left, Seema spun and whirled in fluid movements, hands and face splattered with green and red. He hoped Finn was somewhere far behind, out of the path of immediate harm, but at that moment, a spark of golden red flickered in the corner of his eye. It seemed like only a minute ago when the warehouse had gone silent, causing Ivan to freeze in shock and move too slowly to stop Jack as he rushed headlong inside. Now he was surrounded by many-legged creatures — *koemijari*, Seema had called them — with glistening, hard carapaces and grey eyes that glinted like mica-flecked rock. And him without even a dagger to fight them with.

A slate grey koemijari charged at him. He spun into a side kick. But the arachnoid creature was as spry as an acrobat with its multitude of limbs, and leapt over his leg, tumbling in the air to land on its sharp feet behind him. It had no weapons to speak of — it was a weapon, with those needle-like legs and fangs like a raptor's talons. It sprang at him but made the mistake of announcing its intentions, wiggling its rear like a cat. Ivan met its face with a fist, then cursed as eight legs scratched his arm, trying to hold on while being forced away by his punch.

Hearing a scratching above, he glanced up to see two grey orbs peering down at him, glinting with gleeful malevolence. The creature's brethren swarmed around it, some with a mixture of blood and green goo oozing from their fangs. He dove out of the way, sliding along the warehouse floor face first, as the koemijari dropped down. In between the flash of feet was a flicker of gold. Dread filled his stomach then a shot of adrenalin coursed through his system.

"Finn." He scrambled amongst the feet and flashing blades. But it wasn't Finn he found. He froze for a second then snatched up the other half of the Blade of the Sun. Looking up to see who had witnessed him taking Night's prize, his eyes met Seema's. He scurried back, barely missing another creature descending from above. It glared at him. Another one came down on top of him, stabbing a leg through his own. He grit his teeth to keep from howling: the less attention anyone paid to him the better. He reached around to try to dislodge the koemijari with his free hand. Then he blinked as goo oozed over his face.

"Go, take it to her. I'll cover you." Seema held an elegantly arced blade in her hands. The one that had killed Angelos. He cast his glance around, sussing out where Finn was. He didn't have to look far.

"She doesn't have it. Night doesn't have it." Finn's cheeks were pale — even her freckles seemed paler — as her gaze roved around frantically. "It's not here. We're lost." She still clutched the wrapped blade in one hand, but the other held her strange weapon, a cross between a hammer and a meat tenderizer, with a wicked spike at the end. All of it was covered with the sticky residue of death.

He lay a bloody palm on her cheek, forcing her to look at him. "I have it." She tipped her head, her eyebrows coming together in a question. "She must have dropped it," he continued, grabbing her arm and pulling her into the shadows at the edge of the warehouse.

Finn cursed again, her focus on the two halves of the circular blade as she spoke the words she'd memorized from her father's book in a hushed, hurried chant. She appeared oblivious to the chaos around her. Fortunately, Ivan wasn't, and used her strange weapon to bash a creature mid-air before it dropped on top of Finn, sending it into the nearest pillar with a splat.

"Where are they all coming from?" Seema shouted, dropping down to her knees on the other side of the Smith. Ivan shook his head, and glanced around, looking for some portal. The waves of arachnoid creatures were slowing, but not as fast as they should be. Not fast enough.

A few yards away, Bee fought one of the last werewolves still standing. Ivan recognized her, even in her lupine form. The one who'd betrayed Angelos and been at Night's side from the beginning. From the very beginning, helping to slaughter his clan hundreds of years ago. His fingers itched to join the fray, twitching with a hunger for revenge. But Bee had the werewolf on the defensive, and the limp in the lupine's left leg told him the fight wouldn't last long. He had a more important goal, to protect Finn and Seema as they struggled to stitch the arcane weapon together with some metallurgic magic. Another spidery creature skittered closer, and he drove the spike through its carapace with a crunch. He decided he liked Finn's weapon, and glanced back at his charges to check if they were okay.

"Argh!" Finn shook her fingers and blew on them, dropping the halves of the blade as blue light arced between them.

"Go slowly." Seema took the pieces from her. "Say each word."

Finn's eyes roved the scene around her. Seema grabbed her head, turning it to look in her eyes. "Focus."

Ivan bashed another koemijari with the meat tenderizer. He turned back to Finn. "Listen to her. She's old."

Finn nodded and picked up the blades again. Her lips moved, but whatever she said was drowned out by the battle roaring around him. And he almost missed the moment the two sides stitched together in a line of golden light. He'd expected a thunderclap, a bolt of lightning. But there was nothing.

Until a second later when it shone like a spear of sunlight. Ivan stared at it with a mix of reverence and dread. His heart stopped and the battle sounds muted. Then a koemijari dropped onto the floor right in front of Finn, grey-green slime dripping from its fangs, and he prepared to smash it like he had the others.

"Stop." A crisp, multi-tonal voice rang like crystal over the melee. The combatant's stopped their skirmishes, whichever side they were on, including Ivan.

Everyone around Hana froze, as if there was magic in the word. Everyone except Jack, who took a step towards Night. Even Hana was rooted to the spot, still on her hands and knees. Her breathing had settled, but she tasted bile in her throat.

"Stop." Night's voice was quieter, directed at a specific person now. Mina lay at her feet, and Night's forearm twitched, causing the ordinary sword she held to Mina's torso to glint green in the light. "Or she dies."

Hana didn't need to be a vampire to know it was Mina's blood that dripped from Night's lips. And she was pretty sure the blood smeared across Mina's jaw wasn't a good thing. Another wave of nausea passed through her. Without Mina's help, she didn't expect to survive the night. Just then a shard of light pierced her eye. Glancing towards a broken window, there was a warm cast to the sky — technically she already had. But she didn't expect she'd get off on a technicality.

Except whatever magic Night was working is unfinished. She scanned from face to face, frozen in shock or fear. Or adoration. Her eyes fell on Seema, and with a jolt, realized she held the Blade of the Sun. It was whole, but she obviously had no idea how to use it, despite her ancestors being its guardians. *Night no longer has the Blade of the Sun.*

Hope surged in Hana's veins as she pushed herself to her knees. Maybe, just maybe, she could save Liam and Maggie. Ahead of her, Jack took another step closer to Night. Meanwhile, Mina's back arched, lifting off the floor. Jack charged forward, and the room started moving again, but Hana focused on the werecat.

"Psst." The woman glanced at her. "Throw it here," she mouthed. Either Seema didn't hear or didn't want to listen. Instead, she turned back towards Night. Hana's eyes tracked the werecat, and she saw Mina had shifted onto her side. Her eyes were downcast, her movements were herky-jerky and her skin the colour of ash, but she was alive. And Hana found she was glad for that. Though she didn't have time to dwell on that emotion, as the spidery creatures started closing in again.

Far to the right, Jack was still trying to get to Mina, but the gargoyle blocked his path. He howled and raised his sword to deliver a powerful blow. Hana saw Lin hidden behind the grey creature and shouted. But her warning was too late, even if it hadn't been drowned by the melee. Lin's sword drove into Jack's torso. Hana watched as Jack looked down at his chest and Lin stepped around behind him, bloody tip of her katana pointed down. She couldn't hear what either of them said, but Jack shook his head before he slipped down to his knees.

Brought back to the present, she turned to Seema, determined to get the werecat to give her the blade. She'd used ones like it before, under her grandmother's strict tutelage. Then she watched in horror as Seema prepared to throw it. Lunging towards the woman, she tried to stop her, but was too far away. She cringed as she landed on her hands and knees beside the werecat. But her grimace wasn't because of the hard concrete: the woman's technique was wrong. Her aim was true, but the throw had no power behind it. The circle wobbled in flight before it clattered to the floor in front of Mina.

Mina's eyes opened at the sound, and Hana's breath caught in her throat. The eyes that looked out were completely black, lid to lid, like they'd been injected with India ink. Mina reached out and lay her fingers on the gleaming object, caught in a ray of sunlight. Then Night stepped forward to block the daylight.

"Give it to us." Night's voice was commanding, underlaid with the power of a thousand souls. Hana almost got up to do her bidding. Almost.

"Mina, throw it here," she said instead, her voice a whisper. Mina had moved to her knees, her hands out, palms up, the blade laying flat on them, like an offering on a platter. She tipped her head as she looked at the blade, as if unsure what it was. It certainly looked as much like a crown as a weapon.

Beside Hana, Seema shouted as Night took a step closer to Mina. "Throw me the blade."

Mina glanced at her, then her eyes passed over Hana before making their way back to the blade, sunlight glinting off it. Mina's face took on an expression of reverence. Her jaw relaxed into a smile, fangs full out. Mina knelt before Night, reached out with the blade in one hand, while the other went to the floor beside her.

Hana's gut twisted as Night reached forward to pluck the blade from Mina's fingers.

Mina blinked, trying to dispel the spots of light blinding her. As her vision cleared, she saw the golden blade in her hand. She felt nothing. Emptiness. Lifelessness. But she knew what she had to do. Tipping her head down as a sign of respect, she dropped to her knee and held the blade out in one hand, watching Night's toes come closer.

Then she turned in her crouch and spun the blade towards Hana, hoping her sister-in-law could get it out of the air without her hand being sliced to pieces. She didn't have a chance to see what happened, as green tendrils lashed around her neck and pulsed with burning magic. Her fingers clenched, wrapping around a cold, biting shard of stone.

"You think you can stop me now?" Night took a step closer, and Mina shivered at the freezing void in her eyes. "You've already given me what I need. What I've craved for thousands of years." Her voice rumbled, as if it was a chorus that spoke. "I'm free of that hideous cage, I can walk in the day, —" she nodded at the window, "— and I have enough of my power back to crush you all like insects." Night flicked her hand, turning Mina towards the bright sun shooting through the window, forcing her to close her eyes. "And you have none."

Stars speckled Mina's eyes as she struggled to breathe. "No," she said between ragged gasps. In response, tendrils wrapped around her torso as well. Mina silently cursed as her arms were bound to her sides. She watched out the corner of her eye as Hana threw the blade with more finesse than Seema had. It sliced through the air with barely a wobble.

The blade hit its target, and Night staggered forward a step. The tendrils constricting Mina loosened, and she sighed with relief, but that caused the lariat around her neck to tighten. However, Night was still distracted, and Mina shifted, contorting to work her arm out of the grasp of tentacles. Then she froze as Night laughed, high and wild. "You think a little ring of metal can stop me? It's not powerful when wielded by the powerless."

"No, but maybe this is," Mina said, barely a gasp against the noose around her neck, as she stabbed the obsidian blade into Night's chest. Night peered down at the blade, her lips trying to form words, but none came. Only a howling, whining scream that rose out of her throat as black tendrils streamed from the blade to envelop her. She clawed at them with her hands, drawing blood from her own cheeks and arms. Mina gulped in air as Night's magic dissipated and the tentacles that constricted her disappeared.

Finally, the words came. "No." Night shook her head, and hatred flashed in her eyes, promising death and pain. "Not again."

Mina held her breath, expected to be smote by some final display of power. Then the black ooze completed its job, swallowing Night completely, and the blade reabsorbed it, clattering to the ground. She spun as a howl erupted behind her. The spidery koemijari were melting into puddles of viscous, shiny liquid, the same colour as the obsidian.

Then her eyes fell on Jack, who lay on the concrete, eyes closed, skin the same shade as the floor. Blood had soaked through his clothes from a wound across his torso. Mina slid to her knees in front of him, and gathered him in her arms, cradling him. The others paused an arm's length away. She glared up at them, expecting wariness — after Night's bite, she was no longer a dracul, but she knew she wasn't nosferat either. She was something new. Something different. But it wasn't wariness she saw; it was concern.

She peered down at his face, which didn't even flinch when she moved him. She was sure she was looking at death.

"Please don't." She ran a bloody hand over his ashen cheek.

Then his eyes fluttered open. "Don't what?" His voice was a hoarse whisper. "I don't plan on doing anything at the moment. For some reason, my chest hurts."

Mina's jaw dropped and her eyes teared up. The delirium of death. "You...it...." He coughed, and she realized it was a laugh.

His bloody hand came up to her face. "Might have something to do with the great, gaping wound from Lin's katana. I know. But it wasn't silvered. No poison. I just need a really big drink."

A smile rose unbidden on her face. She pulled him closer to kiss him.

He gasped. "Careful. Maybe we could get some help."

Mina lowered her head as much as she could without moving him. She pressed her lips to his, goo splattered though they both were, then pulled away to look him in the eye. "Maybe we could."

CHAPTER FORTY-SIX

Mina knew she was late for class, but still couldn't open her eyes. Her limbs were leaden, her brain foggy, and her mouth dry. *What did Cam get me into last night?* Whatever it was, it wasn't a good idea. Not when she had school today and needed to meet Dale later at Mr. Whitaker's office. Through her heavy eyelids, she sensed a shadow loom over her. When it came closer, she reached a hand out to snatch it.

"Ow!"

Hana? Mina's eyes shot open. She blinked rapidly, adjusting to the dim light and trying to orient herself. She was in a small room, under the Sanctuary. Her room. She looked at the wrist she held and followed it up to look into Hana's face. The memory of last night came back to her. At least she assumed it was last night. Her eyes drew together, and she pressed her lips tight as a sob rose in her throat. There was no dancing, no beers, no strangers with amber eyes.

She was a vampire. Dale and Cam were both dead. And Jack was grievously injured. Again.

But she was still alive. And Hana was alive. She loosened her grip on her sister-in-law's wrist. "Sorry, I was dreaming."

Hana nodded. "They say your boyfriend will live."

"He's —" Mina started. She wasn't sure what Jack was to her, but he wasn't just a friend. Though she couldn't imagine a happily ever after for vampires: forever was a very long time. "Thanks." Mina shifted to get up out of the chair she'd flopped into, having given Hana the bed.

"I need to get home," Hana said, turning her back to Mina. But she didn't move to leave and, after a second, she looked at Mina. "You can come if you want." Mina's first instinct was to decline; she needed to cut ties with her family. But the thought gave her pause. One last opportunity to see Liam and Maggie, and probably June, since she was babysitting them.

"Okay."

Mina stood on the stoop of Hana and Dale's house, staring at the door. The snow had stopped, and the yard was an unbroken blanket of crystalline white sparkling in the morning sun.

On the other side of the stoop, Hana stood with her hands tucked under her arms. "You don't have to come inside if you don't want to."

Mina glanced at the door. She'd likely never see inside again. She stuffed her hands in her pockets, causing her shoulders to shrug. "I wanted to make sure it was still here. That everything really is okay." Next door, the neighbour's chihuahua started barking, and a movement drew her eyes to the fence. A large, orange-striped cat picked its way deliberately along the top, shaking its paw as it dislodged tufts of snow: Seema. She'd apparently adopted Mina as her new person, and was still more comfortable as cat than woman. And Mina had grown accustomed to her presence, a key member of her preternatural family. Then she glanced at Hana, with her mad fighting skills and her facility with weapons, and a small smile played at her lips. Maybe all families were slightly abnormal. Though Dale had been a perfectly normal older brother. She swallowed hard. "I need to die. I'll squirrel away some money then —" The door opened, and Mina stopped.

Aunt June stood in the entry, hands on her hips, forehead scrunched and her lips in a frown. "Are you two going to come inside and get cleaned up, or are you going to continue to stand out there shocking the neighbours?" Mina's mouth opened, trying to form a retort. She looked at Hana, covered in bruises and scrapes, and spots of dried blood on her clothes. As Hana gave her a sideways glance, she knew, if anything, she looked worse. She couldn't imagine what Aunt June thought.

"I —"

"Pssht!" Aunt June cut the air with her hand then stepped back into the house. "I don't want to hear it, not out here where the neighbours can eavesdrop. They don't need to know there's a Hunter in the house, let alone a vampire in the family."

Mina's mouth dropped open. Hana snorted and stepped through the doorway.

June's gaze slid sideways before she turned around. "And you'd better invite that werecat in before she eats the neighbour's chihuahua."

DID YOU ENJOY A SPELL OF DEATH?

If you enjoyed this book, I'd really appreciate it if you left a review. Reviews really help me get the word out about my books, but they also inspire me to keep writing.

If you like my writing style and want more, join my mailing list over on creneastle.com to hear about new projects in development. If you sign up, I'll send you *A Circus of Devils*, a story from long ago and far away about how Bee came to be a vampire.

I always intended Bloodborne Pathogens as a three-book series. However, I now have all sorts of ideas for spin-offs with some of the characters that I grew to love while writing these books. If you know what you'd like to see next, I'd love to hear it. You can find all the social links and email info at creneastle.com.